HALO

HALO

Frankie Rose

Copyright © 2013 Frankie Rose

All rights reserved.

This Edition Published March 2014 by Frankie Rose

Cover Design: Frankie Rose

Formatted By: Max Effect Author Services

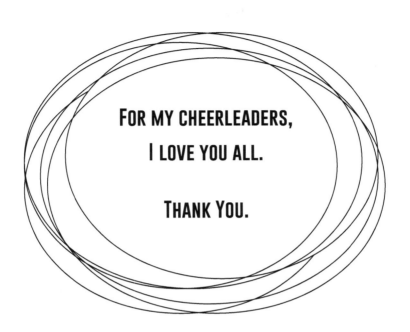

For my cheerleaders,

I love you all.

Thank You.

Pronunciations & Meanings

Halo
A collar-like device which controls the wearer's emotions and pain.

Falin- (fah-LIN)
The Sanctuary's fighting caste. Falin wear halos, and are trained from a young age to fight in the Colosseum

Elin- (eh-LIN)
Pureblooded children of the Sanctuary. The Elin do not wear halos.

Trues
Owners of the fighting houses in the Sanctuary. Parents of the Elin.

Therin- (the-RIN)
Servants of the fighting houses. Therin wear halos.

Tamji- (Tam-Gee)
Freetown's most common fighting caste.

Mashinji-(Mash-IN-gee)
A rogue fighter level. Mashinjis can be called to fight by whomever wishes to match them, and there is no limit to how many matches they can fight in one sitting.

Kansho- (Can-SHO)
The highest level of fighter in Freetown.

HALO

The technician's hands are cold this morning. Everything is cold. The metal gurney pressing against the backs of my naked thighs feels like it's been kept in one of the storage freezers. A clock on the wall, simple and white like everything else, ticks out a long minute while the short woman with the neat brown ponytail fiddles with my halo. She runs her icy fingers around the rim of the metal where it meets my skin, circling my throat. She looks pleased.

"You're competing again today," she says. This isn't so much a question as a statement. I compete in nearly every amphi-match. They're held once a month on the first Saturday. Today is the seventh of March, and it's a match day. I nod my head and the paper gown they've given me to wear rustles like dried leaves. She notes something on the tablet in her hand.

"Okay, I'm going to ask you some questions. Please answer them as honestly as possible."

I nod again. There is no requirement for me to speak yet. She purses her lips into a tight line as she glances down at the tablet, clearly trying to pick a question at random. I've been here so many times that I know them all by heart.

"What did you do this morning?" she asks.

I flex my feet, noticing the skin under my toenails is a violet bruise instead of flushed pink. "I rose with my alarm. I helped my mother—"

"Your mother?" she interrupts. She knows Miranda, the woman I should rightly call Mother, would never need my help with anything. She wouldn't be caught interacting with Falin.

I huff, realising my mistake. "I helped my *birth* mother organise the children for education. Then I met with Falin Asha and we trained for three hours. Following that, we both proceeded here in answer to our call for halo maintenance."

The technician taps some more on the screen. I don't think I've had her before, but it's difficult to know for certain. The technicians follow a script; nothing about them defines themselves from one another, just like everybody else in the Sanctuary. I study her for a moment while she picks another question, wondering how old she is. She could be any age. I'm nearly certain she's never competed before. If she were Falin, her hands would be scarred, and her skin is entirely unblemished. My palms and forearms have been cut to ribbons over and over, rick-racked with slices that have all shed my blood at some point or another. Defensive wounds. My halo's healing components took care of them all.

The technician clears her throat. "Your brother is not competing today, but humour me. How would you feel if he fought and was not successful in his match?" Her voice is flat and monotone, yet there seems to be some open curiosity there. Curiosity isn't outlawed, but it certainly isn't encouraged. I give her a look that tells her I've heard it.

"I would be regretful that he had not applied his training in such a way that ensured his victory."

"You wouldn't be sad?" The technician is already tapping away, and I don't really have to answer. I do anyway, because I am supposed to.

"I wouldn't be sad. My brother and I are both Falin. We know our duty to the Sanctuary and we carry it out accordingly."

"Good. And how do you feel about participating in your own match today? Are you afraid?"

I shake my head. Pull a tight smile. "I have no reason to be afraid."

She makes a small grunting sound that could be construed as a laugh. She knows as well as I do that it is illogical for me to be scared, even if I were capable of it. I am amongst a select few who have never lost a match, even before, when I was a child. Under the age of thirteen, we Falin are pre-mortas, and our matches are a different kind of fighting. All a competitor has to do is land ten points on his or her opponent to be declared victor. Those ten points don't guarantee that the opponent will die, but they usually do. Our knives are sharp. After our thirteenth year, Falin children become post-mortas, and there's no such thing as a ten-point victory anymore. Only the rumble of the Colosseum and blood-soaked dirt. Only death.

The technician frowns and makes sure the leads connecting the electrodes on my temples, over my heart, and on the insides of my wrists are securely attached. She pulls her cheek up to one side in a way that suggests she is confused. They do this sometimes, when they can't work out if I've tricked the equipment or if it is broken somehow. I give nothing away.

"I would have thought some concern would be in order, going into this round, Falin Kitsch, given who you are fighting," the technician muses. The clock ticks out loudly, marking away another minute.

"It doesn't matter who I'm fighting," I tell her. "Only that I win."

"True. It must be difficult to deduce a strategy, though, what with Falin Asha being your training partner. He will be able to anticipate your every move, will he not?"

I snap my head up and narrow my eyes at her. Falin Asha? I have fought and bled with Falin Asha day in, day out since I was old enough to remember. I didn't know I was to be pitched against him today, and the look on my face tells her so. Somewhere, for the very first time, a machine blips. Just once. The technician looks relieved. She slowly nods her head, as though she approves of the fact that I'm not a sterile, emotionless monster of my own volition, and my halo does do its job when it's supposed to. I touch my fingertips to the metal, feeling it warmed and rigid against my skin. I've never responded to the questioning before, and to hear the evidence of emotion spike within me is strange. For some reason, I have always assumed I wouldn't need my halo if I didn't have it. Apparently, I was wrong. The tiny gears inside whir as they recalibrate, something that happens once a day regardless of whether I feel something I shouldn't, and I push my chin down so that it rests on the metal.

The technician hands me a signed slip stating that I comply with current emo-control standards, and gestures me to the door. I pad barefoot into the small changing room, lit with a blazing, stark white light, and get dressed.

My brother will have been here earlier, too. They tend to process the Falin by their Houses, an easy task where mine is concerned, since there are only the two of us. My brother is a year younger than me, but he is quick and agile, and very skilled with his blades. I often think about who would win a match between us. The Sanctuary have been known to pitch blood against blood, and it's with a cold interest that I calculate who would come out on top. Most days I think it would be me. Conversely, I have never thought about who would win a fight between Falin Asha and myself. I suppose tonight we will find out.

I slide my legs into my stiff brown trousers and hike them up, pulling my belt tight. The material is the same as the rest of my combat clothing, taut and heavy duty, difficult to slice with a knife. Once I'm dressed, I leave the changing rooms and head into the compound corridor, where Falin Asha is waiting for me. He leans back against the wall in an odd way that looks like he's slipping down it. Wavy dark brown hair falls into his face, hiding his expression, but I know he will be biting on his lip. His tics might as well be my own; I know them inside out.

His hands are shoved into his pockets. When he sees me coming, he pushes away from the wall and smiles. Warm brown eyes greet me, and I can see myself reflected in them, or at least I can see the gleam of the sun flashing off my halo, anyway. His is hidden beneath the collar of his ratty khaki shirt. I offer out my hand and he takes it.

"So, we're fighting each other today," he says. I look up at him and hear my halo whir, knowing it shouldn't be doing that after only recalibrating a second ago with the technician. He gives me a small smile, pretending he doesn't hear—the polite thing to do.

"I hear we are," I reply. He pulls me towards the exit, down the metal walkway that leads out of the Sanctuary testing area and into the community square. Our footsteps echo off the high walls of the Sanctuary administration buildings, constructed out of grim-looking grey boxes. We hug the wall for no reason other than we've been told to always make sure there's room for other more important people to pass us by. The outskirts of the compound are inhabited, bordered by the low-lying, single storey dwellings of the most important Houses. Beyond those brick buildings lies the Sanctuary's inner boundary, a nine-foot tall wall that is decorated on this side by wooden trellises that drip with sunshine-yellow flowers. The other side is decorated with barbed wire and the occasional patch of graffiti where a Radical has slipped through in the night and tagged the crumbling concrete.

Beyond, a thousand homes spiral outwards from the city's main focal point: the Colosseum. The towering sandstone building soars up on our right hand side as Falin Asha and I navigate our way through the gardens of the Sanctuary's elite, approaching the inner boundary, just like we're supposed to once our business with the technicians is at an end.

A guard with a riot visor and a baton gestures us quickly through the gate, as though our very presence is an offence to the peace and quiet of the hierarchy this side of the wall. We pass under more jagged razor wire that tops the doorway the guard opens for us, and then we are thrust into the real Sanctuary. The city is a dirty grey stain that its people are always trying to paint white. It doesn't matter how hard they try, though. The elements have been conspiring against their attempts to beautify this place for the longest time, and for the most part the wind, rain and sunshine have been winning.

Falin Asha and I stand and stare at it for a moment—the smoke pouring up from the chimney tops; the narrow pathways that snake down the hill we stand upon, which lead to tiny market squares and water fountains; the crowds slipping in between the buildings, all Therin caste mainly, performing the menial labour required for their Households that others are too high-born to carry out. Huge screens adorn the sides of buildings, and smaller ones are erected in the squares, each displaying a rogues' gallery of the fighters who will compete tonight. Details of the current betting odds follow each fighter, a series of spinning numbers that even the youngest inhabitants of the Sanctuary know how to read.

Groups of placid-faced children run between the trees lining the walkways, tying red ribbons on the branches they can reach and awkwardly lifting each other at the waist in order to dress the ones they can't. The ribbons symbolise that it will be raining blood later this evening. Falin Asha pulls me forward and asks a little boy for a couple of the ribbons. The boy's halo is tiny, so small it looks like it would be nothing more than a bangle around my wrist. It's green. There are special instances when they will do that— make the children's halos different colours. It shows that the boy can't be more than four years old, and it also shows that he is Falin. He will be a fighter one day, like us.

He stares up at us with wide eyes and hands over some ribbons almost reverently. I hear his halo clacking away, and this is no great surprise. Children so young can hardly be expected to have mastered their emotions. Falin Asha takes the ribbons and passes me one, and the little boy's expression evens out as the

5

halo's drugs kick in. He turns and wanders back to his task, tying messy bows around the very lowest branches of a young oak sapling. We tie one higher up for him and then move on into the city.

"Are you worried?" Falin Asha asks me. For the past twelve years he has walked me home from training, and today isn't an exception. I twist a red length of ribbon around my finger and don't say anything. I'm not worried, but it would be impolite to directly tell him so.

He bites his lip and stares up at the Colosseum. Red flags flutter from the arched tiers, waving on a breeze that never really penetrates the complicated mass of the city at ground level. It's hot here, which seems at odds with how cold it was in the technician's compound. I look up at Falin Asha.

"Are *you* worried?" We ask each other these questions, because it's sort of expected of us. It's everyone's job to make sure those around them are complying with the emo-control standards. Occasionally, though, I half-expect him to admit to something. Occasionally, I think I will, too, even though it's not true. He gives me a blank look and drags me through the crowds.

The streets are busy on match days. Scores of touts, Therin who have been tossed out of their houses for not working hard enough, sell twists of red tickertape and swatches of crimson cloth. The very poorest of people sell the faded, washed-out rags from match days gone by, having collected them off the floor once the fighting was over. No one really buys from them, and their rags get pinker and pinker and the people get thinner and thinner. You can usually tell when you're unlikely to see a particular tout selling the next month.

Falin Asha holds his hand up as we weave through the sea of people, displaying the fact that we already have our red so no one will bother us. As we travel farther down the hill, reaching the mid-city, we veer off towards the river, where the richest people live beyond the boundary walls. Where I live. Falin Asha, too.

People nod as we pass them by, showing us respect as fighters of high status. The looks they give us are knowing, and I wonder if they've already been told that we are fighting. Have our faces already been doing the rounds on the betting screens? No one will be surprised. The Kitsch and Asha families have been playful competitors for many years. My True father, Lowrence, has probably been waiting for this day for a long time. He likes to win, and a lot of time and money has been invested into turning me into a well-honed weapon. It was probably all in preparation for this specific match.

The Kitsch house borders the waterfront, a position of high power. When we arrive, Falin Asha pulls me away from the glossy red front door, which I'm not supposed to use anyway, and drags me down to the embankment. Sitting on the bank has been a ritual we initiated eight months ago, one we stick to religiously, but today I don't feel like dipping my feet in the water. It's only noon, yet for some reason it feels like time is slipping away and it will be nightfall before I know it.

"What are you thinking?" Falin Asha asks, as he lets go of my hand and sinks with a complete lack of grace onto the grass. I flop down beside him and lean against his shoulder.

"I'm not thinking anything," I say.

"You want to practice?"

I shake my head, which seems stupid really. We should be taking every opportunity we can get to suss one another out. Look for weaknesses. But I already know his weaknesses, and he knows mine. The part of me that is always logical, *always* reasonable, seems to be missing right now. Falin Asha's breath comes out heavy, and I look up at him. His face is so familiar—delicate cheekbones and dark brows that arch a little too high for him not to look permanently surprised. His nose is slightly crooked where I broke it five years ago. He pulls his mouth into a smile but it doesn't seem to reach his eyes. He shrugs me half-heartedly off his shoulder and yanks his shoes and socks off. Rolling his socks together into a ball, he stuffs them into one of his shoes so they won't roll down the embankment and into the water. I slowly follow suit.

Shimmying forward on our backsides, our feet kiss the water. We plunge them in at the same time, knowing it will be cold. Knowing it will be shocking, but doing it all the same. He laces his fingers through mine out of habit.

"This is our place," he says, his voice low.

"I know."

He tilts his head back and stares up at the bare bones of the sky, the faint rippled clouds stretching across the bright blueness of it. "Just don't do this with anyone else."

I feel something bob in my throat, and I realise I'm trying to swallow. Trying and failing. "Of course I won't." Why he thinks I ever would is a mystery to me. Most of the time I can't figure out why *we* do it.

A fleeting shadow passes over Falin Asha's face. He reaches into his pocket and pulls out his last red ribbon, which he then ties gently around my wrist. We stop staring at each other and gaze at our feet, magnified two sizes too big by the water as they turn blue. He's too kind to say anything, but we can both hear it: my halo clicks like crazy.

COLOSSEUM

There are crowds the likes of which I have never seen before, swelling outside the Colosseum. There is an indistinguishable roar in the air, but it is not from shouting or raised voices. The people of the Sanctuary are orderly and peaceable. The roar is because there are simply *so many* of them. It isn't mandatory to attend the amphi-matches, but it feels like everyone is here tonight. Usually, there are families that don't come, especially the poorer families who aren't betting heavily on their Falin. Or, occasionally, as the richer Houses will do, betting heavily *against* their own, weaker Falin—the ones they suspect are getting too old to be of any use in the Colosseum. They call it the Death Bet, because your House will always find a way to pitch you against someone much stronger, much faster than you.

This match between Falin Asha and me is no Death Bet. It's the culmination of some other kind of bet between our True fathers, made sixteen years ago when we were born. It's no wonder Lowrence is so happy this evening, an emotion tempered, of course, with just enough disapproval to let me know he suspects I won't win. His emotional indecision is cataclysmically confusing. Both he and Miranda remain with me as I warm up in the waiting chamber, Miranda eating butter biscuits and drinking tea, and I can't help but stare at their naked necks. The open collar of my father's shirt, displaying his bare skin, seems a little obscene.

"You know what you're doing, don't you, child?" he asks me again. He's already asked me four times, and I keep telling him the same thing: I know precisely what I have to do. I have to kill Falin Asha.

He freaks out every time he hears my halo hum into life, and it's un-customary the way he keeps running his hands across it to make sure it's still adhered to my skin the way it should be. No one, *no one*, should touch another person's halo. Not even if that person *is* your father. He drags his hands back through his steel grey hair, looking stressed.

"Stop doing that, Low. You're going to lose even more hair," Miranda snaps. Hair is a prized commodity to my father's wife, it seems. Whenever she is sitting, she plays with her own soft, golden curls. It was the first habit of hers that I observed when she appeared ten years ago, ushered into our lives out of the blue. I don't listen to her telling off my father; it's better for all parties involved if I pretend they don't exist, and so I go back to my routine, trying to calculate how much money Lowrence has put on me this evening to warrant this level of worry. It must be a lot.

The walkways for the crowds entering the Colosseum are directly overhead, and the thunder of the noise is crushing. I imagine it's akin to what a train would have sounded like long ago when they used to run on the skeletons of the old iron tracks that run through parts of the city. Lowrence and Miranda seem more affected by the noise than I would have thought, but then again they've never been down here with me before. Not once. They probably thought I'd be reading a book in tranquil silence or something. Definitely not practicing at slicing up a rubber dummy with a knife in each hand, trying to reach that warm point when my muscles are loose and I can move quicker than lightning.

At some stage I must have nicked myself because there's blood on the floor, and Lowrence keeps staring at it as though it's his and I've somehow managed to cut him. He checks his bare arms three or four times, and when he doesn't find anything he laces his fingers behind his neck and stares upward. The noise of all the stomping people seems to fall into unison, like they're actually part of some vast machine, churning and surging above us. I ignore him and keep slicing.

"You're sure you're not feeling conflicted?" he says.

I stop thrashing at the dummy and stab the tip of my blade lightly into the material covering my thigh. It doesn't hurt, but I can tell if I push a little harder it will cut through. "No, I'm not conflicted."

"You should tell us if you are, child," he declares, and for a moment I think I see concern in his eye. This is a ridiculous thought because I have no basis to go off what concern might really look like, or any other emotion really, except for the obvious ones. Happiness and anger are easy to work out. Everything else is just messy and confusing. Lowrence's mouth tics at the corner. His face reddens a little, which tells me he's getting annoyed that I haven't answered him.

"I'm not conflicted."

"Good." He blows out a deep breath. "Miranda and I have put a lot on the line for you, child. I hope you understand that."

Miranda turns icy blue eyes on me and nods, like she has had some hand in raising me over the past ten years. As a rule, she barely speaks to my brother and me. I am usually not permitted to stand in her presence as I am taller than her these days, and she believes a True should never have to look up to a Falin. However, since today is a fight day, I am allowed to train, and she sits, observing the whole thing with distaste. I will never be a match for her own children, my half-brothers and sister, all of whom have names and emotions, and love trying to torture the rest of us at House Kitsch into submission.

I know the children understand torture isn't necessary. It is our duty to be submissive to them, and we have no desire to disobey that duty. Being without emotions like jealousy and greed, there is nothing that might tempt us to strive for positions beyond our stations. But my siblings don't care about things like that. They care about things I can't comprehend.

"Remember to smile when my children lead you out tonight," Miranda snaps. She doesn't look at me; I only know she is speaking to me because of her tone of voice—hard and sharp. "I have friends in the boxes. If you embarrass me…"

She doesn't finish her threat. A flicker of curiosity sparks inside me that I immediately suppress, although not before I have chance to wonder how she will punish me if I don't perform to her liking. Will she take away my technology like

11

she does her own children (I have none), or has she a more macabre plan in mind? Without fear or pain as a motivator, she would really need to get creative with me. She knows this, too—I see it in her face when she casts a displeased look in my general direction. "Just make sure you smile, girl."

I test out a smile on my face and it feels like a grimace. Lowrence sees it and growls. He goes pacing again, and for a moment his footsteps fall into time with the crowds above us. There is a knock at the door, and an adjudicator pokes a bald head into the room.

"Five minutes," he says. Lowrence blows out a shaky breath, leans back against the wall. He is wearing a black shirt that probably cost a small fortune, and there are lines pressed down the sleeves where my birth mother has ironed it for him. I'm in my combat gear as usual, the jacket unzipped, and I have Kevlar stretch bandages wound around my wrists. This is allowed during the amphi-matches, but generally fighters don't use them. It's considered a sign of weakness, but the wrists are vulnerable when knife fighting, and I know Falin Asha too well. If he spots any weakness in me, he will use it to his advantage. We're too equally matched in our fighting skills, and I will be doing exactly the same thing.

I have extra knives in my belt tonight. I favour small daggers and throwing knives, but I've added a Karambit, a wicked claw-shaped blade, and a Balisong. The Balisong is a last resort, a foldable butterfly knife that can only lead to dirty, skirmish-style fighting. I don't want to get that close to Falin Asha. I'm hopeful that my throwing knives will remove any need for that, but I can't be too careful.

Another knock at the door reveals the Kitsch Elin; all three of them are dressed in the same royal blue—Andre and Michael in matching suits, and Lexa in a velveteen dress and white socks pulled up to her knobbly knees. I give them each a small smile that none of them return. They roll their eyes at me and hurl themselves at Lowrence, wrapping their arms around his legs and waist. The boys are seven and eight, and Lexa is only five. They all seem to have adopted Miranda's distaste for fraternizing with the lower classes. Michael has a slight pug nose, which he turns up when he glances at me.

"Do we have to do this, Father?" he whines.

Lowrence pats his hand on Michael's head and ruffles his hair. "It's only this once and then you'll never have to step foot on that floor again, okay? Now, you've got to have big smiles this evening. You want to please your mother, don't you?"

All three of them nod, although none of them seem too happy. Andre's blue eyes are cold when he turns to me and says, "You might die tonight. Then we'll never have to see you again."

I don't know what it is I've done to make a seven year old hate me so much, but I can tell that's what he feels—hate. I run my fingers absently across the hilts of the daggers pressing against my hipbones and pull my mouth into a respectful smile. "That's true," I agree.

He scowls, annoyed that I am not crushed by his comment. Surprising, because I'm sure Andre knows I'm not capable of being wounded by anything he has to say to me. The halo would take care of that if I did feel anything, but it's not even necessary. It doesn't click into life around my neck as I stand there rubbing my thumbs slowly over the weapons in my belt. I'm just focusing on what I have to do.

Kill Falin Asha. I have to kill Falin Asha.

When the adjudicator comes for me, the children lead out like they're supposed to, and suddenly they're all smiles and laughter. They leave their mother and father without a backward glance and start walking down the tunnel towards the lit arena beyond. There are flashes of cameras going off up there, and the children seem excited by the prospect of so many thousands of people all looking down on them. Lowrence grabs my arm as I go to follow, and he says in his sternest voice, "Remember, do what you have to do."

I don't get chance to reassure him yet again, because the adjudicator rushes me up the tunnel—dust, echoing chants, adrenalin—and then I am standing in the arena. The first thing I do is check the two massive screens looming at either end of the match floor. On them the twelve most influential Houses are displayed, showing their fighters' names, number of wins, and how much has been bet on them tonight. *Kitsch* sits at the top of the board, right next to the name *Asha*, glowing in brilliant red. Beside our House statistics, an obscene amount of money continues to grow and grow as the late bets roll in. I don't focus on the numbers. I'm concentrating on my surroundings.

It always smells the same down here—musky dirt and blood and sweat. The ground is littered with hundreds of swatches of ruby-coloured cloth, and the air is thick with fluttering red tickertape that the crowds throw down on us in handfuls. Lexa seems thrilled when it drifts down to land in her hair. She smiles at me, open-mouthed, before she realises who I am and turns back to her brothers.

When the music kicks in, a loud, brassy fanfare of trumpets underscored by rumbling drums, the children form a line and start walking towards the triangular court lines where the amphi-match will be held. Miranda must have had them practice, because they walk at the same speed and hold each other's hands, waving with their free ones at the people in the stands. On the other side of the arena, Falin Asha appears from the opposing combatants' entrance. Not to be outdone, his mother and father have sent their one and only Elin, Penny, a tall, red-headed girl, to lead Falin Asha out. She isn't smiling, though, and she looks thoroughly miserable. She's older than Falin Asha by three years, and by rights she should have nothing to do with the fights. She's not a child anymore and it's surprising that she's here.

Falin Asha looks a little pale following behind Penny. Confusingly, he's wearing his knife belt slung low on his waist. Like that, it's only going to impede his movement, and oddly enough he isn't wearing the Kevlar stretch bandages like I assumed he would be. This makes me feel strange, and I touch my halo self-consciously. I don't know if it's working right now because the noise of the conversations going on in the stands overwhelms everything else.

Miranda's potent gaze burns into my back from the Kitsch's box, and I remember I'm supposed to be smiling. I flash my teeth at the crowd but it feels forced and weird. Andre, Michael and Lexa do a few three-sixties when we reach the thick white, painted lines of the match court, etched into a large triangle, and wave enthusiastically at the crowd. Trues and their Elin in the other boxes whoop and cheer at their show, but everyone else in the crowd claps politely, just as custom dictates.

Eventually, the children are ushered away by adjudicators and shown to the box where Miranda and Lowrence wait, but Penny moves off to hover over by the court line. I don't know why, but I had assumed she would join Falin Asha's Trues in their box, strategically placed right next to the Kitsch's. I guess I was wrong. Falin Asha and I pause on the outskirts of the court lines, waiting for the music to stop so that we can enter. He is too far away for me to make out his expression right now, but his shoulders are sloped oddly, and his fingers tap impatiently at the dagger strapped to his thigh, like he is desperate to jump into the arena and finish me off. Maybe he's confident that he can beat me.

Honestly, I have no idea what will happen once we step onto that court. Huge amounts of money will be lost either way, because there have been no other fighters like us. We are both undefeated, and everyone will have a favourite.

The music ends abruptly, which is our cue to step into the triangle. We aren't permitted to draw our weapons until the alarm sounds, but Falin Asha is tapping his dagger again. I frown at him, wondering what he's thinking. The stony set of his face doesn't betray much.

Red paper falls down to rest on the back of my hand and I glance down at it, catching sight of the ribbon Falin Asha tied around my wrist earlier. I tug at it absently until it pokes out above my bandages, and I see him freeze.

The alarm sounds quicker than I was expecting, and for a moment all I can hear are the raucous cries of the people in the boxes around the perimeter of the Colosseum floor going up and up and up. Their wild emotion is almost enough to make up for the fact that no one else in the crowd is experiencing any.

After a moment, I do what is expected of me.

I step forward.

Falin Asha responds.

FIGHT

Falin Asha reaches for a weapon first, and it's not even the dagger he's been tapping at for the past few minutes. This surprises me, and I'm almost too late when he snatches a throwing knife from his belt and darts it at me. I dive forward and roll the way I have a hundred times before, ending up a safe distance from the knife as it spins end over end through the air. It will lose momentum and fall to the dirt long before there's any chance of it hitting someone in the crowd, so I don't stop to check where it's gone.

I grab my own throwing knives and stack all three of them in my hand, ready to flick them out. Crouching low, I stalk closer to the centre of the match court, never taking my eyes off Falin Asha. He's staring at me, too, and I have to remember to watch his hands. He's always excelled at misdirection, and if I'm caught making eye contact with him for too long, he'll have grabbed another knife and thrown it without me even noticing. My index finger on my right hand strokes the length of the sharp knife waiting in my palm. It feels as though the cold steel is humming against my skin, begging to be let loose.

I give in and lunge forward swiftly, raising my hand back towards my chest before flicking my wrist out and letting go. The knife sings as it cuts through the air, making the hairs on my arms stand up. I put a slight curve on the throw, but Falin Asha sees it coming. He ducks back out of its trajectory and drops to the floor. The throwing knife spins past him and buries itself blade-first in the dirt. The crowd hisses, as though they thought it might have all been over by the time we'd both thrown our first blades. Right on cue, the stacks of numbers on the Colosseum screens start spiralling away; the profit and loss cycles of the big Houses have begun.

Falin Asha's hair is pulled back out of his face into a small ponytail, but a few strands have fallen loose. He bats them out of his eyes and smiles at me softly. The hard edge to his face, there only a moment ago, is suddenly gone, and I instantly feel like we're just training. He straightens up and purposefully draws his dagger slow enough that I can see what he's doing. He tosses it over in his hand in a showy fashion, catching it easily by the hilt. "You enjoying yourself, Kit?" he calls to me.

I rock back, confused. He's never called me that before, and there's an odd light shining in his eyes. His smile grows wider at the look on my face. I ready my next throwing knife, ignoring the fact that he clearly thinks we're going to be fighting at close quarters now that he's drawn his dagger. He takes a clumsy step towards me and I flick the knife. I'm surprised when it hits him. It slashes across his arm, actually renting open the material of his combat gear. That material is strong, yet it tears open impossibly easily. Blood blossoms like a scarlet flower through the clean cut in his sleeve, and Falin Asha looks down at it, laughing shakily. Something isn't right here and I know it. He shouldn't be reacting this way.

He's been cut worse than this before and barely even registered the fact. But today it seems like he's actually feeling the pain, and he doesn't seem to like it. I cast my last throwing knife before I can really analyse what any of this means, only knowing that he is distracted and this is good for me. The knife flies forward and sinks into his right thigh. I wasn't aiming for his leg; I was aiming for his stomach—one of the most damaging places to be stabbed—but I take the hit, anyway. An opponent with a leg out of commission is a weak opponent, and I may have just tipped the balance in my favour.

Falin Asha sinks to one knee as I prowl forward, drawing out my daggers. I like fighting with a knife in either hand, and it's good to have a spare to parry and block with while the other one is striking. Falin Asha is back on his feet by the time I'm within range. I keep back, knowing his arms are long. His reach is further than mine, so I'm going to have to lunge and attack, making sure I leave myself an opening to pull back quickly. He's beaten me like that in practice before, and I'm wary not to stray within a metre of him.

I want to wait for him to lead out on the second round of the fight, but he seems hesitant. He keeps staring at me like he's not even paying attention, lost in thought. I clear my throat and growl at him.

"What are you doing?"

"I—" He laughs. *He laughs.* "I have no idea."

"Concentrate!" It's counterproductive to give him advice, but I still do. I know my halo is working overtime, even though I can't hear it. The buzz of it works against my skin, and the drug I can never normally feel is actually present on my tongue. I've never tasted it before. It's an incredibly rare event when anyone does—only during extreme danger, fear, panic. I've heard that it tastes like almonds. It really does.

Falin Asha bites his lip and crouches low. He finally holds his dagger defensively, starting on a circling manoeuvre. This is standard fighting technique and something we've practiced countless times before, but there is something off about the way he moves. It's almost like he's intentionally moving too slow. I do what I've been trained to do and lunge in, slashing with my own dagger. It drags heavily across his chest, and Falin Asha drops to his knees again. The Trues around us at arena level go crazy, slapping their palms against their tables, and for a moment I'm lost. It's only for an instant, though, and Falin Asha rolls out of the drop, springing to his feet. Where I lashed out at him, a large hole gapes in his shirt, and I can see the deep gash that I've scored across his skin.

There's tickertape in his hair now. It seems like he's decorated in a whole heap of red, whereas I have none. This doesn't feel right. Falin Asha's as good as me, and logic dictates that I should have a cut for every one of his. The only conclusion I can come to is that he is doing this on purpose. I just can't figure out why.

He extends his arm and stretches it out a couple of times, hinting that he might be hurt there, too. The pain should be nothing, though, and he shouldn't be showing me any tells. Right now he's basically displaying where I should strike next. It's a rookie mistake to make, and I snake my dagger forward, half expecting him to have been setting me up. I certainly don't expect my dagger to plunge into his shoulder. I drop hold of the hilt and reel backwards, the sickly sweet flavour of almonds flooding my mouth.

Falin Asha just stares at me. I toss my other dagger into my right hand, the hand I'm better at striking with. It takes a long time before he glances down at the knife buried in his shoulder and carefully pulls it out.

"No! What—" I break off. What the hell is he doing? He knows better than that. I did him a favour by leaving that knife in him, and he's just gone and made things a whole lot worse for himself. He's going to be losing blood now. A whole lot of it. He lurches forward and the crowd cheers. I leap away, unprepared for him, and step to the side, tucking myself into a roll, a good way to put distance between yourself and your opponent.

"Kit?" he whispers, stepping closer. I know my eyes are open incredibly wide when I look at him. In my peripherals, Penny paces up and down the court line with her fingertips fluttering at her mouth. Her other arm is wound tight around her body. "Kit?" Falin Asha repeats.

I focus on him and clench my dagger in my hand. The sea of voices swells, and I'm certain I can pick out Miranda's deranged shrieking, yelling over and over again, "*End him! End him!*"

Falin Asha's brown eyes fix on me and it looks for a second like he's crying. That can't be right, though. I hover just out of his reach, staring at him. "What's going on?"

He smiles crookedly and brushes his hair back out of his face. "It's going to be okay, all right? Remember that."

I'm so thrown by his comment that I am utterly unprepared for what he does next. The knife in his hand snakes out toward me, and I skitter away from him to the left. He knows how I react, however, and he moves with me, my mirror image. He darts for me and does the unthinkable, something that spells the end to the fight and me along with it. He grabs hold of my striking arm at the wrist. A low gasp runs around the Colosseum, growing in pitch until it's a rushing echo in my ears. I try and fumble for the Balisong on my belt, hoping I can flick it

19

open and use it, but Falin Asha is there before me. He doesn't knock my hand away, just holds his over it. He pulls me closer to him and sucks in a deep breath.

"Don't let them see," he hisses. With that, I feel a twisting movement between our two bodies, and then his eyes go wide. He looks stunned, the way Elin children do when they fall and they're unsure whether they're supposed to cry or not. I look down and see his own knife submerged up to the handle in his stomach. A cracking, bubbling noise comes out of his throat, and he smiles slowly at me. The whole Colosseum has gone deadly silent.

I gape at him, and for a split second everything is normal as the drugs from my halo force their way into my brain and take over. An angry look sweeps over Falin Asha's face as I feel my expression turn flat, and he reaches up for me. At first I think he's going to touch my face, but he doesn't. His hand crawls along my shoulder with trembling fingers, and I watch the whole time, wondering what he's planning on doing. It's only when he has his fingers hooked underneath my halo that I realise, too late.

He yanks at the metal as hard as he can, dragging me to the floor with him. A scuffle ensues, but Falin Asha's grip goes slack pretty quickly, the energy seeping out of him right along with his blood. I roll out from underneath him and turn him onto his back, listening to the hordes of people in the stands clapping and calling polite victory chants. A cold, grim look sets on Falin Asha's face as he looks up at me. Arena dirt is stuck to his skin, and blood trickles from the corner of his mouth.

His voice is a wet rasp when he says, "Kit, let me…"

I'm too stunned to think straight. I lean down so that our faces are closer, and his hand reaches up again. "Let me," he whispers. "Don't let them see…"

His hand is on my halo again, only this time I stare at him as he seems to draw together every last scrap of energy he possesses. I hold still, and with one final deep breath he yanks on my halo. I scream a little when it rips free over my collarbone, but no one can hear. The shouts, the calls, the laughing of the Trues in the boxes are too loud for anyone to notice my small cry.

I automatically touch my hand to my neck, feeling straight away where the metal has pulled away from my skin. When I look down, Falin Asha's eyes are unfocused. His head has rocked to one side so it looks like he's staring at the throwing knife I buried in the match floor only minutes ago. I've seen so many dead people before, but this—seeing him like this— suddenly makes *me* feel like dying.

Feet race towards us, and then Penny's pulling me back so she can lift Falin Asha's head into her lap. Tears fall down her cheeks and her mouth opens, pulled down in a mask of grief. Her pain is terrible, and I topple backwards onto the arena floor, staring wildly at the thousands of people above me, all waving their hands and throwing down fistfuls of red tickertape. For a moment I really believe it *is* raining blood.

I don't know how to explain it, but my body is reacting. My lungs burn in a way so alien that I panic before I realise that's even what I'm doing. I lurch forward and grab hold of Falin Asha's hand. Penny looks like she wants to pull him away from me, but then she covers her face in her hands, which are red and sticky with blood.

"Zip up your jacket," she sobs through her fingers. I don't respond at first, but when she reaches out and slaps me, I do it. The zip comes up so fast I catch the skin beneath my chin, and a lump rises in my throat. It hurts so much, it makes my eyes water. Then, exactly then, is when I realise: my halo, it isn't working.

Penny gives me a warning look as the adjudicator approaches, smiling with just the right amount of faux happiness on his face. He offers his hand out to me and I take it so he can pull me upright. I don't even help him as he drags me up, and it's only when my feet are firmly underneath me that I swallow hard and look around.

No one is watching what's happening on the arena floor. No one could have seen what just took place. Close by, Miranda and Lowrence stand at the edge of their box, talking with Falin Asha's True father. The man with the same deep brown eyes as Falin Asha shakes his head ruefully while counting out money. He hands it over to Miranda and then his shoulders shake up and down and his face creases, crinkly, because he's laughing at something my father has said.

My head is spinning by the time the alarm sounds out overhead, signalling the victor's announcement. The adjudicator takes hold of my hand carefully as though he expects me to still be hiding a knife up my sleeve.

"Are you ready?" he asks.

"Yes," I tell him. With that, he makes a hand signal to cue up the fanfare, and then we wait a heartbeat. The fanfare kicks in, and the adjudicator lifts my hand into the air, and I lean forward and throw up.

LEAVE

Cooking smells waft into my bedroom like an unwelcome visitor. My birth mother's making me vegetable soup, because she thinks I'm still sick. That kind of explains why I've been sweating and running a fever for the past three days, and why I have locked myself away in my room. I am suffering from the worst kind of withdrawals, and I never even knew I was drugged. The Sanctuary have rules about quarantine, and staying home and avoiding contact with the outside world is number one on the list. I am so relieved that everyone automatically assumed I am ill, because I don't think I could have done it. I couldn't have thought up the lie when it felt like my insides are being crushed. Nothing has ever felt like this.

I want it to stop.

Getting home from the Colosseum was the hardest thing I've ever had to do.

FRANKIE ROSE

It felt like I was crumbling from the inside while I worked overtime, trying to keep the emotion from my face. All those times where I'd thought I could live without my halo, without the *control*—I couldn't have been more wrong. I felt everything—the crushing guilt, the sheer horror—on that journey home, and I had to hide it all. The gaping chasm in my chest just grew and grew, and I could only ever imagine it getting bigger.

Since then I've lain here in my bed, checking my halo over and over again. The only place it is still securely attached is around the back of my neck. Everywhere else it lifts up, free from my skin. A jolting, bewildering sensation shoots through me every time I feel it rub against me.

Thankfully, no one has bothered to visit except my birth mother, who brings me food. It's easy enough to hide my broken halo from her underneath the blankets. I have no idea what I'm going to do, or how I'm going to control this seething mess of raw feeling inside me. All I know is that my friend wanted me to do this for some reason, and I feel like I owe it to him to follow it through.

I'm still buried in my sheets when my mother brings in the vegetable soup. We have the same dark chocolate hair and hazel eyes; I've been told I am going to look just like her when I grow older, and that makes me panic. Will I be making vegetable soup for a child I feel nothing for by the time I am thirty-seven? She flings back my bedroom curtains and lets in the daylight, illuminating the sparseness of my room. The only things in here are me, the bed, a three-drawer tall boy, and the loop of red ribbon that Falin Asha gave me on match day. Whenever I see it, I feel like I'm going to choke.

"You have to be feeling better today," my birth mother tells me. Doesn't look like I'm getting a say in the matter. I make a grumbling noise from beneath the covers. "You had a visitor this morning." She makes clattering noises as she sets down my soup on top of the tall boy. The spoon makes a bright dinging sound when she knocks it accidentally against the side of the bowl. I squint at her. Her hair is braided up neatly on top of her head, not a strand out of place. I ask myself the same question I've been asking myself the last three days—*how can she not see what's happened to me?*

I clear my throat so I can speak without my voice cracking. "Who visited?" I don't care who visited, but I have to ask.

She spreads some butter on the hunk of bread she's cut for me while she says, "The Asha Elin—Penny, is that right? She wanted to speak to you. I told her

23

you were sick, but I suppose you could always go and see her if you're feeling any better?"

Only someone completely devoid of any emotion wouldn't question why Penny would come to see me. She was distraught when Falin Asha died, which is hardly normal behaviour. An Elin mourning a Falin? Usually they would hardly notice he was gone. This means Penny and her brother were close, although he never mentioned her to me once. I get the feeling there are a lot of things Falin Asha didn't discuss with me, though, and maybe this halo thing is part of his relationship with Penny. She either wants to talk to me about what he did, or she wants to kill me for what *I* did. I don't know which prospect sounds more terrible right now.

My mother finishes preparing my lunch and makes to leave. Halfway out of the door, she pauses. "Are you going to get up?"

"Yes," I whisper. "I'll go and see Penny. The fresh air might make me feel better."

"Excellent. Your father is keen for you to start training again. He wants you to partner up with one of the Falin Belcoras."

The concept that my father has already been planning on replacing Falin Asha makes my stomach twist. I want to smash something, but instead I nod my head, feeling my long hair tangling into even more knots against the pillow. She leaves and I eat my soup, sensing the despair inside me shift for the first time in days. It's turning into something more volatile and dangerous.

*****

The Therin looks surprised to see me standing at the front door of the Asha Household. I don't really know if I've used the right protocol because I've never visited an Elin before. When I've come here to see Falin Asha, I've always used the back door, but today I march straight up to the front and hammer on the wood. It feels good to flout whatever I *think* I'm supposed to do.

The Therin woman is docile enough, but I can tell she's a little shaken by my presence. I can have that effect on people sometimes. I think it's all the killing, but it's difficult to know for sure. Technically, she shouldn't be afraid of me at all, but it can happen. A person can sometimes sense, regardless of the drugs, that they're in the presence of death. She goes to fetch Penny and leaves me in the entranceway, running my hand up and down the white paintwork of the doorframe. I never saw Falin Asha go in or out of here, but it still makes me feel

24

like something is burning up in my head. My eyes are pricking when Penny appears. Her hair is drawn back in a tight bun and her face looks washed out. She waves away the Therin and pulls me by my arm into the house.

"I was wondering how long it would take you to come," she says. She doesn't go up the stairs; she sets off into the lower floor of the house, and I follow closely behind her. We walk past the kitchen, where voices leak out into the corridor, and Penny rushes by. I make sure to be as silent as I can, which is very silent. The lower floor of the Asha Household is even bigger than ours, and we walk by five closed doors before Penny stops and opens one, waving me inside.

The room is simple, with a single bed and a small bookshelf above it, where three worn books rest on their side. It smells of Falin Asha in here, a smell I didn't realise I would know absolutely anywhere until now. A pair of his shoes are pushed neatly halfway under the bed. Penny stares at them and tears creep down her face

"I—," I don't know what to tell her. That I was just doing what I was supposed to? That I am sorry? I'm not even sure what it is I'm feeling. All I know is that it hurts more than any physical pain I can put myself through, and since my halo stopped working, I really have tried. Tried to find something that hurts more. There are open scars on the backs of my hands to prove it.

Penny scrubs her hands over her eyes and turns to sink down on Falin Asha's neatly made bed. I picture him here making it before he came to meet for practice on the day of the fight and my heart contracts in a way that makes my breathing uneven. I sit down on the bed with her. "Why did he do it?"

Penny leans forward to prop herself up on her knees, and I notice the back of her neck is all freckly. Those freckles wouldn't be visible if she was wearing a halo. She doesn't bother asking me what I mean.

"Cai—" She winces, like saying the word causes her pain. "Cai wanted to—"

"Cai?"

"Caius. That's the name my brother chose for himself." She blinks at me, like she's waiting for me to approve. Caius. *Caius?* That's going to take some getting used to. Penny's face hardens when she doesn't see the response she's looking for on my face.

"Cai wanted to set you free. I told him not to. I told him it would only lead to trouble, but—"

"Set me free? He thought *this* was setting me free? I'm *trapped*. I need to go to the technicians and get them to fix it, but every time I think about doing it I have to come up with a good explanation as to why I haven't gone sooner. And I can't think of one."

Penny's grey eyes darken a shade, and her eyebrows pinch together. "Cai died so you could have this. Don't you dare throw it away."

"But...*why?*" I can't think of any other question, because I really don't understand. Having my halo broken, having all these feelings rush through me, conflicting with one another, clawing at me, leaves me feeling wretched. Penny makes it sound like Falin Ash—I shake my head, trying to get to grips with such a monumental name change—she makes it sound like *Caius* gave me a gift.

"Cai's halo stopped functioning eight months ago," Penny says, staring at the backs of the shoes on the floor between her feet. "He was always so well behaved. He never caused any trouble. He trained so hard, even when his halo stopped working. I never would have known, but he got angry one day when my father hit me and I worked it out. I kept his secret for him and we became friends. He always wanted to tell you, but I said he shouldn't. And then, when they said you'd be fighting each other, he snapped. He told me what he was going to do but I didn't really believe him."

I bite down on my jaw, feeling my teeth grate against one another. "I had no idea. We trained every day. I never suspected a thing."

"You wouldn't have. He was pretty good at hiding it. Plus he didn't want anything to change. He loved training with you. He loved—well," she blows out a deep breath. "He loved *you.*"

I freeze on the bed, picking apart Penny's mournful expression to see if she is joking. "He *loved* me?"

She nods, saying something else, but I don't hear her. My heart is pounding too hard for me to concentrate. I whisper the words to myself again, testing them out in my mouth to see if I can find some truth in the weight of them on my tongue. I can't. The idea just seems too strange.

Penny grabs hold of my hand, pulling back my focus. "You have to leave."

My head whips to the door, expecting someone to come crashing through. Maybe the Therin that let me in, or even True Father Asha, himself. Penny shakes her head. "No, Kit. You have to leave *the Sanctuary.* It's not safe for you here now. They'll find out. They'll make you wear it again." She points to my neck where my halo still lies, albeit crookedly, beneath my jacket.

"This is ridiculous. Where am I supposed to go?" No one leaves the Sanctuary. Well, no sane person leaves, anyway. There are the Radicals, of course, but they're crazy. Everybody knows to avoid them. They're *wild*.

"There are plenty of places you can go. You just can't stay here. Caius would never forgive me if I didn't make you leave. He wanted you to be free."

"Penny—"

"Kit!"

I grip the edge of the bed until my knuckles turn white. "Why are you calling me that?"

"Because he didn't just rename himself, okay. He renamed *you*. Kitsch. Kit. I don't know why he shortened it. I never asked, but, please, just listen to me. Or at least tell me you'll think about it. He's gone and I couldn't bear it if that's for no reason. He didn't even *try* and fight you. You owe it to him. You have to—"

"Okay!" I hold my hands up. "I'll think about it."

"Promise me you won't go and see the technicians?"

The look in Penny's eyes is desperate, and I'm too stunned by the idea that my friend was in love with me to really think about what I'm promising. "Okay, I won't," I say.

"Good." She stands up and paces back and forth as though she's filled with nervous energy. A second later she drops to her knees and reaches under Cai's bed. She fiddles around for a moment before tugging gently, and when she pulls her arm back, she's holding onto a small holostick. The small, black square of plastic and metal is scuffed and old, an archaic model in the grand scheme of things. "He would want you to have this."

"What's on it?" I take it with shaking hands.

"I don't know but he carried it around with him everywhere. Now it's yours."

I look down at it and panic, wondering what secrets are recorded on the device. It's about two inches square, cold and heavy in my palm. A small blue light flashes on the top and I drop it onto the bed. "I can't. I just can't." If what she says is true, I definitely don't want to see what's on it.

Penny snatches up the holostick and presses it into my hand. "Don't be so selfish!"

She's right. I am being selfish, which is a new experience for me. I let my fingers curl around the device, feeling its corners dig into my skin, and then stow it into the back pocket of my combat gear. I feel like a monster wearing these clothes right now.

"You should probably go," Penny tells me. When I get up to leave, she doesn't join me. "You promised, remember. You won't go to the technicians."

"I know."

"Come and see me in two days. That should be enough time for you to figure out when you're going."

Her faith that I will leave the Sanctuary is surprising, given that the only thing beyond the city limits is a wild and desolate landscape. I stuff my hands into my pockets and take a long look around Falin Asha's old bedroom. He's not here anymore, and I know that whatever happens, I won't be coming back again.

RUN

I don't have the courage to watch the holostick. I don't want to go home either,
even though I can see the Kitsch Household from where I'm standing outside
the place where Cai used to live. Instead, I start walking in the opposite
direction. The houses by the river are well built, from real brick and mortar, but
there are only so many of them. Most of the houses in the Sanctuary are made from
reclaimed wood, but they're put together pretty well. Each small community
generally sees to the upkeep of all the houses, lending the labour of their Therin
whenever something new needs building, in an attempt to lift the social standing
of the area. The Trues, no matter where they live, all have one thing in common:
they want to be better than each other. This competitive betterment seems like a
futile pastime to me now, as I drag myself, numb, through the winding
passageways of an area of lower caste housing commonly known as the Narrows.

HALO

Caius and I used to train here when we were smaller. The houses are pressed so close together, and the roofs almost touch in places. This was our favourite location to come and practice rolls, leaping from one building to the next and tumbling across the uneven wooden shingles or jumbled, mismatched slate tiles. Often we would earn ourselves a cuff on the ear for disrupting the peace, but even back then people were lenient with us. It was like they understood what we would one day become: poster children for the amphi-matches, a common bet, role models for a whole generation of Falin.

People recognise me here as I try to slip unnoticed through the crowds. It's incredibly rare for Trues and Elin to be out walking the streets unless they're visiting friends or travelling to the education compounds, so I don't need to worry about their inquisitive questioning. The people out on the streets today are mainly Therin, carrying water and groceries, sweeping and hawking goods. Some of them nod to me as I pass them by, but mostly they just stare.

These people don't bother me—they know not to talk to me for the most part. It's other Falin I'm worried about seeing. They're the ones who usually stop me, want to know my latest training techniques, what foreign blades I've been gifted by the city for my latest win. It seems to me that every Falin I see will want to talk to me today, because I can guarantee that half the Houses in the Sanctuary have been discussing me. Who is going to replace Cai as my training partner? Which House will have the honour? The Falin won't care themselves, of course, but they will approach me to appease their Trues, and I can't handle that right now.

I keep my head down, the sun warming the back of my head until it feels like my hair is on fire. I duck under the covered walkway out of the glare and shove my hands in my pockets. This pulls my trousers taut and reminds me that I have Caius' holostick on me. Its corners dig into my lower back. I take my hands back out of my pockets, wishing I'd worn my knife belt. Hooking our thumbs through the webbing where it loops around the hips is a habitual trait of nearly all Falin, and I've never found anything better to do with my hands than this. But today I didn't wear my belt. It didn't feel right, and for the very first time I was apprehensive when I looked at it. It is all the blood. I know the blades are sterile because I cleaned them myself, over and over, but I still can't seem to shake the feeling that the metal is tainted, and no amount of scrubbing is ever going to fix that. Maybe I need new knives.

It's a while before I realise I've left the Narrows and hit the poorest parts of the Sanctuary. Here the children walk in the streets wearing nothing but ragged pants and their halos. They're covered in dirt and their eyes have a hungry, hollow look to them as they pass me by. I see two tiny girls, both with pink halos and sticks in their hands, lunging and striking at each other, playing at a real fight. These kids will never make it to the Colosseum, though. Their Houses are too poor to stump up the buy-in for their Falin to compete, and it's more likely these kids will die in a pit fight somewhere out here, in the stinking backstreets where a Falin's life is worth less than a week's food to most families.

The Therin have their work cut out for them on the edges of the city. The streets are filthy and littered with garbage, and their cleaning duties must feel endless. There's no money to afford sturdy materials for any of the houses, and so they're made out of sheets of corrugated plastic and useless off-cuts of wood. Most of the houses rot from the ground up, where mould and damp festers even in the dry months. This is probably where I should turn around and go home, not because anyone will hurt me, but because I am suddenly overcome with a sickened feeling, as I watch the starving children with their rounded little pot bellies and gaunt expressions play at warriors. Yet I don't turn around.

It takes me twenty minutes to make my way through the streets; I don't know my way here, but I head north until the shanties fall away and the land opens out. I've never been this far out of the city, and I'm surprised when I find fields of grass, which are fenced off for as far as the eye can see. In the distance is the forest—everybody knows it's there, but it's one thing hearing about it and another thing entirely seeing it.

I've never seen so many trees. They're different to the ones that grow in the city. These ones don't really have proper leaves, and they are an altogether different kind of green. It's lush and vibrant, and totally new to me. What really surprises me is how close these trees grow together. They're almost on top of one another, lined up in formation, a tree line that runs for miles in either direction.

Directly ahead, before the trees, there are slim, grey chimneys, where billows of dirty white smoke curl up into the afternoon sky. Squat, vast buildings—grey, windowless—surround them, and I know this is the processing compound, where the food for the city's inhabitants is stored, milled, prepared and recycled.

I have no idea why, but I keep walking. No doubt I've been missed back at home by now, but this doesn't seem to matter. A wide, rutted dirt road leads out towards the processing plant, and on either side of it the chain link fences rise up well beyond three times my height. Loops of vicious barbed wire top them for good measure. These fences are well maintained, and there is no way over or under them.

It's eerily silent out here. There isn't a sound apart from a soft hum emanating from the processing plant, and that's so low it's barely audible. All I can hear is my breathing that pulls and blows in and out over my teeth. The world has never been so quiet. As I get closer to the compound I see groups of Therin sitting out in the sunshine, eating from wrinkled paper bags. The men and women are methodical and quick about finishing their lunch. This has a lot to do with the guards standing over them; they're in full body armour, which is the most ridiculous thing I've ever seen. I've never heard of a Therin disobeying anybody before, let alone a Therin who knows how to fight.

Still, the sight of the guards with their black body suits, wrapped in stab vests, with their thick plexi-shields sends a nervous thrill through my body, and I duck down at the side of the road. I'm not sure what would happen if they found me. I could say I was sent here by Lowrence but they'd want to know why, and I don't think I'm capable of lying convincingly.

I hunker down in the tall grass at the roadside and watch for a few minutes as the guards hurry everyone back inside the building to continue their work. When I'm sure they're all gone, I edge forward to get a closer look at what lies past the plant. Concealed within the trees, another huge fence has been erected; it's made from steel struts, spaced evenly, about five metres apart, thicker than some of the tree trunks. The fence itself isn't made out of chain link like the one back by the fields; it's a rigid, cross-hatched steel, and looks incredibly strong. There is an armoured gate about four metres wide just behind the plant, which is how I'm guessing people get to the agricultural fields. They're out there somewhere; I've just never bothered to ask where, or even wondered for that matter. Like I said—curiosity isn't outlawed. It's just not encouraged.

I shrink from the sight of the fence and scurry back up the dirt track in a crouch until I feel I've put a safe enough distance between myself and the compound. When I see the shanties growing from tiny brown smudges to actual dwellings on the horizon, I relax a little. The Colosseum looks foreboding to me now, even from here. It soars up out of the city like an ugly broken tooth, making me feel uneasy. My whole life it has been the place where I went to carry out my work, but now it's the place where I've killed people. Lots of people. The place Cai died.

I hurry back through the city, mindful to keep my head down and avoid eye contact with the multitude of people going about their business. Instead of taking the walkway by the river to get home, I opt for the backstreet. Seeing the spot where Caius and I used to sit and discuss our training, thrust our feet in the water, won't make me feel well at all. My birth mother is waiting for me when I slip through the back door into the kitchen, and she gives me a stiff nod.

"Where have you been?"

"With Penny," I answer.

"All this time?"

"Yes." My first calculated lie. "She wanted me to teach her about the matches." This isn't too far a stretch of the imagination. Lots of Elin are intrigued by the fighting, and most of them even seem to have a bit of a bloodthirsty streak. My birth mother has been with me when I've been stopped in the street before, when Elin want to rehash a certain move I may have pulled in my last fight. She doesn't question my response, just goes back to chopping carrots for dinner.

"Good. I hope she learned everything she needed to know," she says.

I nod, but really I doubt Penny learned anything from our meeting. If anything, *I'm* the one who's learned much today. I've learned some of Cai's biggest secrets. I've also learned there's no way I'm getting out of this city.

6

BELCORAS

"Aren't you really hot right now?" my brother asks. We're waiting outside the Colosseum where we're supposed to be meeting one of the Falin Belcoras to organise a training schedule. I have no idea which one of the Belcoras it will be. There are seven or eight of them, I think, and they all look the same. I glance at my brother and shake my head even though sweat is pouring down my back.

"No. Why do you ask?"

"Because you're wearing your jacket and it's zipped up tight." He reaches for the zipper that is, indeed, drawn all the way up underneath my chin, and I slap his hand away.

"I think I'm still a little sick. You probably shouldn't touch me." This has the desired effect, and my brother puts some space between us. There's no way I can walk around the Sanctuary without my jacket right now, not without someone noticing my halo is almost entirely free from my neck. I woke up before sunrise this morning with it making an odd ticking noise. It took a full hour for it to stop, and I laid there with my heart thrumming in my chest while I panicked that it was going to start working again.

That's what I've decided—that I'm not ready for it to start working again. *Yet.* I keep telling myself I'll only leave it a few more days before I go and see the technicians. Until then, I have to cover my neck.

I have Cai's holostick with me. It's not safe to leave at home, but I feel inconceivably guilty walking around with it on my person. It practically burns a hole in my back pocket, and yet I have absolutely no idea why. It could contain anything inside. It could contain nothing at all. At this rate I'm never going to find out, because I'm too scared to try accessing it. I never knew I was such a coward until now.

All of the red banners and flags have been taken down from the Colosseum, and the four levels of carved sandstone are naked today, as we wait for the Belcoras boy by the main entrance. I'm wearing my knife belt, which feels blissfully normal even though it took a lot for me to strap it on before we left the house. The weight of it, knowing exactly where each and every blade is, the movement and shift of my weapons when I walk, is reassuring. It's only when I consider taking a blade out and using it that I'm filled with alarm.

"What's up with you today?" my brother asks. Belcoras is late, and my brother has never had much patience. He has a pair of throwing knives in one hand. He scissors them back and forth, making them sing. I give him a look that makes him put them away.

"There's nothing wrong with me. I'm just waiting."

"You're not waiting. You're pacing. You're all twitchy."

"I'm *not,*" I insist. My brother shrugs his shoulders and accepts my denial, while I continue to pace and twitch. It feels risky being out here in the open, where anything could happen and any number of events could occur, leading to the discovery that I've been walking around like a ticking time bomb for the last four days. The fact that I haven't told anyone about my halo is a major deal. If I get found out, I don't know what the technicians will do.

In the time we stand there waiting, the subtle pink hue to the morning sky diminishes and clouds begin to amass in the heavens. It won't be long before rain kicks in and the day is a washout; there's electricity on the air and a storm is brewing. Storms mean one thing in the Sanctuary: everybody indoors. Lightning strikes within the city limits are common, and the rain is usually so strong that flash flooding can occur without any warning. Living near the river is a blessing sometimes and a burden at others. When it bursts its banks, we're actually permitted to sleep on the first floor of the house. Miranda says the frequency with which we get flooded is the reason why we don't get carpet on the floor in our living quarters, but I know better.

"Belcoras is here," my brother says, pointing off through the crowds of early morning touts setting up their stalls of fruit and vegetables. I look in the direction he is pointing and pick out a sandy blond head amongst the jostling throng of people. It's a Belcoras, all right. They all have that same dirty, straw-coloured hair. I know because I've killed three of his brothers. As he draws closer, we go out to meet him, and a light rain starts to fall. He's wearing combat gear just like us, but his clothes are worn at the knees and scuffed. No doubt he has to share his clothes with all his siblings.

The boy is probably the same age as me. He's broad and strong and it's obvious he's a trained fighter, even without the faint scars that run down the lengths of his cheekbones. He holds out his hand to greet us and I shake first, noticing the way he holds himself. I do this subconsciously. Studying a fighter is second nature to us, wondering how they handle themselves, how they handle their knives, what their strengths and weaknesses are. I've already ascertained that he favours his right side and that he's probably quick, but not as quick as me, by the time I let his hand go.

He gives me a curt smile, knowing he has been sized up, and I notice that his eyes are mismatched. One is ice blue and one is so dark it's almost black. I've never seen anything like this before, and for a second I'm stunned. A frown flickers over his face, and I realise I'm staring. I look away.

"Good morning," he says. "My Trues have requested we discuss a training schedule. I take it that's why you came?"

"It is," I tell him, organising my face into a mask of nonchalance. "My last partner and I trained every morning from six until nine. Do you think this arrangement might be agreeable?"

Belcoras shakes his head, no. "I work in the mornings four days a week. I can train the other three. Perhaps we can meet later in the evening on the other days?"

I forget that, unlike my brother and I, other Falin from poorer Houses have to work, and for some reason I find his inability to slide neatly into Cai's training schedule very annoying. I'm hostile when I snap, "Fine."

He doesn't seem to notice my temper and nods enthusiastically. "I'm very happy to be able to train with you and your brother. I wasn't able to attend the last amphi-match, but I understand Falin Asha fought poorly. I promise you, I will work hard to ensure I am a worthy partner to you both."

An unpleasant bubbling feeling rises up in my chest, and I struggle to keep my face from reacting to his statement. That's all it is—a statement. But I can't shake the suspicion that he's making a personal remark about Cai. "Falin Asha was *not* an unworthy opponent or training partner."

Belcoras looks surprised at my words, and maybe surprised at the level of anger that even I can hear in them, too. He tilts his head back and a bead of rain strikes his forehead. "Of course. It's just—well, there are a lot of Falin saying that he was sloppy and could have fought better. That he wasn't paying attention."

A low growl works its way up my throat, and both my brother and Belcoras shift uneasily. "Hey, is everything all right?" my brother whispers. I take a step toward Belcoras and automatically draw out the dagger on my right hip. It's my favourite knife. It has top serrations that make it look positively evil. I hold it up in the air and twist it around so he can see.

"Maybe it's just that I'm an excellent fighter. Maybe Falin Asha simply didn't stand a chance." Saying something like that feels horrible, but I'd rather have people believe Cai was out-matched than just an all-out terrible opponent. Belcoras blinks at me, rivulets of water running fast down his face now. His blond hair is plastered to his head, and I have no idea when the rain got so hard.

"Yes, well…I suppose that must be it," he agrees. I can tell he's being polite, because it's not in the nature of a halo-wearer to be argumentative, but I can also tell that he doesn't believe me. This makes me even angrier, and I have to push down the powerful urge to smash my fist into Belcoras' face. I even picture myself doing it, which I'm sure doesn't leave a pleasant expression on my face.

"Sister, we should go," my brother says, reaching out for my hand. I hadn't noticed but there are people who have stopped to stare at me waving my knife under the other boy's nose, and some of them are frowning openly. I pull the knife back and slip it into its sheath in a practiced move that feels fluid. The rain comes down in sheets, and the square outside the Colosseum entranceway already looks like it's pooling water. At least now no one is questioning why I'm wearing my jacket.

Belcoras steps away and gives us a light bow, his halo visible around the back of his neck as he does so. I think I hear it recalibrating, but it's probably just my imagination; he seems completely composed.

"I will see you tomorrow morning, then? Agreed?"

"We look forward to it," my little brother announces, shaking his hand. He seems like an adult when he does this, and it jolts me back to reality. Belcoras smiles and walks away from the Colosseum, the rainwater flicking up from his battered leather shoes as he goes. My brother rounds on me and narrows his eyes.

"What was that about?"

"Hmm?"

He scrubs his hand over his wet hair as the sky above us rumbles angrily. "You were acting strange. You threatened him with your knife."

"No, I didn't"

"*Yes*, you *did*."

I sigh and pull my lips in a tight line. Should I tell him? Should I tell him that I'm spiralling out of control because of all the messed up emotions inside me—the ones I have no idea how to contain? Undoubtedly a bad idea. I set off walking back towards the river and he follows on my heels. "It's nothing."

"I don't mean to disagree with you, but—"

"Then don't."

He wraps a hand around my wrist and yanks me to a stop. "Sister, don't be alarmed but I think there might be something wrong with your halo."

This announcement, with the rain pouring down his face—the calm, innocent way he says it, makes me laugh. The noise rips from me before I can react, and I slap my hand over my mouth to make it stop. My brother just looks at me, his eyes wide and round. A female Therin stops hurrying in the alleyway and stares at me like I have three heads. Laughing was a bad move. A *very* bad move.

"Let me see your halo," my brother hisses, reaching for the zip on my jacket. I flinch back and start heading off down the street in the direction of home, kicking myself for being so stupid. "No. Come on, we have to get inside before this gets much worse."

The clouds have gone from a murky grey to the colour of dark steel in a matter of minutes. It really is important we get back, but it's more important that I avoid letting him see what's happened to my halo. He follows behind me for a few paces before I don't sense him at my back anymore. I turn and find him standing in the middle of the deserted alleyway with water dripping from the cuffs of his shirtsleeves.

"Let me see it," he says.

I stare at him, trying to work out what to do next. He walks purposefully towards me and goes for the zip on my jacket again, but I sidestep out of the way and hold my hands to my throat. "Just—there's nothing the matter with it. Let's go."

A deep roil of thunder claps out overhead and my brother takes a step away from me. "We're going to get this fixed," he whispers. "Everything's going to be okay." He sets off in a run back towards our house, dodging around me as he goes. I try and grab hold of him, but his hand is wet and slips free from my grasp. I know what he's going to do. He's going to race home and tell Lowrence and Miranda that there's something wrong with me, because this is what he's been brought up to do. It's his duty, and he doesn't realise what he's doing. Running after him is an option; I'm faster than he is, but then what?

There's nothing I can do or say to him that will persuade him to keep my secret, not with him so indoctrinated by what we've been told we should and shouldn't do.

I make up my mind there and then. I'm not going after him. I'm not going back. The rain blurs the image of my brother as he races off down the alleyway as fast as he can, and I freeze the picture in my mind. This might be the last time I see him, after all. He pauses at the end of the alleyway and looks back at me, like he knows I'm just standing there in the rain watching him go. For a moment I think he will come back and talk to me, but then he balls up his fists and he is gone.

RUN

The same Therin that answered the door to me yesterday opens up the back door at the Asha Household. Her eyes are a weak blue and rheumy, and I wonder if she can even see me at all. "Yes?"

"I need to see Penny."

The Therin shakes her head. "Now really isn't the best time. Penny has come down with a chill. You should come back in a couple of days."

She goes to shut the door but I shove my booted foot in the gap and growl. This can have a useful effect on people, I'm learning. She shrinks back and stares at me like I'm mad.

"I just need to speak to her for a minute. Please." I try not to sound like I'm on the brink of giving in to the tidal wave of panic and fear and adrenaline smashing through my veins, making me want to start breaking things. That really wouldn't help matters. She gathers the hem of her pale green shirt in her hand and scrunches it up while she glares at me.

"Her father won't like it," she says.

"Don't tell him I'm here, then. Just go and get Penny."

The Therin nods hesitantly and backs away from the door, and I'm left trying to work out if it was a massive mistake coming here. She could be telling Penny's father that there's a mad girl handing out orders on his back doorstep right this second. He would most definitely drag me straight back to the Kitsch Household. It would be all over then. Rain or no rain, Lowrence would force me kicking screaming up to the technicians compound, and then I would be dealing with a whole new world of trouble.

Doubt gets the better of me, and I'm about to make a dash for it when Penny stumbles down the stairs in a violet dressing gown and her hair in a tangled auburn mess about her head. I gasp when I see her face; a fierce-looking bruise purples beneath her right eye, the hue complementing that of her dressing gown quite nicely. Her lip is badly swollen and split. She grimaces at me and pulls me out of the rain.

"What are you doing here?"

"My brother found out. He's telling my family right now. What happened to you?"

She brushes my hand away when I go to touch her cheek, and ducks her head so that her hair falls over her face. It doesn't hide the bruise though, or the fact that she's been crying.

"My father...he—"

"Oh."

She'd said yesterday that her father hit her and that Cai had been angry when he'd found out, but still, I'd somehow convinced myself that was a one-time thing. It obviously wasn't. She pulls her dressing gown tight around her small frame and hurries us into the kitchen. The rain hammers against the window, and the sound almost steals away her whispered voice as she says, "If your family finds out—"

"I know. I have to go."

A pained smile pulls at one side of Penny's mouth, the side that isn't three times its normal size and bleeding. "You'll need things to keep you going." She whips herself into action and finds a leather satchel hanging in the pantry, which she starts stuffing with food. I'm standing there like an idiot when the Therin from before enters the kitchen and takes a sharp breath.

"Uh—" I clear my throat. "Penny?"

Penny turns around and scowls at the Therin. "Don't just stand there. Help me."

The woman starts like she's been caught slacking off and joins Penny in dumping small rolls of bread and hunks of cheese into the satchel. A few oranges find their way in there too, and a flask of water. Penny shoves the bag into my hand and leads me back to the door.

"I have no idea how I'm going to do this," I groan. "You don't understand. There's a fence and guards and—"

"Whatever you do, don't try to clear the fence," she says hurriedly.

"Then what? How am I supposed to get out?"

Penny glances over her shoulder as the stairs creak loudly, signalling someone is coming down. "Penny? What are you doing? Who's at the door?" It's her father. A look of fear washes over her face.

"Follow the river. You can get out that way."

"But how?"

The creaking of the stairs turns into actual footsteps, and Penny panics, pushing me out of the door. "I don't know, Kit. Cai just said that he'd found a way. Maybe it's on the stick. Watch it." She pauses for a fraction of a second to reach through the slim gap in the door. She squeezes my hand. "Good luck."

"Thank you."

She closes the door, and I hear shouting on the other side.

******

The material of my clothes is kind of water resistant, but once it's been exposed to a sheeting downpour for more than a couple of hours it gives up any pretence that it's going to be useful and starts taking on water. This makes running very hard, but I keep going. All in all, this was probably the best and worst time for me to decide to leave the Sanctuary. The city was abandoned while the storm raged on like the world was ending, and not one person confronted me as I raced through the richer areas, where the river flows. Like everywhere else in the Sanctuary, the salubrious side to the city eventually petered out and gave way to slums. Both of those places are behind me now. Now, there is just the narrow pathway between the fenced-in fields on one side of me, and the river on the other, which is swollen and angry.

The rain keeps coming and I don't think it's planning on stopping any time soon. I wonder if Lowrence has informed the authorities that I'm missing, and if they'll have any idea of what I'm planning to do. It would be surprising if they did, because I don't have a clue, myself. Some point soon, I have to find shelter—somewhere dry where I can rest for a minute and do like Penny said. I need to watch Cai's holostick to figure out how I'm supposed to get out of here.

Doing that isn't going to be easy. The land outside the city is flat for miles and miles in every direction. This highlights two major problems, which are these: First, I know there is nowhere for me to stop because these fields are seemingly endless, and there are no buildings or even any trees in sight. And even if there were, I wouldn't be able to get to them. Just like yesterday on the dirt track to the processing plant, there are chain link fences, only here not only do they go up remarkably high on either side of the water, but they then curve over to meet directly overhead. I am fenced in.

Second, it's a major problem that the land is so flat because that means it's incredibly easy for the river to burst its banks. And, referring back to problem one, I am fenced in. Right now I'm running on a very narrow pathway next to a raging body of water that's incrementally getting bigger and bigger, and I have nowhere to go.

Turning back is impossible. The water has been rising gradually the whole time I've been running, and I wouldn't get a mile before my situation becomes dire. My only option is to push forward as hard as I can and hope against hope that I hit *something* that can help me get out of this cage. Otherwise I'm going in the water, and I don't like my chances of surviving that since I've never been swimming in my life.

If my halo were working right now, I'd probably be able to deal with this situation a whole lot better. But, logically, if my halo were working right now, I most definitely wouldn't be in this situation at all. I ignore these kinds of thoughts while I push myself forward. My back's been aching for the last eight miles mainly because the stupid satchel Penny gave me wasn't designed to be worn while running, and it continually slams against my spine.

My brother's face keeps flashing into my mind when he told me that everything was going to be okay, and I feel hideous for leaving him. It's not as though he's going to be personally offended that I've abandoned him, but it still stings. I should have persuaded him to come with me. Forced him to if need be. Not that his presence would help with what's happening right now. My legs feel heavier with every step I take, and when I stumble and almost slip into the surging grey water, my heart rises up and threatens to burst out of my throat.

I have to stop here and watch the stick before I don't get a chance. With shaking hands I take the small plastic square from my back pocket, and fat raindrops instantly begin to bead on its surface. I hunch my body over to shield it and then frown, my finger pressing firmly on the play button. Nothing. Absolutely nothing happens. I form half a word in my mouth before I realise I don't know a curse word strong enough for this particular moment. Cai, albeit sensibly, given his non-functioning-halo status, has screwed me completely by encoding the holostick. I'm furiously wracking my brain, trying to work out if the four-digit code might be something I know, when my feet suddenly go cold.

I look down and the water is fast approaching my ankles. I let out a frustrated growl and close my hand around the stick. Shucking the satchel off my back, I root around inside, pulling out the small black flask that Penny filled with water for me. I open it and empty it out, figuring that water hardly seems to be a problem for me right now, and then I shove the stick inside, fastening the lid on tight. It goes back inside the satchel, and I triple knot the drawstrings so I'm not in danger of losing anything inside.

The food is going to be ruined but there's nothing I can do about that. By the time I've done all of this, the water is inching up towards my knees. There's no point trying to run now; I wade forward as quickly as I can, but the rushing water against the backs of my legs makes staying upright tough. It doesn't take long before I lose my balance and fall forward onto all fours. The word 'irony' held very little meaning for me before Cai ripped my halo off, but I'm truly beginning to understand its meaning now. For years I have been thrown into countless scenarios during my amphi-matches where I could easily have died over and over again, and yet I didn't. And now, when all I need to do is get from one point to another, it looks like my number's up. I laugh for the second time in my life, only it sticks like a bitter gasp in my throat.

The river surges forward, and I am swept away.

FLOOD

bright light shines into my eyes, and I briefly think someone's come into my room and opened my curtains too early. My body feels like it did the day after I fought and barely beat Falin Hetzin. It's hard to breathe; my ribs ache, and my left forearm burns like crazy. It takes me a while to figure out why. I panic when I crack my eyes open. It's stopped raining and the sun is shining, but I'm still half submerged in the river. My back is pressed against the siding of a small brick aqueduct. The river roars through it, disappearing down a long, dark tunnel. I'm within reach of the embankment, but I have no hope of pulling myself out of the water, because a huge tree limb is pinning me against my chest, crushing me back against the wall. On top of this, there's a gash on my arm, and my blood is swirling into the water and rushing away with it.

Weirdly, my jacket is gone, which is bad but not the very worst thing. The worst thing is that the satchel is gone, too. I consider the massive tree trunk pressing me back into the smooth surface of the cool bricks and think how a person wearing a functioning halo would react in this situation. I can't even begin to imagine. There are so many conflicting feelings stabbing through me right now that it seems impossible that I'll find a way out of this mess. I need to pick one emotion and go with it otherwise I'm going to be stuck here forever. I choose anger.

I smash my fists against the tree branch for a while, before I realise that it's not doing me any good, and my knuckles begin to bleed. I focus all the fury that I have pent up inside me so that I can try pushing the branch away from me, but the current of the water is far too strong. By the time I've exhausted all of my energy, all of my anger is gone too, and I'm left with little more than fear.

Fear has to be the most unpleasant feeling I've ever experienced. It leaves me frantic and filled with self-pity, and I end up getting angry all over again at how pathetic I'm being. I slump forward and lean into the branch, burying my face into my arms, careful to avoid the burning cut.

I'm pinned there for longer than I care to admit before a miracle happens. Another huge log sweeps down the river and collides with the limb trapping me. The thing splits in two with an ear-jarring, splintering noise. I see it all happening in slow motion, and I reach out and grab onto a fistful of tangled tree roots before the log breaks, clinging on for dear life when the current tries to take me, too. I scramble up the embankment, my boots squelching, my legs numb and threatening to crumple. Once I'm safe, I collapse beside the brick aqueduct. It hurts far too much when I try and breathe. There's a very real chance I have some broken ribs.

Everything is freezing cold. I roll onto my back and concentrate on trying to breathe through the pain coursing through my body. Who knows, though? Maybe I'm not suffering that much pain at all, and if I hadn't lived my whole life with a damned halo glued around my neck, I would be able to deal with this more efficiently. But I have had the halo, and I'm not dealing with the pain at all. My own muffled cries keep on surprising me with how weak they sound.

I fall asleep for a while, and when I wake up the sun is starting to sink. My clothes have dried out at least, but I still feel like vomiting from the pain in my ribs. I get up stiffly and take in my surroundings for the first time. The fence is still there, of course, and it sweeps out to the left and the right for I don't know how far. It's eventually swallowed by trees, but I know that just because it's hidden doesn't mean it ends. The river now cuts through the fence via the aqueduct tunnel, and it's the only way I can see myself getting through.

The thought that Cai has probably stood here, calculating how to swim through this tunnel makes me dizzy. I don't know if he ever tried it, but if he did then it will have been when the water was less insane. He might have even been able to wade through with his combat pants rolled up around his ankles, and the whole thing had been a pleasant experience. Right now the water is so high and charging so hard that there's barely a gap at the top of the tunnel. White foam spews up when it hits the brickwork, causing spray to shoot three feet into the air.

I back away from the water and lean against the fencing like I have another option and I'm just waiting for it to hit me. Nothing hits me. As soon as the sun goes down I'm going to be in trouble. I'm exhausted and I'm hurt, and if I don't get this done now there's no way I'm going to be strong enough in the morning when the cold, hard ground has leached away what little reserves I have left.

A small voice inside my head suggests that maybe the water levels will have dropped by morning, but there's no way of telling with how hard the rain fell earlier. It could be like this for days, and then I really would be screwed. I feel half drunk when I stumble back down the embankment and dip my feet in the water.

My body convulses when the biting, icy current skirls around my toes. Doesn't bode well for how I'm going to react when I have to submerge my whole body in it. I do the only thing I can think of to get this over with quickly and plunge myself in. I immediately regret it. The water is so deep I can't touch the bottom, but that doesn't really matter, because it's moving so fast I wouldn't have been able stand even if I'd wanted to. In a split second I'm caught up and dragged under the water. When I come up, spluttering, it's dark and I've been sucked into the tunnel. There are only a few inches at the top of the water where I can breathe, and I tip my head back and pull in a wheezing gasp. Before I can take a second something strikes me in my stomach, hard, and I go back under.

The water is filthy and filled with debris, and silt pours up my nose. I thrust my hand out to try and stop myself or grab hold of something. My knuckles smash against the side of the tunnel and a spiralling pain shoots up my arm. It's only when I breach the surface again and the sun is shining above me that the frigid fingers of fear loosen their grip around my heart. It's still slamming in my chest, but at least I now know I'm not going to drown in the dark. If I die, it'll be with sunlight on my back.

HALO

On the other side of the tunnel the river spins in a dangerous current, whipping the water to create a green-brown foam that floats on the surface. Tree branches and shattered wood clog up my exit to the banks on both my left and my right; the fast flowing water picks some of them up before smashing them up and spitting them out again ten metres away. There's something up ahead there—a line of black, jagged rocks dam the river, and the water turns white where it collides with a brutal force against them.

I'm considering screaming when I see something flashing out of the corner of my eye. There's someone beside the river, and they're rushing forward toward the rocks as quickly as I am. This keeps me from making a sound. If I'm going to be dashed to pieces, then I'm damn well going to retain my dignity while I do it. My boots feel like leaden weights as I start to kick, trying to guide myself away from the scariest, sharpest-looking boulders. My efforts have no effect, and within seconds I'm thrown directly into the middle of the piled rocks. The air huffs out of my lungs as I impact, holding out my hands in the vain hope that I'll be able to brace myself. A biting pain spasms through the right hand side of my body, and I pull in a startled breath. More water than air fills my mouth. I'm spluttering and scrabbling frantically when the blurry outline of a person steps out onto the rocks with nimble, bare feet.

No way am I hanging around to find out who this is or what they want. From somewhere—I have no idea where—I find enough energy to shove myself away from the approaching figure. Gripping hold of the wet stone until it feels like I'm going to rip out my own fingernails, I claw myself towards the other side of the bank. I'm almost shocked when I manage to reach the other side. I roll myself out of the water onto the mud and lie flat on my back, gasping.

"Well, that was unnecessary," a low voice calls. I ignore it and tuck my legs up to my chest, wincing as my stomach cramps. I turn onto my side and throw up all of the water I've swallowed. It looks brackish and foul even on the way out. When I eventually find it in me to sit up, there's a boy crouching down on the other side of the narrow river, staring at me. No halo.

His hair is bright blond and tied back into a messy ponytail. It's so short I can tell he must have to re-tie it fifty times a day. Strands of it hang down into his face even now. His eyes are startlingly dark, a very intense brown. His shirt is filthy—black, or at least it was at some point. It's splattered with mud that's obviously been there for a while, because it's cracked and turned white in places where it's dried out under the sun. His sleeves are rolled up to his elbows, revealing tiny, centimetre long black lines that run along the underside of his forearm from his wrist to his elbow. I can't tell if they keep going but I'm willing to bet they do.

I prop myself onto my knees and spit out the disgusting taste in my mouth. He makes a surprised huffing sound out of his nose, barely audible over the dull roar of the water.

"Charming."

No way I'm responding to that. Instead I sink back onto my heels and glare at him. "What do you want?"

He folds his arms across his body and pulls up the corner of his mouth into a smirk. I've only ever seen a smile like that on Lowrence before, and it makes me want to hit him repeatedly in the face. "What do I *want*?" he says.

I nod, trying to be covert as I run dirty palms up over my thighs. I relax when I hit the webbing of my knife belt, although my fingers only find my daggers there. Everything else seems to be gone. "Yes. What do you want?"

"No, *Who are you?* No, *Thanks for risking your life to come and save me?*"

Now it's my turn to snort. "I didn't need saving. I got out on my own, didn't I?"

The boy nods his head thoughtfully. "Yes. You were very graceful."

The tone of his voice makes the hairs on the back of my neck bristle. "Did my father send you?"

"Depends on who your father is."

"Lowrence Kitsch, of Household Kitsch."

The boy thinks on this and then shakes his head. "Nope."

"Well, then, why are you here?"

He rises slowly from his crouch, revealing that he's wearing a knife belt over his dark pants, which are as filthy as his shirt. They're soaking wet at the bottom, presumably from where he waded over the rocks to try and reach me. The handles of his knives look like they're made out of steel instead of plastic or wood. Expensive. They glint brightly where the sunlight lances down through the surrounding trees.

"Anyone ever told you it's impolite to eye up a man's hardware?" he asks. I pull a sour face at him and draw out my daggers, wiping their blades back and forth across my thighs to dry them. "You're not a man," I tell him. "You're a boy."

This makes him clench his jaw. "I'm eighteen. That qualifies for manhood

49

where I come from."

"Then we clearly don't come from the same place."

He scowls. "Okay. Fine. I'm glad you didn't drown. Sort of. Good luck with whatever it is you're doing out here."

I square off my shoulders at him and lock my jaw. "Thanks."

He's still barefoot when he backs away from the other side of the river, the mud oozing up between his toes. He doesn't turn away from me until there are a good few trees around him. Maybe he suspects I'll send a knife his way, although I'm sure he must have noticed that my throwing blades are gone. I feel my mouth curling into a weird expression as he melts into the forest, and I raise my fingertips up to my lips to see what they feel like.

KIT

The forest is freezing at night and filled with sounds I don't recognise. Every shadow or rustling sound is Lowrence or even Cai's True father coming to get me, and I must only sleep half an hour at a time. I have no idea what I'm supposed to do now, and a part of me regrets not wheedling some information out of that stranger on the far side of the river. He did try to help me, I think, but I can't be sure. I was just so battered both mentally and physically from the water that I didn't really think properly. I shouldn't have let him leave.

The ground is unbelievably hard, and when the sun finally steps out over the horizon, I think my bones are more bruised than when I laid down to try and sleep. Everything hurts. Everything throbs. My halo has somehow found its way out and over my shirt in the night, and I'm panicked when I tuck it back under my clothes. The smooth, rigid metal is icy cold. Makes me suck in a sharp breath when it hits my skin. It's entirely free from my body now. All of the tumbling and the thrashing yesterday must have finally worked it loose from the back of my neck. The skin definitely feels sore there, anyway. I prod the metal with my fingers underneath my shirt, and the whole thing rotates around my neck.

I shake my head and clamber to my feet, and that's when I notice I'm covered in small, brown insects. They're everywhere, crawling all over me. I make a very high pitched noise and start slapping at my clothes, my skin, my hair. Their tiny little bodies have worked their way down the back of my shirt, I'm sure of it. I'm not satisfied they're all gone until I've ripped off my clothes and hopped around for fifteen minutes, swatting at any speck of dirt or faint mark on my body.

I don't hear anybody approaching, and that's a mistake. I should be paying attention, should be on guard, but I'm too freaked out to realise I'm not alone. When I look up, standing there in my underwear, I meet a pair of sombre brown eyes. My hand automatically goes to my waist where my knife belt should be, but it's not there. It's on the ground, still attached to my combat gear. The brown eyes watch carefully as I step back and sink to the ground, reaching out for a blade.

Having a dagger in my hand feels good and helps me think I'm in control, but when he starts walking forward, four legs— *four legs!*— on the ground, I panic.

"Stop!" My voice jars in the heavy silence of the morning, and something comes to life in a tree above me. Long, extended wings rustle and take to the sky in a flash of black and grey, with a sheen of blue-green. A bird. My first bird. I've only ever seen them represented by distant specks of black against the sky before; they never land in the Sanctuary, like they know the place is simply off limits. I'm so shocked by the sight of the small animal taking flight now that I don't realise the creature in front of me has crept forward. A feeling, a wet rasping across the back of my hand, startles me, and I shriek. Not very smart at all.

The animal drops into a hunched position straight away, looking up at me with curiosity in his eyes. There's hair all over his body, tan and black, and he smells musky and warm like the earth. I know he's a dog, I just never expected to see one. He looks equally as astounded to be seeing me, too.

Dogs aren't supposed to be friendly. They're supposed to be vicious meat eaters, and I have no trouble believing this when he opens his mouth and a large, pink tongue lolls over his gigantic canines. Ripping, tearing teeth. I stagger backwards and stoop low to gather up my clothes. I'm slipping my legs into my pants when he tips his head to one side and lets out a small bark, which is enough to make me topple over backwards. Lying on the floor, wrestling the rest of my clothes on takes but a few seconds. I'm warily watching the dog, tugging my boots back on, when he darts forward.

For a moment I freeze, unsure what to do. His face is in my face, and his tongue is still lolling as he breathes in and out and in and out. His breath stinks like day-old stew. I'm sure he's going to attack me, and I brace for it.

He licks my cheek instead.

I resist the urge to scrub at my face with the back of my hand, because the way he's watching me, his head bobbing up and down as he pants, sort of makes it look like he's laughing. My apprehension falls away, and I find myself laughing, too. This is the first time I've ever enjoyed the sensation of laughing. It bubbles out of me, rises up from my belly, and I listen to it echoing off the crowded lengths of the tree trunks that stretch on forever.

I get up eventually, and the dog shadows me, flicking his pricked ears back and forth behind him as he listens to things I can't hear. I begin to make my way further into the forest, and he whines. His whine becomes a bark when I continue walking, and I stop and turn to look at him. He's stood watching me, his body still, as though he's waiting for me to do something.

"What?"

He cocks his head to the side again and nods at me impatiently. I have no idea what this means. He circles quickly and waits again, and I make back towards him to see what he wants. As soon as I take a step, he spins and bounds off through the forest, back towards the river. He stops after six or seven paces, looking over his shoulder to see if I'm still there. I could be wrong, but I think he wants me to follow him.

"I'm not going back in that water."

He barks, and I think we're on the same page. I trudge after him, not particularly enjoying the way that my boots are still squishy and damp inside. After an hour we're back by the river, and the water is even more ferocious than it was yesterday. Good thing I came through when I did, because the brickwork aqueduct is no longer visible, and the seething vein of water floods and rushes straight over it, bursting through the fence. A shiver runs the length of my body, and the dog makes a hushed yip.

"I don't know what you're so nervous about," I tell him. He wags his tail and

53

starts off away from the fence, following a trail that hugs the side of the river. It looks like a real pathway, although it's overgrown and difficult to navigate in places. I constantly have to clamber over fallen logs and fight my way through overgrown plants with long, vibrant green fronds. The dog patiently waits for me.

By midday the fact that I haven't eaten or drunk anything in a while begins to become a problem. I have no clue what I'm going to do about this. There's no food out here but at least there's water. I stop every twenty minutes, cupping my hands gingerly into the raging river that we follow, drinking draught after draught until my stomach feels like it's going to split. This takes away the hunger pains for a while, but it's not long before they're replaced by a whole new kind of pain.

The sweating comes on hard, and I can feel the buds of my perspiration pushing their way out of every single pore on my body. My skin feels irritated and flushed. About an hour after the sweating starts, I begin to throw up. The experience is new, painful and violent, and it goes on and on until I feel like I'm going to pass out. The dog comes and stands by me dutifully as I kneel in the dirt, staring at the filthy half crescents of muck under my nails. I can tell he wants to get moving but I can't. I feel like I'm dying.

I roll onto my back and pluck out one of my daggers from my knife belt because it's comforting to have it in my hand. I know its weight. I know the texture of its handle beneath my fingertips. It's the only thing familiar to me in this alien world. I stare up at a chink of blue sky that's visible through the forest canopy, waiting for my body to stop trembling. I lie there for a long time before the dog whines softly and then sinks down beside me, pressing his warm, musky body against mine. I go to sleep thinking of Cai.

10

RYKA

Hot. Something feels blisteringly hot, too close to my face. I sit up quickly and a wave of vertigo punches through my body. Without a doubt, if there was anything left inside me I would throw it up. The dog is gone. I'm not where I fell asleep anymore, either. I'm sitting on some sort of blue foam mat, and there's a balled-up wad of dark material behind me where my head was resting. A fire crackles about a metre away from me. I shuffle away from it, worried by its proximity.

"What's the matter? Don't like being warm?" a voice, *that* voice, asks me. I try to focus my eyes in the dark, but they've been blinded by the bright flames and it takes me a second to locate him. The blond boy leans against a rotten tree stump on the other side of the fire, and the dog is nestled into his side. *Traitor.*

"Of course I like being warm. I've just never been this close to a fire before,"

I grumble.

"*Never?*" He seems incredulous.

"No. The Sanctuary has strict rules about fire. Too easy for it to get out of control. It could take out the whole city in one go."

He seems to think about this. His face is a little rosy from sitting too close to the flames. I take the opportunity to make a quick study of him, looking for his tells. The way he holds himself is confident and a little cocky, even just sitting there. His muscles are tensed in a way that suggests he's not as comfortable as he's pretending he is, though. He's still wearing his knife belt, although he must have taken mine off me because it's bundled up neatly at my side. I was wrong before; there isn't much boy left in him. He's at that almost grown stage where all he needs to do is fill out a little more and he'll be worryingly big. Fat chance I'm admitting this to him, though.

"How did you find me?" I ask him.

"Jada," he replies, scrubbing his hand against the back of the dog's neck. The dog perks up his ears, recognising his name.

"You sent a dog to spy on me." This is a ridiculous concept, but that's what it seems like he's saying.

"I couldn't cross the river for a while. She could. I knew she'd find you. She's good at finding people."

"She?" I don't know why, but I'd never even questioned the fact that the dog was male.

The blond guy stretches his legs out and crosses his ankles. "I've had her since she was a puppy."

"Oh." Now would probably an appropriate time to ask what he plans on doing with me, but instead I slump back against the blue mat and stack my hands across my stomach. It feels tender and sore.

We remain there in silence with the fire snapping and sending embers skirling off into the night air. They twist and spiral upwards around one another, burning orange and yellow, and watching them makes my breath catch in my throat. After a while the blond guy says, "I'm leaving early in the morning. If you want to come with me, you should get some rest. Go back to sleep."

"Who says I want to go with you?"

The blond guy chuckles and tosses another log onto the fire, making it spit. "You're right. You were doing so well on your own. I shouldn't have made any assumptions."

"No, you shouldn't."

"You're really hostile, you know that?"

I have no idea what he means. All I know is that I don't like his attitude or the way he looks at me with that smirk on his face. I roll onto my side, away from him and away from the fire. "I'm getting some sleep."

"Good. *If* you decide to come with me in the morning, I can take you to someone who can help."

I bend my arm under my head and use it as a pillow, but it's really not that effective. Despite the mat, I can tell this is going to be just as uncomfortable as last night. "Help with what?"

He pauses for a long second before he says, "With getting that thing off your neck."

My body tenses and I pull in a sharp breath. "You know what it is?"

"Oh, I know what it is. And I know you really mustn't have wanted it on you anymore to have torn it off."

If I had any energy, I might have told him that it wasn't my choice. Every part of my body hurts, though, and talking about how my halo came to be ripped from me will only serve to make my heart hurt, too. I don't go to sleep; I just lie there on my side listening to the boy and the dog shift quietly. As I grow drowsy, an impulsive part of me forces me to ask, "What's your name?"

I think he's fallen asleep for a moment, but then he says, "Ryka. My name is Ryka."

"Huh." Ryka feels too short. He is so close to my age and he's wearing a knife belt. Seems to me he should be a Falin of some Household, and a rich one by the looks of his blades. But he's clearly not. I chew on my thumbnail, wondering where he's come from and whether he's grown up his whole life without a halo.

"You feel like telling me who *you* are?" he asks, his voice low.

I try to figure out if I even know the answer to that myself. "I don't really have a name."

"What? But...you must be called something. How do people usually address you?"

"They don't."

Ryka sighs, loud enough to make Jada whine. "You're being difficult."

"I—ugh—" I hold my hands up to my face and flex them out. My knuckles are caked with dried-on blood and swollen, which is no doubt why it hurts so much to move them. "I am Falin Kitsch."

"Wow. Clinical. I'm not calling you that."

"Okay."

"*Okay?* Come on, you have to think of something shorter. I'm not referring to you as *hey, you* all day tomorrow."

I squint up into the sky where one of the stars, a distant silver pinprick, looks to be moving ever so slowly across the bruised blue of the heavens. "Kit, then," I say. "I guess you can call me Kit."

CHOKEHOLD

I wake up to find Ryka pouring water over the burning embers of the fire and Jada licking furiously at an empty wooden bowl. Her tongue makes wet tearing noises as she goes to work. My clothes feel damp and cold, and my bones ache almost as much as yesterday. Almost.

I'm trying to work out how I'm supposed to retract my previous statement—the one about not wanting to go with Ryka—whilst retaining my dignity, when I see it. The satchel. The one Penny gave me. It sits on the ground next to a more rugged-looking black bag, which was definitely designed for hiking and running. My heart does a small summersault when I realise Cai's holostick is probably still in the water flask.

"That's mine," I say, pointing at the satchel. My first words of the day are broken, my voice cracking from disuse. Ryka looks at me sharply.

"I don't know about that."

"It is. I lost it when I was in the river."

"Exactly. You lost it. I found it."

My face reddens as I scramble to my feet, suddenly very, very awake. "Give it to me."

Ryka laughs, flashing white, straight teeth. "I don't think so. That's not how things work out here."

"I don't care how things work *out here*. I want my bag back."

"Why? What's so important? Are you partial to sodden bread and water-logged cheese?"

My urge to scream is incredibly strong, and I have to fix my jaw to stop myself. "I just want the water flask."

Jada looks up from her bowl and studies Ryka and me with inquisitive eyes. It's like she can sense that I'm about to lose my temper and fly at him.

"Just the water flask?" he asks. There's a small smile ticking at his mouth.

"*Yes.*"

Ryka makes a show of slowly stooping down and collecting up the satchel. The leather is still soaking wet, and water drips from it when he picks it up. The small black water flask is the very first thing he pulls out. "You mean this?"

"Yes. Give it to me." I lunge forward and try and snatch it from him, but he's quick, just like I thought he would be. He twists his body around so I can't reach the flask and a wicked smile breaks out across his face. He opens it without taking his eyes off me, and pulls out the tiny piece of metal and plastic. For a moment I'm so relieved that it wasn't damaged in the water that I feel like I'm choking. Ryka pops the lid back onto the water flask and then holds it out to me. The holostick remains gripped firmly in his other hand.

"Here you are. One water flask."

This is just too much. I may have only just woken up, and my body may be stiffer than it ever has been before, but I somehow find it in me to dive for my knife belt and snag one of my daggers. Perhaps he wasn't expecting this, because Ryka's smile wavers a little before he slips the holostick into his pocket and plucks out one of his own knives. A narrow stiletto blade, four inches long and beautifully sharp. A puncturing blade. It shines like molten silver.

"I guess it's time we got this out of the way," he tells me.

"What do you mean?"

60

"Well, you're a girl walking around with a knife belt like it belongs to you. Some people might consider that asking for trouble."

"It *does* belong to me. And I'm not asking for trouble. I'm asking for *what belongs to me*," I snap. I drop down so that my centre of gravity is lower and flick my dagger over in my hand so the spine presses flat against my forearm.

"C'mon, *Kit*. Who did you steal them from?"

"I didn't steal anything. These daggers were given to me by the Sanctuary municipality in recognition of my fiftieth match win. They gave me some throwing blades in recognition of my hundredth but I lost them in the river."

Ryka grins, dropping into a wide guard stance I'm not familiar with. He holds his knife like it's an extension of his body, a part of him. "I almost believed you before, but now I know you're lying. Even those heartless bastards in Lockdown wouldn't put a girl in the arena. And fifty wins? Should have said five. That would have been unbelievable enough."

I growl at him, tightening my grip around the dagger handle. If he doesn't believe me then that's his problem. But I'm getting that holostick back, one way or another. He's too busy grinning at me to see what I'm doing with my feet. I angle my back leg so that it's turned at a forty five degree angle to my body— a good, solid position to ground me. It only takes a slight lunge and I'm right up close. I keep my back foot planted and kick swiftly upwards with my front leg, feeling the energy twist from the floor through my body, travelling out when I make contact with the heel of his palm. His arm flies back and he lets go of his stiletto, which arcs upwards into the air before pivoting gracefully and falling point down. The knife strikes vertically and buries itself an inch in the dirt between us. Closer to me than him. I bend at the waist, never taking my eyes off him, and I snatch it up, sliding it into one of the free loops on my belt.

"I take it this is how things work out here, Ryka? You lost something. I found it. That makes it mine, right?"

Ryka's face is very different to how it was a minute ago. His liquid brown eyes are wide and round, and his smile seems to have vanished altogether. He must have thought I would start slashing wildly just because I had sharpened steel in my hand. But why dirty my equipment when my feet are just as good a weapon as anything else?

"You'd better give me back that knife," he tells me.

I curl my lips in a way that I think mirrors his smug smile from before. It feels good, and I can almost understand why he was doing it. "I don't think so."

A muscle jumps at Ryka's jaw, and he runs his hand back through the bright blond hair that's fallen loose from his ponytail. When he sweeps it out of his face, I catch a glimpse of the markings on his forearm again, a stack of evenly spaced black lines disappearing up underneath his shirtsleeve.

"Don't get cocky," he says. "Just because you surprised me doesn't mean you're a knife fighter. Now give it back."

"Give me back the holostick."

Ryka shoves his thumbs through the loops on his knife belt. I guess everyone that wears one everywhere in the world must do it. "No."

I shrug my shoulders. "Well, you're not likely to get this pretty piece of silver back then, are you?" I trace my thumb over the warm hilt of the knife, watching Ryka flinch as I do.

His shoulders tense, and even though his eyes are locked on mine I know what's coming. When he leaps forward, a double-edged dagger of his own suddenly in his hands, I have already dodged to the side. There's a cold fury to the way he snakes after me, like he's angry I was prepared for him. He strikes out with his dagger and I duck low, hearing the metal whistle through the air. I drop and roll backwards, righting myself into a crouch. I balance with a hand lightly resting on the dirt and the other one held out, point first. A warning. Baring my teeth. If he comes any closer, I'll strike.

Ryka blows out a frustrated breath and steps an inch closer, daring me. I explode up from the ground, but clearly not how he expects me to. I lean my body weight on my right side, my strong side, making him think that's where I'll be moving. A small glimmer of a smile flashes over his face when he jumps to the left, thinking he's outsmarted me. But that's where I meet him. My body slams into his and we fall backwards, landing on Ryka's bag and the satchel.

His boots kick up clouds of acrid dust from the charred remains of the fire. He shoves me roughly with his free hand, pushing me away. I can tell he's not using all his strength with me, though. That's a mistake. He's quick, sure, but I'm quick, too. If he considered me a real threat even for a second, he would be using his strength against me. In the arena it would be the only thing between winning and dying a brutal death. His lack of conviction that I'm half the fighter I say I am makes me see red, and I decide to teach him a lesson. I whip my body around while he's still scrabbling to get up, and I hook my legs around his neck.

Before he can react, or slip out of the hold, or even *blink*, I tighten my thighs and squeeze. I've killed someone like this before. Admittedly the crowd was displeased—you are technically supposed to overcome your opponent with your knives—but there are no set rules. And like I said, when it's a matter of life and death, winning or losing, you should always use your strengths to overcome your opponent.

Ryka knows he's in trouble. He reaches up and tries prising my legs free from his throat but it's too late for that. I could probably sit back and relax until he passes out, but I don't. I'm still polluted with this ridiculous anger, so I lean forward and nick his forearm instead—just a small cut, but it has a purpose. It tells him that I'm in the position of power right now, and if I wanted to, I could easily do a lot worse. When I unravel my legs from around him, Ryka pulls in a wheezing gasp and rolls away from me, clutching at his throat.

"What the hell?"

I get up, feeling pretty pleased with myself. He looks like he wants to murder me. Maybe I let my guard down because I think he is still recovering, or maybe it's that Ryka's quicker than I thought, but I barely have time to ready my dagger before I'm back on the floor and he's on top of me. We're both gasping for breath, and Ryka's holding his dagger to my throat. There's a flash in his eyes that I've seen a hundred times before in the arena—that look people get when they think they've already won. Confidence. Or maybe it's just relief. Anyway, like all of those other people who wore that look before him, it's a false sense of victory. His expression changes when he realises I have my dagger pressed against his windpipe, too.

His eyes harden and grow a little darker. "Are you going to give me back my knife?" he hisses.

"Are you going to give me back the holostick?"

A stubborn look sets over him. I can feel his heart pounding against my chest. He must be able to feel mine as well. His eyes flicker momentarily to my halo, which has worked free from under my shirt and fallen back to rest on the hand he has pressed against my neck.

"No. You can't have it."

"Fine," I spit. "Then get off me." The fact that he's touching my halo, or that my halo is touching him, really, makes my cheeks flame.

Ryka pulls back and sinks onto his heels, scooting away from me as quickly as he can. "I'm not sure you *should* come with me today," he sulks.

I sit up, still holding out the knife in case he thinks he can rush me again. "Actually, I've thought about that and I've decided it's a fantastic idea."

A small, hard laugh works free from his chest, and Jada barks. "Fat lot of good you are," he tells her. The dog comes up to me and licks my hand. Maybe she isn't a traitor, after all. Ryka regards her with poorly concealed disgust, which only increases when he looks at me. "If you're coming with me, you're going to want to change your ideas about being some sort of knife-fighting queen. In fact, you're going to want to re-think carrying knives in general."

"And why's that?"

"Because," he says, getting to his feet, "women don't fight where I come from. And they certainly don't cut random men." His fingers twitch like he wants to touch the spot on his arm where I sliced him.

"It was a tiny scratch," I tell him.

"I know. But where I come from it means something. Come on." He slips his dagger back into his belt and steps forward, holding his hand out to me. I'm not stupid enough to think he won't reach for his stiletto if I let him pull me up, so I kick back and stand without his help. He quirks an eyebrow at me.

"You really are something else."

"So are you." I don't say this with quite as much admiration as he did.

"Just don't say I didn't warn you, okay?" he says. "You're really going to wish you'd listened to me."

COLLAR

Ryka gives me back the satchel now that there's nothing in it I want, and we set off walking. It's less than an hour before I start feeling sick again, and the sweating comes on hard. I must look flushed because Ryka stops stalking through the forest like he's hell bent on leaving me behind and makes me rest. I think if he wasn't so desperate to get his knife back he really would leave me. The way he keeps glancing at the stiletto sitting above my hip reminds of the hungry look in the starving children's eyes when I passed through the shanties. That feels like a lifetime ago.

"When was the last time you ate?" he asks.

I spit into the undergrowth, trying to rid my mouth of the sensation that I'm going to throw up. "I don't know. Two days ago?"

"*Two*—"He rolls his eyes. "And what about water?"

I blow out a heavy breath, wishing he'd go back to being silent. It feels distinctly like I'm being told off. "Yesterday. I drank about five litres of water from the river."

Ryka looks accusingly at Jada, who watches us with her tongue unfurled over her teeth, puffing. He shakes his head. "I thought I told you to fetch her back in one piece," he tells the dog. She tenses when he puts his hand in his pocket and pulls out something that he throws into the undergrowth. She bounds off after it, sniffing madly. Ryka loses his smile when he turns to me.

"Don't you know anything? You have to boil water like that if you want to drink it, even if it is fast flowing. It's got all kinds of filth in it."

I feel too terrible to argue with him, so I just breathe deeply and try to piece myself together. I'm kneeling in a sea of green ferns, biting back a groan, when his hand descends into my field of vision. In it is a speckled apple, green for the most part and tinged with pink.

"Eat it," he says. "You're going to pass out otherwise, and I'm not carrying you."

I begrudgingly take the apple and wait for him to back off before I bite into it. We don't have apples like this in the Sanctuary. This apple is imperfect, where as every piece of fruit and vegetable we consume back home is a uniform shape and a uniform size and a uniform colour. The taste is the same, though. Sweet and granular on my tongue. I haven't realised how hungry I am until now, and I make short work of the apple, even eating most of the core.

"How far do we have to go?" I ask. Ryka's been sitting on a rotted-out tree stump watching me eat with blatant curiosity. Gives me the same sort of feeling I used to get when I knew thousands of people were watching, waiting for me to kill someone in a match. I don't want to feel like that right now. I toss what's left of the apple core, and Jada comes barrelling out of nowhere and snatches it up before it hits the ground. "Well?"

He pulls his mouth to one side, looking up at the sky. It must be a few days since he's shaved, because there's a shadow across his jaw, a darker blond than his head. "If we can get moving, we should be there before nightfall."

I nod, thinking. Another night out in the open doesn't sound appealing, but finding the energy to push on seems impossible. There's a little hesitation in me now as well. I hadn't really considered the logistics of leaving the Sanctuary—where I would go, what I would do. Everything just happened so fast.

"This place were going," I say. "Does it have a name?"

Ryka rocks back on the tree stump, giving the knife another furtive look. "Freetown."

"Free*town?*" I must look horrified with my mouth hanging open.

"Yeah. What did you expect?"

"I don't know, I…how many people are there?"

Ryka pulls the corners of his mouth down and shrugs. "Twenty thousand or so."

I mouth the words, *twenty thousand* feeling the apple in my stomach twist. "I had no idea. I had absolutely no idea there were so many."

Ryka snorts and gets to his feet. "What, so you're all shut away in your little city on top of the hill thinking the rest of the world just doesn't exist?"

I look up at him, startled. "Yes!"

"Ha ha! That's possibly the funniest thing I've ever heard. What did they tell you?"

I frown, trying to process this information. "We've always been told there are only small bands of Radicals out here in the forest, maybe ten or fifteen people per group. Certainly no more. I've never really thought about it, I guess, but I figured maybe there were a couple of hundred people living beyond the city walls."

"Radicals?" Ryka narrows his eyes at me. "That's what you call us?"

"Uh-huh."

"Well, that's ironic."

"Why do you say that?"

"Because you're the radical ones. Your government thinks you can't be trusted, can't be civilised enough to handle your own emotions, so they collared the whole population like dogs. Turned you all into walking zombies." He kicks at a small rock with the toe of his boot, and it rolls to a stop in front of me. I pick it up and turn it over in my hands.

"It's not like that. It's for the greater—"

"Are you about to say it's for the *greater good?*" His voice rises in pitch at the end.

I go to answer yes, but then I catch myself. I'm just repeating what they've told me since I was old enough to understand, what I've been brought up to believe was the truth. Except now I know they've lied, maybe about everything. That knowledge makes me feel very small. Remarkably lost. I stare at the rock, pressing its sharp edges into my fingertips until the skin underneath my nails turns white. "I don't know what's good or what's bad anymore."

"I bet. You said you've fought over a hundred matches in Lockdown. That makes you a killer on a pretty grand scale. That can't feel all that good."

I snap my head up at him, biting on my lip. I taste blood before I open my mouth to speak. "I'm not thinking about that."

Ryka laughs loud enough that three birds launch themselves out of the tree branches above us. He ignores them but I follow their flight path upwards until they disappear from view. "You think it's that simple, do you? You think you can just not think about it and it goes away?" He blows out a sharp breath. "I'm telling you now, *if* you ever *do* kill someone, you'll see how absolutely stupid that statement was."

I slump forward and scrub my face in my hands. "You still don't believe me?"

"No way!"

"Urgh! Whatever." The time for wallowing in the dirt, trying to ignore Ryka's scathing comments is over. I'm shaky as hell when I get to my feet, but at least the apple stays down and I feel minutely better. "We should go," I say. Jada lopes off into the forest on a pathway I can't see but she seems to know well. I set off walking, but Ryka catches me by the arm.

"I really am gonna need that knife back before we reach Freetown."

"All you have to do is give me the stick."

He gives me a guarded look. "And I will. But you have to tell me what's on it first."

"I don't know."

"You've gotta be kidding me."

I shake my head. "It belonged to a friend of mine. He used to record himself on it apparently. I haven't had chance to watch it yet."

"So you're telling me you went head to head with a Tamji fighter to get some *diary* back? One you haven't even watched yet? Gee." He rolls his eyes and sets off walking, releasing my arm. "I figured it was something important."

"It *is* important."

"Uh-huh. So where's this important friend of yours right now, huh?"

I hold my breath in my mouth, feeling the words hovering over the tip of my tongue. I keep it short. "He's dead."

Ryka's pace slows. "How?"

"He lost his match."

"Who was he fighting?"

He's going to find this laughable, so I try and lend some weight to my voice when I say, "*Me*."

"Of course." In his words, I can hear the stupid, annoying smile he's wearing. I pretend I don't notice. Better not to acknowledge it at all.

"What's a Tamji fighter?"

Ryka clears his throat. "We have progressions of fighting in Freetown. Everywhere else that I've ever heard of, too."

"There are other places?"

He slows a little more so that he falls into step alongside me. "There are *lots* of other places, other cities," he says. He's mocking me with the way he speaks to me, like I'm a small child. "A Tamji is a fighter of high honour. I've been Tamji for six months. Everyone keeps saying I'll be upgraded after the next few bouts. I'm not sure, though. It depends."

"On what?" I can't help but ask. Their system of fighting sounds so different to the one back home.

Ryka chews on his lip. "On the priestesses. Fighters are upgraded during the blood ceremonies, which are held before each match. The town's priestesses have visions. They call men from the ranks and upgrade them when it is their time."

"So, you aren't promoted based on your skill?"

"It's supposed to be that way, I guess. Loosely. We just go when the priestesses call us."

I screw my face up. Is he lying? He could be for all I can tell; I'm still no good at differentiating the truth from anything else. "That doesn't make any sense."

"Why not?"

"Because! What if someone with no skill is called up to become a *Tamji*," I say, emphasising the term, "and he's not ready?"

"Then it must be his time to die." Ryka says this with such nonchalance that I'm stunned. I try not to let my horror show but it's getting tougher; there are no half measures for me anymore. Everything is either the very best or the very worst thing ever. Mostly the very worst.

"Who are these priestesses? They must be monsters to pitch two unevenly skilled fighters against one another. That's not a match. That's murder."

Ryka blows out a sharp breath from his nose and glares at me. "Firstly, it's *all* murder, no matter how you look at it. And secondly, the Priestesses are revered. Be careful saying stuff like that in future, especially if you want to stay in Freetown. You'll get yourself killed otherwise. Don't you have the Faith in Lockdown?"

"No." The only religion I've ever known is the religion of routine, of training, the religion of fighting.

"Huh. Explains a lot," Ryka says. "No religion, no feelings, no freedom. All of those things go hand in hand. You're all just a bunch of collared animals with no idea that you're being held captive in the first place."

I feel my muscles twitch, not liking the way he's talking. There's a hard edge to the timbre of his voice, incredibly bitter. "Do animals wear collars?" I ask.

"Yes, they do."

Weird concept. I can't really picture it; an animal is still a lump of meat on a plate to me. "But Jada doesn't?"

"No, she doesn't," Ryka gives me a stern look, tucking his hair behind his ears. "Even she has more freedom than you did in Lockdown."

The hard, bright light in his eyes is really more aggressive than it needs to be. I don't know him and he doesn't know me, so why does he look like he's personally offended? Not that it matters. Who cares what he thinks, anyway? Sadly, I guess *I* do, because I find myself snapping at him. "It's not the same, okay. Stop calling it a collar. I'm not an animal, and this is a *halo*." I tug at the hard metal hanging loose around my neck.

Ryka looks at me for a moment before bursting into laughter. I want more than anything in the world to slap him across his face. Jada runs back to us and starts barking like she wants in on the joke.

"What's so funny?" I snap.

"Your *halo?*" He reaches out to hook his finger under it. I can barely believe he's done it for a moment, can barely believe his finger is touching the skin on my neck beneath the ring of heavy metal. I haven't even been brave enough to touch that skin yet; it just felt wrong when I thought about it. I flinch away like his touch burns me, wide eyed. This sobers him up, and he stops laughing.

"You can't have any idea what a halo truly is," he says. "Or if you do, you should know...yours has well and truly slipped."

FREETOWN

I hear Freetown before I see it. A surging, pumping, throbbing sound punctuated by the call of individual voices. Some laugh, some shout, some cheer. Jada abandons us about fifteen minutes later. She freezes in the darkness, one paw lifted, ears still as she listens. Ryka, nothing more than a shadowy outline in front of me, his hair turned to silver by the stark moonlight, lets out a sharp, low whistle and hisses, "Go home, Jada."

She obeys and bolts, leaving the two of us to make our slow, stumbling progress towards the town. It's not long before I start seeing the burning orange glow of fires, and red and green lights dancing up ahead. Ryka halts and rounds on me, quicker than I like.

"The knife," he says, holding out his hand.

The lights up ahead are reflected in the deep pools of his dark eyes, making the colour hard and flat. He shoves Cai's holostick towards me and I take it and slip it into my back pocket before he can snatch it back. I don't even get the chance to give him the knife; he steps forward until there can't be any more than six inches between us, and he reaches down and draws it from my belt. It disappears back into the corresponding loop on his belt where it belongs.

"You must really love that knife," I say. There are at least eight weapons on his belt, so it's odd that he got so bent out of shape for just one. It's pretty, certainly, but it isn't the most impressive piece of metalwork he's wearing.

Ryka pulls his lips into a tight line and his breath blows hot against my cheek. "I don't love knives," he says, his voice stiff. "A knife is a tool—a utensil. It's used for defending yourself when you have to. I love being *alive*."

My first thought is that he seems overly angry by my statement, but I don't say anything. It won't get me anywhere, and right now I have bigger things to worry about.

Freetown.

Ryka stares at me a moment more, way too close for comfort, and then steps back. "Come on. There might be some hot food left if we're lucky." He pushes forward and I follow a little slower than before. How am I going to be received here? I have no clue what these people will be like or what they know about the Sanctuary. If everyone here thinks like Ryka, I might not get the warmest of welcomes. And why *would* they welcome me? I'm an escaped member of a restrictive society, without any money or skill, other than in killing, of course, and let's face it—I have nothing to offer them. I'm a burden. A mouth to feed. I shuck off the creeping, uncomfortable sensation just in time for Ryka to breach the boundary of the tree line. And there it is.

The river we've been following this whole time stands between us and the bright scar of a town nestled into the valley up ahead. Dark silhouettes make up the skyline, shifting with every gust of air that breathes out across the water. Tents. Thousands of them. Some are tiny and could barely fit two crouched people inside, others so big they look palatial. Even from here it's obvious they have many rooms and sleeping quarters. In the dark, they're all a muted brown shade, but I get the feeling that will be different in the daylight.

This isn't what I was expecting. When Ryka said Freetown was an actual town with twenty thousand people, I assumed there would be buildings. Solid structures. Street lights and actual streets to put them on. There are no streets here, though. Only muddied walkways that weave haphazardly through the seas of flapping material. Hundreds of night fires burn, some dangerously close to the fabric of tattered, worn tents. The ink-black shapes of people flicker and twist around the flames, nothing more than tiny specks from this distance.

Ryka points to a small wooden bridge that spans the river, turned green with moss and lichen at the edges of its rickety nailed planks. "Are you ready?"

"Yes." I sound pretty convincing, but I know the sad truth. I'm a liar. Shame I can't trick myself along with Ryka. Regardless of my nerves, I have choices to make about who I want to be now, though, and I don't want to be a coward. "Where are you going to take me?" I don't even know that Ryka is going to take me anywhere. He could abandon me as soon as we walk into Freetown. There's nothing stopping him from doing that, and after all the arguing and face-pulling he's done since we met, he will probably be glad to see the back of me. He starts walking towards the wooden bridge, more confident now that home is in sight. "To Grandfather Jack," he says. "He's in charge here. Along with the priestesses, of course."

"And people call him Grandfather?"

A dry look passes over Ryka. "They do."

"But he's not really their Grandfather, surely?"

"You're smart for someone who's done nothing but crush skulls and bite peoples' ears off their whole life."

My mouth drops open. "I've never bitten anyone's ears off!"

"Finally! The truth!" Ryka hits the bridge and his boots make a hollow clomping noise as he takes long strides to the other side. The planks of wood feel spongy underfoot. They are probably well past a little maintenance and in need of replacing altogether. I hurry across, trying to dispel the images of falling through the rotten wood and plunging into the water below. My legs are jelly by the time I get to the other side.

Ryka rolls the sleeves down on his shirt and pulls the band from his ponytail so he can re-tie it, capturing the wisps of blond that have escaped. "Whatever you do, don't tell Jack your little fantasy story, okay? That story doesn't end well."

I grit my teeth and consider jamming the knuckle of my bent index finger into his side. That would really hurt, and seeing him squirm would frankly make my day. He stalks off towards the tent line before I can do more than picture it, and I trail along behind him. My hands start to shake as we pass the first haphazardly

73

pitched tents.

Some of their flaps are open, and inside there are families eating and women in long skirts rocking babies to sleep. In others, groups of teenage boys play cards and roughhouse, scrubbing each other's heads with their knuckles, laughing raucously and shoving one another over. The smell from the night fires is everywhere—a bitter, biting constant that should make me panic, but instead seems to calm my nerves. Intermingling with it are a thousand other smells, some more pleasant than others. Cloves, cinnamon, and anise flood my senses, forming a map of memories on my tongue; spiced meats and sugary scents, unwashed bodies and soiled clothing, butter and yeast and excrement—all of these are underpinned by the crisp, clean smell from the forest, which wafts on the breeze. It cleanses the palate, wiping away everything before it.

Every time we pass a fire where people gather around it, Ryka inclines his head and grunts out a greeting. More often than not the people crouching around the flames rise as he passes, averting their eyes politely. Some of them don't, though. Some of them jeer and grin at him, laughing when he makes some joking remark about beating them bloody at training in the morning.

I watch everything. There's a strong possibility that I'm not going to be able to stay here, and I want to be able to find my way back to the bridge if I have to make a quick exit. Ryka leads me through a maze of tents, occasionally skating on the mud where the pathway turns muddy. Wooden planks have been placed down so people can navigate the boggiest areas, but my boots are still clogged with stinking brown sludge. I knock them against one another as I walk, trying to scrape some of it away, but it only makes it worse. The foul mud doesn't seem to bother Ryka. He waves at a group of girls that pass us; they wear long, flowing skirts like the women I saw back in the tents, with colourful shirts and scarves swirling around them as they move. They must have small bells sewn into the material, because they tinkle musically as they pass, giving me hard stares from their beautiful, kohled eyes.

I duck my head and keep close to Ryka, unsure of how I'm supposed to react to such open curiosity. We walk for a long time before Ryka takes yet another sharp turn and we find ourselves in an open marketplace. The noise is furious, like the rushing of the river when it was at its maddest, the undulating pitch and fall of countless voices all talking at once.

There have to be at least a hundred stalls, all organised in a grid pattern, with a snaking walkway that winds through them. Leather bags and belts, clothes, silver bangles and bracelets with tiny bells attached to them, small wooden instruments that people press up to their lips and play as we walk by, food merchants and drinks stalls. For every stall of one kind, however, there are at least two knife stalls. Every single kind of knife under the sun. I could spend hours here running my fingers across sharp blades, lost in the glimmer of bright metal.

I almost lose Ryka three times before we're half way across the market place. The confusion of bodies, all pushing and pulling and pressing together, is overwhelming. He glances over his shoulder, no doubt expecting me to be getting trampled, and frowns. "Here." He holds out his hand.

I take it, scowling. If I don't, I'm getting lost and that's for certain. His hand is so much bigger than mine, and strong. He could probably crush my finger bones right now if he really wanted to. Hopefully he won't. I get pulled through the crowds, casting my eyes to floor so I don't have to catch the irritated expressions on people's faces as I stumble into them and trip over their feet. There is nowhere like this in the Sanctuary. I've never borne witness to so many people all gathered in one place, laughing and talking and *feeling* so openly. Not even in the Colosseum. There, the crowds are huge, sure, but it is mainly made up of Therin. They only discuss the bets they've placed on behalf of their Trues, or talk reservedly amongst themselves, discussing tactics and fighting favourites. They're not frantic or harried like everyone here. The chaos of it makes my legs wobble.

"We have to hurry," Ryka tells me. He sounds a little annoyed that I'm not moving as fast as he would like, but something in his tone makes me think he's at least trying to be nicer.

"Why?"

"Because," he says, "the man we're going to see holds court until after dinner and then he goes home. And he really doesn't like to bothered by people at home."

"Oh."

Ryka pauses abruptly and I walk into his back, my nose pressing up against his shirt. He smells like sweat and Jada and something fresh and green. A crowd of people have halted right in front of him to peruse some of the stalls selling fried food. He growls low in his throat and pushes roughly through them. I manage to struggle through after him in the gap he makes before it closes, and I see the end of the market up ahead.

"Maybe I should go see him in the morning?" I suggest.

"Not an option."

"Why?"

"Because then I'll have to figure out what to do with you until morning, and I seriously don't have the energy for that."

Of course. I was right: he can't wait to be rid of me. "Fine," I say, "I don't want to be stuck with you longer than necessary, either."

Ryka turns and throws a casual smile over his shoulder, his face lit up by the final stalls that sell multi-coloured candles and storm lanterns. "Oh, come on. I'm charming and pleasant to be around. You, on the other hand—"

I dig my thumb into his back, hard, without thinking. "You're lucky I need you right now."

"Or what?"

"Or you'd find yourself on the floor, trying to worm your way out of another chokehold is what."

The crowd breaks and Ryka picks up the pace, pulling me forward beyond the marketplace. We're in a small square, thick with mud, which is bordered on three sides by huge white canvas tents. Their guy ropes are staked out as close to their structures as possible, presumably to stop people from tripping over them. Ryka whips around and pulls me to him. The muscles in his body are no less tense, but his scowl seems to have disappeared. Maybe it isn't a permanent feature, after all. "Look, can you—can you just not tell anyone about that. I've never fought a girl before. I didn't want to hurt you."

I fold my arms across my chest and stare at him. "As I recall, I was the one doing the hurting."

"I *know*," he says. He scrubs his hand over his face, blowing out an exhausted sigh through his fingers. "Look, any time you want a rematch I'm all for it. Just please—don't go round telling people you cut me. It won't end well."

I consider his request, taking into account that he didn't shout it, or flat out order it of me. "All right. So, it's not considered manly to be beaten by a girl in Freetown. I won't breathe a word."

Ryka nods slowly, not taking his eyes off me. I can tell he's searching my face, seeing if I am someone who means what they say. I used to see Trues do this to one another all the time. He turns and walks off without taking my hand this time, quickly skirting the back of the tent to our right. When he reaches the corner of the square where the tent finishes, he steps over the tangle of ropes and disappears through gap between them.

I follow, distributing my weight carefully so I don't fall onto the tensed lines. Ryka waits on the other side, leaning against a steel support that forms part of the entrance to the tent we just walked beside. "Remember what I said," he tells me. Then he pulls back the mud splattered canvas doorway and vanishes inside.

14

JACK

Afire rages in a pit located in the very centre of the huge tent. This is undoubtedly a very bad idea. A strong breeze could catch an ember and the whole thing could go up. A thousand tents make up Freetown, though, and there seem to be just as many fires. I can only imagine they must know what they're doing. Or at least I hope they do.

I hide behind Ryka as we walk into the room, trying to find a calm space in my head where I can convince myself everything is going to be all right. Along one side of the tent, six stacks of chairs form a line, varying in height. The one closest to us is overloaded, and the tower leans forward like it might topple over any minute. Four gas burners sit in the corners of the single large room, flickering inconsistently and throwing off shadows, which dance where the light fades. There is nothing in here apart from the fire, the stacks of chairs, the gas burners, the sticky mud floor, and the small group of people sitting close to the fire.

"Well!" A voice calls out, low and gruff. "Look who it is. The wanderer returns."

I peek around Ryka's shoulder and see three faces gazing back at me. The eldest, a man of at least sixty, looks startled when he catches sight of me. "And he's brought someone with him. You been hunting wild people in the woods again, Ryka?"

"Wild is *definitely* the word," Ryka replies.

Since I've been spotted, I side step out from behind Ryka and eye up the people around the fire. The man who spoke lounges back in his chair, his legs thrust out before him, crossed at the ankles. The toes of his boots have gone grey where the caked-on mud has dried in a thick crust. His hair is shaggy and steel grey, swept back out of his face. He wears a loose blue shirt, which pulls a little tight over his considerable belly. Quick, intelligent dark eyes study me back. They seem so much younger than the rest of him. Bright.

The other two, a woman and a man, have a more polished look about them. The woman reminds me of my mother— my birth mother. Her dark hair is coiled in a tight braid on the back of her head, and gentle creases line the delicate skin around her eyes and her mouth. She looks like she must smile a lot. The dark-haired man beside her wears nothing about his personality on his face. He is devoid of anything but cool curiosity as his stony eyes pick over me. He doesn't look friendly, not like the old man or the woman. There is something of Lowrence to him, even though he looks nothing like my father. I'm ashamed to say I don't hold his gaze for long.

"Well," the older man says, "are you going to tell us where you've been and who you've got with you?"

Ryka looks at me and frowns. "I went where I always go. And she," he gestures to me with his thumb, "says she's called Kit."

The old man uncrosses his legs and then crosses them the other way with a small smile on his face. "Kit, hey?"

"Yes, Kit. My name's Kit. Well, not really, but—"

The old man bursts out laughing, rocking back on his chair. When he reaches up to brush his hair out of his face, I see the same thin stack of marks trailing up the back of his arm. The ink has faded, though—gone blue and fuzzy, unlike Ryka's crisp lines.

"You don't seem to know who you are, child," he says around his smile. He's more right that he can ever know. I kick my toe against the back of my other boot and pull a wry face. He takes this as some sort of response. Turning to the woman and man at his side, he says, "Perhaps we can discuss your proposition in the morning, Ella. As for you James, my answer was no yesterday, it's no today, and if you're half as smart a man as I think you are, you can probably guess what the answer will be tomorrow." He chuckles when he speaks, knocking James' boot with his, but James doesn't smile. He gets to his feet stiffly, his back ram-rod straight.

"Thank you, Grandfather." He holds his hand out to shake with the old man. His face is expressionless and well contained but I know body language. The guy is furious. Ella leans forward and kisses Grandfather Jack on the cheek, squeezing his hand.

"Good night."

James doesn't say anything as he stalks out of the tent, but Ella smiles broadly at me and winks. "Lovely to meet you, Kit. Ryka." She inclines her head to him like the people around the fires before did, and then they're both gone.

"Come and sit down, the pair of you," Grandfather Jack says.

Ryka moves off and sinks down in the chair next to the old man with ease. My hands prickle as I join them.

"So," the old man grins at me, leaning forward to prop his elbows on his knees. "Kit," he offers me his hand. "You can call me Jack."

I lean forward so I can shake his hand, noticing that Ryka's staring at Jack with his mouth open. I ignore him.

"I'm very honoured to meet you, Jack."

He laughs. It's a low, rumbling sound that might come from as deep down as the soles of his boots. "Likewise. Now, where have you come from?"

I let my gaze flicker over to Ryka, trying to work out how much of my 'fantastical story' I'm not supposed to tell. He rolls his eyes.

"She's from Lockdown. She was drowning in the river when I first found her."

"I was *not!*" I answer hotly. "I was doing just fine, thank you very much."

"Uh-huh. She drank her body weight in river water and nearly died of exposure," Ryka says.

"All right, now, never mind that. So you escaped Lockdown, then?" His eyes creep down towards my neck, and my cheeks start burning. I know what he's wondering. I tug down the neck of my shirt to reveal the halo around my neck. With the back of my fingernail I lift it up, a little afraid to touch it. He nods his head, lacing his fingers across his belly. "I see."

He doesn't seem even remotely fazed. I tuck my halo away. It feels wrong that Ryka should be looking at it—at *me*—with such unveiled horror in his eyes. Jack raises an eyebrow.

"I have to say, I thought you'd be different."

My heart stutters. "What?" Maybe he has some preconceived ideas about what people from the Sanctuary are supposed to look like. Green spots, three heads, something like that.

"The Sanctuary put out a radio broadcast two days ago. Said one of their fighters had gone missing. There's a reward on your head, Kit. They're offering an astronomical amount of money to get you back."

I stare at him until the heat from the fire forces me to blink. A number of things run through my head, the first of which is how best I should escape from this tent. Jack is pretty old, but it's wrong to underestimate someone based on their age. He could be a proficient killer for all I know. Secondly, I'm wondering who put up the money. Was it Lowrence and Miranda, or could it possibly have been the Sanctuary municipality themselves? I'm worth a lot of cash to both parties. I shouldn't be surprised that they would do this. Ryka leans forward in his chair. "Why would they be willing to pay a small fortune for her?"

Jack *tsks*. "I just told you, boy. She's one of their amphi-fighters. Pay attention."

I'm well and truly over Ryka's belief that I'm a frivolous, lying little girl. I ignore the dumbfounded look on his face. "What are you going to do?" I say to Jack.

He purses his lips and squints one eye—a pretty strange look. "I'm not going to do anything, I shouldn't think. What do I want with a basket full of money? We don't use it here. Everything we have is traded or worked for. The only place I could spend money would be in Lockdown, and the likelihood that I'll be headed there any time soon is, well, nil."

This doesn't reassure me. Jack knows as well as I do that the Sanctuary will give him food and clothes and technology in place of money if he wants it. I shrink back into my chair, still thinking about running. Jack smiles easily, rocking on his chair legs.

"I'd heard about you even before your escape act, child. You're quite famous. We listen to the match reports every month. And every month it's your name they're repeating over the airwaves."

"I didn't know you got their match reports," Ryka breathes. There's a combination of excitement and annoyance in his voice.

"I'm sure there are a lot of things that I know and you don't, Ry," Jack says. Ryka pulls a face and slouches back into his chair. He's not showing the same reverence to Jack that Ella and James did just now, but the old man seems to expect it from him. "We like to keep abreast of the news in your city," he says to me. "Frankly, we've been waiting for a rebellion to break out for a long time. Surprised it's not happened by now, in fact."

"Why? Why would there be a rebellion?" I ask.

"Do you think you're the only one with a halo that doesn't work? There are plenty of people, Falin and Therin, all over the Sanctuary that go about their daily lives, living and breathing and *feeling*. They've organised themselves into cells in some parts of the city, mainly the Narrows and the poorer areas. They've been waiting to strike. It's only a matter of time."

My jaw hangs slack. "I...I had no idea." I could have gone to someone. Someone inside the city could have helped me. Wonderful news after everything I went through to get out.

"That's a good thing," Jack says. "Means the Sanctuary don't either. We've been talking to people on the inside for years, trying to help them make a break for it. Things are beginning to ramp up."

"So, you're helping them?"

He gives me a cursory nod. "There's only so much we can do, but we do it gladly."

"And...you're not going to turn me over to them?"

He stares into the fire, watching it pop and flare brightly against the relative darkness of the tent. Ryka's eyes are on me but I don't look at him. I'm too desperate for Jack to say something that will reassure me. Make me believe I am safe.

"We've never turned anyone away from Freetown. This place is a home to anyone who can live by its rules. I have to say, Kit, things are different here. Your life will be different, but that can be a good thing if you let it. Can you accept that?"

"Do you mean," I look at Ryka, "I'm not supposed to fight?"

Jack nods. "You're not *allowed* to fight. You can't let your temper get the better of you. How long has it been since your halo came free?"

I think back, shocked by the short space of time it's been. "Six days since it got ripped—" I hesitate. "Since it came off partially. Two days since it came free completely."

"Then you're still withdrawing. You've got a way to go before the drugs leave your system."

All the air vanishes from my lungs, one long, painful sigh. "You mean I'm not feeling everything right now?"

"Not even close."

I slump forward and hide my face in my hands. I've been waiting for this whole overwhelmed feeling to get better, but that's not going to happen. It's going to get worse.

"You don't have to do this if you don't want to, you know," Jack says. I can't see him with my face in my hands but his voice sounds like he's got a frown on his face. I peek through my fingers, and he has. "No one would blame you if you wanted to go back to wearing it. It's incredibly hard to come to terms with powerful emotions when you've never experienced them before. Especially if you've...*done things* that might make you feel bad."

A shallow, surprised laugh slips out of me. "Let's not skirt around the matter here," I say. "You mean, *especially if I've killed a whole bunch of people.*"

Ryka makes a strangled noise, and I glimpse at him out of the corner of my eye. He looks morbidly fascinated by me, and there's the tiniest hint of a smile playing at the corner of his lips. The light warms his hair to a honeyed gold, his skin a sun-kissed bronze. I want to shake that strange expression off his face with my bare hands.

"Don't look at me like that," I say.

"Sorry. I just thought—"

"Yeah, I know. You thought I was lying. I got that." The weight of my halo resting unnaturally against the back of my neck feels like a forceful hand pushing me down. Half the time I'm comforted by it; the other half of the time I feel like it's strangling me. I touch it through my shirt, feel the material whisper across its surface.

"We could fix it for you if that's what you really want," Jack says.

Ryka leaps out of his chair so quick that it wobbles dangerously. "What? Why on earth would she want *that?*"

"Calm down. You don't have a clue what she's going through. It *could* be what she wants. Maybe she doesn't want to deal with any of the things she's going to feel. It's certainly not gonna make her happy, now, is it?"

"How do we know what she's going to feel? She could be happy. She could feel—"

"Guilty," I say, staring into the fire. The flames have leapt from the pit and are burning in my mind. In my heart. I blink to take away the strange pricking in the corners of my eyes.

Jack and Ryka stop talking and stare at me. I feel both their eyes boring into the side of my face, but I'm not ready to look at either of them.

"I want it *off,*" I whisper, clenching my fingers around the halo through my thin shirt. Claustrophobia floods through me; I want it off right now and I feel like I'll scream if I have to wait one more moment.

"Good," Jack says quietly. I don't notice when he rises from his chair. I only feel his hand on mine, and I realise I've been pulling at the metal band really hard. The back of my neck burns from the release of pressure when I stop.

"We can't do anything about it now, sweetheart. In the morning, though. August will be able to take care of you in the morning."

"Okay." I ball my fists up and rub my eyes, which are itchy from the smoke and the way that I *feel.*

"Ryka will show you where you can sleep. We'll set up a tent for you soon, all right? Get some rest. Tomorrow will be a big day."

I don't say another word as we leave the tent. Jack trails behind us and squeezes my shoulder by way of a goodbye.

"I'll see you at home," Jack says to Ryka, and then he goes back inside.

OLIVIA

I wake up with sunlight shining on my face, warming my hair. The tent Ryka showed me to sits beside the river, and from my low metal cot I can hear water splashing and women singing. It's beautiful. Calming.

After finding some food for me last night, Ryka led me here, explaining that it was a shared tent for people travelling through. He left, saying he'd come by in the morning at some point to take me to August. Now morning is here and my bones don't feel as weak as they did when I was sleeping on the forest floor. I'm grateful for that, but my resolve is nowhere near as strong as it was yesterday. I keep having to remind myself why I'm doing this. Why I left my family; why I nearly killed myself escaping; why I want to have the halo removed.

Cai.

He died so I could do all of those things.

HALO

I sit up stiffly in the bed and shuffle forward so I can reach my pants. The holostick is still where I left it, in the back pocket. I grab it and fling myself back under the covers, blocking out the sound of people getting ready for the day beyond the tent.

For a moment I just sit there, pressing the device to my lips. There's no question that I should watch it. I'm just having trouble finding the strength. Plus there's still the small problem of the encryption code keeping it locked. If I am right, though, that might not remain a problem for long. I stare down at the four silver buttons: play, stop, forward and back. A combination of those four buttons unlocks the secrets held inside that Cai recorded. I think back to our days of training and I can hear his voice in my head, always saying the same thing. *Defence is sometimes the best form of attack, Falin Kitsch. First we defend, we defend again, we block...and then, when our opponent least expects us to, that is when we attack.* Defend, defend, parry, attack. I've been thinking it for a while now and the riddle seems pretty clear. With timid fingers I hit the stop button twice. I follow that up with the back button, and then I hesitate. This could be wrong. *I* could be wrong. If I am, then I'm risking the potential that the device will shut down forever. Cai could have put all kinds of safety measures in place to prevent his secrets from falling into the wrong hands. I only have a second to make up my mind. My index finger hits the play button and I hold my breath, torn by two drastically opposing forces—the desire to see my friend's face again, and panic over what he will say if I do.

I don't get chance to worry for long. A blue light flashes on top of the holostick and it whirs into life, vibrating in the palm of my hand. Usually new holosticks compress images and the recording comes out small, a fist sized representation of whoever makes the recording. Since this piece of technology looks like it's older than I am, I should be unsurprised when Cai's form leaps into existence, not fist-sized, but *full*-sized. I am not unsurprised, though; I'm freaked out. I squeal, throwing back the covers on my cot as a larger-than-life Cai is projected from the stick.

"I'm feeling pretty proud right now, Kit," he says, his eyes angled just right so that somehow he's looking right at me. I gasp and fling the holostick from my hand, breaking the connection that makes it play. Cai's wavering, semi-transparent form vanishes in a split second, leaving me panting and tangled up in my bed sheets.

How? How did he know I would watch this? How is the first thing he says directed right at me? My heart is pounding and it feels like I can't breathe right. I struggle with the frantic urge to curl up into a small ball, knowing that if I do I will fall apart into a million pieces and I will never be able to put myself back together again. Instead I take a deep breath and collect up the stick, blinking at the small screen on the side that is now illuminated. *29 Stored Files. Continue File 1?* blinks back at me. I pull myself upright, preparing myself this time. When I hit play and Cai reappears, I'm ready. Kind of. He smiles a little before he begins speaking and my throat throbs, like I've just swallowed one of my own knives. How can this hurt so very, very much?

"I'm feeling pretty proud right now, Kit," he tells me again. All six foot three of him is standing right in front of me, uneven nose, hands stuffed in pockets, dark hair tumbling into his face, the works. If it weren't for the fact that I can see right through him, I'd be sure I could reach out and touch him.

"*We won't do the whole,* sorry I can't be with you *bit. That's overplayed, and besides... wherever you are, if you're watching this and I'm not with you, then that means I did something stupid to get you out. I'm sorry if that's the case. The plan right now,*" he says, smiling, "*is to do something stupid to get us* both *out. So...*"

My eyes are burning like I've been hit with a dose of the pepper spray the Sanctuary guards carry on their belts. I knew it was going to be bad, but this? It's destroying me. My breathing just won't come out straight, feels like I'm fighting to hold back this overwhelming urge to scream and cry at the same time. I am powerless and fragile as Cai continues.

"*...I guess you want to know what's been going on? Maybe Penny or Opa have already told you. I'll just start from the beginning anyway, in case you're coming into this blind. I guess... I guess I should tell you that all this is happening because my halo stopped working. I don't know why.*" He pulls his scruffy shirt down at the front to reveal the slim band of silver metal encircling his throat. "*It's still stuck here. Can't seem to get the damn thing off. Still...Opa says it's good camouflage.*"

A flicker passes over his face, and Cai's shoulders tense. "*I have to go now. You're here to train, and we can't have* you *talking to* you*, now, can we?*" He shrugs his shoulders and he reaches out, like he's going to switch off the recorder on the stick. For a second he pauses. "*Just know, Kit. After seventeen years, I'm* *finally awake. And I'm going to find a way to wake you up, too."*

Cai's figure disappears and the holostick in my hand buzzes impatiently, flashing *Play File 2?* My stomach lurches at the prospect, making me feel even worse than I did back out in the forest. Ten minutes ago I wouldn't have thought that possible.

And I'm going to find a way to wake you up, too.

He really did find a way. It involved him stabbing himself in the chest with his own knife, while my hands were locked around the handle. Why did he have to be so stupid? Seeing his face, hearing his voice has done nothing to make me feel better. If anything my pain is amplified, because now I want to feel his hand in mine and the urge is desperate, overriding everything else. I have no idea who this Opa person is, either, and the added mystery of that makes me strangely anxious.

I hold my finger down on the off button until the little screen goes blank and then I put it away, hyperventilating. I've watched one file. One file and I'm already freaking out. This is going to be hard, and it's going to get harder every day. I'm going to keep feeling more and more, which means the guilt and pain in my chest are going to keep growing. But isn't this what I deserve for getting to live when Cai didn't?

I drag myself off the bed, feeling hideous for cowering back here like a child. Cai got up and faced every single day, glad of the fact that he could be normal, even though he couldn't show it. He made the best of his situation and started planning his life. A life he gave up for me. How ungrateful am I that I'm stuck in here hiding from the world? Shame eventually gets the better of me.

When I go outside, the sunlight is so bright I have to squint to see. There are four women standing on the banks of the river and, worryingly, they are completely buck-naked.

"Hey!" a young blonde girl calls when she notices me. "Hey! Come over here." I *really* don't want to go over there. The last thing in the world I want to do is go over there. I'm still spinning out from being confronted with Cai's smiling face. Besides, they're naked, and I've never even seen *myself* naked before. Not properly, anyway. The girl starts walking towards me, smiling, her thick wavy hair swaying with each step, and I realise that if she comes any closer, the tent won't block her from view and the whole town will get a show. Unwillingly, I step forward. I haven't put my boots on yet, so when I place my foot onto the steep slope down towards the water, mud squeezes up like toothpaste between my toes.

"Hey," the blonde girl says breezily. "You came in last night, didn't you? You're from Lockdown?" She leans forward and gives me a kiss on the cheek before I can flap my arms and reach for a knife or swat her away. She's smiling too broadly to have noticed the look of abject horror on my face.

"Yeah, I—I did. I am."

"I'm Olivia," she says, grinning. She turns and points at the other girls. "That's Aura and Melody. Hey, where did Simone go?" The girl with shoulder-length ginger hair and bright green eyes, Aura, shrugs, laughing lightly. She has freckles. *Everywhere.*

"She got embarrassed!" she giggles.

I can understand Simone's discomfort. Melody is blonde too, only more burned honey than Olivia's bright, sunshine hair—a strangely familiar hue of gold. "She's not from around here," Melody says. "People are a little more uptight where she was raised."

"I can relate," I say.

They seem to find this hilarious and start laughing so hard Aura's pale skin flushes red. I smirk, but I'm too ill at ease to join them.

"Are you gonna wash up?" Olivia asks.

"That's what you're doing? In the river?"

She nods.

"Don't people drink from here?"

All three of them burst out laughing again. "We draw our water by the bridge," Aura explains. "Everything further down is fine for swimming and washing."

"Oh. Ah. I don't think so." There's no way I'm taking my clothes off around a bunch of women.

Olivia wrinkles her nose. "I'm not being funny, but you really should."

It takes a second for me to realise what she means. I'm filthy. The past few days I've been running, swept through a dirty river, fought like a hell cat, rolled around on a forest floor—a lot—and been sleeping in my clothes. I must stink. And I dread to think what's happening on top of my head. I could definitely use a wash.

"Come on." Olivia takes my hand. "I'll wash your hair for you if you like. Just let me get dressed." Every muscle in my body relaxes when she says this. I think she can tell because she sets off laughing and the others join her again.

They disappear off up the bank together, leaving me behind. Soap and a folded washcloth have been left on a sun-warmed rock down by the river—kinda looks like they've been expecting me. I duck down quickly and strip to my underwear. It takes five minutes to wade out knee deep into the river, scrub my body with the coarse, flat piece of soap, and rinse off. My skin's burning by the time I tiptoe back to the rock and pat myself down. My combat gear is so dirty it can almost stand up by itself. I'm glaring at it, trying to work out whether I should put it back on, when Olivia appears over the embankment. She's wearing a jade dress that falls to her knees with small bells dangling from the hem. They jangle as she makes her way down to me, mixing in with her giggles. I do my best to fight the urge to run and hide behind the rock.

She carries a stack of folded clothes in her hand. "Here," she says, offering them out to me. I try and act casual as I take them. I pray it's not a dress. Anything but a dress.

"They're some of my old clothes. I've never worn them. I wanted to give you something pretty but my brother said you'd probably want trousers."

Her brother said I'd probably want trousers? Fantastic. I narrow my eyes at her. "You're Ryka's sister?"

Olivia lets out a deep sigh. "Unfortunately. Come on. Get dressed so I can wash your hair."

I see the familial resemblances now. Their hair is the same colour and her eyes are a deep chocolate, just like his. They're both incredibly bossy as well, although when Olivia tells me to do something, it doesn't sound like she'll clobber me if I don't comply. I immediately like this about her.

The black trousers she's given me fit perfectly, but they're made from a light cotton, no use in a fight. The material would split after being *shown* a knife. The shirt is white and a little tighter than I'm used to, but it smells fresh and clean. I feel like a new person when I put them on.

No one has ever washed my hair before, and it's the most relaxing thing I've ever experienced. Olivia doesn't really talk while she works through the messy tangles with her delicate fingers, just hums quietly. When it's time for her to rinse the soap out, she walks me to the edge of the river so she can pour the freezing cold water over the back of my head with a white tin pail. I lean forward and she falters, just for a second. Not long enough to be rude but long enough for me to notice. I know the sight of my halo has thrown her.

"I'm getting it taken off today," I say quietly. She empties the pail a second time over my hair, and I wince as some of the frigid water runs down the back of my shirt.

"It's none of my business," she says. "You don't have to explain anything to me."

Gratitude swamps me right then, and an odd lump forms in my throat. "I don't mind," I tell her. "You can ask me if you want."

She hesitates before saying carefully, "What did it feel like? The first time? You know, when you felt something? Was it wonderful?"

I clear my throat. "Ahh…not really. I'd just—someone had just died, and—"

"Oh! I'm sorry. Ignore me. Pretend I didn't ask." She wrings out my hair frantically and then throws the towel over my head, scrubbing like crazy. With hair like mine, she's re-creating all of the knots she just worked out.

"Olivia!" I stagger back, flinching as the rocky river bed bites into the tender soles of my bare feet. "It's okay. Calm down."

When I manage to push my hair back out of my face, Olivia's wringing her hands instead. "I'm just not going to open my mouth again," she says.

I shake out my hair and toss the towel onto the rock. "Don't worry. I don't mind. I guess…I guess I haven't really experienced *wonderful* yet. But I'll let you know if and when I do."

A smile spreads on her face. "It's now my personal mission to make that happen soon. Do you think you're ready to go now?"

"Go where?"

"Oh," she says, "Ryka asked me to take you to August. He's busy this morning. He missed a week's worth of practices and the Tamjis frown on solitary training. They want everyone to know what they're up against."

It's no surprise that Ryka found an excuse not to come and deal with me himself. I'm glad he did, too. His sister is much more pleasant to be around than he is. What's surprising is that the Tamjis all train together, especially when there's no logic to the way they are called to fight. Everything is based on what the priestesses decree, according to Ryka. If I were fighting in a system like that, I'd want to hide my weaknesses and my strengths to maintain an edge over my opponents. Olivia takes my hand and guides me back towards the tent, where I clean off my feet and pull on my boots and my knife belt. She looks at me strangely but doesn't say anything. It's one thing agreeing not to fight here, but another thing entirely not wearing my knives. It's a habit that's going to take more than one night to crack.

HALO

"Are you nervous?" she asks.

"About what?"

She points to her neck, smiling so that her left cheek pulls up to the side.

"Yeah, I'm nervous," I tell her. Because I am. I really am.

AUGUST

The walk through Freetown is terrifying, if only because Olivia knows everyone and they all want to talk to her. I stand behind her, trying to look inconspicuous, but I'm not very good at that, so people end up giving me cautious looks and moving on quickly, pulling their gawking children behind them.

Olivia barters for two cups of sliced fruit, tugging three of the small silver bells from the sleeve of her dress in payment. Seems like an odd system to me, but it appears to be working for the residents of this strange refugee town. We eat as we walk through the hawkers' market, which thankfully isn't as busy as it was last night.

"What do you do when you run out of bells?" I ask.

She slips a piece of melon into her mouth and chews. "Sew more on."

"Huh. And what about the men? Surely they don't walk around with bells sewn into their clothes?" I can't imagine Ryka tinkling every time he walks. Olivia opens her mouth to answer, but before she gets a chance her brother falls in alongside us, smirking casually. He is shirtless, the tanned skin across his shoulders beaded with sweat, and his black pants are covered in mud. His hair is the exact same colour as his sisters; it's surprising that I didn't make the connection between them straight away. My cheeks flush when his eyes skirt over me, studying my clothes and my expression.

"The men pay for their services in blood and sweat," he says.

"I thought you were training." Olivia scowls, though I can tell she's pleased to see him. She elbows him and offers out her fruit cup. Ryka takes a piece of fruit and tosses it into his mouth, still staring.

"I was. We finished early." He narrows his eyes, squinting at me. His gaze lingers on my neck, even though my halo is hidden. "I came to see if she was gonna go through with it."

I know he's referring to the decision I made last night. He thinks I'm going to back out of getting the thing removed. "Of course I am going through with it. I said I would, didn't I?" I don't know why, but it takes work to peel my eyes off his naked chest. Once I accomplish that, I studiously ignore him as we tromp our way through Freetown.

"Are you headed to see the priestesses later?" Ryka asks his sister.

"Yes, I am. You should come with me, Kit. The Keep where the priestesses live is beyond that hill over there. You see the pathway leading over it? They call it the Holy Walk."

The hill Olivia points out lies in the distance beyond the farthest reaches of Freetown. A green swell rises up out of a copse of matchstick-like trees, where I can make out the pathway she's talking about. It zigzags back and forth in a pale yellow line until it disappears over the top of the hill.

"They have a house over there?"

Olivia laughs. "It's more than a house. It's incredible, really. I won't ruin it for you by trying to describe it."

"It's creepy, Liv. You're the only person who likes going there," Ryka adds. He skirts around a broken wooden plank half submerged in the mud. "She cooks for the priestesses. Doesn't shut up about them."

Olivia slaps his arm and the scowl she put on when he showed up suddenly looks a little more convincing. "Shut up, Ry. And for crying out loud, put some clothes on."

Laughing, he does as his sister says, producing a shirt that was slipped out of sight in the back waistband of his pants. It goes over his head, but not before his eye catches mine and he winks. I flinch and go back to ignoring him.

Olivia pelts a piece of fruit at him and Ryka pokes her in the side, making her squeal. She kicks out at him, missing entirely. "You shouldn't speak that way, anyway. This one," she says, pointing at her brother, "went to the Keep when he was eight. He nearly died in his first proper match, but the priestesses cared for him and brought him back to health." She turns to Ryka, eyebrows raised. "I would have thought you'd be a bit more grateful, seeing as how they saved you."

My eyes round out. "How were you hurt?" Ryka smirks again, revealing a deep dimple in his left cheek.

"It was nothing. My sister likes to exaggerate."

"Nothing? He was stabbed in the thigh. It wasn't really that deep, but he was so young that they thought he might not make it. He pulled through, though. I think that's what started people off thinking that this fool is invincible."

"Ha ha! They think that?" I break out laughing before I can stop myself.

A flash of pride burns across Olivia's face. "No one's ever beaten him before."

I try not to laugh anymore because it looks like she might be upset if I do. She might be even more upset if I tell her that I pinned her brother and could have killed him if I'd wanted to. I just smile and nod. "That's very impressive." It certainly explains Ryka's social status and why he thinks so highly of himself. He just rolls his eyes and pulls at Olivia's arm. "Jack wants to see you at home, Liv. I can take our new friend to see August, after all."

An excited look passes over Olivia's face. "Did he mention anything about feathers?"

Ryka frowns. "He did actually."

A blindingly happy smile explodes across Olivia's face. She spins and pulls me into a tight, overwhelming embrace before I can do anything about it. "I'll come and see you later. And don't feel bad about telling me if my brother is awful to you. I'll sort him right out." She points a warning finger at Ryka before running off into the crowd, jangling like a set of keys.

"Feathers?" I ask, confused.

One of Ryka's shoulders pulls up in half a shrug. "I never know what those two are up to. Our grandfather has a major soft spot for Liv. She reminds him of our mother." He walks onwards, not looking at me, and I study the back of his neck while I decide whether I really want to question him. Eventually I decide that I do. "Does Jack like your mother?"

"Used to."

"But not anymore?"

"She's dead. She was his daughter."

The nonchalance in Ryka's tone betrays much, as do his words; the way he removed himself entirely from the equation—*Jack's daughter* is dead, instead of *my mother* is dead—has deleted himself entirely from any personal involvement with his mother's demise. He is either dead inside, or completely torn apart. The steely resolve in his eyes tells me little. It does tell me that he doesn't want to talk about it, though. "Wait, so Jack actually *is* your grandfather?"

"Yes."

"And yet you don't call him that?"

"No."

"But everyone else does? And he's *not* their grandfather?"

"Yes."

"I'm confused."

"I can imagine." Sighing, Ryka stops dead and faces me, rolling his shirtsleeves up to his elbows. "The people call him that out of respect. He was voted to lead Freetown a long time ago, and they've always likened him to the leader of a family. A big, messy, twenty-thousand-strong family." With his arms stretched wide at his sides, Ryka gestures to the tent city around us, and the people all shoving and pushing past. "We stopped calling him grandfather when we were tiny. It just didn't mean the same thing anymore."

Running my hand just underneath my halo, I focus on the shallow indentation in his cheek, where his dimple revealed itself moments ago. "Then why did he tell *me* to call him Jack?" I ask.

Brown eyes pick over my face, pausing to stare at my lips. "I wondered that myself. Come on. August's forge is just up ahead."

August's forge is a squat, sprawling tent that sits practically on top of the river. Billows of dirty white smoke pour out of the back of it, and once again I wonder about the practicalities of having fire of any kind inside a building made out of cloth.

"August!" Ryka tosses back the tent flap and skips inside, leaving me to edge nervously in behind him. A middle-aged man with a heavy, tooled leather apron greets us. His hair is black as jet and pulled into a tight ponytail. Head to toe, he is filthy. He stands by a huge fire pit burning in the centre of the room, holding a length of metal into the flames. Its end glows like a burning white star. Everything smells like chemicals and warm metal. I've never been inside a forge. I don't even know if the Sanctuary has any forges. The way August's tent is so immaculately clean and tidy surprises me. Ironmongery seems like it would be a messy job, but everything is in order here.

Two long trestle tables run the length of the room, pushed back from the fire, which are laden with heavy iron tongs and chisels. I don't know the names of most of the tools, but they are arranged in neat rows, and each one is clean. At the far end of the room, the back wall of the tent is missing and the edge of the river runs less than four feet from it.

August flashes us a broad smile when he sees us and withdraws the length of metal from the fire with a set of tongs. He carries it quickly to the river and plunges it in. A loud hiss erupts from the searing hot metal, and a cloud of smoke rises in the air. The smoke blows into the tent on the breeze, and I bite back choking gasps as August comes back inside.

"Ah, come on. It's not that bad," he says, laughing. He leans forward and slaps Ryka on the top of his arm. For a second I think August is contemplating hugging me. That's the last thing I need, but he apparently already knows this. His eyes skirt over me and he smiles, revealing that one of his front teeth is blackened.

"You must be Kit," he says, setting down his work. I shake the hand he offers me. This I can do. "I've been waiting for you all morning. What time do you call this?" he jokes.

"Midday. Apparently that's what time people in Lockdown wake up," Ryka replies.

"Actually, we usually get up before sunrise. I was just very—" I break off when Ryka starts chuckling. I have to stamp down the urge to pinch him really hard. I clench hold of my dagger hilts instead, trying to calm my spike of anger. It's a powerful tide washing over me, almost blinding me with its ferocity. Surely it can't be this bad all the time, and for such a small thing? August *tsks* at Ryka.

"Careful, son. She'll have an eye out with one of those blades if you're not

97

careful. Wait." August's eyes pause on my knife belt, growing in size. "Well, well," he says. He holds out his hand again. "May I?"

"Uh—sure." I pull out my daggers and offer them to him, handle first, unsure why I should feel so nervous. August flips them both over in his hands with the practiced skill of someone who handles weapons every day, catching them up before twisting and throwing them behind him out of the tent. A zipping sound fills the air and then a juddering *thunk, thunk*. Both daggers slam into a tree trunk by the water's edge, wobbling from the force of their impact. August hoots and claps his hands together.

"Still perfectly balanced!" he cries. "You've taken care of these knives, haven't you?"

"Yes, sir, I have. You recognise them?"

"Recognise them?" When he spins back to me, he is grinning from ear to ear. "I made them. Got a very good haul for them, too. How on earth do you have 'em?"

"They were a gift from the Sanctuary."

"A gift?" He nods to himself. "That's appropriate. A gift. Some of my finest work right there." He points at my daggers still buried in the tree, and I slip past him so I can go and get them. It takes a good, hard yank to free them from the wood, and I polish the edges of their blades on the bottom of my shirt. August's grin hasn't slipped an inch by the time I get back. He shakes his head like he's just run into an old friend he never thought he'd see again.

"I understand you're here to have your halo removed, then?" he says. There's no beating about the bush; he comes right out with it.

"Yes, I am."

The next twenty minutes are torture. They consist of this: August's hacksaw banging me repeatedly in the back of the head; Ryka's demeanour going from indifferent, to intrigued, to (vaguely) worried; burning hot metal digging into my throat; and finally a jarring shock that nearly unseats me.

"Okay. Tip your head slowly to the right," August says.

I do as I'm told, and the warped arm of my halo moves across my field of vision. A soft smile pulls at the corners of Ryka's mouth, and for a second there is no bravado on his face; he just looks pleased. I touch my fingers up to my neck and find... nothing.

"Here you are." August slips around the chair and deposits a twist of shining silver metal into my lap. Still gripping on to the sides of the chair, I stare at it blankly. It looks slim and fragile resting on my legs. But that's it. That bent, broken halo is the reason I'm here. Why I left. I reach out and touch it cautiously, and suddenly I can't see. A bolt of panic rushes through me, and I blink hard. My eyes feel wet. My eyes feel *wet.* I shouldn't feel so terrified by the fact that I'm crying, but I am. I brush the hot drops of water out of my eyes angrily with the backs of my hands and cough to try and mask the hideous occurrence.

"It's okay," August says, laying a hand on my shoulder. "You don't need to be embarrassed. Anyone would be happy to have that thing off them."

A distorted smile works its way onto my face when I look up. August thinks I'm crying because I'm happy. I don't contradict him; it's probably for the best that he thinks that. But from Ryka's intense, penetrating gaze, I get the feeling he might suspect otherwise.

"You want to keep it?" August asks. "Or shall I melt it down?"

I hold my hand out quickly, stopping him before he can do just that. "No, wait! Wait." I try to ignore the hard look on Ryka's face. "Do you think…do you think you could try to fix it?"

August stares at me like I've just grown another head. "Uh…sure. I can try, Kit, but I'm a smith, not an engineer. This is probably well beyond my capabilities. It'd be useless making you any promises."

"That's okay," I tell him. "Whatever you can do."

TAMJI

Another two nights pass by where I sleep in the shared tent with Aura and Melody. And when I say sleep, I mean lie absolutely still in the darkness, trying to get my mind to calm down. I am hyper-aware of everything, of my heart thumping in my chest, of the sick feeling in my stomach, and the panic I experience whenever I start thinking about my brother still trapped in the Sanctuary.

During the time I find myself alone, I watch Cai's holostick, despite how bad it makes me feel. He doesn't say much about how he handled the awakening of his emotions, but the recordings do reveal one thing: he really did care about me. The last file I watch makes my throat close up. Cai looks so boyish and *real*, standing at the foot of my cot.

You move like flowing water when you fight. It's breathtaking, really.

You're so powerful. Graceful. I have to struggle not to touch you. All I want to do is reach out and run my hand through your hair. That's weird, right? Sorry..." he says, grinning. *"But then you usually kick me in the face and, well...it's hard to feel romantic towards someone kicking you in the face.*

I'm not calling you you *anymore. I'll think of something temporary until you can decide for yourself. You deserve a name. You deserve so much more than you have right now. I want to be the one to give you everything you could ever desire. I find it impossible that you're not in there somewhere, waiting to wake up.*

Maybe there's a way. If there is, I'll find it. I have to. For me and for you.

He looks so impossibly sad by the end. It's funny how two days ago I'd never cried, and now I seem to make a habit of it. I'm going to put off watching any more until I feel stronger.

Today's the first day I'm going to be working with Olivia. She cooks for the priestesses, and she's arranged it so that I'll be working with her from now on. Cooking is a completely new concept to me; I've never done it before, not once. Not that I have any idea how to clean or take care of the elderly or small children, which were the other options open to me, so working with Olivia seems like the best bet.

She's an hour early when she comes to get me, but I'm washed and dressed already. I see her approaching through the mottled ocean of multi-coloured tents and go out to meet her. A large woven sling hangs over her shoulder, weighting her down to one side, which makes her list as she walks through the mud, her tiny bells tinkling.

"Hey!" she cries. "I brought you more clothes!"

"More cl—" I break off, take a deep breath. "I don't need more clothes!"

"Of course you do. Ryka said it would be nice if you had something different to wear."

"Ryka?" Inside the bag, a tangled mess of orange and green and blue and red awaits, along with the flash of silver sewn along the hems. Bells. It's not just clothes she's giving me. She's giving me money, too. "I can't take these."

"You can and you will." For the first time, Olivia looks a little fierce. She cracks a grin at me but I can tell she's not going to take no for an answer. Stooping down, she plucks a sheer green slip from the sling, holding it up for me to see. I narrow my eyes at her.

"It's a dress."

"It is."

"I'm not wearing a dress."

Olivia flashes her teeth at me in an entertained smile. "And why not?"

"Because I won't be able to move properly. I won't be able to run." Automatically, my thumbs move to my knife belt.

"What do you think you're going to have to run from here?" she laughs.

Everything, I think, but I don't say it. "It's just not going to happen."

Olivia pushes past me and staggers through the open doorway to the tent, dumping the sling onto my cot. She flexes out her hands and turns to give me a hard glance. "My brother said you'd say that. He also said I had to make you see sense. I know you haven't exactly been out wandering though town, Kit, but people are still talking. They know there's a girl walking around with a knife belt, and they don't like it. If it were up to me, you'd be able to arm yourself to the teeth and have at it. But there are a lot of people here who follow the Faith and the old ways, and—"

"And?"

"And women don't carry knives. Not here. Jack said you knew about the changes you'd have to make in order to stay?"

"Jack said I couldn't fight. I couldn't lose my temper. He didn't say anything about not wearing my knives." Ryka may have told me it was a bad idea out in the woods, but I've decided that his advice doesn't count. The concept of stepping foot into Freetown without a weapon makes a cold sweat break out across my shoulder blades. It wouldn't feel right.

Olivia's eyebrows draw together in a tight knit line, a comically frustrated look on her. "It's for the best, Kit. You can't come to work wearing them. You have to be a little flexible. Please? Can you just wear this to the kitchens with me? You can change back afterwards, I swear."

The green dress hanging from her outstretched hand looks like something Miranda would wear. Long and flowing. I stare at it for a full minute before I reach out and take it from Olivia's hand. "Ugh, fine."

"Thank you!" she squeals, launching herself at me. No one's ever hugged me before, not really, and for a moment I don't know what I'm supposed to do. With my arms pinned to my sides there's not much I *can* do, anyway. Olivia's eyes are bright when she pulls back, studying me intensely. "I'm so glad." Her face screws up. "I'm going to enjoy telling him how wrong he was."

"Who?"

Her facial expression levels out, back to bright and happy. "My stupid brother. He said you were more stubborn than me. What was the other word he used? Yes, that's right, indoctrinated. He said you'd never do as you were told."

I hold my breath for a moment, because I feel strange. It literally seems like I have to push down a swell of hot pressure in my throat. It doesn't really subside, just gets a little less intense, until I can eventually talk around it. Why the hell do I care what Ryka says to his sister about me? I only met him three days ago and during that time he's miraculously managed to get under my skin. "Where does he train?"

Olivia blinks, clearly reading the hard look on my face. She turns away and runs her fingers over the green dress lying over my cot. "Over on the river bank close to the Holy Walk. But Kit, don't pay attention to anything he says. He acts like a fool half the time. The other half, he's saying stupid things he doesn't really mean."

I stare down at the dress and clench my jaw. "Oh, I'm sure he means it. Will you come with me?"

"Where?"

"I want to talk to him."

Olivia sighs and picks up the dress. "I don't suppose you're going to wear this anymore, are you?"

I look at it and all I see is Ryka laughing at me. "No."

******

The sound of small children squealing reaches us before we turn the corner on the path following the river to the Keep. "Hey. Hey, Kit—" Olivia reaches out and pulls me back to her side. "You can't storm over there and start giving him hell, okay? He's only going to react badly in front of the others. Just wait until he comes to us, all right?"

If Ryka wants to react badly then that is fine by me, but I get the feeling Olivia is going out on a limb for me right now, and if I make a scene it would definitely reflect poorly on her. I screw my mouth up and give her a begrudging nod.

"Okay. Come on." She leads me around the narrow, rocky finger of claystone, which shelters the fighter's training ground, and suddenly we're on a beach. Or at least I think it's a beach. I've never exactly been on one before, but I know what sand looks like and there's an awful lot of it lying around. White and powdery with speckles of black through it. The knoll that shields the Keep, grassed on the side facing Freetown, turns into a sheer cliff face where it fronts the river, creating a sort of cove.

Fifty feet away, a group of men parry and lunge around one another, their bare feet kicking up sand as they move. Sunlight gleams off their naked shoulders, slick with sweat. As we approach, a group of small children come running out of the river, their skinny, naked bodies drenched, screaming and laughing. They don't seem remotely fazed by the fact that thirty men are fighting only feet away. The flash of metal in the fighters' hands means only one thing: they are using real weapons to train with, and worryingly there is a lot of bare skin on show. Olivia points over to the farthest group of fighters closest to the water's edge. "He's over there."

I had already spied him. Ryka's bright blond hair is unmistakeable, especially as we draw closer and I see that it has mostly fallen loose from his ponytail. Stupid to have hair that length when you are a fighter. Too long to keep out of your eyes, yet too short to successfully keep back. At least I can tie mine back tight. I'm still thinking about this as the first men on the beach notice our arrival. Three of them stop what they are doing and pause to stare as Olivia leads me to a low, flat boulder that breaches the sand at the very base of the rock face behind them. She tugs on my arm and sits, gesturing for me to do the same.

"He'll know we're here for him. We'll just wait."

There's an awkward look in her eye, and it doesn't take a genius to figure out the reason. Over half the men have stopped training and are catching their breath, causally shooting glances at us as they talk amongst themselves and flick their knives into the sand. Nearly all of them are muscular and tall, and absolutely every single one of them wears the same tattoos tracing up the backs of their arms. The majority of the stacked lines stop mid-tricep, but some of the fighters have lines that travel all the way to the tops of their shoulders.

Olivia notices me studying them. "They're counters," she says, arranging her skirt so it covers her knees. The bells jangle against her shins and make bright metallic sounds where they *tink* against the rock. "They get a line either side for every fight they win."

I look back at the men, squinting against the sunlight. From here it's impossible to try and count those thin black lines, but it would take a lot to get to the elbow let alone the shoulder. All of these men are killers. All of them dangerous. I can't help but study the ones fighting, still oblivious to our presence, wondering if I would be able to take them.

Ryka is among them. He wheels around the figure of a broad man with dark hair, the sounds of their fight echoing off the buttressing walls of the cove. Slash, retreat, slash, retreat, over and over. He's quicker than when he fought me in the forest, which makes me even more annoyed. I'd suspected that he'd held back, and this is solid proof. The man fighting him is bigger and more muscular, and definitely older. It takes me a moment to figure out where I recognise him from: it's James, the man who was in Jack's tent the night I arrived.

His face is just as controlled as it was then, but there's something extra—something dangerous in his eyes. When he pivots to avoid a broad cut from Ryka, I see that his tattoos sweep up over his shoulder blades and almost meet at the back of his neck.

"Huh. So James is a good fighter, then?" I ask.

Olivia grunts and folds her hands nervously in her lap. "He's Kansho, the highest level of fighter. The *only* Kansho."

"So how does that work, then? Does that mean he can stop fighting soon?"

Olivia looks at me and laughs. "Any of them can stop fighting, Kit. They can give up any time they like. But if they do, they give up all hope of attaining a position on the council that helps Jack run Freetown. Plus people...I don't know. People have strange ideas about men who don't fight. There's a stigma attached to it, like you're less of a man."

This is possibly the stupidest thing I've ever heard. "So they kill each other and die out of pride?"

"You could put it like that," she says. "They don't see it that way, though. It's more about honour."

A derisive laugh bubbles out of me, louder than I'd intended. A dozen faces turn towards us and Ryka's is among them. Recognition flashes across his face as he sees me sitting next to his sister. A frown follows, severe and quick, before he spins back to face James, baring his teeth. James dances back, graceful really, considering his size. He twitches his knife over the back of his hand and darts forward. It almost catches Ryka's wrist, but he tucks himself up and rolls from James' reach. Olivia sucks in a sharp breath, her eyes wide.

"What?" I ask. Sure, James had nearly had the drop on Ryka, but the knife would have barely grazed him. Olivia fidgets, pulling at her shirtsleeve.

"James nearly drew blood," she murmurs.

"It was a good move," I say. "Probably wouldn't have hurt, though."

Confusion flits across Olivia's face as she watches the two of them. "Don't you have the blood demand in Lockdown?"

"No. What's the blood demand?"

"All blood must be answered with blood here. It's the way it's always been. If a fighter gets cut, even if it's an accident, it has to be answered in the pits. And a fight in the pits is a fight to the death."

A jolt runs through me as I turn back to watch Ryka and James skirt around each other. This time I notice the effort on both their parts not to make good on their strikes. They are just training, after all. Ryka makes eye contact with me and I glare at him. Suddenly his comments out in the forest make a lot more sense. His anger, too. I'd cut him. I'd marked him with his own blood, and where he came from that meant a fight to the death.

Suddenly, something else seems mighty suspicious. "And what happens if their opponent takes their weapon?"

Olivia goes pale. "That's just about the most shameful thing that can happen to a man here. They get cast out of Freetown for good."

I knew it. If Ryka had walked back into Freetown and I had been wearing his stiletto, he would have been humiliated and made to leave. I wouldn't have wanted that for him, even back then, but he still could have been less of a jerk.

"Why?" Olivia asks, turning away from her brother as he topples backwards into the sand. James stands over him and laughs, holding his hand out to help Ryka up. It appears their match is over.

"No reason," I lie. It's becoming too easy.

Ryka looks rueful as he stalks barefoot toward us over the sand. On the way, he gathers his hair and re-ties it so that it's out of his face. For the first time I notice that his tattoos reach his shoulders and curl over the top. Not as high as some of the other fighters, but definitely high enough to make him a force to be reckoned with. I scowl at him, hard, and he stiffens up.

"What are you doing here, Liv?" he demands. He may have addressed his sister, but he is looking straight at me.

"Kit wanted—"

"I wanted to come and thank you for encouraging your sister to restock my wardrobe. There was no need, though. I'm not wearing any of it." I shoot Olivia an apologetic look. "Sorry."

"That's okay," she sighs. I narrow my eyes, refocusing on Ryka.

"Olivia was just filling me in on some of the differences between Freetown and the Sanctuary. It's been really interesting. I had no idea about the blood demand, or what would happen to a fighter should he lose his weapon."

I don't get the reaction from him I thought I would. In place of his warning glare, a lazy smile rolls across Ryka's face. He laughs, an easy, delicious sound that makes my skin prickle. "There are many differences between here and Lockdown," he says. "I'm sure there are plenty of things you have to learn and adapt to before you fit in, Kit." His eyes flicker down to the neckline of my black shirt, which is low enough to reveal my missing halo. That makes him pause. His reactions are weird, and him staring at the naked skin where my halo used to be makes me uncomfortable.

"Oh, I'm all for learning the rules and rituals here." I give him a sharp smile. "That doesn't mean I'm going to walk around with jangling bells sewn into my clothes, though. And I'm certainly not going to wear dresses because you think you can goad me into it."

Ryka shrugs, the movement causing a strand of his hair to fall loose already. "No big deal. If you want Jack to kick you out of Freetown, then that's your business. There are plenty of other places you can go. Try Sweeton. I've heard they treat their women wonderfully there."

"Ry!" Olivia is a blur of gold as she leaps to her feet. "The only women in Sweeton are *prostitutes*!" she hisses. "Don't you dare even *suggest* she go there!"

Ryka smiles, dusting his hands free of sand. "You're probably right. Any man who tried to go near her would end up castrated, anyway. But—" he holds up his index finger, looking at me. "They do use coins instead of bells in Sweeton. Would solve your aversion to *jangling*."

He spins around and saunters away before I can open my mouth to say anything in response. My cheeks feel like they're on fire. The muscles shift in his back, still marbled down his left side with sand as he walks away. I can't help it. My hands automatically shift to my hips, searching for my daggers. Olivia gives me a wild look and grabs hold of my arm.

"Ignore him. Jack would never make you leave. My grandfather's an old sweetheart. Come on, let's get out of here before I end up an only child."

PRIESTESS

I don't like the look of the Keep. Columns of black rock jut out of the hillside like stone spears fifty meters high. At their base the same rock lies in shattered ruins where one of the pillars must have tumbled to the earth long ago. It can't have happened in my lifetime. Fat layers of springy green moss have swallowed some of the great boulders, camouflaging them against the rest of landscape. The undergrowth is thick and damp and smells like rot. Once a dry, narrow track on the other side of the hill, the Holy Walk is now the Holy Wade. Mud sucks up to my ankles, and for the third time in as many days I feel like swearing. Olivia holds her skirts up in one hand as she trudges through the filthy mire in bare feet. The thought of doing the same makes me feel queasy.

"Where are we going?" I ask, as we navigate our way across the base of the valley floor. Olivia points towards the soaring rock formation and smiles.

"The entrance is at the foot of the tallest tower. They're hollow inside. That's where the priestesses' chambers are. The prayer vaults are below ground. Beautiful, aren't they?"

Beautiful isn't a word I would use. Sinister seems more appropriate. The sun vanished as we summited the hill blocking the Keep, and now a low lying level of cloud presses down on the world, throwing stretched out shadows off the spears of rock like crooked fingers. It could be the shadows or it could be the residual anger from my encounter with Ryka, but an unwelcome sense of foreboding sits heavy in the pit of my stomach. If it was an option, I might have reconsidered taking care of the children instead of cooking for the priestesses. But Olivia can't stop grinning, and I think she likes the idea of working with me, so I don't suggest it.

By the time we get close enough for me to make out the dark silhouette of an opening in the rock ahead of us, or the tiny slanted rents in the towers that act as windows, I am covered in mud. It's even flecked across the backs of my hands.

There's no sound other than Olivia's bells for a few minutes as we finally make it onto a gravel pathway that snakes up to the Keep. After that there's the crunch of my boots as well. Olivia somehow manages to make it the whole way across the sharp rocks with bare feet. A rusted iron trough sits on the ground when we reach the entranceway, and Olivia dips her feet in, wiggling them around until they emerge pink and clean.

"You have to clean your boots off," she tells me. I look down at the churned up mess caking my boots and frown. Underneath all that fresh sludge there's about five days worth of dried mud.

"Or you can just take them off," Olivia laughs, reading my mind. "You're kind of supposed to anyway." I sit down on the worn rock step, resigning myself to the fact that I have to go into the creepy looking Keep with freezing cold feet. I'm fighting with my laces when I feel a presence behind me. Olivia's smile falls off her face and she bows her head.

"Good afternoon, Sister," she says quietly. I look up at Olivia, wondering if I'm supposed to jump to my feet and bow or do...something. I have no idea how a person is supposed to act around the priestesses. Olivia offers me her hand and helps pull me up. The slender priestess standing in the entrance doesn't do anything. From head to toe, she is covered in some kind of crimson veil. The material looks incredibly thin, and it's obvious that she is wearing many layers of it over her body. The only place covered by a single, fine layer is her face. Or where her face should be, anyway. A pure white mask, blank and staring, greets us, only faintly shielded by the red material. Narrow black lines rim the mask just like the counters, the tattoos that mark the fighter's arms. The priestess doesn't say a word, just turns and disappears back inside the Keep.

Olivia picks up my boots and dispatches them by the iron trough, and then pulls me inside after her.

"Why is she wearing a mask?" I hiss, as we follow the priestess down narrow, darkened corridors, lit occasionally with burning gas lamps. The chemical smell coming off them snaps in the air, a bright, acidic burning.

"They're ceramic. The priestesses never show their faces," Olivia says, loud enough that it echoes off the walls. I flinch, knowing the woman must have heard her, but Olivia only laughs. "Don't worry. It's okay to talk about them. She's not allowed to respond, though. They prefer that we act like they're not even there. It's said they See more clearly if they can move among us without being acknowledged."

"They'd probably see more clearly if they didn't wear masks and red veils over their faces," I countered.

"Not see like that, Kit. *See*. Like visions."

"Oh." Ryka mentioned something about that before. The priestesses divided and promoted the fighters into differing categories, depending on their visions. Sounds like a load of nonsense to me. From the way Olivia greeted the priestess, though, she clearly does place some stock in it, and it would be unwise to comment.

We follow the priestess through a rabbit warren of tunnels until we reach a split in the corridor, where a narrow stairway leads up. Daylight streams in through a tapered slit in the rock, a welcome reminder that the world outside is only a couple of feet away. I have no idea how Olivia walks around with bare feet all day, because by the time we're half way up the coarse steps, my toes have gone numb and I've spiked the sensitive skin on my soles too many time to keep track of. The priestess leaves us at the top of the stairs and Olivia thanks her. She vanishes as Olivia guides me into a bright, high ceilinged circular room, where four other women stand at stations by polished marble counter tops. It smells of spices in here and cooking meat. A huge bowl sits on a marble plinth in the centre of the room, filled with exotic looking fruit. The women pause in their work, picking me over with their kohled, dark eyes. Intrigue, confusion, irritation, not a single smile among them. Olivia grins at me, ignoring the overwhelming silence.

"We'll be cleaning vegetables today." She disappears into a small side room and comes back with a heavy wicker basket, loaded with potatoes and carrots and long white bulbs that I've never seen before. They're all covered in mud and whiskery with roots.

A long afternoon stretches out where Olivia does most of the talking and I pretend I'm listening. Mostly, I do my best to ignore the hushed whispering of the other women. They don't seem too impressed by me at all.

Four hours after our arrival, the other women have produced a rich, thick stew and Olivia and I have chapped our hands washing the vegetables in freezing cold water. Olivia ladles out two considerable portions of the stew under the watchful eye of the others, and we eat in silence before she drags me down the staircase. I try to pay attention to where we're going as we head back to the entrance but there are just too many turns. A priestess is waiting for us when we arrive back at the iron trough. Oddly, my boots are clean. She holds out a smooth wooden bowl and in it are dozens of tiny bronze bells. Olivia leans forward and plucks out four. She hands them to me and then takes four for herself. Four bells for four hours work. I have no idea what the value of a bronze bell is but I'm hoping it's a lot. Cleaning vegetables is really not fun. I slip them into my pocket and the priestess places her hand on Olivia's shoulder. She bows her head and then nods.

"Hey, I think I'm needed. I sometimes do extra duties after my shift in the kitchens. Think you can make your own way back?"

I shift my gaze from Olivia to the priestess and back again. Over Olivia's shoulder the faint outline of the boggy trail can be made out. "Sure."

She hugs me again, but this time I'm prepared. I let my hands rest on her back for a second as she squeezes me, and when she pulls back she's wearing a pleased smile. "Don't worry. You'll get used to it," she laughs.

I watch her slip back into the Keep and the priestess follows without whispering a word; she turns and gives me a slow look over her shoulder, just before the darkness swallows the red of her dress and the white of her mask. In that moment, I swear I can see a set of pale blue eyes shine from within.

******

Three steps off the gravel path my boots are filthy again. By the time I get halfway back up the slope they are just as dirty as they were before. I find it hard to concentrate on that, though; a solitary figure paces back and forth at the crest of the hill, turned to a dark silhouette by the sun setting beyond. I know who it is even before I have a chance to see properly. The way he keeps tucking his hair behind his ears is a dead giveaway.

I manage a taut smile when I arrive next to Ryka, trying to hide the fact that I'm a little out of breath. "Hi," I say, walking straight past him. When he jogs after me and takes hold of my arm, I can't say I'm surprised.

"Come with me," he says.

I tug my arm free and stop walking, staring at him. "Why?"

His brown eyes are calm, but a small muscle jumps in his jaw. "The Tamjis from training made comments about you today. They're not pleased that you invaded our training session, strutting around with that knife belt on. I told you there'd be trouble if you didn't stop wearing them. Jack's waiting for us."

"Jack?" I blow out a deep breath. If Jack is waiting for us, then am I in trouble? Am I about to get kicked out, just like Ryka said I would? "All right. Lead on." Surprise flits across Ryka's face. Maybe he wants me to protest, but I don't. There's no point. If I'm getting booted out for nonconformity, then so be it. I set off walking, tracing the pads of my thumbs over the heels of my daggers. Ryka pushes ahead, swinging his arms so that his rolled-up shirtsleeves ride up, revealing glimpses of his tattoos. He shoots me a glance over his shoulder, his face unreadable.

"Do you like fighting, Kit?"

I stare at the black ink on his arms, quiet for a moment. "With you or in general?" I eventually say.

He laughs softly. "Both."

"No, I don't *like* it."

"Then why do you do it?"

"I don't, not any more. I didn't have a choice in the Sanctuary, but now—"

"I'm not talking about physically. I'm talking about how defensive you are." Ryka slows so that we walk side by side. He tucks his hands into his pockets and studies the darkening sky as we make our way towards Freetown. He's quiet, and seems genuinely interested in my response. I don't rightly know what to say that doesn't sound stupid. In the end, I just tell him the truth.

"I don't know how else to be." I look at him out of the corner of my eye to find him smiling. It's not the first time I've seen him do that, but the sight isn't getting any less confronting. "What's so entertaining?"

"Oh, nothing. I just think we're pretty alike, you and I."

I want to laugh at the thought, but he's not being a complete jerk as per usual so I don't. "That's an interesting theory."

"Yup."

We walk down the hill in silence and it's not until we reach the outskirts of the camp that he speaks again. "I'm sorry, okay? For the way I've been the past few days. I know it may be hard to believe, but I'm not usually like that."

Patiently, I wait for the caustic comment that will ruin his apology. It doesn't come. "So why have you been?"

He shrugs, wrestling with himself. I have to give him credit; he seems to be trying really hard. "You put me on my ass in the forest," he says eventually. "I massively underestimated you. And now, well, with Freetown's traditions, you kind of...own me."

"*What?*" I choke on my breath. "I kind of *own you?*"

Ryka tenses. "Sheez, don't say it so loud! It's just some stupid tradition."

"How can I own you? That's the most ridiculous thing I've ever heard."

"You *cut* me. You own me."

I shake my head so vigorously that I briefly panic about brain damage. "No, no, no, that's not right! Olivia said that if I cut you, you would have to fight me to the death!"

He smirks a little, but I can see he's still freaked out. "Only if a *fighter* cuts another *fighter.* You're a girl, Kit. When a girl cuts a guy, it's like—it's the most personal thing that can happen between a guy and a girl, okay? It's basically like the guy's surrendering to her, giving her his life."

Holy crap! My hands are shaking as I shove them into my pockets, trying not to look at him. "I don't think it counts in this instance," I say, and horrifyingly my voice sounds uneven.

Ryka nods, giving me a cautious look out the corner of his eye. "Still. You really, *really* shouldn't tell anyone that happened."

"Would it be bad for you if they found out?"

Ryka stops dead. It seems as though he really wants to confuse the hell out of me, because he reaches out and places his hand on my cheek, and I can do nothing but stare up at him with wide eyes. Why the hell is he touching me? His gaze travels over my face, pausing on my lips for a second longer than is comfortable. "Bad for me. Bad for you," he says softly. "Let's just pretend it never happened, okay?"

This freeze frame in time is just too overwhelming. I back away slowly, out of his reach. His hand remains for a second before he allows it to drop to his side. Looking down at his boots, he clears his throat. "Agreed?"

I swallow and nod, because that's all I'm capable of. We set off walking again, my cheek burning where he touched me. Suddenly I don't want to be around him anymore.

"Is Jack in the tent you took me to the other night? I think I can make it there myself." I really can if I have to. That tent is like Freetown's version of the Colosseum; it can be seen from any vantage point within the city's limits.

Ryka shakes his head. "Sorry, little Kit. The way those guys were talking this morning, they want to take those knives off you personally. Jack'll kill me if I knew about that and didn't make sure you got to him safely. Once you're with him, don't worry. I won't be hanging around."

It seems like all of Freetown knows I'm being taken to their leader as Ryka shoves his way through the market place. Whole crowds of people stop talking as I follow him towards Jack's tent. When we pitch up outside our destination, Ryka tugs open the canvas flap and holds it aside, his face completely blank. No smiling or scowling. I kind of get the feeling I've done something to piss him off, which is nothing new, but this time he doesn't want me to know it.

"Thanks." I slip by him into the tent, unsurprised to find Jack sitting in the centre of the dusty room. There are no other chairs drawn up beside him this time; even the wobbling stacks are gone. The fire in the pit burns low, barely lit. A broad smile flashes across Jack's face when he catches sight of us.

"Come to see me again so soon!" he laughs. "How are you, Kit? Ryka, stop pulling that face."

So much for not coming in. Ryka hasn't made good on his promise to leave as soon as he dropped me off. Standing at my side, I can see exactly which face Jack is referring to. Ryka's eyebrows are pulled together, his mouth pressed into a tight line. "She won't take off her knives," he tells Jack.

Grandfather Jack raises his eyebrows at me. "Is that so?"

I nod. "If you say I'm not allowed to wear them, I'll respect that."

Ryka rocks on his heels, shoving his hands into the back pockets of his pants. "So you'll take them off if he tells you to? Just not anyone else?"

"No." I push down the bubbling, sharp feeling in my chest. "I can't take them off. I'll leave."

"Oh, come on! You're being ridiculous."

"I will. I don't feel safe without them."

Jack interrupts, preventing Ryka from saying anything else. "You don't have to leave, Kit, and you don't have to take off your knives. I really wish you would, but I'm not going to make you. I've already told the others they're not to bother you."

Ryka's eyes go wide. "But—"

"But nothing, Ry. If we make the girl leave, they'll find her and haul her back to Lockdown. Do you want that?"

A nimbus of blond hair falls into Ryka's face, disguising his expression when he mumbles, "It doesn't make any difference to me."

Jack stares at him for a second and then shakes his head. "You're too stubborn for your own good, boy. I'm sure your father wasn't as stern as you when he was your age. Your mother definitely wasn't!" Ryka's face loses all expression at the mention of his parents. I can practically feel a chill rolling off him.

"Thank you for understanding," I tell Jack. The old man stops studying Ryka, who remains still and silent, and gives me a small nod.

"Of course I understand. If you've grown up with those things on you at all times, it's going to take a while to break the habit. You will eventually, though, Kit. You're not going to need them here. Before too long, you'll realise Freetown is entirely different to the Sanctuary. The people are different. The way we are with one another is very different. Hell, even the way we fight is different. Maybe it's time you saw for that for yourself."

Ryka twitches, looking at me out of the corner of his eye. "The pits are no place for her, Jack."

"Don't be stupid, boy. Everyone in Freetown comes to the fights. If your sister can go, I see no reason why Kit can't." He shrugs and sinks further into his chair, looking up at us both.

"Fine, Liv can take her," Ryka sighs. He looks tired, and the fight seems to slide right off him. He turns to face me and I think I catch a flicker of concern. Could he really feel that? For me? His words say no, but his body language disagrees. He's wound up like an impossibly taut bowstring. "You think you can handle seeing it? I mean, spilled blood when you're anesthetised is one thing. When your hands are covered in it and you can smell it in the air, knowing what it means...that's entirely something else." Ryka pauses, but I don't get to tell him I'll be fine. It's like a switch gets thrown somewhere inside him. He pivots on his heel and Jack and I watch his back as he quietly leaves the tent. When I spin back around, there's a twisted smile on Jack's face. I'm definitely not smiling, though.

"Is he always this confusing?"

Jack curves a bushy steel grey eyebrow at me. They seem to be the most expressive part of his body. "My grandson can be a little misunderstood, sweet-heart. I may give him a hard time, but he's a good kid. He just worries about a lot of things."

"Well, why would he be worried about me?" Jack just looks at me, smiling softly. He doesn't reply, and it takes me a while to realise he's not going to. It's like he's waiting for me to work out the answer to my question on my own, which is really annoying. I don't even try. "Olivia's going to take me to the blood ceremony? That's different from a fight how?" I'd never considered what it might be like watching matches instead of fighting in them, and for some reason there's a dark curiosity in me.

"Blood ceremonies take place a few days before matches, when the priestesses alter fighters' rankings. We don't have one every match. Only if one of the priestesses have had a vision."

"And they've had one now?"

Jack nods, folding his hands over his belly. "They've had one now.

19

MASHINJI

"Close your eyes!" Olivia shouts. There's excitement in her voice, loud over the shrieks of the crowd pressing at our backs. I close my eyes immediately, knowing what's coming. I've just watched the teenaged boy on the pit floor spray a whole bucket of blood up into the gathering masses that circle the pit, dousing them bright crimson. The skin on my face tingles as a fine mist hit me. Olivia laughs brightly when I open my eyes. Her whole face is speckled with vivid red dots.

"Don't worry," she tells me, smiling. "It's only pig's blood."

I'm not worried about being covered with pig's blood. I'm more concerned by the fact that it stinks really badly, rotten and old. The tickertape and swatches of red cloth from the Colosseum seem very civilised to me right now. At least they only represented blood. The residents of Freetown are apparently a more literal people. I wipe my hand over my face and Olivia laughs harder. "What?"

"You have more blood on your hands than you did on your face. You've just made it ten times worse. You look quite scary now."

When I look down, I see that she's right. My hands are covered in blood and so is the front of the loose, flowing green shirt Olivia persuaded me to wear. Six feet down on the pit floor, the guy who threw the blood starts howling out a loud chant, side skipping around the circular pit. His chest is bare, marked with bloody handprints. The stack of lines running up from his wrists is small. Only a few kills. The crowd responds, and a call goes up from the hundreds of people thronging to get a get a better view. It sounds like a beating pulse at first, quickly growing in pitch until the noise of the voices around us turns into a crashing roar.

Raksha! Raksha! Raksha!

Olivia joins in, her eyes bright with the reflections from the fires that light up the hill on the other side of pit. With the blood and excitement on her face, she looks a little mad. "*Raksha! Raksha!*" she hollers, elbowing me to join her.

"What are they shouting?"

She starts slapping her palm against her thigh like some of the other women surrounding the pit, making the bells on her dress sing. "*Raksha!* We shout it when fighters are promoted. It symbolises the voices of all the men who have died before in the pit. It's their death chant, calling for fresh blood to the other side. The most brutal fights always take place after the blood ceremonies. The step up in ability is too much for some men. They don't fare too well against the more seasoned fighters."

That sounds like a pretty morbid tradition. I shudder, noticing that there is more than one kind of fire reflected in Olivia's eyes. A fever burns there, which is surprising. For such a sweet girl, she seems completely swept away in the furore around us. Jack was right: this is totally different to what I'm used to in the arena. Maybe it's the sheer volume of people, shouting and bloody themselves, all eager to find out which fighters have been chosen to move up in the ranks. Maybe it's the fact that Olivia and I are balanced precariously on the edge of the massive, yawning hole that dips down into the earth and rough hands keep shoving at us from behind. Whatever it is, I don't feel all that well. Was Ryka right? Is this going to be too much for me? There's a knot in my belly that I just can't seem to shake. My hand flutters to my neck, subconsciously checking to see if my halo is whirring. I feel stupid when I realise it isn't there. Olivia notices and stops clapping her hand to her thigh, reaching over to take hold of mine.

"Don't worry. This is all normal," she tells me. "There's no fighting tonight." Her lips continue to move, but I can't hear her words. The swell of voices soars, growing impossibly loud. "They're here!" Olivia hollers, clenching hold of my arm. The crowd parts on the other side of the pit, the people forming a narrow walkway between them. A flash of red appears through the press of people and that's when Olivia starts trembling. "The High Priestess!" she shouts. I can tell she's not just pointing out the High Priestess' arrival; she is genuinely excited. The calls of *Raksha! Raksha!* grow louder as the staggering figure of a stooped woman lumbers into view, wearing the same fine red robe I saw earlier on the other priestess at the Keep.

Her back is so hunched over that it looks painful for her to walk. A handful of men gathered at the side of the pit leap down into the dirt, barely flinching at the drop. From there they hold their arms out and the fragile figure steps forward, letting them lower her to the pit floor. It looks like they're lifting a small child; she mustn't weigh anything. A roar goes up as soon as her feet hit the floor, and the men and the teenager who started the chanting vault up and drag themselves out of the fighting arena. As soon as the last man is up and the High Priestess is alone below, a silence falls across the crowd. It takes a moment for the people at the very back of the audience to realise everyone is waiting for them to shut up.

I look around and can't help but notice the people's faces: expressions of awe are echoed everywhere. Absolute reverence fills their eyes, men, women and children alike. Olivia is no exception.

"What's going on?" I hiss.

Olivia shakes her head and shushes me. About five seconds pass before a loud voice cuts through the night air, echoing in the silence. The High Priestess.

"Calden Moore!" she shouts. Her voice is powerful and strong, entirely at odds with her fragile stature. A low muttering travels through the crowds, and people push back as a young guy with dark hair threads through them. He emerges four feet to our right, pausing to jerk his shirt over his head, where he throws it to the ground and drops down into the pit. Tattoos mark him past his elbows.

"Tamji!" the High Priestess shrieks, throwing her arms high above her head. A wild surge of noise ripples through the air, making the hairs on the back of my neck stand on end. I swallow a lump in my throat, wondering if Calden Moore is ready to be promoted to Tamji. The guy definitely looks surprised as he paces towards the High Priestess. He holds his right hand out when he reaches her and a pale hand appears from within the red folds of delicate material.

The unmistakeable flash of a knife glints in the High Priestess' hand, and before I can ask Olivia what she's about to do, the woman in red plunges down into Calden's palm. The blade cuts through, sticking straight out the other side, and Calden remains completely silent. No way had I been expecting that. I look around to see if anyone else is as stunned as me, but the people gathered around the pit just look anxious, like they're waiting. Calden blinks slowly, never taking his eyes off the High Priestess. She holds his hand in hers, unmoving, watching him. It's like there's some tense showdown between the High Priestess and Calden and everyone is holding their breath to see what happens. The jagged silence is only broken by the snap of dry wood crackling on the fires close by. Several moments pass before the bent old lady suddenly whips into life, thrusting Calden's wounded hand high above her head.

"*Rashatta!*" she screams, muffled by the ceramic white mask that I can now see beneath the slowly fluttering veil across her face.

The crowd howls the word in response, louder and louder each time. The chant is still being hollered by the people of Freetown as the woman takes hold of the blade embedded in Calden's hand and yanks it free.

Calden's face remains neutral, entirely still and lifeless. He bows low in front of the High Priestess, and it's only as he jogs back to the pit wall that he cradles his hand to his chest, wincing.

"He did well," Olivia says into my ear as people reach down for Calden's arms and pull him out of the pit.

"Do fighters dull their pain?" I ask. Why else wouldn't Calden have scream-ed out when he was stabbed? Olivia shakes her head.

"No. Fighters have to take a cut from the High Priestess and show no pain or fear before they can be ranked. The last time Calden flinched when the High Priestess sliced his shoulder. He's been waiting for the opportunity to prove himself again for a long time. He was only supposed to be raised one grouping, though. He just climbed three."

I look back down on the High Priestess and shiver. "And she stabbed him through the hand this time, just to make it harder?"

"They have to be sure."

"Sure of *what?*" My voice is strained, and Olivia gives me a startled look.

121

"That they're worthy to die, of course."

Before I can open my mouth, because I'm longing to, the High Priestess calls out another name. I don't hear it, only the sea of people reacting around me, jostling me forward. My boots are pressed so close to the edge of the pit that the earth crumbles and skitters downwards, marking the same path I will take if I get shoved one more time. I push back, anger spiking in my chest. This is different, though. I thought I knew anger, but I was wrong. The power of the emotion pulsing through my body leaves me breathless and for a moment I consider turning and bolting through the crowds. I want to, only I don't know how safe Olivia would be if I left her.

Three more men are called forward, Tamjis each one. They leap down and take the cuts that the High Priestess offers them. Only one of the wounds she inflicts is as severe as Calden's. The last man called, Lettin Corr, a giant of a man with a bold chest tattoo to accompany the countless scores up his arms, jumps down and strides with purpose to the High Priestess. She reaches up before he even stops walking and slashes with frightening precision at the side of his head. The people in the crowd go wild, and fresh blood sprays down into the pit. A second or two passes before I can see the extent of the damage the High Priestess has inflicted. Lettin gets helped up out of the pit right beside Olivia and I, and as he pulls himself up the last few feet, I understand. His right ear has been sliced clean through, rending straight through the cartilage. The very top part of his ear hangs off by a thread, dangling and bloody, and yet Lettin grins at us when he stands. Even his eyes don't betray his pain. His friends clap him on his back and he disappears into the swell of bodies.

"I think I'm ready to go," I shout out to Olivia. She looks at me, confused, and as she does so the tall man standing beside her rocks forward, pushing her closer to the pit edge. She squeals and I instinctively reach out and grab her arm. She stares back at me as I hold onto her, her body leaning out over the drop.

"Kit!" she shrieks, "pull me back in!" There's fear in her eyes when I tug her forward. She falls into me and her legs collapse out from underneath her; the man responsible for knocking her off balance is suddenly in our faces, apologising and wringing his hands, pushing the people around us back.

"You shouldn't be standing at the edge," he scolds. There's a reprimand in his voice but the expression on his face says he's scared.

"It's okay," Olivia breathes. "I didn't fall." I don't understand why both of them are so terrified. The fall would only have been six feet, not far enough to warrant this much panic. They're acting like it was a near death experience for both Olivia and for the man. He smiles nervously and backs away, allowing a hesitant line of men to push after him. They stand well back from me and Olivia this time, though.

"Thank you." Olivia turns back to me. "Thank you for catching hold of me." Her face is slightly green, and I'm about to ask her what the big deal is when the High Priestess' voice splinters through the air once more.

"*Mashinji! Mashinji!*" In the silence that follows, I look around to find people staring blankly into the pit. Olivia's hand tightens on mine. "Did...did she just call Mashinji?"

I blink at her, wondering why everyone has frozen still. Wondering who the High Priestess called while I was pulling Olivia back to safety. "Yes. What's Mashinji?"

She swallows, her eyes big and round. "It's a level of fighter. We haven't had anyone called to be Mashinji in, well, forever. Since before, when I was really small. The last person—" She trails off, glancing around her. It takes a full minute for a pathway to clear on the opposite side of the pit, and when Ryka walks through, shrugging off his tight black long sleeved shirt, a strangled gasp erupts from Olivia.

"No," she whispers. It's as though Ryka somehow hears the word over the incessant, rustling whispers of the crowd and his eyes snap up. They lock onto Olivia's. They look softer than usual, which is an odd contrast to his facial expression—harder than ever. He gives her a curt nod and drops gracefully down into the pit.

Olivia steps back and grabs hold of my arm. "We should leave," she says.

"What?" All the excitement and shine has dropped right out of her. "I don't understand."

"Mashinji—" She swallows like she's trying to remember how to breathe. "Mashinji is a rogue level. It means the fighter can be called to fight anyone at any time. More importantly, he can be called by a fighter instead of the priestesses."

I look back down on Ryka standing in the pit before the High Priestess. His eyes have finally gone hard, the way I'm used to seeing them.

"How many levels are there above Tamji?" I whisper.

Olivia turns and looks at me, biting on her lip. "Three."

Three. Three levels of fighters above the skill level Ryka has been training with. In his new ranking, Ryka could be called by people far more skilled than he is. "There was a danger he could have been called to one of the higher ranks, anyway," I tell Olivia. She looks like she needs comforting, but my words don't seem to have the desired effect.

"You don't understand. Usually a fighter only has to participate in one match per night. It's different for Mashinji. They can be called to every single fight in an evening if the others want to match him. People have used that to their advantage before—pitched the Mashinji against a handful of inexperienced men at first to tire him out, and then when he's good and exhausted they'll put him up against someone far better than they are. It's a sure fire way of killing off a strong competitor."

So, it turns out Freetown has its own version of the Death Bet. I take this on board, wondering why it feels like I'm going to throw up. "And is Ryka a strong competitor?"

A pained look flashes across Olivia's face. "Yes."

The High Priestess steps forward and gestures for Ryka's hand, and for a minute I think she's going to repeat her actions with Calden. Ryka doesn't give anything away. If I didn't know any better I'd suspect him of wearing a halo from the completely void expression he wears. I feel Olivia pull in a sharp breath as the High Priestess throws her arm over her head. The anticipation of what will come next draws us both back to the very edge of the pit. The blade gleams for a split second before the High Priestess plunges down once more, but this time she stops. The point of the blade is so close to Ryka's skin that it has to be puncturing his palm. The woman in red grips hold of his hand and pulls him closer, at which point she leans down and gently slices the edge of the metal across the very tip of his index finger.

The smallest of cuts. Olivia looks at me, just as confused as I am. The crowd of people watching along side us burst into laughter and raucous shouts, clapping their hands. When the High Priestess lets Ryka go, he immediately paces back to the opposite side of the pit and jumps, lifting himself out before anyone has chance to offer him help.

"Did you see that?" a man behind us laughs to his friends. "Even the Priestess isn't going to test Ryka's worthiness. The Gods know he's fit to die."

Olivia spins around and glares at the man behind us. The second he sees her face, his smile vanishes.

"Apologies, Miss Olivia. I didn't see you there. I should be more careful with my words."

"Yes," she snaps. "You should." With that, she grabs hold of my hand and storms off, leaving behind the crumbled earth where we'd stood and watched her brother accept his death sentence.

20

SING

Under a blanket of stars I finally find the place I am looking for. After the crush and madness of the blood ceremonies, this is exactly what I need. Silent, secluded, far from the outskirts of the Freetown and its inquisitive inhabitants, the small clearing is perfect. More perfect still is the solitary tree growing in its centre, gnarled and twisted in every direction, like it forgot which way was up. When I look at it, I see a tool, the exact tool I need to practice with. I kick my boots through the wet grass, enjoying the slick catching noise it makes against the muddy toes of the leather.

Once I reach the tree I slip out my daggers, one in each hand, and I begin. It takes three minutes to warm up, another five to find my rhythm, and another to become fluid. I continue slashing and blocking against the tree, driving my knife into the bark, only to rip it free and attack anew. My muscles burn and my limbs are weak, but the feeling is so good. I am made for this. I used to be a machine, created for this specific purpose, and right now I am finding out which parts of me still work after being switched off for so long. Luckily, it seems I am just in need of a little oiling.

By the time I can hardly hold my knife up anymore, there are wood chips in my hair and the tree is covered in deep gouges, bark-less in places. I step back and admire my handiwork, only to jump out of my skin at the voice behind me.

"What did it ever do to you?"

I spin around to find Ryka sitting in the grass, legs crossed, watching me. He looks completely different to the last time I saw him leaping out of the pit. Balancing the tip of a knife on his index finger, shifting his hand slightly back and forth to keep it upright, he looks relaxed and untroubled. "Bad night?" he asks, smirking.

I curse at myself for not paying attention. He totally sneaked up on me and I didn't hear a peep. "No," I tell him. "I wanted to come and train a little. Can I do that in peace?"

"I'm not disturbing you, am I?" he asks brightly, falling back into the grass. His knife disappears back into his belt.

"Yes, you are, actually."

"You know that tree was about four hundred years old, don't you?" he asks, ignoring the frustrated tone in my voice.

"What? Trees live that long?"

"Much longer if you don't stab them to death."

"I didn't stab it to death. It'll grow back."

Ryka lifts his head up and looks at me, smiling. "Sadly, no. It doesn't just *grow back*. I'm afraid you just spelled the end for that tree. Bad karma, too, since it's a prayer tree."

"Prayer tree?"

He nods. "Look up."

I tilt my head back and that's when I notice the thin strips of material tied around the branches higher up. In the dark, they're all a murky grey colour but I know without a doubt that they will be red in the daylight. It's just like back in the Sanctuary: a small green halo, clacking away; red ribbons in tiny hands, tying them to branches; Cai and me, the day I killed him. I shiver and focus on the tree. "Well, damn."

"Yeah. You might not want to own up to that. "Ryka chuckles and lays back down in the grass.

"You just sat there and watched me! You could have said something."

"I know better than to surprise you when you have something sharp in your hand, little Kit."

I make my way over to him with a sinking feeling setting over me. Now I'm killing things without even realising it. When I reach Ryka, he is lying on the ground with his eyes closed and his shirt hiked up a little, exposing a strip of skin across his stomach.

"Want to join me?" he asks, his hands rising and falling where they are stacked on his chest.

"I don't think so. Why are you even here?"

He opens one eye. "I was coming to pray. Dangerous pastime, though, by the looks of things."

He's lying, I can tell. "Try again."

A resigned sigh works out of him as he opens the other eye and heaves himself up into a sitting position. "I'm here to make sure you don't get skewered on one of Jack's traps. And before you even start with the, *I don't need looking after, I know everything* speech, just take a look at that poor, brutally murdered tree over there and consider how much you really do know about being out here."

I glance at the tree. Four hundred years of doing just fine and then I come along. "Point taken," I concede. "I just wanted to warm up my knives. I'll know better next time."

"Yes, next time come and see me. I'll help you train. I told you I'd be up for a rematch any time, didn't I?" Ryka grins at me, even more pleased when he sees that I am blushing.

"Good night, Ryka." I turn and set off back towards Freetown, moving quickly in the hope I'll be able to get a decent head start on him.

"Wait!"

I pause, hands on my dagger hilts. Why the hell did I stop? I should just keep going. I'm about to do just that when he says, "I'm serious. Come on, if you really want to train, then I'll help you."

I turn slowly to find him standing a few feet behind me, hands shoved in his pockets. He doesn't look like he's making fun of me. Doesn't sound like it, either.

"Why would you do that? You've made it very clear you don't think I should even have knives in the first place."

With a shrug, Ryka plucks a dagger from his knife belt and toys with it in his hands. "There are only so many trees out here, Kit. I'm just trying to save the forest."

"Tell the truth!"

"Okay, fine," he sighs. "I'm Mashinji now. I'm not allowed to train with any of the other fighters."

"Why not?"

"I'm just not. It's part of the rules."

"I see. So I'd actually be doing you a huge favour, and after you gave me such a hard time about my knives, too, right?"

Ryka spins around, ignoring me, and throws his knife, hard, so that it *thunks* into a tree trunk. Apparently not ready to admit to such a thing, he stalks off to retrieve his blade while I think. Should I take him up on his offer? It's not like I have anyone else to partner with. Of course, fighting him would be easier if I didn't feel so strangely nervous. I have no idea where this bizarre fluttering feeling has suddenly come from. It's annoying as hell, and gets much worse when I remember my body locking around his, wrestling with him the first time we met. In the darkness, I catch Ryka's eyes dilating and I'm almost one hundred percent sure he's remembering that, too. His smile broadens, and my hands start to itch. I can't let him make me feel so strange. I won't. "Okay, then. You're on." I begin to pace back toward him, but he holds his hand up, stopping me in my tracks.

"Whoa, wait a minute. You have to connect with your weapons a little first. You've just thrashed the living hell out of them."

I quirk an eyebrow at him, wondering what on earth he's talking about. "They're knives. Tools. You said as much yourself when we were in the forest. Now, are you going to fight me or not?"

"I was a little pissed off, if you'll recall. And yes, a weapon is a tool, sure, but it's also a living thing, has a personality. You need to treat it with the proper love and respect." He levels me in his gaze, holding out his dagger point-first. The moonlight glints off its wickedly sharp tip. "Close your eyes," he tells me.

"What? No way!" He's crazy if he thinks I'm putting myself at such a disadvantage around him. He drops the knife to his side, huffing.

"You're impossible. Just do it. Close your eyes. I'm not going to hurt you, I swear."

129

I study him—the way every muscle in his body is slack, and how his eyes seem gentle—and I find my scowl fading. "Fine." I snap my eyes closed but I'm too wary to trust him completely. I leave my left eye cracked a little, enough that I can discern his blurry shadow as he makes his way silently towards me. He just stands there, looking at me, for a moment. I have no idea what he finds so interesting, but it's awkward that I'm standing here with my dagger held out in front of me, and he's just staring.

"Well?" I ask. He shakes his head and pulls a face, and it's all I can do not to react. I don't want him to know I'm peeking, though, so I keep my blank expression trained on my face. He steps closer, and closer still, and with every step he takes I get more and more uneasy. It starts as an unsettled feeling in my stomach, a low flutter that grows and grows until I feel oddly short of breath. When he's finally standing in front of me, my dagger pointed behind him out toward the trees, I feel like I'm going to pass out. His breath comes out in slow, long exhalations, brushing across the skin on my cheek. Ryka tips his head to one side, and the look in his eyes is so invasive that I can't do it anymore; I scrunch both eyes shut, unable to bear it.

"That's better," he whispers.

I could say something waspish, but I don't. I just keep my arm raised, my knife out like he showed me, waiting. He shifts around and then I feel it—he presses something against the edge of blade. A slow drawing motion slides up and down my knife, putting pressure against it. My arm moves under the tension, but Ryka tuts.

"Push back. Gentle," he says softly.

I do as I'm told, and a low hum travels up my arm, flowing like electricity all the way to my shoulder. It's a vibrating, tingling sensation that feels kind of amazing. The slow movement across my knife becomes rhythmic and I find myself copying the motion, drawing back when Ryka does, easing forward a second later. What he's doing quickly becomes apparent. I know the feeling of metal on metal, know what two sharp edges feel like together. His knife is working mine, sharpening it. A soft, low, humming sound develops in the silence. "There," he whispers. "That's how you make them sing."

I want to open my eyes, but I'm too trapped to do it. Trapped in how peaceful and strangely intimate the moment is.

"You do this with all your Tamji buddies?" I ask him.

Ryka laughs gently. "Not quite." He inhales and then I feel him move, closing the gap between us. "I'm going to stop now." His hand closes around my wrist as the pressure ceases, and I open my eyes to find him staring down at me. I feel ridiculous still brandishing my knife up at him, and since I can't lower my arm—he still has hold of my wrist—I lower my eyes instead.

"Are you blushing, Kit?" he whispers.

"I—maybe." There's no point in lying; my face feels like it is on fire, and my bright red cheeks must be visible even in the darkness. Ryka narrows his eyes slightly, searching my face.

"Why do you think that is?"

I have no idea why he's asking me. I mean, how am I supposed to know? Suddenly, far too warm, I panic. I pull back and go to shove my knife back in my belt, but my quick movement startles him. He goes to grab hold of me, following which a searing pain burns into the skin above my hip.

"Ow!"

"Kit! Gods, I am so sorry!" Ryka lets go of my arm and drops his knife on the ground, fumbling with my shirt.

"What—what the hell are you doing!" My cries don't deter him; he grabs hold of my shirt, lifts it a couple of inches, and then freezes. His whole body goes still.

"Oh," he says quietly.

"Oh? *Oh?!* You just stabbed me with your knife, Ry! I'm bleeding, for crying out loud!"

Ryka inches upwards until he is standing straight again, and looks down at his feet. "I did *not* mean to do that."

"What, stab me or nearly tear my shirt off?"

"Either. And I didn't stab you. I barely broke the skin."

I look down at the bleeding cut just above my hipbone and see that he's right. It's only an inch long and a millimetre deep, but still. I'm not used to pain yet, how much it actually *hurts,* and this fairly innocuous graze stings like crazy. I glare at him, but that doesn't seem like enough. I follow up my unhappy look with a hard slap across his arm.

"Hey! It was an accident!"

"Yeah, right. I bet you've just been itching to get back at me since the woods."

An odd, crumpled expression flashes across Ryka's face. "I promise you, if that were the case, I would just kick your ass. I definitely wouldn't cut you with a knife."

It takes me a beat to figure out why he's so freaked out, and when I do all the blood drains from my face. "Oh. Wow. So I cut you, and now you cut me. What does that mean?"

Ryka just looks at me, his brown eyes piercing mine.

"I don't want to know, do I?"

He shakes his head, a tiny, nervous smile playing at the corners of his mouth. "Nope. I'm guessing you don't." He ducks down and reaches for my shirt again. I slap his hand, but he shoots me an *I'm-not-messing-around* look, and I avoid the otherwise inevitable argument by letting him continue. He lifts my shirt slowly and frowns at the single line of blood running down towards my knife belt. With slow, careful movements, he traces his finger along my stomach and catches the droplet before it hits the fabric. He studies it for a second before stooping and grabbing his knife from the grass, clenching his hand—the one with my blood on it—into a fist.

"Why did you do that?" I demand, as he sets off walking towards the trees. "What did you just do?" He throws a smirk at me over his shoulder. The look is ruinous, will be the end of me, I'm sure.

"Nothing, little Kit. Nothing at all."

DECAY

The next morning I'm woken by a scraping sound against the side of my tent. It's still dark and I'm particularly unhappy about being woken up.

"Come on, little Kit. Time to get up and train with me."

It's him. Standing outside my tent. Dragging his fingernails across the fabric. I hide my head under my blankets, waiting to see if he goes away, but he doesn't. The scraping continues, setting my teeth on edge.

"All right! All right! Sheez!" I get up, sulking enough that Ryka pretends to cower when I fling back the tent flap and stalk towards the river to wash up. "I thought you were joking when you said you would train with me."

"You thought, or you *hoped?*" he replies, leaning against a tree, watching me as I splash cold water onto my face. "I don't know why you're bothering with that. You're only going to get dirty again."

HALO

I scowl up at him, freezing cold water running into my eyes. "Some of us don't look or feel as great as you obviously do first thing in the morning."

"I look great first thing in the morning?" Ryka grins and that dimple appears in his cheek, deep and pronounced. A jolt of adrenaline and goodness knows what else makes my heart start flip-flopping in my chest. *Damn. Well, I guess I walked into that one.*

"Don't get smart, mister. I'm sorely tempted to climb back into bed."

"And miss out on the opportunity to twirl those blades of yours around? I don't think so. You should be nicer to me, Grumpy Morning Kit."

I scramble back up the riverbank, doing my best to ignore his wicked smirk. It's tough, though. I end up sneaking a glance at him as he falls into step alongside me. He's looking straight ahead but his smile hasn't slipped a bit, and I get the feeling he knows he's being watched. He ducks his head, his eyes shining brightly, and I see that his hair grows in a tiny, perfect whorl at the back of his neck. Shaking my head, I tear my eyes away and clench my teeth. Noticing things like that is only going to get me into trouble.

"Don't pretend like I'm not helping you out here," I say, shoving past him to grab my knife belt from inside my tent. "You're kind of without a training partner right now, yourself, remember."

Ryka's eyebrows pull together a fraction. "Fine, I'll admit it. You're helping me out. We should probably keep our little arrangement under wraps, by the way. The both of us could end up in hot water over this."

"You more than me, I think."

He shrugs. "Probably. Still, I think it's going to be fun. Oh, and you're going to need to bring a bag with food and water. We've got a long hike ahead of us."

"Where the hell are you taking me?"

Ryka pauses when Jack's voice breaks the silence of the morning, calling his name. I raise an eyebrow at him to see if he'll respond, and he mirrors me, raising his own. "I'm taking you back to the Colosseum. Now come on, before I get roped into field work."

******

We walk for three hours straight, and the whole time Ryka refuses to clarify what he means about taking me back to the Colosseum. All I know is that he's not

134

taking me back to the Sanctuary, because we're walking in the opposite direction. A series of questions are fired at me, each one more confusing than the next. Why he wants to know such random things about me is a mystery, and my deep contemplation over each enquiry is a source of constant frustration for Ryka.

"You're not supposed to think about it, you're just supposed to know. Come on, what's your favourite colour?"

"Uhhh...green?"

"Are you asking me, or are you telling me that your favourite colour is green?"

"Um. Telling. I think."

He sighs, the sound exaggerated and unnecessary. "Okay, since you started feeling again, what's been your favourite moment?"

"My favourite moment?"

"Yeah."

"People have those?"

"Sure they do. I have lots." He looks over his shoulder and there's that dimple again.

"Well..." I feel really, really stupid trying to think of a moment I favour above all others since I left the Sanctuary. There have been few truly happy moments. "Last night was interesting," I say, my cheeks burning a little. "The knives, I mean. When you made them sing like that."

Ryka turns around and walks backwards, hooking his thumbs under the shoulder straps of his bag. I didn't think it was possible, but somehow his smile just got wider. My cheeks burn, and he shakes his head, laughing at me.

"And what was your earliest childhood memory?"

"I don't know. I guess...I guess meeting Cai for the first time. We were learning to train, so I must have been around four years old."

"Huh." He nods, as though he's thinking this over, and turns back around. He goes quiet for a while after that, and neither of us speaks. I begin to feel the pressure of the silence between us, like something happened that I don't know about, like maybe I said the wrong thing. I could be doing this whole conversation thing wrong for all I know. It's not like I've done it much before, apart from with Olivia, and sometimes she's just content to be silent. I love her for that. This isn't like that kind of silence. Maybe I should be asking questions, too. This whole social etiquette thing is far more complex than I had first imagined.

It takes me a while to pluck up the courage to ask a question, and when I do I kind of blurt it out in a rush. "What was *your* first memory?"

"My father," he says simply. He doesn't expand on that, and I don't push. We walk for another hour or so before he says, "We're there. Are you ready?"

"For what?"

"For a *real* city."

The trees thin out and suddenly I see exactly what he means. A city. A huge, sprawling, ruined, over-run city stands off in the distance, buildings taller than I have ever imagined possible, some standing majestically, others a tumble of ruins, leaning drunkenly against one another. A cracked concrete pathway emerges out of the forest, leading directly into the heart of it.

"Wha—how?" It's the most amazing, terrifying thing I've ever seen. It's just so big. Sunlight glints off broken glass in the distance, the shards broken teeth in the open maw of countless smashed windows. "What happened?" I'm literally breathless as I try to take it all in, but it's just too much. I look at Ryka and he's watching my reaction with a soft smile on his face. It seems secret, though, as though the smile, unlike many of his others, is purely for himself. A smile of pure pleasure.

"Didn't they tell you about the world before?" he asks quietly. I shake my head, trying to find words, but they just won't come. "The country was covered in cities like this one before the collapse. In fact, from what I can gather this city was pretty small in the scheme of things." He considers me for a second before shoving me gently with his shoulder. "Come on, I want to show you."

And he does.

We spend the next few hours trailing through an obstacle course of crumbling rubble and abandoned items that confuse and intrigue me. Ryka seems to know what most of them are, although a few remain a mystery to the both of us. Large wire baskets on wheels, rusted and stacked in huge piles that tower two storeys high, litter the walkways between the buildings. Peeling orange and brown metal shells of cars lay abandoned everywhere, with fronds of green ferns and vines twisting around their decaying skeletons. The city is dead in so many ways, but alive in so many others. It feels like there are a thousand pairs of eyes peering down on us as we travel towards a destination that only Ryka knows, and it's hard to work out if there are actual people lurking in the surrounding buildings, or if it's just the ghosts of the past watching over us.

"What happened to all the people?" I ask. I can't even imagine how many of them there would have been all in one place, to justify a settlement this huge.

"War." Ryka shrugs, gazing up at the toppling building next to us. "Swiftly followed by his friends Disease, Famine and Death. *We* happened, I guess. The same crap we do to one another now, only with better technology and on a grander scale."

He leads me from one building to another until we finally arrive at a squat, gigantic building that he declares was a version of the Colosseum, once upon a time. It's true that when we walk through the tunnels and find ourselves in a large, open space, surrounded by thousands and thousands of seats, all looking down upon us, red and cracked and rusted, I immediately think of the Colosseum back in the Sanctuary. Except this is so much bigger. This place could literally seat every single inhabitant of the Sanctuary and then some.

"So this is where we train today," Ryka tells me. He yanks his shirt over his head with one hand and tosses it into the knee-high grass that grows from the arena floor of this huge gathering place. "Are you ready?"

Somehow I find that I am, even though I'm completely overwhelmed by the morning we've had together and the things we've seen. We spend the next three hours lunging and parrying, learning the way the other moves. It becomes a dance after a while. Our bodies are in tune in a way that I've never experienced before, not even with Cai. Would Cai and I have been like this if things had been different? I'll never know, but something deep within me suspects that this kind of alignment is something I'm only meant to share with Ryka. And the thought scares me stupid.

By the time we're done, we have created an almost perfect circle of flattened grass where we've been stalking around one another. I sink to the ground, exhausted from not training for weeks, and Ryka follows, grinning. He's not even out of breath.

"Did your last training partner run circles around you, too?" he asks brightly, propping himself up on one arm. I pull a face, but I know he's only joking so I let the comment slide.

"We were pretty evenly matched, Cai and me," I tell him through laboured breaths. "We both broke each other's bones. Gave as good as we got."

"Huh." Ryka falls onto his back, his eyes unfocused as he stares up at the sky. "Do you think I could have beaten him?" he asks slowly.

I frown, turning to look at him. Why would he ask something like that? "I don't know. You're...you're good. Maybe."

"Mmmm."

We lie there in silence for a while, watching the sky, such a stark hue of blue that it looks faded and washed out. The sun disappears for a moment when a teased out, wispy cloud passes over it. "I would have liked to meet him," Ryka says softly.

"Really? Why?"

He blinks, pulling one shoulder up in a half-hearted shrug. "I don't know. You were obviously very close, even with the halos. Seems like I can't understand you without understanding him a little, too."

A prickle of heat dances across my skin, burning at the base of my neck. That he's even thinking things like that makes me feel...odd. "Well...I suppose... you could *kind of* meet him."

Ryka frowns and sits up, the skin on his back still slick with sweat. "What do you mean?"

Cringing, I wonder if I should have even said anything. He looks intrigued now, intrigued and intense, and I don't know that I can face seeing them together side by side. "Uh...forget it. It's stupid actually."

"No, come on, tell me. What did you mean?"

I know from the look on his face that he won't let this go now. I really should learn to think before opening my big mouth. This is going to either be horrendous or, well...horrendous.

"I mean...this." I hesitatingly remove the holostick out of my pocket, where it always lives when I'm not in my tent.

"Ah. The incredibly important holostick. So you've watched it, have you?"

"Some."

"Let's have it, then." A grim set takes over Ryka's face, like he's bracing himself for a very unpleasant experience, and my hands tremble as I scroll through the file numbers, trying to come across one I've already watched that won't make me feel too weird or embarrassed. I don't find one. Ryka leans forward and peers over my shoulder, so close I can smell him, feel his heat burning into my arm.

"That one. Go back. I wanna see that one," he says, pointing at the screen. *File Eighteen. Play?* flashes on the screen at us.

"Number eighteen? Why that one?"

"Eighteen's as good a number as any and you're taking forever. Here." He reaches out and stabs at the play button with his index finger and suddenly Cai's there, crouched along side us, looking us both in the face.

Ryka tenses and I know he's surprised about the full-formed version of my ex-training partner staring us down. Like me, he's probably only seen the smaller, compressed images coming from a holostick. Cai shifts, and Ryka leans back, studying him. I try to see Cai the way Ryka is seeing him, for the first time: scruffy brown hair; dark eyes; his crooked nose and serious expression. There's power in his shoulders and a fluid, intrinsically confident vibe that comes off him in the easy way he holds himself. I try to work out if he is good looking, and I'm a little shocked when I realise that he is.

"I couldn't explain before, but there's no harm in it now," Cai says. Without the small smile that always seems to be hovering over his lips in his other recordings, he looks older. Tired. *"We planted a device in the technicians' compound, and yesterday it was supposed to go off. One of Opa's connections was supposed to arm the device so that it detonated during the matches. No real damage would have been done, but it would have created enough chaos to let them know we're here. That we're fighting back. Only..."* he sighs and casts his eyes to the floor. Slowly, Cai's ghostly image stands, and he scratches at the back of his neck. *"It didn't go off. Nothing happened. I won my match, waited in the tunnels for the signal that we were going ahead, but...there was nothing. Opa says his connection is dead, that we would all be dead if he was still alive. They would have slapped a working halo on him and he would have told them all about us, otherwise."*

I listen, horrified, as Cai explains their failed plan to incite disorder, knowing that he's right. The man who was supposed to trip their device, whoever he was, is now almost certainly dead. Ryka listens, too. He studies every inch of Cai—his face, his clothes, the way he moves. Carefully, he gets to his feet and circles around the hologram figure—as different as night and day, the two of them only have one thing in common: their solemnity. The sun comes back out and lances down through Cai, scattering the image for a second. Ryka frowns and stops, fixed solely on Cai.

"If only you were free of your halo, Kit. This would all be so much easier if I had you here with me. I get nervous sometimes. I panic about what will happen when you're free and can make decisions of your own. Will you want the name

I've selfishly given you? Will you still want to sit on the riverbank and dip your toes in the water? Will you want...will you want me?" Sorrow fills Cai face, and I know that when he recorded this, he really could have used a friend. I feel horrible that I wasn't there for him in the way he needed me to be. I also feel horrible about the awkward look on Ryka's face. He runs his hands through his hair, exhaling deeply as the recording ends and Cai disappears. I don't say anything. I wouldn't have a clue where to start. Ryka paces quietly in the trodden down grass for a moment before crouching down beside me. He reaches out and curls my hand closed around the holostick, giving me a lop-sided smile. My heart burns in my chest when his fingers linger over mine.

"I think I would have liked him," he says softly. "I'm sorry that he's gone."

22

PRIVACY

Olivia finds me in the next morning, exhausted from arriving home so late after my day with Ryka, but strangely happy. She kidnaps me and delivers me to my new home, a relatively large tent set back from the bustle of Freetown proper. It sits right next to the river, completely secluded and hidden from prying eyes. I have no neighbours bar one other tent, the one Olivia shares with Jack and Ryka. It is a monstrous thing, all oranges and browns and greens, and sits across a small wooded clearing, fifty metres away. She insists on holding her small hands over my eyes as she walks me into the place I will now sleep every night. Giggling, she pulls me inside, and I see that my things are already here. Fresh pine and woodsy smells tickle my sinuses. A small table and a chair sit against one side of the canvas, and in the corner a small hollow has been dug, presumably for a fire. I smile to myself, knowing I'm never going to light a fire in here no matter how cold it gets. To the right, lovely white voile material hangs from the highest point of the domed tent, creating a divide. When Olivia pulls it back, there is an actual bed. A real wooden frame with a mattress and soft blankets, finished off with pillows that are piled high. My jaw falls open.

"You like it, don't you?" Olivia grins.

"I—I love it." I walk into the room and trace my fingers over the smooth surface of the headboard, which has been carved with delicate looking flowers. "I've never seen anything so beautiful."

"I knew it!" Olivia tackles me from behind and bear hugs me. "I'm sorry this place took so long to organise but the bed was a while in the making. The men have to split their work between the workshops and the fields, and they had to find the perfect materials for it first." She throws herself back on my new bed, bouncing.

My eyes sting like crazy as I grin back at her. "No one's ever done anything like this for me before."

"Get used to it. I like doing nice things for people. It's a simple joy in life, making others happy."

I go and sit down on the bed next to her, staring down at my hands. I could literally cry, but for the very first time it isn't because I'm angry or it feels like my heart has been ripped out of my chest.

"Well, you have." I tell her quietly. "You've made me really happy. Thank you."

She leaves after that, promising to return later, and I decide that since my new tent is now hidden from the rest of the town, I have very little excuse for not washing properly. My hair is disgusting and my skin feels like I have ten layers of grime caked on it, to boot. Fifteen minutes later, the frigid water of the river is rushing around my shoulders when I notice I'm not alone. Four men stand on the bank, each with a strange glint in his eye.

"Little Warrior!" a balding man calls out. The tatty leather waistcoat he's wearing looks like it might have been stained red once upon a time, but now it's a dirty brown colour. His teeth are an unfortunate shade of yellow. "I see you do take your blades off for some things?" He reaches down and plucks up my knife belt, which looks tragically empty with just two daggers sheathed in it.

"Put that down!" I twist in the water, unsure what to do. I want to charge out of the river and grab them straight out of his grubby-looking hands, but I can't.

The fact that I'm naked— well, there's no way I'm getting out of the water naked. I don't want these leering freaks to see me without any clothes on. I do the only thing I can think of, hoping she will hear me. "Livia! Olivia!"

The balding man laughs, pulling one of my daggers from my belt. "Oh, come on. She's not going to hear you, not over the sound of all this rushing water. *I* barely heard that pathetic scream."

The three men standing around him guffaw at his remark, which makes me hate them. They're as rough as their leader, but none of them seem quite as ready to taunt me.

"Just put that down and leave," I hiss.

"And where would be the fun in that? I think you should come and get them. What do you think, boys? Should our little hellion come and take her knives back?"

"Joshua!" Before any of his friends can answer, another figure emerges through the trees. For a second I think it's Ryka and my stomach drops through the floor, but it isn't him. James, the man who was with Grandfather Jack the night I arrived in Freetown, the man who fought Ryka on the beach, appears. His dark hair falls into his face as he surveys the scene in front of him: Joshua and his buddies on the bank, my knife belt in his hand, and me, shivering in the water like a coward.

"What are you doing?" he asks, narrowing his eyes at Joshua.

"We—we were just having some fun," the other man stammers. "We didn't mean anything by it."

"That's fortunate." James steps forward and takes my dagger out of his hand. "Because you were told Grandfather Jack wants this one left alone. I'd hate to see you breaking Freetown's rules. You voted Grandfather Jack in as our leader, did you not?"

Joshua looks around at his friends, but they all seem to be looking elsewhere. "Yes, I voted for him."

"So it really wouldn't make any sense to be disobeying him now, would it?"

Joshua shakes his head, making his double chin wobble from side to side. "No. No sense at all."

"Good." James takes a step forward and the group of men react, moving backwards as one.

"We have fields to tend," Joshua announces, and all four of them turn and hurry off into the trees. I'm positive I must be blue by the time James turns and looks at me.

"Come here," he says.

I stare at him for a moment, unsure what he means.

"Come here," he repeats, his voice a little harder this time. Suddenly I'm not sure what just happened. Did James come and save me from those creeps, or was he just getting rid of them so he could...I don't know what?

"I'm not wearing anything," I say through chattering teeth.

James' eyes flash as he walks towards the riverbank. A startled shout erupts out of my mouth when he wades into the water, fully clothed, and comes for me. My dagger is still in his hand, and there's a cold expression on his face. I spend half a second trying to come up with a way to disarm him and defend myself, but I remember Olivia telling me that James is Kansho, the highest level of fighter here. I'm chilled to the bone and naked, and he's an undefeated warrior. Instead of lashing out when he reaches me, I do something I've never done before: I freeze with panic.

"You are making life hard for yourself," James hisses, grabbing hold of my wrist. "You think I haven't seen a naked girl before?"

In an awkward second, he's dragging me out of the water and up the side of the embankment. He lets go as soon as I'm back beside my pile of clothes and spins to face me. "You'll give yourself hypothermia protecting your modesty around here."

"I'd rather get hypothermia!" My hands are shaking as I scrabble to pick up my clothes. I'm welled up with so much embarrassment and pure fury that I fumble, and James reaches down and snatches my shirt out of my hand.

"You can't carry on like this," he tells me. "It'll only continue. People around here like a little sport, in case you haven't noticed. They're going to keep coming, keep finding ways of getting you alone, unless you do something about it."

I eye my balled up shirt in his hand, calculating whether I'd be able to grab it from him. Probably not. "What would you have me do?"

"What you're told," he snaps, shaking his head. "You think you have a right to be walking around with these?" He holds my dagger in the air, pinching the blade between his fingers.

"As much right as you!"

"Well, then, prove it. Change yourself. Don't ever back down." Quicker than I had imagined, James rushes forwards and grabs hold of my hair. I kick out at him, hard, landing a solid strike on his thigh. He pushes his leg out in the same direction as the strike, the way I was taught to when blocking a kick.

"What are you doing?" I yell. My heart starts thumping so hard in my chest that it feels like it's trying to burst through my ribcage.

"If you don't want to act like a girl in this town, you can't afford to look like one." He strikes out quickly, slashing at my hair with my own dagger. There's a tearing sound, like silk being quickly ripped apart, and a startling weightlessness on my neck. When James lets me go again, he throws my dagger and a seven-inch-long knot of my hair down at my filthy feet. I suck in a surprised gasp and stare down at it, not brave enough to reach up and find out what he's done.

"Do you know what happens to men in Freetown if someone takes their knives?" James asks quietly. His eyes never leave mine, never once slip over my naked body. I swallow and clench my hands into fists.

"Yes, they're cast out."

"Good. The next time someone takes your weapon from you, think about that."

"It won't happen again," I spit.

"Yes," he says. "It will."

He turns and marches off into the forest before I can say or do anything else. Instead of trying to tug my scrunched up clothes over my damp skin, I gather them up and run into my tent, fighting down the urge to sob.

23

CUT

By nightfall I'm starving but too ashamed to come out of my tent. If only I could hole myself away back here for the next few weeks, the horror of being so defenceless might subside and I could face the world again. But there's Olivia, of course. It's not really possible to knock on a tent; instead, she sings when she lets herself in, hallooing to announce her presence. I consider throwing myself under the beautiful covers of my new bed and hiding, but what would that accomplish?

Her eyes go wide when she spots me sitting on the edge of the feather mattress. From the expression on her face, my hair must look pretty bad. "Kit! What—?" Her mouth falls open and she loses the ability to speak. An irritated flash plays over her face after that. "Did you do this yourself?" she says. I hear the accusation in her voice, that she thinks my new haircut is a drastic way of rebelling.

"Of course not!" I'm a little snappy, but I can't help it. I really need some time alone, and I just don't have it in me to be polite.

"What happened, then?" She sits beside me on my bed, hitching her skirt up a little so she can tuck one leg underneath her. She reaches out to touch my hair but I flinch and she lets her hand drop into her lap.

"Some men—" I start. A really bad start.

Olivia grows a bright red. "Oh, Gods, Kit. What happened? Who was it? Did...did they—"

"No!"

She ignores my protests and pulls me into a hug. "Don't worry, I'm going to tell Jack. He'll make them pay for what they did."

"They didn't do it, Olivia. It was James."

She stops fussing and pulls back. "*James?*"

I nod and run my fingers over the ends of my hair. It only just reaches my jaw line now. "Yes. He said if I didn't want to act like a woman of Freetown, I shouldn't look like one either."

"I can't believe he would do that."

"Believe it."

She shakes her head. "No, you don't understand. James has been canvassing for women to have their own matches for years."

"What? Why would he do that? Hardly seems like he would care if the women here are treated like second-class citizens."

Olivia shoots me a disparaging look. "It's not equality for women he's after. It's equal rights for the *men*. James thinks men should be allowed to be priests. The women who work in the kitchens at the Keep say he'd have himself as the High Priest before nightfall the day Jack and the priestesses ever allowed that to happen." She takes a deep breath. "James is just about the most power hungry individual in Freetown. He'll do anything to get ahead, even if that means faking his beliefs in the Faith. Or putting women in the pits. He figures that you can't change one tradition without changing the other."

"That's really messed up." I screw up my nose and sink back onto my bed, feeling my hair fan out around my head in a way it never did before. "Are you going to tell Jack what happened?"

"No." Olivia finds my hand and squeezes it. "It's not my place. You should be the one to tell him."

I eye her in my peripherals. "Can we just let him think I did it myself?"

A vaguely irritated expression flashes across her features. "It's your decision. You have to do one thing, though."

"What?"

"You have to let me tidy it up for you."

Olivia disappears and returns a few minutes later with a pair of slim, narrow scissors, and spends the next twenty minutes trimming my hair into what she deems 'tidy'. I sit on the floor at her feet, trying my hardest not to think of my halo, or how I took it back to August to get it fixed. If he had said he was able to repair it, if there *was* an easy fix, I might already have been wearing it. With hair this short, barely brushing the bottom of my ears, I'll never be able to hide a collar around my neck in Freetown. Everyone will know if I put the thing back on, and that scares me half to death. I'm already a social pariah, and with that loop of metal flattening out my emotions, I really would have no place in the world. No place but the Sanctuary.

24

BEAUTIFUL

Sky-blue eyes widen at me as Olivia and I walk across a clearing in the vast tent maze. I can't see the girl's whole face; half of it is hidden by a male shoulder, which she is looking over. The guy's back is broad, and even before I see his hair, I know it's Ryka. The way his body weight rests on his left foot. The way his shoulder slopes down as he whispers into her ear. After all of our time spent together training the other day, I now know the way he holds himself, and that makes me feel conflicted. So does the way he angles into her as he continues to talk into her ear, too close to notice the surprise on her face, presumably at seeing me.

I'm really turning heads with this new haircut. I can't say that I'm enjoying the attention, although Olivia warned me I can't be shy about it if I want to pretend I did it myself. For a few panicked moments after leaving my brand new tent, I worried about what I was going to say when people asked me why I'd done it. Shouldn't have worried, though: of course, no one breathes a word to me. They just stare.

Blue Eyes blushes as Olivia and I drew closer, and I can't help but wonder what Ryka is saying to her to make her react that way. He shifts his weight slightly and reveals more of her: flowing red dress with bronze bells, stitched into the gentle pleats of the material; very slim, with softly curled brown hair all the way down her back. I'm pretty sure my hair used to look like that only this morning.

"I didn't know he was going to be here," I hiss. For some reason I feel self-conscious about seeing Ryka after our day together. Olivia pivots to smirk at me over her shoulder. There are tiny white flowers woven into her hair, painfully pretty.

"I didn't know he would be, either." Her smirk gets wider. "He told me he had better things to do. I didn't realise he meant Simone. Oh well, if he's all distracted with her then he won't bother us. That's not a problem, is it?"

Something tells me she's trying to goad a reaction out of me. I shake my head and bite my tongue between my teeth quickly, just enough so that I taste copper. "No. No, of course it's not a problem."

Olivia tuts, giving me a weird look. I ignore it and let her grab hold of my hand, and she draws me farther into the clearing, where a huge fire licks and spits at the sky. A horrible feeling wells up inside me, one that makes me feel sour and a little angry. I try to put aside the awful, niggling sensation, try not to wonder who the girl is and what she and Ryka are doing together, but it doesn't seem to work.

The only thing that distracts me from my line of thought are the looks I'm getting as we make our way through the crowds. The hair. It has to be the hair. It's better to believe that, anyway. It will grow back eventually, and it's nice to dream that as it does, people's interest in me will diminish.

"Come on, Melody's over there. I promised we'd meet her." Olivia pulls me in the red-haired girl's direction, close to the fire on the other side of the clearing. Standing beside her are two guys, about the same age as Ryka, and as the light plays over their skin I see the tattoos on their arms. They're fighters. Melody squeals when she sees us, but then her happy expression dissolves the second her eyes hit me.

"What happened?"

My hand hesitantly goes to the short ends of hair. "It's nothing. I— my hair's very thick. It's been really hot, so I cut it off."

"Is that a Sanctuary thing?" one of the boys asks. His eyebrows are pinched together, and I can't decide whether he's being confrontational or if he's just interested. His blue eyes are sharp.

I nod my head. "It just makes sense."

"Mmm. It seems like everything in Lockdown is more sense than the natural order of things," he says.

"Oh, come on, Max. We came here to enjoy ourselves." Olivia playfully slaps his arm, and Max smiles. The sharpness fades from his eyes the instant she touches his skin.

"It was just an observation, Liv. Didn't mean anything by it." He offers me his hand, still smiling. There's no concealed malice in his face, nothing to make me wary. "I'm Max. This is my brother, Callum. We're celebrating tonight. This loser has finally made Tamji."

The guy Max gestures to steps into the light to shake my hand as well. His black hair is ruffled and falls into his face, almost disguising the same colour blue eyes he shares with Max. The boys are so similar that I find myself confused.

"Yeah," Olivia laughs, "they're twins."

"Twins?"

"Yeah, you know, born at the same time?"

I can't hide my shock. "*You mean from the same woman?*"

Everyone but me laughs. Hard. My cheeks burn like crazy but I'm too concerned over the idea that a woman can carry two children at one time. "How do they not die?" I exclaim.

"Well, sometimes they do," Olivia tells me. "But Cal and Max's mother was just fine. They were just tiny when they were born is all. They're identical. Cal's hair is longer, though. And if you can't tell them apart by that, then their personalities are a dead giveaway. Callum's a whole lot nicer than his brother."

"Hey!" Max lunges at Olivia and throws her over his shoulder, making her squeal. She reaches out to me for help, eyes bright, her pleas gasped through her laughter. I just shrug my shoulders. Twins? I've never heard of anything so strange. Max runs off through the tents behind us, crowing, with Olivia still doubled over his shoulder. Melody sighs. "One day they're going to stop pretending they're not in love with each other."

Callum laughs. "The day my brother admits to anything other than a fierce

151

need to pound his fist into something, the Gods will crown me king of Freetown."

Melody rolls her eyes. "Come on, he may play the tough guy but he knows Olivia wants to join the priestesses. I think if her plans were different, he would have Claimed her already."

"What?" This is news to me. I tug nervously at the hem of the loose shirt Olivia picked out for me. "Priestesses? And what do you mean, *Claimed her?*"

The look on Melody's face is pure conflict. "Oh—I shouldn't have said anything. She hasn't told Ryka or Grandfather Jack yet. She's waiting to see if she's accepted into the order first. As for the Claiming thing, that's pretty straight-forward. If a man wants a woman for himself, he Claims her. Sometimes someone else wants to Claim the same woman, so there's a challenge. Whoever wins the fight, wins the girl. Isn't that how it's done in the Sanctuary?"

"No!"

Callum clears his throat. "No, it's much more civilised there. Women are just given away by their Trues, right?"

When he puts it that way, it does sound pretty bad. That was the future I had to look forward to. If I lived long enough to make it out of the colosseum, that is. "There's an algorithm that selects cohesive partners. That's how they work out if two people will work well together," I tell them.

"And where's the fun in that?" Callum's eyes rove over my face. It's like he's trying to work out if I believe in what I'm telling him.

"Is it supposed to be fun?"

The laugh that bursts out of Melody is so loud that people turn to look at us. Across the fire, Ryka's head lifts and our eyes lock. "Yes," Melody says. "It *is* supposed to be fun. You definitely want to have a little more than *cohesion* with your partner."

"You mean love?" I ask. My eyes remain locked on Ryka, trapped by the way he's staring at me, unblinking, still leaning into Little Miss Blue Eyes. "How can a girl fall in love with someone who 'Claims' her? It's a little barbaric, don't you think?" My cheeks feel warmer than they should, even by the fire. I manage to force my gaze back to Melody and Callum.

"I'll take barbarians over cold-blooded scientists any day," Melody sighs. Her face becomes serious. "No offense, of course."

No offense? I'm so past taking offense at anything anyone says these days. "None taken."

"Besides, times have changed. The Claim is more of a traditional thing now. People usually fall in love and agree to be together. If a woman is Claimed and doesn't want the guy who did it, she can always object."

"I think we should go back to the old ways," Callum adds. "Knock 'em over the head and drag them back to the cave, that's what I say." He's clearly joking, but if that were going to happen anywhere, it's in Freetown. Anything could happen here, with so much *life* happening all at once. Max puffs as he arrives back at our group, tipping Olivia off his shoulder with a pretend roughness that makes her squeal again. He catches her up at the last second and sets her on her feet gently, all the while grinning at her.

"Jerk," she slings at him, but she can't keep the smile off her face. Max crosses his arms and grins, too.

"Whatever. We all know you're too privileged to walk anywhere on those dainty little feet of yours. I was doing you a favour."

Olivia's cheeks blush deeply, and Melody thumps his arm. "Rude."

"Sorry." He's not sorry. If he were, he wouldn't still be grinning. "Hey, while we're talking about archaic traditions, how about you three girls get up at the crack of dawn and bring us our breakfast? Cal's finally joining us down on the beach for Tamji training. 'Bout time, too."

Callum folds his arms across his chest, the very replica of his brother, and scowls. "You were only called to Tamji last month. You make it sound as though you're so much more advanced now that you've been getting knocked on your ass four weeks longer than me."

"Four weeks is a long time in Tamji training. I *am* way more advanced than you now."

"Well, if we're taking into consideration the fact that I was born eighteen minutes before you, and I'm an inch taller, then maybe, *maybe* we'll be even on the pit floor now."

"Pssshhh!" Max shoves Callum roughly and tips his head back, laughing. "Even? I've been beating you for the past three years!"

"In your dreams, perhaps." The sound of a new voice cuts into the conversation. I go very, very still, and it's not just me. Ryka seems to have some sort of an effect on everyone, everywhere he goes. He's standing a few inches behind me, and I can't help but wonder if Blue Eyes is with him, too. What did Olivia call her? Simone?

"Thank you! Finally, someone who knows what they're talking about!" Callum smiles, shooting a smug look at Max.

"You'd better watch yourself, Ryka," Max says, rocking on his heels. "I might call you into the pit for that!" His teeth flash in a broad smile and everyone laughs. Well, Melody, Max, Callum, and even Ryka laughs—a strange, unexpected sound—but Olivia doesn't. Neither do I. My cheeks flame, and my insides constrict until it feels like I'm going to throw up. All because Max joked about calling Ryka? It takes two seconds for Max to notice my expression, one I'm trying desperately to hide. He shifts uncomfortably and shrugs his shoulders.

"Oh, ah, sorry, 'Livia. Kit. I was only playing. I'd never call Ryka."

"Of course you wouldn't." Ryka finally steps forward into my field of vision. His hair is a burnished gold in the flickering light cast by the fire, fallen loose from his ponytail in places and tucked behind his ears. He's grinning like a mad man. "You know better than to call someone who'd skin you alive in two seconds flat." He looks at his sister. "You don't need to apologise to Liv. She worries about everyone and everything. It would be abnormal if she *wasn't* worried. As for Kit—" he looks me up and down. "She's always stony faced. Yet to develop a sense of humour, aren't you, Falin Kitsch?"

Falin Kitsch? What the hell? It feels like he's slapped me. I have no idea why he's being so hostile; the past few days have been great. No arguments, no fighting. Well, no fighting that wasn't calculated training, anyway. After the prayer tree and the ruined city, I thought things were finally okay with us, if not admittedly a little confusing. Whatever the case, I feel like Ryka's discovered the very name that will hurt me the most and used it. My mouth goes dry. I can feel eyes on me, yet I refuse to meet them. I stare at the floor, at my mud caked boots. "Yeah," I reply. "You're right. I find very little funny these days."

Olivia's hand finds mine and I draw in a deep breath. It's the work of a second to force my head up, but it feels like there's a colossal weight trying to push me back down. "The truth is, Ryka, I've no idea why, but I don't think it's funny that you're Mashinji. That you can be called to fight by anyone during the matches, or that you could be exhausted and beaten bloody and still have to fight another round for your right to live. It seems unfair to me that *anyone* should have to go through that. But occasionally, Ryka...Occasionally..."

I pivot on my heel and manage to slip free from Olivia's grasp before she can stop me. Not ready. I'm not ready to deal with this, and Ryka's the last person I want to follow after me. But he does.

"Ry, leave her alone!" Olivia calls after us, as I pace quickly into the darkened walkways. Hopefully they'll lead me back to my tent, but honestly I have no idea where I'm going. The dark hides too many switchbacks and narrow paths for me to remember the way here. I don't really care, though. So long as I get to where I really need to go: away.

"Kit!"

I consider breaking into a run but that seems too pathetic, even for me right now. The anger pumping around my veins won't let me appear weak, so I keep stomping through the mud.

"*Kit!*" A hand grabs hold of my shoulder and I wheel around before he can pull me. Ryka's facial expression is stunned when I growl at him.

"Do you like hurting people?" I snarl.

"I'm good at it," he breathes, his eyes locked on mine. "But no. I don't like it. It just...seems to happen."

"Don't give me that. This level of antagonism takes some real effort. Falin Kitsch? Why would you call me that? One minute you're helping me, the next you're trying to shove me back into a box that *you,*" I stab my finger into his chest, "wanted to drag me out of. Why?" Ryka's hand, still on my shoulder, feels like it's burning me. I shrug it off. He clenches his jaw and swipes his hair behind his ear. The jerk's too shocked to say anything. Or at least I think he is, until he frowns.

"What happened to your hair?"

"*What happened to my hair?* You're so annoying, you know that? Why can't you just answer a simple question?"

A steely look transforms his face. "Because I don't know how to treat you, Kit. I'm...I'm no good at this, okay. And I called you Falin because I had a very rude awakening today."

"What...what do you mean?"

"August came to find me. He asked me to let you know that he's fixed your stupid halo and you should go and pick it up tomorrow. And now you're going to run along like a good little Sanctuary puppet and slip the thing back on, aren't you?"

"That's it? You're *this* mad at me because you think I'm going to just give up at the drop of a hat. You don't know me, Ryka."

"YOU don't know you! Jeez! A month ago you were a walking zombie.

155

You're only just becoming a real person now. You're full of these feelings and you have no idea what the hell you're supposed to be doing with them. And let me tell you, so far you're not handling them all that well."

"*What?*"

"Don't pretend like you don't know what I'm talking about, Kit. I'm gonna let you in on a little secret. Just because you don't want to feel something—it's not convenient, or you just want to ignore it—doesn't mean it's going to go away. It's only going to make you miserable, and that goes for the other people that your decisions affect, too."

I gape at him, my mouth hanging open. "None of my decisions affect other people. You're not making any sense." His eyes blaze, filled with so much frustration and anger that I want to take a step back, but I can't. I'm rooted to the spot, trying to figure out what on earth is happening.

"I'm making perfect sense," Ryka huffs, stepping closer. "And, yes, you're decisions effect *me*. I'm stupid to let them, but they do, okay?"

I flinch away from his words, too stunned to respond. I have to get out of here, and the quicker I can do that, the better. Jack's meeting tent looms off in the distance, a pale white ghost. I gather my bearings from it, heading off in the direction of the only place I can consider home, back to my tent. I know Ryka's still behind me.

"Why are you running away? Just tell me, Kit! Are you going to put that piece of metal back around your neck?"

Dizzy with the amount of turns I've made, I curl my hands into fists. "I don't know. I don't know what I want. Just because it's fixed doesn't mean I'm going to wear it again. It's—it's just an option."

"Well, it shouldn't be! Kit? Kit, stop. You're walking in circles." Ryka's hand lands on my shoulder again, pulling me back. I try to tug free, but he doesn't let go. "Tell me why your hair is so short."

"Because I cut it. Thought you'd be smart enough to work that out."

"I am." Jerking me backwards, Ryka manages to slip by so that he's standing in front of me. He catches hold of my hips with his hands, preventing me from moving around him. "Tell me."

"What's to tell? It's hot. My hair is too thick, so I cut it."

"I'm going to find out, y'know. You wouldn't have cut it."

"Oh? What makes you think you have any idea what I would or wouldn't do?"

"Because you lived through summers just as hot in Lockdown and it looked like you'd grown your hair out for years. If you were the type of person to be utilitarian about their appearance, it would have been then, when it would have been *logical*. But you didn't. Ergo you wouldn't cut it off now."

I work my jaw, trying to keep from shouting. "I'm sorry you hate my hair, Ryka. I know it's ugly. I know I'm not beautiful like that girl you were flirting with. I'm sorry I'm not petite and fragile and feminine. But you know what? It really doesn't matter. I'm nothing to you. At best, I'm your sister's friend. Forget about training together. You don't need to acknowledge me in future. In fact, I think I'd prefer it if you didn't."

I snatch myself out of his hands and move to get around him. He has hold of me again in a second. "I don't hate your hair, and it's certainly not ugly." He brushes the tips of the strands swaying just above my jawline and his fingers graze my ear lobe, making me shiver. He sees my reaction and pulls in a sharp breath through his nose. "Simone is—"

"Beautiful," I repeat.

He lets out the breath he's holding. "Yes. But nowhere near as beautiful as you."

I immediately stop struggling. " *What?*"

He studies me intensely and then shakes his head, his expression all frustration. "I'm the one who found you and brought you here, so you're never going to just be my sister's friend. I'm always going to feel responsible for you."

I bite down on the inside of my cheek to stop myself from snapping. "You're not responsible for me. I can take care of myself. Is this about the blood? Because if it is, then we already decided that it didn't count and we should—"

"It's not about that. Well, it is a little. Whether you believe in it or not, the Gods or our traditions, any of it, you've shed my blood and I've shed yours. That means something here. Damn it, it means something to *me*. Not because of the Faith. It's just...it's just who we are." He steps back and gives me some room. "And for the record, it doesn't matter that you're not petite or fragile. In fact, I admire that about you. As for being feminine—" His eyes travel over my body and I can't help but blush. I feel like I'm still standing next to the fire back in the clearing. Actually, I feel like I'm standing *in* the fire.

"The way your cheeks go red is pretty girly," he says, saving himself, and me, from the awkward silence. "I wouldn't worry too much about the feminine thing."

Words have never really failed me before, but right now? Yeah, I've got nothing. What am I supposed to say to any of this? It would really help if I even had a damn clue what is going on. Ryka is standing here, telling me that he cares about me. *Me.*

"I have to go," I tell him. I snake my way around him and this time he doesn't follow. He does call after me, though.

"Kit?"

"What?" I slow ever so slightly.

"I just—I have to—" Stammering is really out of character for him. He inhales and then rushes it out. "Kit, I have to know. Are you going to wear it again?"

The burn in my cheeks grows to inferno-like temperatures. "I...I don't know, okay!" And that's when I give in. No matter how weak it makes me look, I run away.

HAZE

It takes a long time to find the way back to my tent. All I can think of is how badly I want to slip into bed and pretend like the whole nightmare conversation with Ryka didn't just happen. But it did. There won't be any forgetting what was said tonight, not even if my life depended on it. Why did he have to go and do that? We were doing just fine; things were just starting to calm down between us. And now? Now, things are even more explosive. I just want to put it all out of my mind and sink into unconsciousness, a feat I can only accomplish once I eventually locate my new home. Storming through the small opening, I see my goal ahead, but then a figure steps out of the shadows, blocking the entry way.

"Olivia, I just want to go to sleep," I say. "Sorry, I don't mean to be rude. I just don't think I'm going to be very good company right now."

"Fighter," a low voice says, and in the thick silence the word sounds strangely muffled. My pace slows instantly, while I peer into the night, trying to work out who is waiting for me. "You and I have business," the voice says.

The person is definitely male—tall and really broad. A black mask disguises his face, one I recognise, and it takes me a beat to remember where from. The priestesses—they wear masks like these, except theirs are white with black counters running around the rim. This one is coal-black, complete with white counter, an exact inverse.

"What—what kind of business could you have with me?"

The stranger's head tips to one side and the effect is altogether eerie and disturbing. "Surely there is only one kind?" he responds. A flash of silver in the moonlight betrays the blade he's holding in his hand, his arms hanging loosely to his sides. I suck in a breath and ready myself. It's instinctual; I have my own knives in my hands in a heartbeat.

"Listen, I've done nothing wrong. I don't want to fi—"

It doesn't matter what I want. In a flash, the stranger with the black mask leaps forward, flinging a hand out towards me, and a plume of dusty white powder explodes in the air, hitting me square in the face. I choke on the burning sensation that sears down my throat, trying to spin and meet my attacker. He's quick. Quicker than anyone I've ever fought, or seen fight before. The blades in his hands spin so fast that it's like the night air is filled with molten silver. I sink into a defensive stance, but everything is suddenly off kilter, strange and unfamiliar. Blurry eyes, shaking hands, pounding heart, panic racing through my veins like wildfire. The fight might well be over before my attacker even makes his first move, because I know in the pit of my stomach that I've just been drugged and I'm about to get my ass kicked. I've never felt so disjointed and confused, and the effects are devastating.

He comes at me, lethal and silent, and I dodge the edge of his knife as it cuts towards my stomach. One staggering step backwards. He responds by easing to the side, blocking my path back out into the forest. My attacker darts forward with both knifepoints extended, ready to spear me through my chest, but I drop just in time. I react finally and kick out at his legs, aiming to take them out from underneath him, but the man in the mask literally jumps, avoiding my strike. His leg comes down in an axe kick aimed directly at my head. I roll out of the way, only to receive a dazzling blow to the temple. I somehow manage to climb to my feet, but my efforts are all futile, and the stranger makes short work of pinning me into the dirt. My head is spinning, my mouth filled with a sharp, acidic taste, and it feels like my stomach is about to purge itself.

"Interesting," the man in the mask says, as he kneels over me. "Most people can't stand for ten seconds after a hit of the Haze. You're very strong."

If I wanted to reply, if I had any sort of motor function at all and wasn't completely incapable of speech, then I'd tell this guy that I'm stronger than he thinks. Sadly, I'm like a puppet with cut strings, and I can do nothing but stare up at him with glassy eyes, trying to discern which of the five figures looming over me is the real one.

"They've Seen you," he says, his words rasping against the ceramic mask covering his face. "They've Seen what will happen if you stay here. The Sanctuary will find you and bring destruction down upon the heads of all free people. The last person to threaten our safety in this way was dealt with, and so it shall be with you."

The black and white mask distorts as my eyes roll back into my head, but not before I see the glimmer of metal descending toward my throat. I have the wherewithal to acknowledge that this is it; this is the moment when all the fighting, the struggling, the pushing and pulling finally ends for good. The thought is actually kind of peaceful.

"*Stop!*"

The roar sounds like it's coming from the forest, like the massed body of countless trees all inhaled and bellowed the word in unison, rocking the ground. The ground, however, continues to spin long after the word dies on the wind, and I pitch onto my side, retching into the dirt.

"Leave the girl be." I recognise the voice now, the deep rumble of it, and I know that Jack has found me. "Leave. Immediately," he says.

A pressure lifts from my body as the man in the black mask stands, stepping over me, his knives still clenched firmly in his hands. "Will you prevent the will of the Gods, Grandfather?" he asks.

"The will of the Gods takes place on the pit floor, not hidden in the shadows out of view from the world."

"Exceptions shall be made," the man retorts flatly.

"*None* shall be made. Leave, or the town will hear of this."

Miraculously, my attacker doesn't persist. "So be it," he says, his voice hard and irritated. He moves stealthily towards the tree line, but Jack lunges and grabs hold of his arm. "If you think I don't know what's going on here, then you're sadly mistaken. I won't allow this to happen again. You tell them."

The black mask turns to face Jack head on, and the figure appears to stare at the old man before ripping his arm free and melting into the darkness. Jack's boots make their way over to me; they're all I can see from my doubled-over foetal position on the floor. He tuts and bends down, his shaggy grey hair and concerned frown coming into view.

"Well, well, young Kit. Seems like you're in a bit of a state."

******

Groggy, sore and miserable, I recover enough by the next day to go hunting with Jack. My lungs burn the whole time and it takes every ounce of strength I have just to keep up with the old man. The forest is littered with snare traps, so eloquently hidden that I would never see them if Jack wasn't there to point them out. Sharp metal teeth hide in the hollows of dead, rotted out tree trunks, and incredibly thin wires pause, taught, ready to sink into the flesh of an ankle or a neck. It's fairly obvious why there are no people wandering around out here: there are just too many ways to die.

"Are we going to talk about what happened last night?" I ask, as we navigate our way through the invisible gauntlet.

"What do you want to talk about?"

I gawp at the back of his head, raising my hands in sheer frustration. "Oh, I don't know. How about the fact that *someone tried to kill me*? Who *was* that?"

"Could have been a number of people. I have my suspicions, however."

"Care to share them?"

Jack shakes his head and grunts, crouching to study some track in the undergrowth that I'm completely blind to. "No point in guessing. Only makes people paranoid."

"Uhh…I think I'm going to be paranoid, regardless, now."

"Still." Jack straightens and sets off again. "All I can tell you is that he was sent by the priestesses."

I had assumed as much, but having Jack confirm that the priestesses sent out an assassin to murder me makes my blood run cold. "Why would they do that?"

"I couldn't say. You should keep well out of their way for the time being, until I can get to the bottom of the matter. I'll go and see the High Priestess."

None of that makes me feel any better. I stalk sullenly after him for a while, feeling like my insides got ripped out and squashed back in all the wrong places. "What was in that stuff I breathed in last night, anyway? And what did you mean when you told that guy you knew what was going on? That you wouldn't allow it to happen again?"

More grunting follows as Jack stoops to collect a dead rabbit from a trap, its body limp and broken, which makes me feel remarkably sorry for the poor animal. "The Haze is a compound the priestesses make up to enter their trance-like states. I have no idea what's in it, but I've heard it's powerful stuff. And I do know what's going on—when they're trying to pull strings and work things to their favour. I said I wouldn't allow it to happen again, because this isn't the first time the priestesses have caused hurt within my family. I aim to protect mine and those they love."

My brow crinkles as I take this in. Is Jack telling me he thinks of me as one of his family? "What do you mean?"

He sighs, looking at me like I'm just not getting something. "Have my grandchildren ever told you how their father died?"

I shake my head, no.

"Ryka's father was a good man. He loved my daughter so much, and those children...you know, most young boys idolise their fathers. Ryka did idolise his father, but Matthew—" Another deep sigh. "Matthew worshipped the ground his children walked on. He couldn't have been a better father. It was hard when we lost him. That loss is still a rancour that eats away at Ryka every day. He'll never admit it, but losing his father destroyed the gentle part of him. Or at least buried it so deeply that it barely sees the light of day anymore. He's protective over his sister and me. That he's been spending so much time with you says a lot about what he thinks of you, too."

I don't say anything, because uncomfortable memories of last night, before I got attacked, rise to the surface: Ryka and I arguing over my halo and our blood.

"Matthew was Mashinji," Jack continues. His eyes are on his scarred hand, weaving through the grass. He doesn't look at me. "He was a real character. Everyone in Freetown loved him. He was always quick to laugh and joke with people. Always available to help whenever he was needed. It was a shock when he was called as Mashinji. Mirry, my daughter, worried about Matthew being called into the pits, but no one else really thought much of it. There had been Mashinji fighters before and no one ever called them. It was always left to the High Priestess to pair them with an opponent. It was that way with Matthew for a while. Six months, in fact. I think we all got used to the idea that Matthew's ranking was little more than a title that meant he couldn't train with his friends. It was a surprise when he was actually called. Ryka was eight, Olivia six. She was with her mother, thank the Gods, but Ryka was with me. He was never usually allowed to watch his father fight, but for some reason, that night, I—" Jack shook his head. "A low ranking fighter called Matthew first."

My stomach twists instantly. It is the word *first* that's done it. I know the way this story plays out. Olivia practically told me herself the night of the blood ceremony. Jack clears his throat and continues. "After Matthew won that match, he was called to fight three more. It was clear there was some kind of collaboration, because they were all low ranked fighters."

"They were wearing him out," I say. My chest squeezes when Jack tilts his head into a small nod. "Why would they agree to that?" It's impossible to work out why low ranked fighters would be willing to call an experienced opponent, knowing they're probably going to die.

"Because of the priestesses, of course. People here border on fanatical when it comes to their faith. They'll give up their homes, their families, their lives even, if they're asked to."

"And you think the priestesses asked them to?"

He nods. "Matthew was exhausted after four fights. That's when he was called by the last fighter. He made short work of my son-in-law and Ryka watched the whole thing. I should have taken him home; I know that now. But Matthew and I were close, and I knew what was coming. I didn't want to leave him to die alone."

Hot streaks trace down my cheeks as I realise I'm crying. I don't feel too foolish, because Jack's face is wet as well. "I'm sorry," I whisper.

"Not half as sorry as I am," he returns. He straightens his back and takes a deep breath. "Anyway. Ryka's his father's son through and through. He's going to be a good man and a good father one day."

Jack's statement makes me feel strange. The thought of Ryka as someone's father is completely laughable, but I'm too caught up on Jack's first statement to find it funny. *Ryka is his father's son, through and through.* He really is. He's Mashinji.

"Who was the fighter that called Matthew last?" I ask.

Jack finally looks at me, his eyes hollow. "It was James, young Kit. James is the man who killed my daughter's husband, but I know that the priestesses were involved. So you see, my grandchildren have been dealt enough pain by those robed witches to last a lifetime, and I won't allow them to suffer any more. They both care about you in one way or another, and until that changes I will protect you as best I can."

*****

It's dark when we hear a loud cracking through the forest. Jack hitches the rabbits we caught higher onto his shoulder and lets out a low whistle. A pair of bright eyes flash at us in the dark. Jada comes bounding out of the trees and slams into Jack's legs, sniffing madly around him. No wonder he hitched the rabbits up; the dog is clearly more interested in the meat than saying hello to us.

"Come on, girl. Come on. Move or you won't be getting anything at all." Jack growls, but it's pretty clear Jada's belly will be full by the end of the night. The way her tongue hangs sideways out of her mouth, giving her a broad smile, says she knows it, too.

"Thought you were dead, old man." More branches snap underfoot and Ryka emerges from the darkness, his black clothes making it hard to pick him out of the shadows. His eyes travel briefly over me but move on before I can read him.

"See you had a helper," he says.

"I did." Jack reaches up and throws a pair of rabbits at Ryka, who catches them out of the air. It feels hard to breathe when I look at him now. I still can't believe that James, *James*, the man he was sparring on the beach with only a few days ago, who cut off my hair, is responsible for killing his father. Ryka is silent as he turns around and melts into the darkness, back the way he came. We follow after him with a hungry-looking Jada on our heels. I pat her head as we walk, trying to work out if she is Ryka's only real friend.

"You left it late coming back," Ryka says quietly.

"Ahhh, don't tell me you were worried about us?" Jack teases. Ryka just grunts into the dark.

"More like I assumed you'd gotten yourself caught up in one of your own traps. You're forgetful in your old age, y'know."

Jack's shoulders shake with silent laughter as we move through the night. Nothing else is said for a while, until the lights and sounds of Freetown slowly grow from a distant hum to a raucous clamour.

Jada runs back to Ryka's side as we near the bridge crossing the river. She pauses, looking up at him. "Jada, go home!" he hisses. She takes one last look at him and bolts.

"I'm going home, too," Jack announces, thrusting the last two rabbits he carries at me. "The pair of you can take these up to the Keep."

"What?" Ryka halts half way across the bridge, his boots clomping against the wood. I remain stock-still, myself, wondering why, after last night and our conversation today, Jack would send me anywhere near the Keep. He winks at me, which is even more confusing.

"Come now, you wouldn't make an *old man* walk up that steep hill in the dark, would you?" There's a wicked smile on Jack's face as he swaggers off without us. I slip past Ryka, swiping the rabbits off his shoulder as I do so.

"What do you think you're doing?" he demands.

"I'm taking the rabbits up to the Keep. It's okay, you can go home, too." If Jack seems to think it's safe for me to go there, I might as well go alone. That way I can try to talk to one of them, figure out why the hell they want me dead.

"Like hell you are." Ryka pushes in front of me and tries to take the dead animals, but fails. "Give them to me."

"No! I'm capable of walking another mile."

He rolls his eyes. "I know you're capable of walking. It's just not safe for people to be out on their own at night."

I almost laugh out loud at the gigantic lie that slips easily from my lips. "I don't feel threatened here."

"Are you sure?" He reaches up and touches the tips of my hair, just like he did last night. The gesture throws me, and I'm glaring when I turn on him, angry that he's right. Freetown's people are out to get me, and he doesn't even know about the priestesses' assassin.

"What do you think you're doing, Ry?"

"Did you just call me Ry?" he asks, grinning.

I scowl and shake my head. "Everyone does. It was an accident. Don't worry, I won't do it again."

"You can call me that if you want. I'm sure you've called me worse, anyway," he says, jumping to catch up as I set off without him. "And I touched your hair because I know you're not telling me the truth. You didn't cut it off yourself."

"I *did*."

"You did not." His grin widens. "Olivia told me what happened."

My mouth hangs open for a second before I manage to close it. She swore she wasn't going to say anything, especially to him. How could she? She wouldn't do that. No, she couldn't. "You're lying," I snap.

"Ha! So, something *did* happen. Kit, come on. I can't look out for you if you let people bully you and don't tell me about it."

I walk quicker, slamming my boots into the mud. "You're not my keeper, okay? You can drop this whole *I'm going to watch out for you*, bit. It's getting old."

"Does it offend you that much? That I *want* to look out for you?"

I blow out an exasperated growl. "You've changed your tune. Seriously, not long ago you were shouting at me for not taking my knives off and generally being a jerk. Now you're telling me you want to take care of me? It's a little hard to buy."

"I didn't say I wanted to take care of you. I said *look out for*. There's a difference."

"Right. You wanna make sure I keep out of trouble while you *take care* of Simone, is that it?" I flinch as soon as the words leave my mouth, not sure why in hell I said them in the first place. The back of my throat burns like I'm going to throw up. I walk faster.

"Uhhh, Kit?"

"*No.*"

"You can't just say no. You don't know what I'm going to say." He's laughing and it makes me feel ridiculous. My cheeks are bright red again.

"I can if I know what you're about to say. And I do. I don't care if something was going on with you and Simone last night. And I don't care to know, either."

"Nothing was going on with Simone," he says, his voice suddenly serious. I glance at him and the smile is gone from his face.

"I'm sorry to hear that." I keep on stomping, keep on wishing I could stop talking.

"Jeez, woman! Are you really going to pretend that I didn't pretty much come straight out with it last night and tell you that I like you?" He goes for the rabbits again and I swing them away, rounding on him.

"You're acting weird, Ryka. You hate me one minute and the next minute you're saying bizarre things to me, and…urgh! The next minute you're this! You have to forgive me for not understanding."

"I can forgive you. But you have to forgive me, too. I've been hostile, but I explained that. My pride was bruised."

"No kidding," I snap. He just laughs, which makes me angrier. "So why have you decided to be nice to me now?"

"Because—" He touches my hair again and my cheeks flame. What the hell is going on with my body? "I don't like the thought of someone doing this to you, Kit. Tell me what happened."

He looks so serious that I almost consider telling him for a second. Consider telling him everything—James, Joshua, even about the priestesses' assassin. I have the words poised on my tongue, ready, when Ryka squints off up the Holy Walk.

"Hey, is that Olivia?" he says.

I follow his gaze and squint, too, struggling to make out the figure running towards us. The gentle tinkle of bells reaches us long before she does. Sure enough, it's Olivia. She falls into Ryka's arms, laughing hysterically.

"Ry! They said yes!" she cries. "They finally said yes!"

"What are you talking about?" He stands her up, laughing with her, although there's confusion in his eyes.

"The priestesses, Ry! They accepted me. They're going to let me join them. Isn't this the best news? Oh, Kit! I didn't tell either of you. I wanted to wait until I was sure they were going to—"

"You're joking," Ryka whispers. In three seconds his body language has changed dramatically from amused to horrified. "You can *not* be serious." His words mirror my own thoughts exactly. There's no way she can go into the Keep, not when I know how dangerous and manipulative they are.

Olivia's smile falters. "Be happy for me, brother. I may not have said anything but you've always known this is what I wanted." Ryka steps back; he laces his hands behind his head, his whole body shaking.

"I'm not going to be happy for you! This is a huge mistake, Liv. You're throwing your life away!"

Olivia's shoulders tense; she looks like she's about to explode. "How is serving the Gods throwing my life away?" she whispers.

"We both know you're not going to inter yourself in that mausoleum of a Keep because you want to serve the Gods. Jeez, she's not in there, Livy! She's gone. She's *dead!*' That word echoes off the hillside, repeating harshly, and all three of us wince. With her hands tucked into the pockets of her skirts, Olivia seems to grow smaller.

"You can think what you want, Ryka. We've no proof that she's dead. Of course she's in the Keep." She runs off down the path towards Freetown and I watch her go, unsure what I'm supposed to do. Ryka and I stand side by side in silence and it's long after Olivia has disappeared from sight before I turn to him. He immediately looks away, but not quick enough to hide the fact that there are tears in his eyes. I'm too stunned to say anything.

"Go after her. Make sure she's okay," he says quietly. I know he's not telling me what to do. He's asking me, pleading with me, so I won't see him cry. I drop the rabbits at his feet and run after Olivia.

*****

The news of Olivia's acceptance as a priestess travels quickly around Freetown. Over the next week I see Ryka and Jack a total of three times, always together, and both of them look tired and worried. Few words are exchanged between us, mainly regarding Olivia's determination to follow through on her plan, no matter what her brother and her grandfather say. I spend time with Olivia as usual, and she seems to have forgotten all about her exchange with Ryka on the Holy Walk. She goes back to being intensely happy about her upcoming move into the Keep, and now I know why.

Olivia explained that her mother went missing after Matthew's death, and no one knew where she went. She was heartbroken over the loss of her husband and took to walking in the forest. One day she just didn't come back. Months later, bones were found out in the middle of nowhere and that was that; everyone accepted that Jack's daughter was dead. Everyone except Olivia, that is. Mirry was a devout woman, and Olivia is sure her mother consigned herself to the priestesses' care, giving over the rest of her life to work in the service of others. Her conviction unshakeable, Olivia believes that when she becomes a priestess, she will be reunited with her mother. The whole town is buzzing with the news and it's all I seem to hear about.

Today, there are other reasons why Freetown is alive with chatter, though. The countdown to the matches has begun, and there are three days until the first round of fights. Ryka's fights. It seems everyone is on edge and filled with energy, and I spend my time continually looking over my shoulder, black-masked faces always standing in my peripherals. There's never anyone there when I look, of course.

The smell of roasting pork fills the air all over the tent city as families slaughter their animals to prepare the blood for the festivities. In Lockdown, I'd never thought of pork as an actual animal. I'd never even considered where it came from. All that mattered was that I received enough protein with each meal to repair my muscles and build new ones. That made me a better fighter, stronger, quicker. Now that I've seen the actual animal, smelled its thickened blood sprayed into my clothes, well...I'm not sure I'll ever eat pork again, no matter how good it smells. Olivia, on the other hand, doesn't seem to have a problem with it.

"Mmmm, this is so good," she groans, wiping juice from her chin as she finishes her barbecued meat. "You could have bought some for yourself if you were wearing that pretty purple skirt I gave you." She's stopped using up her little bells on me since she gave me all of her clothes— I get the feeling I'm quite well off now— but I don't care. I'd rather be hungry than noisy any day of the week. My tight smile tells her as much, and she elbows me in my ribs. "What's up with you anyway? You've been quiet for days."

I search the sky for the right way to tell her that I don't want her disappearing into that Keep, that the priestesses are pretty much evil and tried to have me killed. If she goes with them, I'm worried I'll never see her again. Technically, I won't. She'll be covered head to heel in that red, floating material, never permitted to speak again. My traitorous throat closes up and I feel my eyes prick. I'm really getting the hang of this crying thing.

"Hey, you don't need to be sad," Olivia says.

"I'm just worried. There's...there's something you should know..."

"I've been waiting for you to tell me," she says softly. "Jack already explained what happened to you the other night. I know he thinks the priestesses ordered someone to attack you, but I promise you, Kit, they would never do something like that. They are holy women. They value life above everything else. This man, whoever he was, is going straight to hell for daring to wear that sacred mask." She loops her arm through mine and pulls me towards our destination, the crowd parting for us as we go. "Now, I'm sorry that happened to you, but I've heard it all from my grandfather. I won't change my mind. Just be content that I'm happy and setting off on a journey to do something important. It's not like I'm going to be dead or anything. You can come up to the Keep whenever you want. I might not be able to talk with you but you'll know it's me. I'll make sure of it."

"I'm—I'm not sure I'll be staying in Freetown," I mumble. I feel like my legs have been pulled out from underneath me now that I know Jack's already told her what happened to me. I was so sure she would rethink once she heard about the assassin and the way he drugged me.

Olivia makes a *tsk*ing sound. "And why would you leave? *How* could you leave now that I had that beautiful big bed made for you?"

I touch my fingers to my neck, something I haven't done in a while. *It's not there, stupid.* Chastising myself won't do much good, though. Learning to deal with the thickness of emotions is the only way any of it gets better, I know. Still, it's so hard. "I won't have any reason to stay here," I tell her. My voice stays level and that in itself is a small miracle.

"You have so many reasons," Olivia says. "My grandfather is quite taken with you, infamous warrior of the Sanctuary Colosseum. And what about Ryka?"

I glare down at my boots. "I'm not the same person that left the Sanctuary. A warrior doesn't burst into tears when someone cuts off her hair. And Ryka? I'll be gone a week before he even notices I'm not here."

"You're so ridiculous. You're lying to yourself, you know that, don't you?" Olivia lets go of my arm as we reach the pits where Ryka was called as Mashinji. "Even *I* know my brother's developed quite the infatuation with you."

"I'm not so sure about that," I say, but something warm and not entirely unpleasant burns in my chest. I pray it'll just go away; I pray I'm not attracted to Ryka.

Just because you don't want to feel something—it's not convenient, or you just want to ignore it—doesn't mean it's going to go away. It's only going to make you miserable, and that goes for the other people that your decisions affect, too.

I know Olivia's grinning at me, because I can feel her over-excited eyes on my skin. "I'm going to be a lot more peaceful in my decision if I know my brother has someone he can turn to, Kit. He needs that."

"He doesn't need me."

"You both need each other," she corrects. "I have to say, I thought you would be the first to realise that, not Ry."

"What does that mean?"

"It means what it means," she says breezily, scanning the people around us. We're waiting for August. He has lists of supplies Jack asked us to collect before nightfall; the smith is organising a weapons market before the matches start, giving the fighters the opportunity to purchase new weapons and trade in old ones. Apparently the markets bring in a lot of trade from outside Freetown, and I can't help but worry. Somehow, August's daggers found their way to me inside the Sanctuary. There's every chance someone from Lockdown will be attending the markets. Bad news for me. Bad news for everyone here if I'm recognised and Jack refuses to let them take me. I've agreed to keep a low profile when the fights are on, sticking to my tent. Definitely for the best, in my mind. Olivia's acceptance ritual is taking place right after the matches, and I don't want say goodbye, anyway.

"He's here," Olivia says, craning her neck to see over the crowds. "Callum's with him."

"Callum? Max's brother?"

"He's August's apprentice. He'll be selling his own knives this market. First time, I think."

August and Callum make their way though the thrum of people, and Callum looks righteously annoyed by the time we greet them. He obviously cares for large groups of people as much as I do. We shoot each other consolatory glances by way of greeting. August shakes my hand. "Hello, Kit. How are you treating those blades of mine?"

I lift the hem of my shirt and show him my gleaming daggers, freshly cleaned, sharpened and polished. Old habits are hard to break.

"Good girl." He swipes an arm around me and pulls me into a rough hug. The man smells like smoke and the earth, strangely comforting, honest smells. "You should come by and see me later. I have something for you." *My halo.* Ryka's angry expression invades my mind, and I have to fight to push it out. "Here are the supplies I need," August says, fishing a dirty piece of paper from his pocket. He hands it over and thanks us for meeting him. "I'll see you later, Kit, yes?"

"Sure."

He showcases his blackened front tooth in a broad smile before slapping

Callum on the back. "All right, son. Consider your work day over. Go and do something downright mischievous with these two young ladies."

Callum's cheeks blush red first, then Olivia's. Figuring out why takes a while, by which time August's laughing so hard tears are practically rolling down his face. It's a long time for him to marshal himself. "I didn't mean it like that, but I can see your young minds aren't so young anymore. Whatever blows your hair back." He winks and I finally blush, too.

"That man lives to destroy my social credibility," Callum declares, stuffing his hands into his pockets. The small black lines on his arms are on display today, terminating just above his elbow. Turns out Callum's pretty badass, even if he's only just made it to Tamji. "Come on," Callum says. "Max mentioned something about a Claiming down by the river this afternoon."

Olivia's eyes light up. She claps her hands together and giggles, bouncing next to me until she realises I'm nowhere near as excited as she is. "You people are so unromantic," she pouts, slapping my arm. Once again, I find myself thinking just how *un*romantic a Claiming sounds.

The throngs of people grow thicker as we approach the waterfront close to the tent I stayed in when I first arrived in Freetown. The familiar area brings back none of the sentimentality I already feel for my new tent. Swarms of young women have gathered, eyes heavily kohled, flowers woven into their hair, and they all talk behind their hands, whispering to one another. Groups of men, both young and old, look on with poorly veiled amusement, as the women chatter and scan the faces around them. I frown and lean into Callum so he can hear me over the rumble of voices.

"Which girl is being Claimed?"

He shakes his head. "Don't know yet. No one will know until the guy calls out the Claim."

"So she could have no idea?"

Callum says this is so, and Olivia shakes next to me, all ill-contained energy. "How can you not think that's romantic? Imagine if it was you. Wouldn't that be amazing, for someone to stand up and say that they want to be partnered with you in front of the Gods forever, for everyone to see?"

"No." I shudder at the thought. "How are you supposed to say no if you don't like the guy? There's so much pressure— all these people staring at you." It would basically be my worst nightmare.

Olivia shoves me playfully, and Callum's hand goes to the small of my back as I stumble into him. "Steady," he laughs. His breath tickles the bare skin on the back of my neck, and I jump at the unexpected sensation. Eyes wide, I glare at Olivia, but she is oblivious.

"Wait, look, there's Max! Hey, Max!" she calls. Max doesn't see us. Oddly, he looks quite green, and a tall man with a shock of grey hair is talking to him intensely.

"What's my dad doing here?" Callum says, stepping around me so he can see his brother better. A small frown creases his brow. The tall man places both hands on Max's shoulders and Max nods. Callum's frown deepens. "Oh," he says. Now he's the one with wide eyes. "*Oh*."

A look of horror forms on Olivia's face as Max takes a step back from his father and takes a deep breath. Suddenly it's as though everyone around Max realises he's about to do something. Groups cut short their conversations, elbowing those around them until a silence spreads throughout the crowd by the water. Olivia can't seem to look away from Max. Callum covers his eyes with his hand, as though he can block out what's about to happen, but he can't. His twin inhales, his chest rising sharply, before he shouts out, "I make a Claim!"

The last word echoes through the crowd as a hundred different girls all repeat it. Everyone but Olivia and me. Her face is ashen. She staggers backwards and reaches out for my hand. "I can't do this," she whispers. "How could he? He knows I'm joining the priestesses. I can't back out now. I can't accept him. This is...this is *cruel*," she stammers.

It *is* cruel. I feel foolish for having just remarked on how hard it would be to say no to someone in front of all these people. Olivia is about to find out how hard. Callum just keeps shaking his head. His hand has slipped from his eyes, now covering his mouth instead.

"I don't think—" he begins, but before he can say anything else, Max shouts again.

"I make a Claim before the Gods. I say the words, with an open heart, on my knees, I pray that the woman I choose accepts me. I Claim Simone Altern for my wife. I challenge all who would—"

All I can hear is my own heartbeat in my ears. That and the subtle, pained gasp that comes out of Olivia's mouth. "What did he just say?" I breathe.

"Simone," Olivia whimpers. As she backs away from the gathering, Simone, the girl Ryka whispered to at the bonfire, steps out of the crowd and places a small, pale hand into Max's. I stagger backwards after Olivia just as Max looks up. He's not looking at me, though. He looks past me, straight at Olivia. Clenching his jaw, he swallows hard and then turns back to Simone. It's almost visible how hard it was for him to do it. But it's done. Callum sighs as everyone else around us starts cheering.

"I'm so sorry, Livy," he says. Olivia is well past hearing; she's running, tearing and shoving to get by all of the people pressing forward to congratulate Max and Simone. I run after her, giving her space to decide which direction to go in, although it seems like she's just running with no thought as to where she ends up. Eventually we hit the boundary of forest, the town's sprawling madness behind us, and she collapses. Carefully, I sit next to her and just let her cry.

"Did that just really happen?" she gasps. The way she clutches at her chest, it's as though it's physically hurting.

"Yeah, I think it did." My voice is so quiet, I barely hear it myself.

"How is this my life?" she wheezes. "How is this my life?" I scoot closer to her and place my hand on her back. That's all it takes; Olivia throws herself into my arms and clings onto me, her slim body shaking with the force of her tears. I rub my hand up and down her back, stroking her hair.

"I thought...I thought he was going to Claim *me*," she sobs. I hold her tighter and for the first time I finally see what it looks like to be heartbroken. I pray that all I have to do is see it. It seems to me that feeling what Olivia feels right now would be worse than dying.

******

"Is she okay?" Ryka wears a troubled grimace, one I think I have etched into my own face.

"Kind of. She's asleep," I tell him. He tucks his hair behind his ears and gestures behind me. He seems nervous. I don't ask him in, I just move back so he can slide past me through the narrowing opening. He casts his eyes around briefly, taking everything in. The voile divider in my tent has been tied back, so he can see his sister passed out under the covers in my bed. Her blonde hair is fanned out across the pillow, and she almost looks peaceful. Her swollen eyelids tell a different story once you get up close. Ryka stares down at her for a second before sitting

175

carefully on the edge of the bed at her side.

"She cried for weeks when our mother went missing," he says softly. "She looked just like this, only smaller." It doesn't feel right that I'm here for this. It seems like a personal moment, one Ryka should spend with his sister alone. But he keeps on talking. "She'd crawl into my bed back then. Looks like she's found someone more reliable to comfort her these days." He gives me a smile that's altogether boyish and apologetic. "Thank you, Kit. Thanks for looking after her."

I have no idea what to say, so I shrug my shoulders. Ryka brushes his hand slowly against Olivia's hair and then stands up. "Do you mind just letting her sleep here? She might not want to deal with me and Jack just yet."

"Sure. It's not—" I pause as Ryka stoops down to gently draw the holostick out from underneath my pillow. "It's not a problem," I finish clearing my throat.

"You still watching this?" he asks me, curling his fingers around the small square.

"Yeah. Sometimes."

He nods. Slipping it back under the pillow, he straightens and then looks at me, his eyes distant. "You miss him still?"

I can't answer for a moment. It takes longer than it should to find my voice. "I don't really know anymore. Every time I think about Cai these days, it's about the day he died. It's like nothing really existed for me before that."

Ryka's chin dips towards his chest. He pulls in a deep breath, a brisk sound. "He sacrificed himself for you, didn't he?"

My mouth falls open. "I never said that. He—I—"

"No, but...come on, Kit. I saw the way he looked when he was talking about being with you. How scared he was that you wouldn't want him. He loved you, even with your halo. It's pretty obvious he would have died to save you. Hey, are you okay?" Ryka's at my side in a heartbeat, placing his hand tentatively at my back, the same way Callum did earlier down by the river at the Claiming. I feel like I'm going to throw up. An image of Cai's face, blood trickling from his mouth as he looks up at me, dying, burns in my mind. His pale, cracked lips open and his voice is a whispered accusation. '*You did this to me.*'

I blink back tears, straightening out my shirt. "Yeah, it just hits me sometimes. I think I need some air." I back out of the tent and draw the cool air into my lungs, willing myself not to let this guilt crush me.

"I'm not very good at it, but you can talk to me, you know?" Ryka murmurs.

I swallow and cup the back of my neck with my hand, not looking at him. Jada emerges out of the tree line and creeps forward stealthily, tongue lolling as ever. She thrusts her head under my hand, wanting to be stroked.

"Or you can talk to Jada," he adds. "She's pretty trustworthy. Never told anyone my secrets, anyway."

I allow myself a small smile. "Seems like you tell it pretty straight, Ryka. I somehow doubt you're keeping many secrets."

"I have tons," he shoots back. "More than I care to count."

I *mmm* doubtfully, scratching Jada behind her ears. She seems to like that. Cai's face is gone now, although who knows how long the reprieve will be. When I look up, Ryka is watching me pet Jada.

"She likes you," he says.

"You sound surprised."

"I'm not. My sister's a good judge of character. If Liv likes you that pretty much means everyone else will. Including my fickle dog." He whistles softly and Jada pricks her ears at the sound.

"And you?" I ask.

He smiles. "Seriously?"

I nod, and his mouth pulls up to one side in a way that makes my heart race. He looks wicked.

"Well, we're friends. In that weird way where you're eternally mad at me, and I'm eternally imagining what you look like naked."

"What!" I go to slap his arm but he ducks out of reach, grinning. From the way my insides react to his words, it feels like I've swallowed something entirely too hot. Is this normal? Is this what liking someone feels like? It's confusing and frustrating and frankly—okay, I'll admit it—kind of wonderful. But what the hell am I supposed to do with that? How do I change who I am, sixteen years of fighting, a life of blood? How do I trade in all that confrontation for something a little sweeter? I think it's probably too late.

"I really didn't do myself any favours when I met you, did I? You still don't trust me?" Ryka tips his head forward, smiling ruefully at his feet when I shake my head. "In that case I suppose it's pointless asking if you've fallen in love with me yet?"

The boy is determined to make me die a death this evening. It's all I can do not to choke as I shake my head. "Sadly, no. I don't think I want to kill you

177

anymore, though. So there's that."

In the moonlight, Ryka's eyes bow as he smiles broadly. "There *is* that. We'll have to see what we can do to change your mind, though. I've never been very good at waiting for anything I want." He shoves me gently with his shoulder and my heart stumbles.

"You want me?"

Ryka's smile is devastatingly sharp. "You own me, remember. And now, after the other night...I guess I kinda own you, too."

This time I can't prevent the choking. My face must be purple by the time I can catch a breath. Ryka just grins, enjoying my reaction.

"What can I do to convince you I'm a good person?" he asks.

"I already think you're a good person."

"No, you don't."

"Okay, I'm halfway there."

"Tell me what I can do to get you the other fifty percent." He laughs, but his words are quiet. Serious. The tone in his voice has my insides doing strange things again.

"I'm not sure. You could tell me one of your many secrets," I say. No way is he telling me anything. The way his shoulders stiffen makes me think I'm right, but then he holds out his hand.

"Okay, come with me."

A jolt of panic surges through my body as I look down at his outstretched hand. He waits patiently for me to take it, probably longer than most people would. His fingers close around mine when I finally find the nerve to accept, and he starts guiding us through the trees.

"It's dark, we're going to break our legs," I tell him. I'm not really scared; I just need something to say.

"Not going far. My secret is down by the water." His hand tightens around mine, his grip confident and strong. It takes less than a minute to get to the embankment, but Ryka walks us along a little ways, until we're actually around the back of the tent he shares with Olivia and Jack.

"Here," he says. He lets go of my hand and jumps down the five-foot drop, fluidly landing in a crouched position. He seems surprised when he turns to find me right behind him, having jumped down too.

"That's right," he says. "You're not a normal girl."

"What were you going to do?" I laugh. "Lift me down?"

Ryka runs his hand back through his hair and flashes his teeth in an easy smile. "Well, yeah."

I suddenly wish I hadn't been so hasty in jumping. "I saved you some back pain. What's the big secret, then?"

Even though he doesn't need to, Ryka takes my hand again and we walk down the water's edge. The moonlight slides across the rippling water, making it look like twisting pale silk. I drop down to touch my fingertips to the surface of the water, feeling its cold kiss against my skin.

"Freezing?" Ryka asks.

"Freezing," I agree.

"Great." He starts unbuttoning his shirt.

"Wait, what are you doing? You don't have three nipples do you? That's not your secret?"

Ryka laughs so hard he snorts. The shirt falls off his shoulders and he lets it drop onto the pebbly shore by the river. "Not quite. I'm sure you and everyone else in Freetown would have noticed that when I train. I spend half the day without a shirt on."

It's true, he does. Although, right now is different to every other time I've seen him shirtless. This time I'm close. Really, really close. "So why are you getting undressed, then?" I pretend not to study the way his muscles contract and move underneath his skin. How broad and muscular he is. He tucks his hair behind his ears again, doing his own fair share of pretending– mainly that he doesn't notice me studying him.

"Because I want at least one item of dry clothing for when I come out," he says, smiling.

"Out?" Suddenly I realise he's going in the water. I go to grab hold of him, but he dances out of my reach.

"I thought you wanted to know my secret?"

"I do, but you're going to catch your death if you go in there right now!"

Ryka shrugs and backs away, not even flinching when his bare toes hit the water. "I'm a big boy. I'll be fine." With that he turns and dives into the river, making me gasp on his behalf. Shocking. Water that cold would be truly shocking. He comes up in the middle of the river, laughing.

"I hope you appreciate this!" he cries. I don't get a chance to tell him that I do. He dives back into the water and he's gone for what feels like forever. I'm trying to figure out if I'm brave enough to go in after him when he breaches the surface, gasping in a breath. His pale blond hair is plastered to his head as he hurries out of the water, carrying a fat, oblong rock in his hands. His teeth chatter as he rushes towards me, throwing the small boulder to the ground at his feet. The moonlight catches on the water beading across his chest, running down his arms, and his black pants stick to his legs, soaking wet. I collect his shirt from the ground just as he shakes his hair out, spraying me full in the face.

"Arrrghh! Thank...you...?"

Ryka chuckles, grabbing his shirt out of my hands. He lunges forward and wipes it across my face before I can object. "There. You're welcome."

He slips the now damp shirt on and does up a button halfway down, leaving the rest open. Having accomplished that, he looks down at the rock at our feet.

"What is it?" I ask.

He gives me a pained look. "What does it look like?"

"A rock."

"Congratulations. Your powers of deduction are impressive." I shoot him a withering glance, which wipes the smile off his face. "All right. Look at this." He motions me down with him and we both crouch beside the rock. It's slimy and covered in green algae, which smells really bad. Hefting it over with the heel of his hand, Ryka points at a faint mark on the underside. He lets it go and the rock lands with a weighty grinding noise. On the underside are marks. Letters, in fact. The jagged engravings are two Ms, side by side. Beneath them, an O and an R are carved with careful precision.

"My dad did this," Ryka says quietly, tracing his fingers over the marks. "We were little, but I remember." He nods, as though reassuring himself that he actually does. "My dad was telling Liv and me about all the different kinds of rocks there are around Freetown. He tried to explain how they were all formed and which were good as building materials. We were too young to understand at the time, but we loved hearing him tell us anyway. He was a pretty smart man."

"Sounds like it." My voice is hushed, but it still feels too loud. Ryka's eyes shine in the muted light, meeting mine.

"We wanted to know which one was the strongest of all the rocks. He told us it was marble, but there wasn't any around here. Apparently, volcanic rock is pretty strong though." He slaps the wet boulder and chews on his lip. "He explained that even though they're really strong and difficult to mark, all rocks are eventually reduced to nothing. He said it would take millions of years, but it would happen one day. At the time we didn't believe him. The buttress by the river, the stone of the Keep, all of it just seemed so solid and immoveable. My father took out his penknife and said he would prove it to us. All morning he spent carving our initials into this rock—his, my mother's, mine and Liv's. After that we kind of had to believe him, y'know?" Ryka falls silent for a minute, and I can tell the memories are painful for him. He presses his palm to the boulder, gently this time, the muscles in his neck working overtime.

"He said, 'Son, there are many things in life that may seem indestructible. But remember, family is always stronger. Those are the only bonds that are truly unbreakable.'" Tracing his fingers over the markings one last time, Ryka picks up the rock and swings, launching it back into the river.

"What are you doing!"

The look he gives me is a hard one. "My family was worn away a long time ago. My father was wrong. That bond was broken when he left us, so I'm letting nature do what he said it would. One day that boulder will be nothing but sand and there'll be no evidence that any of us ever even existed."

"And that's your secret? That you're pissed off with your dad for lying to you because life isn't perfect?" My head hurts. Hell, my chest, my eyes, my heart hurts. Ryka grins, at odds with how horribly I feel for him.

"No. Liv's been looking for that rock for about five years now. That's my secret. She's never going to find it." A look flashes over his face. "*She's never going to find it*," he says. "Okay?"

It's painfully unfair that Ryka's cynicism is robbing Olivia of something sweet their father did, but this is Ryka's secret. He's trusting me with it. "Fine," I tell him. "I won't say a word."

*****

"I've been waiting on you, Kit. Didn't Ryka give you my message?" August's thick mess of wavy hair kicks up in the breeze that teases the tents this morning, causing their canvas sides to undulate. It looks for all the world like they're breathing, the soft movement a casual draw and pull of lungs.

"Yes, he did. I was going to come yesterday but Olivia was upset."

Two tiny lines form between August's eyebrows. "Yes, well, I heard about that. Callum explained what happened. Pass on my regards to her for me, will you?"

"Sure." August's regards probably aren't going to do much to alleviate Olivia's sudden absence of life. The crying has stopped this morning, but in its place is a distinct lack of everything *Olivia*. Her cheeks sunken in, she left after waking, not a word passing over her lips. Without her boisterous presence pulling me in one direction or another, I drifted towards the forge without even realising. August hands me a beaten metal mug of tea and a butter biscuit, and I can't help it: I immediately think of Miranda's words in the Colosseum before my match with Cai. I seethe at how unaffected I was by her cold, calculated demands back then—*be nice to my hideous children, pretend that we love you. Smile*. I swear if I never see Miranda's haughty face again, it'll be too soon.

"So, do you want it?" August says. Thankfully his voice brings me back, sweeps Miranda's blank, pitiless expression from my mind.

"Yes," I tell him.

Five seconds later, the thing is in August's hands—my halo. Last time I saw it, it was battered and twisted out of shape, and now, to be honest, it doesn't look much better. The once smooth, shining silver surface is scarred from where August used his tools to pry it from around my neck. At least it's circular again, though. Kind of. It was never going to be perfect. He offers it out to me and I take it, immediately noticing that he hasn't soldered it together. A small gap exists, breaking the circle.

"Have you thought about whether you want to put it back on yet?"

I shake my head, turning over the piece of metal in my hands. Its weight is so familiar. "I'm not ready. I just need to know—will it work? If I do decide to put it back on?"

August's mouth pulls down, a grim, unhappy expression. "Yes. I fought with myself as to whether I ought to give it back to you, you know. The inner mechanisms were well beyond my ken, but there are others here who have first-hand experience with these things. They were able to assist in the repairs."

There are other people in Freetown who know about the halos—how they work and what literally makes them tick? I make a mental note to question Jack about them later. "And the drugs? It'll still produce the drugs?"

"It's probably capable of producing around another year's worth of the toxin. After that, I don't know. I suppose we could try and work out how it's formulated in the first place. Once we know how, it's possible that we might be able to reproduce it."

Toxin.

I say drug, August says *toxin*. That's how everyone here sees the halo and what it does to a person. Before, I thought of it exactly how the administrators in the Sanctuary wanted me to—as a medication. I slip the halo into my leather bag and clasp it close to my body. It's scary having it so close to me again, but also comforting. I wish there was some half measure between being affected by the halo and still being able to experience my own emotions. A dulled down, manageable kind of ache would be preferable over the loud roar of guilt I feel most days. Maybe I can just wear it at night. If there's a chance it would hold back the night-mares—Cai's bleached out, lifeless face—then I'd even think it might be worth it. But, of course, there is no half measure. It's either off or it's on, because I'm not stupid enough to believe that I'll be strong enough to remove it once I'm blissfully numb to the world again.

"Thanks for this, August." I give him a bleak smile and we part ways, but not before he gives me a firm hug. I'm slowly getting used to them.

Halfway back to my tent, I catch sight of Ryka running in the distance. He looks like he's heading towards the Holy Walk, probably to train, and I have to dismiss the immediate urge to go after him. He doesn't need me distracting him. Freetown's matches are two days away now, and the whole place is buzzing with a static hum I'm more than used to. It was the same back in the Sanctuary, only this time I'm *awake* and I can feel the anticipation, the electricity in the air. It's not a pleasant sensation for me, now that I've associated it with death and blood.

I take my halo home and hide it under my bed. The day is my own after that, and I sneak through the stalls of August's market, careful to make eye contact with no one as I survey all the glinting hardware. It's not just Freetown's smith's work that is showcased; a whole armoury of blades in all shapes and sizes are displayed, each exhibiting the signature of its creator. Short squat men with stubby fingers demonstrate the benefits of small handled throwing knives, whilst others, men with too much flair to have ever been fighters themselves, flaunt flashy folding blades, twirling the silver in the air to appreciative gasps from the crowds. Even Callum has his own stall. A small selection of slender pieces are arranged carefully on a folded cloth when I find him on the outskirts of the market place.

"Hi, Kit," he greets, the ghost of a smile on his lips.

"These are beautiful," I tell him, running a hand over the nearest knife, a six-inch stiletto blade. They really are impressive. I gesture to the table, asking if I can touch. Callum grins and tosses the stiletto at me so I have to catch it out of the air. My hand snaps out and I flip the knife over quickly, testing the balance and the weight.

"Figured you'd know how to handle that," Callum says, his eyes watching me as I spin it.

I pull my cheek to one side, half a smile. "So you aren't of the opinion that women shouldn't touch weaponry?" Ryka would probably have a fit if he saw me now, touching a knife in public, attitude adjustment or no. Callum doesn't seem fazed one bit.

"James thinks women should have the right to fight if they want to. Everyone else argues that the population would suffer too greatly if women were dying all over the place."

"What, even more than if it was a guy dying in the pits?"

"Well, yeah. I mean, one guy can get a lot of women pregnant, y'know? Women can only bear one child a year, realistically. That's how some people look at it: hard figures."

"And what do you think?"

"About women fighting? I don't see how it would be a bad thing, so long as they fight other women. It wouldn't be fair otherwise." A short snort of laughter tells Callum what I think of that statement. His blue eyes cloud over. "I mean, it makes sense. Men are so much stronger than women. We're supposed to be hunters. Fighters."

"Doesn't make the slightest bit of difference whether you're male or female when you've been trained with one of these properly," I tell him, holding up his knife. Doesn't matter if you've been trained for twelve years in the art of killing. The smallest of women can bring down the most monstrous of men in the blink of an eye. I should know, after all.

I take a closer look at Callum's work, noticing that his signature is a soft engraving into the metal of the blades. It's pretty really, decorative, but that doesn't mean the equipment is just for show. The edges are honed and bitingly sharp.

"I may have to buy one of these from you," I tell him. The empty sheaths on my knife belt are irritating, and it would be nice to feel them full again. "How much for this one?"

A little pride peppers Callum's tone. "I don't think any of these are the right knives for you, Kit. Give me a week. I've been working on something I think would be perfect. And we can discuss price later."

Gratitude floods me. Not only is Callum not trying to remove my knives from my hands, he's actually willing to give me more. Grinning, I know I'll pretty much pay him anything for the weapon he makes me. The quality of the blade will be excellent, but Callum's given me something more than a knife. He's given me respect enough to believe I could use it. Even if he somehow thinks it should only be against other women. I smirk and toss the stiletto one last time before placing it back on the folded cloth.

"Nice work, Cal." The voice takes Callum by surprise, but honestly, I've kind of been expecting *him* to show up. Waiting to see his face, or maybe I've been hoping? I turn and Ryka's leaning against the stall, absentmindedly prodding the tip of his index finger with his own knife. The author of his weaponry is the same as the daggers I wear on my hips: August.

"Sold much?" Ryka steps forward to take a look at what remains on the table.

"Nearly all of it," Callum replies, another swell of pride in his voice. "All my best pieces are gone. These are just what's left."

"Then the others must have been amazing." Ryka tests the same stiletto I held a minute ago. His dark eyes focus on the tilt of the knife as he weighs it in his hand. "I'll take this one."

Callum beams. No bells exchange hands, but Ryka and I walk away from the stall under the understanding that Ryka is now in for a twenty-five hour trade in labour with Callum. "What on earth would Callum need you to do for twenty-five hours for him?" I ask. Our shoulders bump together as we move through the jostling crowd, and the contact makes me feel slightly disorientated.

"He can ask me to help him with anything. Usually, trade and craftsmen get their buyers to take their places on their shifts out in the fields. Every man in Freetown gets allotted them, regardless of their business. If a customer works the allocated time they're supposed to be tending to the crops, the craftsmen are free to work at their trade. It happens a lot. That's why there are men who spend most of their time labouring, and you never see bakers or carpenters or smiths with a till in their hands."

"Huh." I am still yet to see these fields, a mile out past the Keep, further than I've dared explore outside Freetown's limits.

"It was nice of you to buy the knife, anyway," I tell him. It really *was* nice of him. It's clear Max and his brother look up to Ryka, and that one sale is probably worth more to Callum than all the others combined. Ryka drags his hair back out of his eyes and gives me a look. Nervous? Does he look nervous?

"Here." He quickly holds out the stiletto to me. "You can have it."

For five paces I stare dumbly at the flashing silver weapon he's offering me, not sure which is more shocking: Ryka giving me a gift, or the fact that the gift is actually a knife.

He sucks his bottom lip into his mouth and exhales through his nose. "Look, you don't have to take it if you don't want it. It probably doesn't match your daggers or something. Girls worry about that, right? I can always—"

I snatch it out of his hands before he can even think of rescinding his offer. "You're giving this to me?" I raise an eyebrow at him.

He scowls, but he doesn't mean it. I can tell. "I heard you ask how much it was. I thought you wanted it."

A strange prickle chases across my cheeks. "I did. I *do*," I say.

"Good. Now put it away before anyone notices."

That's more like it; he's not entirely on board with me arming myself while others can see. I smirk as I tuck the stiletto into my knife belt, drawing my shirt back over it to keep it from view. "You didn't need to do that, y'know. Olivia gave me—well, I think I'd struggle to walk under the weight of all the bells she gave me. I probably could have afforded that without you needing to sweat it out for twenty-five hours." A flat look passes over Ryka's face and somehow, strangely, I know I've hurt him. "It's not that I don't appreciate the gesture. I—"

"It's okay," he says quietly. "Manual labour's a good workout." He clenches his jaw and we walk through the market without saying much of anything else for a while. It's only when we reach the huge bonfire at the far end of the market that Ryka breathes out a curse and pauses.

"What is it?" I follow his gaze and struggle to pick out what could have put him on edge. The bright flames of the fire steal my ability to differentiate much in the surrounding darkness.

"There," he points. "Olivia. And Max."

Sure enough, Olivia's bright blonde hair gleams like a beacon in the shadows. Max is bent close to her ear, talking hurriedly. Olivia shakes her head, one arm wrapped around her stomach, the other hanging listlessly down at her side. An uncomfortable groan clues me in to the fact that Ryka's just as conflicted as I am right now.

"Should we go over?" he asks.

"I have no idea. I don't think so."

Ryka sighs. "He would have been good for her. Everyone's thought they were going to be together since they were kids."

"You don't think she'll change her mind? About going to the priestesses?"

Ryka shakes his head. "She can barely remember our parents. Liv's always been happy enough, but there's been this hole in her life that our mother should have filled. Until she finally figures out that our mother isn't in that Keep, she's going to be immoveable. They're going to wind that red cloth around her body and then she's going to discover she was wrong after all. But by then—" His voice goes stiff.

"It will be too late to leave?"

He bites his lip. Nods. "Way too late."

We're still watching them when Simone approaches. The girl with the cornflower blue eyes has a timid way about her as she slowly makes her presence known. I hold my breath. From the way Ryka stills at my side, he's holding his breath, too. Pain flashes across Max's face—I am getting too good at recognising that emotion—and Olivia's shoulders sag. I've seen women here in Freetown argue. Their heated, high-pitched voices resonate around the campfires after dark. It would be out of character for Olivia to start shouting, but something tells me that with feelings like this, people are liable to surprise you with how they act.

Olivia proves me wrong. She rushes the slender girl, whose eyes round out to twice their normal size. Where some women might have slapped or attacked, Olivia pulls Simone into a fierce hug. A burning sensation ignites at the back of my throat.

"Oh."

"I know." Ryka breathes. Then he does something that makes my throat close up entirely: he takes me hand. He's done it before, but this is different. He's so incredibly gentle, conscious of what he's doing. "Come on," he says, "I can't watch her do this to herself."

Neither can I. Freetown blurs past us, a carousel of laughing, ruddy faces flashing one after the other, as Ryka guides us away from the melee of the night markets and the weapons and his sister's broken heart.

"Where are we going?"

"Somewhere quiet," he replies, gently urging me along behind him. It's nice not being dragged for once. Feels like my presence is being requested instead of demanded.

It takes ten minutes to find our way to the beach, the one the Tamjis train on in the mornings. Ryka is soundless as he pulls his boots off at the edge of the sand. I follow suit and discard my own boots alongside his so that they sit side by side underneath a gnarled oak tree.

"I feel so trapped back there sometimes," he tells me. Blond hair gets tucked behind his ears again. "Everyone knows everything about everyone else. It's like a thousand people are watching Olivia and Max like they'd watch a fight. People's private lives should be just that—private." His hand closes around mine again, naturally, and the contact makes my head swim.

"Why do people care so much?" I ask.

Ryka hitches up a shoulder in half a shrug. We walk onto the cool sand, and it feels pretty amazing on my bare feet. I see why Ryka walks around like this half the time. "Perhaps," he says, after a while, "they're all so interested because, aside from the fights, there's not much happening here. Freetown's small. We don't welcome trade from other towns all that often. It's not safe. So we look to our own for entertainment. Isn't it that way in Lockdown?"

Entertainment is a moot point in the Sanctuary. "Not really. Curiosity isn't something that's encouraged. We have roles to perform. Most of us go about our day without wondering what anyone else is doing."

"But what about your parents? They have emotions, right? What do they do all day?"

"They—I—I really don't know." How have I never realised that I know so little about Lowrence and Miranda? Any other True for that matter. My lack of knowledge is stunning, considering that I lived for sixteen years in the Kitsch Household. I never once wondered what was going on above my own head. "Sometimes we'd hear running footsteps. The children, I think," I tell Ryka. "Laughter, too. It sounded like my father was laughing with his children."

"That didn't make you sad?"

I feel cold inside when I say, "No. Nothing made me sad." Ryka's silence tells me a lot; he feels sorry for me. "It's not like it mattered, though. I mean, I didn't know any better," I add.

"And now? What did it feel like to have the halo control you, now that you know what it's like to live without it?"

I think about the metal ring, hammered roughly into shape, back in my tent. Think about its cool, indifferent grasp around my neck. "Hollow," I say. "It felt hollow." Do I want to feel hollow again? The night terrors I suffer, that stomach churning sickness in my core when I wake, would have me saying yes in a heartbeat. If it weren't for this glimmer of something else I feel now as Ryka holds my hand. Now, I just don't know.

I don't want to talk about me. About the halo. We find our way over to the smooth slab of rock Olivia and I sat on the first time we came here, and Ryka and I watch the river pass us by. Even as we sit there, breathing evenly together in the darkness, that water is rushing over the rock Matthew carved his family's names into, wearing them away. It passed by the Kitsch Household, too, at some point earlier in the day.

"Do you think your mother is still alive?" I whisper, not sure if I'm breaking this fragile bond I now share with the boy sitting next to me. He doesn't react, doesn't tense up. Doesn't say anything for a while. I barely hear him when he says, "Sometimes. She just walked off into the forest one morning. There are a hundred ways to die out there. But there are plenty of ways to survive, too."

I know it instinctively—that that's what Ryka's doing all those times he goes out into the forest on his own. His absences from Freetown, though confusing to everyone else, make perfect sense to me. Ryka and Olivia are both still looking for their mother. They're just looking in different places.

26

FIGHT

The air smells different. Braced against the heavy sky, the emerald flush of the tree line struggles to hold up the weight of the impending horizon this morning. Maybe because things felt different when I woke. Maybe because the steel colour of the clouds promises a mighty storm and there's electricity vibrating in my lungs with every breath I take. But maybe…maybe it's because today is a fight day.

Freetown is whipped into a mad frenzy as I go to find Olivia down by the pits. She left early, before the sun rose, and Jack had to tell me where to find her. It's not in me to be annoyed with her for not coming to see me on her last day before she joins the priestesses. I'm too sad for that. Sad and terrified. I lose Olivia today. Worryingly, there's a chance I could lose Ryka as well, even though he's not really mine to lose. I see Cai's face everywhere I look as I hurry through the bustling crowds of people preparing for the night's festivities, and an overwhelming tide of remorse seeps into my bones. What will I feel if Ryka dies today? Will the emotion, whatever it may be, override the guilt I feel over killing Cai? My conscience is clearly not going to let that happen this morning. Won't let me really contemplate Ryka losing his match, either. At least I don't have to watch. Since I'm staying in my tent, there's comfort in the knowledge that whatever happens, I won't be traumatised with the memories of it for the rest of my natural life.

I find Olivia just where Jack said she would be, sitting on the lip of the pit with her legs dangling in. She raises her head as I approach.

"Hi, Kit." She smiles brightly. Brighter than I would have expected given everything that has happened, is *going* to happen today. Evidence of Max and Simone's Claiming ceremony is everywhere. Boughs of weeping willow hang from the openings of nearly every tent I passed on the way here, a sign of celebration and of coming together. The event will take place after the first fight of the evening. My heart bleeds for Olivia as she rises to meet me. "You're up early," she says.

"So is everyone else."

"True. No one gets to sleep in Freetown on match days. Have you come to help me prepare?"

I suck back a sharp breath. "What kind of help?" If there's one thing I don't feel like doing right now, it's helping Olivia sign herself over to the priestesses.

"My hair needs to be washed," she says. "Not until later, though. I need to be cleansed so I am worthy to be accepted."

I have no idea what is involved in the ritual Olivia will undergo in front of Freetown later, but I agree to help her anyway. Even if I don't like it, she's been my only real friend here and I don't want to let her down. She walks with me back through the tent city and we gravitate towards the river where we first met.

"Have you spoken to Ryka and Jack about this?" I ask her quietly.

"Of course. Endlessly. You've met my brother and my grandfather, right? Both as stubborn and relentless as each other. They think I'm crazy, and that's fine. I don't expect them to understand. They shouldn't want to stop me from doing my duty to the Gods, though."

"But your mother, Ryka said she's not—"

"Ry says a lot of things." Olivia places her hand over mine and squeezes. "If I'm wrong about my mother, then at least I am dedicating my life to a worthy cause. The priestesses are invaluable to Freetown. Their prayers and rituals have kept the people of our settlement safe for a long time."

It's on the tip of my tongue to tell her what I truly suspect— that the knives of the city's skilled fighters have more to do with their relative safety. It definitely isn't down to some hokey chanting in supplication to a bunch of unknown Gods. It would be rude to say that, though. I just smile as we sit on the riverbank, smile and nod my head.

"I know you don't believe," Olivia says. "But you don't really know what the Faith is all about, do you?"

"I guess not."

She starts snicking the bells free from her skirts with a small, delicate knife, designed specifically for that job. The rattling silver orbs pile up as she speaks. "The Old One is the first of the Gods. He created the planet and the sun, the sky and the stars. We pray to him to give thanks and to keep safe those who pass before us. He died long ago and travelled onto the other side to stand watch over the bodies of the fallen. The Old One welcomes fighters into the Rest, mothers who die in childbirth, children who perish from sickness. His is the face that greets them when they arrive home.

"The Essence is the Goddess of life, of inspiration and of wisdom. We pray to her for all three, and it's to her that we dedicate the fights. The blood is tribute to her for the life that we hold here, and it is shed with reverence.

"Lastly there is Potentis, God of what is to come. We pray to Potentis for all the things we desire for our futures: rains for a good harvest, healing for the sick, good fortune for those who travel." Olivia's eyes start to shine. "We hold ceremonies to Potentis when babies are born, to bless the future of the child and to mark out its path as a strong fighter, or a benevolent mother."

She goes quiet for a while and I ponder her words, trying to make sense of them. It all sounds very nice, but there's very little in me that can find truth in what she says. "What makes you believe these Gods exist?" I ask her.

Olivia finishes up with her little bells and gathers them, smiling softly. "My mother taught me how to recognise the signs of The Essence in my life, the signature of The Old One in nature, everywhere we look. She used to sing to me about Potentis, observing our needs and blessing us with the gifts and trials we need the most. Everything I feel for the Gods stems from her teachings. I can understand how it would be hard for an adult to convert to a religion that provides no proof of its legitimacy, and asks for something many people just don't possess."

"What's that?"

"Faith." She smiles. "Faith is a fragile thing. More often than not, it gets broken and worn away by life. It requires us to be willing to fight for a belief, to *choose* to believe it. Maybe that's why it's something passed down from mother to daughter, father to son. Only a child can believe with a pure trust that what they're being told is the truth. After we grow into adulthood, we are taught or we learn the hard way to question everything."

"And Ryka? Did your father teach him the same way your mother taught you?"

Olivia sucks on her lip thoughtfully. "My father was the same as Jack. He believed that there is a higher power, a creator, but he didn't know with a certainty what or who that was. He believed in doing good and being as he wished others would be. Believed in giving thanks for what he had. He said if he lived his life that way, then he surely couldn't offend whoever created him. I think maybe Ryka feels the same way. It's not something he talks about."

"Mmmm." Matthew's version of religion sounds like covering all bases to me, but it's one I can understand. If I had any reason to believe in an all-powerful being, I would live like Matthew and Jack.

We don't talk any more of religion. We spend the day talking of Max and how she went to wish him well with his joining to Simone. I wash Olivia's hair when the time comes, the same way she washed mine when we first met, the saddest of symmetries, and as darkness falls she hugs me to her and gives me the bells she plucked off her clothes.

"I'm not going to need them anymore," she tells me, squeezing me to her small frame. My eyes burn like crazy, and I give up any pretence that I'm not going to cry.

"Promise me, Kit. Promise me you will come to the Keep. I know it makes you uncomfortable, but I'll find a way to let you know I'm there. That I'm okay. Promise me," she says through her own tears.

"I will, I promise." A promise I intend to keep. I'll make sure she's alive and happy in her new life if it's the last thing I do, and if she's not happy, or worse…if she's not *alive*, I will raze the priestesses' fortress to the ground.

"Good." She wipes her eyes, sniffing. "Now promise me the other thing."

A low horn vibrates through the trees as I go to ask her what she means.

Her eyes widen. "I have to go. The High Priestess is leaving the Keep. Tell me that you'll look after my brother, Kit. He needs you."

I start to shake my head. "Ryka's capable of looking after himself. He doesn't need anyone."

"I'm sure he'd like to believe that," she rolls her eyes, "and it might be true. He could get by, keeping to himself and bearing the weight of all that self-inflicted responsibility he carries around with him twenty-four hours a day. It shouldn't have to be that way, though. He should have someone. Someone who will be there to help carry his burdens. Soften his heart up a little, y'know?"

"I'm not sure I'm the one to do—"

She cuts me off. "You are. You are the only one." Another sad smile breaks across her face. "And it would make me immensely happy to think of you both happy together out here from time to time. That you are my sister, that you are a part of my family."

A choked sound works its way out of my mouth, and I can't speak. I nod, grabbing her and hugging her one last time. The first time I have ever initiated close contact like that.

"I need to find my brother. I need to say goodbye," she rushes out.

"I hope—" I can't finish.

"I know," she says. "Me, too."

As Olivia turns and runs back towards the activity of Freetown, I really do hope. I hope she finds her mother in those shattered black spines of rock. I hope she can be happy.

******

The horns sound for a long time, and from the muted cheers that go up after a while, I know I have missed Max and Simone's Claiming ceremony. I can only pray that Olivia didn't have to watch, or if she did then she was able to take peace in the knowledge that Max is going to find some level of happiness after she is gone.

I kick myself, forcing myself to stop thinking like that. Olivia isn't dying. She's still going to be alive, still going to be the same girl underneath all that red. And if I'm honest, I know she's not going to be taking any peace from knowing Max is with someone else. It just wouldn't be possible, surely? Time ticks by slowly, and I wrestle with the coiled discomfort in my belly. Is Olivia going through the rituals now? What will they do to her? Disgusted with myself though I am, there's also a more urgent question on my mind. One I have been trying not to think about. Is Ryka okay? Has he been called? In my head, I see James dropping down into the pit and growling up at the cheering mob, yelling out Ryka's name. I had no idea I would feel this... *terrified* for him. Not a nice feeling. How do the families of the fighters deal with this level of panic every single month? It's a crushing, fiercely powerful alarm that makes my palms sweat and my heart race.

With nothing to do in my tent, I find myself staring blankly down at my halo, running my fingers across it's dinted surface. If I hold it close to my ear, I can hear a ticking sound now. Did it always do that? I can't remember. The whir of gears was a familiar occurrence, but I can't ever recall a ticking.

A horn, so loud the ground vibrates through the soles of my boots, fills the night air. It makes the canvas of my tent walls tremor with its low rumble. Who knows what it symbolises. It could mean someone is dead, for all I know. I start pacing the length of my bed, chewing on my thumbnail. I need something to take my mind off what is happening out there.

I reach for the holostick and scroll forward to a random number, just needing to hear my friend's voice.

"Your brother busted me sitting outside your bedroom window tonight, and I had trouble convincing him that I wasn't doing anything weird. He lives on the brink of feeling, your brother. Something tells me he's fighting against his halo all day, every day. He asked me why I insist on coming to the matches to watch your fights, even when I'm not fighting myself. I told him my Trues asked me to observe you. I could hardly have told him that if I know you're in that arena, I'll go crazy unless I can watch over you. Even if that means I have to witness your complete lack of humanity every time you kill. It's worth it. Stupid, I know. If anything ever happened to you, there's very little I would be able to do to stop it. I wouldn't be able to stop myself, either, though. My world would end if you died in that Colosseum, Kit. I love you more than life itself. Maybe that's why I go. Because if you did die, I wouldn't want to live either. I would throw myself into the arena and kill whoever took your life, and I would welcome the hail of gunfire that took me out afterwards."

Choking, I hit stop. I can't look at Cai when he's saying things like that to me. The passion, the intensity in his eyes is so raw that I know he means every word. His declaration is a portentous omen, and it feels like this moment—the moment when he recorded this file—was the exact moment when he decided he would die for me. I hate it. I hate that he felt that way when I didn't. It's horrifying to realise it, but the reason why he always attended my fights is the exact same reason I want to—no, *have* to go to the pit now. He came because he loved me. I have to go for Ryka. Does that mean that I love him? Cai's solemn eyes burn into my mind, but I try not to think about those bigger questions. What it all possibly means.

Because that would only slow me down as I run.

******

Jack sees me before I see him. I'm puffing hard as I pull up on the outer rim of the crowd gathered around the pit. The old man rushes me from out of nowhere and throws a cowled cloak around my shoulders.

"Are you crazy?" he hisses. The lines of his stacked tattoos, his kills, fill my vision as he yanks up the hood and arranges it around my face. "There are people here who know your face, child! I thought you understood the gravity of someone placing you here?"

"I'm sorry." Oxygen slams into my body as I inhale, exhale, inhale. "I had to see..." I trail off, searching him out. Ryka. He's standing on the opposite side of the pit at the very edge, burning a pathway straight for me, like he knows where I am in the crush. There isn't a scratch on him, and he's still wearing one of his standard black shirts. From his calm demeanour, it's clear he hasn't yet been called to the pit.

"Olivia said you would come," Jack says, his voice incredibly tight. "I thought you had more sense."

"Has she gone?"

Jack drags me forward. The crowd parts for their leader, and whispers of *'Grandfather'* fall like hushed, respectful caresses on my ears as we move closer to the edge of the pit. Once we're standing at the very edge, I can see what is taking place below. Olivia is leaning back against a priestess in an odd slump, and three other women move around her body, carefully feeding red material over and under, over and under. Her body is slowly being cocooned in swathes of the thin material. Her face is tilted up at the stars, but she lacks any expression. Those brown eyes, so similar to her brothers, are utterly blank.

"What's wrong with her? What did they do?"

"The Haze," he says simply.

"They...they *drugged* her?"

Jack nods, a sour look on his face. "Stops the girls from backing out, I imagine."

"This isn't right." I'm suddenly all hot and bothered over how Jack actually let this happen. He should have forbidden her, done something to prevent all of this. I'm of a mind to get angry with him, but when I look at the old man, his cheeks are wet and I don't have the heart. Feeling the pressure of a hot stare on the top of my head, I glance up and find Ryka pinning me with his gaze. Strange. He swallows, his throat bobbing, and I can tell he's fighting tears, too. It's maddening that between the three of us, we couldn't talk her out of this.

The priestesses wrap the never-ending red veil around Olivia's body once more, but this time the material is looped over her arms, pinning them to the sides of her body. My instant claustrophobia can't be quashed, even as I breathe through the panic, reminding myself it's not me being trussed up like I'm being prepared for a funeral pyre.

"Don't watch, child," Jack says, pressing his large, heavy hand into my back. It's comforting, having it there. He shouldn't be comforting me, though. He's saying goodbye to his granddaughter. I have no idea how he's going to ever fill up the void hollowing out his insides—the same void eating away at mine

As the red cloth moves up Olivia's body, the priestesses start to wail. Their low keening is eerie as it vibrates out of the pit, individual voices undulating and harmonising one minute, rising in pitch into total discord the next. Women in the crowd start to cry. A heavy sadness fills the air, pouring into my lungs, and it's hard to breathe around the weight of it. It's not a few women standing around the tableau below shedding tears; it's with surprise that I note every single woman is sobbing.

The men stand with hardened glares and clenched jaws, and I feel it deep in my bones: they're humming. It starts low, a pressure building with increasing force, and soon it's a tidal wave that causes the very molecules that make up my body to jitter. My teeth rattle together in my head. It's unbearably sad that I can feel the bass timbre of Jack's voice travelling down his arm and into my body. I'm sharing his grief this way. On top of my own, it's overwhelming.

As soon as Olivia's face is covered, the howling and the humming ceases. It's like someone threw a switch somewhere, and every single member of Freetown just...stops. I'm locked onto the red cocoon of Olivia's body when the pristine white petals start falling down onto the kicked up muddy floor of the pit. Handfuls of them flutter, listing on the breeze, and in the absolute quiet it is like their flights are plotted downwards on the very silence itself.

"It's done," Jack whispers. Certain things happen after that: Olivia's body is lifted by strong arms out of the pit, and then the priestesses take her, a sea of shifting anonymous crimson bodies, accepting her into their fold. As they pass him by, Ryka reaches out his hand, a parting gesture, but the priestesses shy back from his touch. Keep him from making contact with his sister. The devastation on Ryka's face makes my skin flame. I hate the priestesses so very much in that instant. *Hate* them.

Then they're gone. With them, they take something incredibly precious. It feels like they're taking away the sun.

I'm numb as the noise floods back into the pit. Shouting and cheering, the sadness that reigned down with the silken white petals only minutes earlier turns into furious celebration. Bastards, all of them. It's hard to understand how women can mourn one second and then be frantically happy the next. To have such easy control over their emotions makes them all liars. I kick my boot against the hard-pressed dirt and rub the pads of my thumbs into my dagger hilts, working my jaw. On the other side of the pit Ryka is a mirror of me. I tamp down my hostility only because the crowd starts pushing and shoving.

"The High Priestess is coming!" someone cheers.

"Stay here. Keep that hood pulled up and try not to make eye contact with anyone." Jack drops down into the pit, leaving me with a cold impression on the base of my spine where the warmth of his hand used to be. "People of Freetown!" he yells. "Tonight is the first of three. Tonight we celebrate the tradition of our warriors' sacrifice. The Gods smile down upon us as we honour our dead and send more to the Rest. Who will bear the blood of their brothers on their hands tonight?"

If I thought the humming was loud before, the '*Haroo!*' that splits the air apart is truly deafening. Ryka's voice is amongst them. How I think I can hear him over everyone else is ridiculous, but I swear I do. Bodies surge forward as a pathway is formed on my side of the pit, but I don't waste time watching the frail figure of the High Priestess step down into Jack's open arms. I'm watching Ryka. Even though his eyes are elsewhere, it seems like his body is tilted towards me, zoning in on my exact location in the crowd. I tap my foot nervously, wondering how this is going to play out. Will it be like the Colosseum matches? The pomp and ceremony held on a match day back in the Sanctuary seems positively sophisticated compared to the rushing and shouting and pounding here. I somehow doubt there will be an adjudicator to judge the fights fairly. It's going to be a free-for-all, and I'm poised to watch the whole thing voluntarily. *Leave, leave, leave,* my heart pounds out, but I can't. I'm too worried, my fear toxic, spreading like a river of poison through my veins.

Somewhere a dull drumbeat kicks up. It's not long before feet join in the rhythm, trying to beat into submission earth that already yielded long ago. I remain motionless. I'm not becoming a part of this wild machine, baying for the blood of Freetown's men. I just refuse. My body is jostled side to side by other bodies, pressed too close, and I fight to hold my place. Elbows, knees, hips, shoulders. Elbows to the ribs, knees to my legs, hip against hip, shoulder against shoulder. Half of me thinks the rough treatment is intentional, but when I cast a look around, no one is paying me any attention. All eyes are fixed on the High Priestess and Jack standing together down in the pit. Right now I am just another faceless person in a swell of surging bodies. At any other time this would feel good, but right now—right now I want to vault across the yawning gap between Ryka and I, grab his hand, and run.

That's what I want to do. Run. With him.

I press my lips together and count the faces I can see, doing my best not to think about that. How on earth would that ever even work? Would he come with me? In the pit below, the High Priestess' unwavering voice fills the night air.

"*Raksha!*" she screams.

A thousand other voices join hers, yelling the word, pushing it upwards so it rises in one hot breath that seems to come from everywhere and nowhere all at once. It sinks into my skin and drops through me like a stone. My heart beats louder than the drum, louder than the rushing water when I escaped the Sanctuary, louder than my guilt and fear and worry.

Raksha.

HALO

It symbolises the voices of all the men who have died before in the pit. It's their death chant, calling for fresh blood to the other side. Right now it does feel like the dead are chanting. And they definitely want fresh blood. I try to find Ryka in the press opposite, but it looks as though the fighters are gathering, weaving through the maze to meet at a point to my left. Ryka has departed there, too, and I know instinctively that they're getting ready to fight.

Of all the possible times I could freak out, this is probably the worst. There's little I can do about it, though. My heart's pounding. With the heavy cloak Jack draped over me dragging through the dirt, I shove against the crowd, meeting immediate resistance. I have to get there, though; I have to get to Ryka. What I'll do when I reach him is a mystery, but I can't help but worry that he's going to be the first person called. The scene plays out on a loop, getting worse and worse with every rendition: James crying out Ryka's name; James gripping onto the back of Ryka's head, a fist full of blond hair as he drives his glinting quicksilver into his chest.

That faded out look, the one I've seen so many times before as the light well and truly goes out in someone's eyes, that's what will happen to Ryka if James gets him into the pit. I scramble uselessly against the body next to me, struggling to shift what turns out to be a mountain of a man. I look up at him and our eyes meet. It's the fighter from the blood ceremonies who had his ear sliced in two. Lettin. That's his name: Lettin Corr. He's shirtless again, his huge chest tattoo slicked with sweat. He smiles at me and I arrange my face into what I suppose to be a polite response, when something happens. I'm shoved.

The smile on Lettin's face slides off like water running down rock. I don't have time to reach out for him, although Lettin does make a grab for me. He catches hold of the cloak, a great bunch of material wadded up in his massive hand, but it's not enough. Suddenly, helplessly, I'm falling…

…into the pit.

SACRIFICE

Six feet isn't so far to fall. When you land hard on your back, though, breathing can become a problem. Above me, Lettin and the small woman standing next to him both look horrified. The cloak that remained behind as I fell flaps in Lettin's hand like a billowing flag, and his knuckles are white where he's clenching onto it. It takes a while to shake the jarring impact from my head, and it's when the stars clear from my vision that I notice everyone is quiet. *Everyone.*

Not a single person makes a sound as I lie flat out on my back on the pit floor. I go to get up and the woman next to Lettin, the little, petite one, finally gasps. Her hand flies to her mouth and her eyes appear as large as the silver disc of the moon hanging in the sky over her shoulder. Why does everyone look so terrified?

"Oh, Kit." The sigh comes from Jack. He appears right next to me. "What have you done?"

"Done?" I lift my head and survey myself, confused. Toppling into the pit was hardly an intentional thing. The short tempered part of me wants to point that out but frankly I'm too concerned with the abject horror I'm witnessing. Raised eyebrows, open mouths, tensed muscle everywhere. It seems as though I just made a mistake. A big one.

"What's going on?" I hiss to Jack. When I catch sight of the old man, my stomach back-flips. Words seem to fail him. He gives me a sharp glare and then looks down at his feet.

"It wasn't her fault," a voice calls out from the crowd.

I scan the people standing above me, trying to find the owner of the voice. My gaze falls on Jack again, though, and I stop. All I can see is the bottomless regret etched into the worn lines of his face. He won't meet my eye.

"She was pushed," the same voice repeats. "She cannot be held accountable."

Jack's jaw locks and he exhales through his nose. "This isn't about accountability, James. You know that as well as anyone."

James? Confusion swamps me as I look again, finding the dark-haired fighter standing above us. His strong arms are crossed over his chest, and thick veins of tension stand out in his neck. He stares at me, and the look in his eyes is fearsome.

"Then what is it about?" he says, addressing Jack. "The old ways? The Faith? These traditions are barbaric. It's time for them to end."

A rustle of shocked voices goes up through the throng. It reminds me of another sound from a long time ago: the dry leaf sound of the paper gown I wore the last time I was interviewed by one of the technicians. Except this is louder. And this time I am not the picture of placidity; I am terror personified. Jack steps closer to me but his presence doesn't make me feel any better. The High Priestess moves around him, her red robed form looming over me.

"Our laws are not traditions, fighter. They are exactly that: laws, passed down to us by the Gods. This girl came to the pit floor uncalled for. This is sacred ground, and she has offered herself up as sacrifice. You know what must be done."

As a furore leaps up around her words, my heart stops. Sacrifice? They're going to *kill me* because I fell onto the pit floor? Suddenly it all makes sense. Well, it makes absolutely no sense at all, but at least now I know why Olivia was so thankful when I grabbed hold of her at the blood ceremonies. If she had fallen as I just did, she knew what would happen to her. They would offer her up as a sacrifice to the Gods.

"*No!*" Another shout punctures up above the rumble of excited voices—Callum's. I know him well enough to recognise his voice. Sure enough, he fights his way forward and rushes to stand beside James. I shakily get to my feet. My legs feel like they're likely to give out on me any second, but I don't let them. There's no time for that. I'm too busy inching away from the High Priestess like the frail little woman is going to take me on herself. Where the hell is Ryka? Every single part of me is screaming that I need to find him.

"We must depart," the High Priestess says, offering out her hand to Jack. He looks at me with too much sorrow on his face for me to think he's going to do anything about this. Which is why I'm surprised when he doesn't accept the small, gnarled hand and he clambers out of the pit to stand beside James.

"I know what must be done, and yet I cannot agree with it. I reject the sacrifice," he cries.

More shocked voices. More rustling and awkward shifting from the masses.

"I also reject the sacrifice," James shouts.

Callum follows suit. "I, too, reject."

Am I allowed to reject myself as sacrifice? I definitely reject myself as sacrifice. Surprisingly there are a few more voices offered up, close to the pit and further away, who call out on my behalf. I can only imagine if they are people I know. Maybe Melody and August. Maybe Max is still here somewhere, too. A thick silence follows. A well of fear is building in the back of my throat when finally another voice echoes out into the night air.

"I reject the sacrifice!"

Ryka.

Even though his voice was impossibly close, it takes a long time to pinpoint him in the crowd. My mistake is that I am looking for him at head height. And he is on his knees. In the hammered down, sticky mud, Ryka is on his knees. "I reject the sacrifice!" he all but screams.

"Not enough." The High Priestess moves effortlessly to the side of the pit, where a handful of men reach down and pluck her out. Her stooped form turns and faces me.

"The consequences of tainting sacred ground are too much for this town to bear. The people know it is unwise to incur wrath where offering is required. The offering of one for the good of the many. Who will claim this honour?"

I'm stunned. This is really happening. Two days ago, Olivia sobbed into my shirt and asked me if this was really her life. Now I'm left wondering the same question. Am I really going to get killed by a member of Freetown? Ryka rocks back and gets to his feet, although the effort looks like it kills him.

"No one dare," he says, his voice low and menacing.

"This is not your place, boy," the High Priestess says calmly. "If you do not stand down, you will be nominated to commit the act yourself. Would this please you?"

"Put me in that pit and I won't be going after *her* with a knife." The threat in his voice is clear, and everyone hears it. A loud shout goes up and the fighters gathered around Ryka flinch away from him like his brand of idiocy is contagious. I will him not to do anything stupid, but it might already be too late for that. He glares up at the High Priestess from underneath drawn brows and I can tell he means it. Good Gods, he means it.

A soft clicking sound comes from underneath the woman's veils. Unfazed by Ryka's insinuation, she point-blank ignores him. "I ask again. Who will claim this honour?"

The spit of the burning fires is all I hear for a moment, but then a buzz explodes further back in the crowds. A pathway clears and a tall, broad man stalks his way forward. A jagged scar runs down the right hand side of his face, and it's too neat and tidy to be a defensive scar. Self-imposed, more likely. He falters when he catches sight of me.

"I didn't know it was a girl," he says. His knife is still in his hand, though.

"It matters not whether the sacrifice is male or female. She volunteered herself. It must be done."

"I fell!" Finally I find my voice, and with it my anger. It rushes over me so forcefully that I can't keep my hands from shaking. My whole body, in fact. "I didn't volunteer for anything. I'm not fighting."

"You're right in that, child. You are not supposed to fight. You are supposed to die," the High Priestess tells me.

Like hell I am.

I lock onto Ryka—see the horror on his face. He looks from me to the fighter now dropping down into the pit, and I watch it happen: he explodes. He goes to jump into the pit after the fighter, but the men around him catch him by his arms. It takes six of them to hold him back and in the end there's nothing he can do. They pin him to the floor while he strains and kicks. "Don't you dare, Sam! Don't you dare!"

The fighter, Sam, hesitates for a second. The look he gives me is almost apologetic. Spinning a short, ugly looking blade over his hand, he shakes his head. "I'm really sorry, girl. This is just the way of it. Why don't you lie down? I'll make it easy for you."

And just like that, I snap. I'm not lying down. I'm sick to death of lying down. "How about I make this easy for *you*. Leave," I say, menace in my voice. My hands hover over my knife belt, still concealed under my shirt. If he takes one step towards me, I'll have steel in both hands before he can blink.

"Don't you touch her!" Ryka hollers, still restrained on his back. His boots dig uselessly into the ground as he tries to get away. The people surrounding the struggling fighters are all statues, clearly conflicted as to what the hell they should be doing. Most of them know Ryka, and his fury mars the air enough for them to keep quiet. Not so on the other side of the pit. The chant starts up low, but it gradually grows in strength as more and more people take it up.

"*Raksha! Raksha! Raksha!*"

The stupid call galvanises Sam, who, up until this moment, hasn't really been all that convincing in his role cast as my murderer. The glint in his eye definitely gives the impression he's starting to take his position seriously.

One step.

He takes one step and I do what I said I would. My daggers are a part of me, an extension of my body in a heartbeat. Sam hesitates.

"Oh, come now, girl. This doesn't need to be a difficult. It can all be over in one quick thrust. I swear, you'll hardly feel a thing. If you go up against me—"

"You'll die," I snap. Good thing my voice sounds confident, because I really don't feel it. This is a first for me. A terrifying, raw first. I am not wearing my halo.

Before there were consequences to my fights, some of which remain the same now. If Sam wins, I die. If I win, Sam dies. Other consequences are different, however. If Sam cuts me, it'll hurt. If he attacks me, my heart rate will elevate and I'll be scared and I won't be able to breathe and Iwillfeellike...thewallsofthe pitare... closinginaroundmeand...

"*Kit!*"

The shout warns me just in time. Sam dodges forward with his crude blade, and the sweep he lashes out with would have slashed my stomach open if I hadn't leaped back. I glare at him incredulously.

"One strike, huh? You obviously don't know human anatomy very well. It can take days for a stomach wound to kill a person."

Sam hunkers down and everything about him says, *defend!* "I'll take what I can get to put you down first, girl," he tells me.

"Fine. So long as we both know where we stand." I dip so that my centre of gravity is close to the ground and I flick my daggers over in my hands. In this stance the hammering in my chest seems to ease. This is something I can do without thinking normally, but now I have to concentrate to process everything that's happening over the roar of my emotions. It's hard, but I can still do it. My body remembers what is required of it, and I strike out. Flashing metal sings through the air, and I'm the driving force behind it, urging it to seek out flesh and bone. My rapid manoeuvre has Sam on the back foot, literally, and I don't take the kill I could rightly claim. Instead, I just graze his neck.

A stark line of red blossoms across his skin, and howls go up all around us.

The warning slice I've given him doesn't serve its purpose. It takes five seconds of staring at Sam's dismayed face before I realise I haven't made things better for myself by showing him I'm capable. I've just sealed my fate. Rather than extricating myself from one ridiculous ritual, I've landed myself well and truly into another: the blood demand. I made him bleed, and no one here is foolish enough to pass this off as a symbolic cut between a man and a woman. We are fighters, both, regardless of our sex.

Freetown witnessed me taking the lifeblood of another, and, strict record keeper that the town is, a debt now exists between Sam and I. A debt that can only be paid with my blood. From the expressions on the people hovering at the edges of the pit, payment is due immediately.

Sam takes a dazed look around and then starts circling me. I let him prowl for a moment, subconsciously keeping track of him while I watch Ryka buck, still trying to get out from under his friends. What is he going to do if he actually manages to get free? If he steps one foot on the pit floor without being called for, the High Priestess will demand his death, just like mine. That can't happen.

I find Jack still standing next to James, and oddly both the men don't look as worried as they did a few minutes ago. "What am I supposed to do?" I call up to them.

Jack's eyes flash—steel and resolution. "What you need to," he says. He's telling me I need to kill Sam. He knows as well as I do, along with everyone else, that that's the only way I'm climbing out of this pit. Maybe even then that won't be enough. James folds his arms across his chest and just stares down on me. The look in his eyes says one thing: impress me.

Sam is heavy-footed and clumsy in his second attack, but I have to give it to him—he's fast. Just not fast enough. He lunges from behind, a coward's strike by anyone's standards, with his knifepoint honing in on my kidneys, and I spin, throwing a wide kick. My foot connects with Sam's forearm and the force of the blow is more than enough to knock away his weapon. A displeased grumble from our audience tells me that I'm not the favourite in this match. Surprise, surprise.

Immediately, Sam has another weapon from the belt at his waist, and this time he approaches slower. I let him come to me again, not willing to play the dart and dodge game. I want this over. I've weighed Sam, weighed his brash attack mode and the way he favours his right side, and now I've set my body on pause. I've fought people like him before, and the inevitable always happens. They get too close.

He's a foot away and I'm breathing slowly, trying to calm the thunder in my chest, when Ryka breaks free. He jumps to his feet and immediately goes to leap down into the pit, but Jack's seen what is happening and comes out of nowhere, bear-hugging his grandson before he can leap. Above all the noise and the chanting and the jeering, I hear Jack yell, "Just stop, Ryka! She doesn't need it. Watch! She doesn't need saving!"

Sam circles closer, his movement predatory, his shoulders tensed. "That's it," he coos. "Don't worry. It'll all be over in a moment." I almost laugh when I realise he thinks I'm panicking or something and I don't know what to do. Fine. I let him believe it. Jack sees me for what I really am. What I'm capable of. Soon everyone else in Freetown will, too. An inch closer. Another inch—

"Do you have family, girl?" Sam whispers.

His question throws me. "What?"

"Tell me their names. I'll make sure they're cared for."

My voice cracks when I say, "I have no one." Not because I miss my brother or my birth mother. But because he asked me in the first place. Suddenly, I have to fight to keep myself still. It's not right that I have to kill this man. It's not right that I need to murder someone to satisfy some stupid superstitious ritual.

HALO

"You don't need to do this," I tell Sam.

"I'm sorry," he breathes, "but I do."

I close my eyes, and he leaps. I'm not where he thinks I will be, of course. With a swift spin, I pivot on my heel and lock the hilt of my dagger against the flat, open palm of my free hand. I bring it to the side of my rib cage just below my breast, and I twist around Sam's body as his intended deathblow meets with thin air. There's not much to it from here. A final rotation of my upper body; a transference of energy as potential turns to kinetic, travelling up from the floor, through my body, pushing outwards with very little exertion. Metal grinds on bone, and a wet gurgle wheezes out of Sam. One punctured lung. He sinks to his knees... and all hell breaks loose.

The crowd starts screaming. I look up at Jack and Ryka, and Ryka has gone still in the old man's arms. He's just looking at me, eyes wide, and all I can think of is Cai's recording. How he watched me kill endlessly, harrowed out by my inhumanity. Well, right now I'm chock full of humanity but I'm still capable of destroying life. Is Ryka horrified by me now? He should be. I horrify myself. His eyes grow wider and I think I can see how disgusted he is by me, but then his mouth opens and the shape of a soundless warning masks his face. Something's wrong. I duck instinctively and feel the biting sting of pain slash across my arm. I'm on fire, my nerve endings protesting angrily, as I roll away from the danger.

Sam is on his feet, blood spilling from his mouth and dripping from his knife. My blood. I don't dare touch my fingers to the searing wound on my upper arm. Who knows how deep it is, and I can't worry about that right now. I have to focus on finishing this, otherwise we're going to cut each other away piece by piece until nothing remains but the red earth. Ultimately, I don't want to die just yet, and it's this thought that pushes me forwards at a near run. Sam weaves as I charge him, my tactics completely changed now, and it's not a considered dodge that saves him from my blade; it's his body collapsing as he spits up more shiny, viscous blood from his mouth. To his credit, he doesn't pause. He kicks my legs out from underneath me and then we're grappling on the ground. I don't want this kind of a fight. Even though he's injured, Sam's reach is much greater than mine and there is strength in his muscled, heavy arms. I strike out with both feet, trying to put some distance between us, but Sam covers my body with his, pressing me downwards.

He spends two seconds trying to pry my dagger from my hands before he gives in and manfully flips me onto my front, shoving my face down into the dirt.

He almost has my arm locked behind my back when I push my hips up and unseat him, flinging him off me.

From there, things happen quickly. My hands are full of his death and Sam sees it. He has time to rise to his knees as I spring up and scissor the blades; they sing as the metal scrapes together but soon they're both buried in Sam's neck. It takes a lot of power to follow through with the sweeping motions, but I make good. His head makes a dull thumping sound as it hits the pit floor, and a jet of red arterial blood sprays up at me, soaking the front of my shirt, my face, my hands

I take a deep breath. I can't...what the...? I can't breathe. I drop my knives, panicking that Sam somehow managed to puncture one of *my* lungs without me noticing, but he hasn't. I just...can't...breathe...

I rest my hands on my knees, leaning forward in an attempt to get some air into my lungs, but my head won't stop spinning. The roaring sound in my ears is my blood pounding, pounding, pounding. It's also the voices of every single member of Freetown losing their minds.

28

RASHATTA

I'm floating. When the High Priestess approaches me, still leaning over Sam, I've totally checked out of my body. I'm somewhere above us, watching everything play out, and honestly I don't really care what happens next. I'm just too spaced out by the reality of what just happened to locate any of my self-preservation instincts. The hunched figure places a hand on my shoulder, close to the painful gash Sam gave me, and I wince. The old lady has a powerful grip on her.

"*Rashatta!*" she screams. I can't remember what that one means, but I'm glad it's not freaking Raksha. If I never hear that word again, I'll die happy. Unlike before, the crowd doesn't respond immediately. Their objections over what I just did echo long after the High Priestess' call fades in the night air. She calls it again, and this time there's a demanding note to her tone. By increments, a cautious, unhappy silence develops.

"The sacrifice is satisfied. The blood debt is satisfied," the old woman cries. Her hand tightens on my shoulder and I wince through the pain. She draws me upright and I can see the slow rise and fall of her chest as she breathes. It's the only thing that makes this small pillar of red material a real person. That is, of course, until she starts lifting the veils back from her face.

A frightened whisper begins to run around the crowd. Whatever she is doing, I don't think I want to stick around for it. The way people are reacting says a lot. They're freaking out, and I probably should be too. "Can I go?"

"*Rashatta!*" she screams. I suddenly remember when she used the word before, back at the blood ceremony when she started calling the fighters to be ranked. It makes no sense that she's calling it now, but maybe it's a part of other ceremonies, too. Other ceremonies that hopefully don't involve me killing any more people or dying myself.

In a slow brush backwards, the High Priestess removes her final veil to reveal the white porcelain mask that covers her face, just like the one that covers all the priestesses. Olivia, too, by now, I think. You can hear a pin drop as her watery blue eyes peer out at me from behind the smooth white mask, bordered by black counters. We stare at each other for what seems like forever before she reaches up quickly and rips the mask from her face.

A collective gasp goes up around us, so sharp that if it had happened indoors, all of the oxygen would have been sucked clean out of the room. I look up and no one—*no one*—not Jack, not Ryka, nor James or any other person, is looking at the High Priestess. Every single set of eyes are averted to the ground, some closed entirely. The women start crying again, but this time it's not showy wailing. It's gentle whimpers trapped behind bitten lips. They're frightened.

I turn and face the woman before me, determined not to let the town's reaction affect me. Tough, though, when the subject of their fear has a face like this woman's. To say it is ruined would be a kindness. A maze of violent scars crosshatch her face, angry and purple. Some look like they could be really old, but it's obvious none of them have been allowed to heal properly.

She lifts her hand high over her head and brings the mask down to the ground, hard. The impact is enough to shatter it into three jagged pieces. She doesn't say anything, just produces a knife, showing me the blade. Her pale blue eyes are on me when she draws that over her head, too. Suddenly I know what's happening. I have no time to figure out if I *want* it to happen. The knife slashes out like a cruel claw in the High Priestess' hand, and it scores me along the already brutally painful injury on my arm. It's inside me—a scream so great I feel like my teeth will work free if I let it out. I bite it back, but it's not only for fear of losing my teeth. If I made a sound, if I so much as flinch…

The old woman weighs me the same way I weighed Sam just now as I sit on the waves of pain pulsing through my body, begging me to cry out. All it would take is one small grimace and she will cast me out of the pit. But I can't. It's just not in me to purposefully fail a test like this. The High Priestess nods, grinning when I refuse to react. What have I done? I know what this means, even before she opens her mouth to call out one last time. I'm one of them now. I'm a fighter.

Her lips peel back, revealing a row of blackened teeth, and the High Priestess smiles. "Tamji!" she hollers. The word rocks through me to my very boots. Tamji. She's named me one of the higher-ranking fighters in Freetown. As the kickback of her announcement rides over the people still gathered by the pit, I feel faint. I must be mad. I escaped the Sanctuary and washed the blood from my hands only to find myself standing here, the death of another person on my conscience again.

"Who will stain your skin with the sacrifice of this man?" the High Priestess asks me. I stare at her gormlessly for a moment before I realise what she's saying. She wants me tattooed. I look up and see the only person I can bare the thought of touching me.

"Ryka," I say.

His eyes meet mine and the blood in my veins runs a little cold. He's never looked at me like this before—sad, angry and confused. He bites down, his jaw clenching. "No," he says quietly. "I won't do it."

"You have been nominated, boy," the High Priestess tells him. He glowers at me, still careful not to look at the High Priestess, and all the while the muscles in his body twitch, like he's considering turning on his heel and walking away. He doesn't, though. Jack nudges him in the back and Ryka reluctantly drops down into the pit. All the while, I'm sinking. Sinking into the pit floor, growing smaller and smaller under the furious heat emanating from him. I don't really notice when he reaches me. Don't notice him grabbing my hands in turn and firmly drumming the sharp point of a blackened blade into the hard bone underneath my wrists. It all happens in a blur, because my brain is still frozen on the moment when Ryka said no. The moment when he wanted to turn his back and walk away.

CHOOSE

A fever the likes of which I have never experienced before rips through me for the next six days. For the most part I'm unconscious, although occasionally I sense another presence in the tent with me. Funny how I can discern who stands over my bed just by the quality of their silence. Jack is pensive and paces, and August sits on a chair by my side, so incredibly quiet. From the complete lack of worry in the air whilst he is with me, I get the feeling he's asleep most of the time.

Ryka, on the other hand, hovers on the peripheries. The powerful tension that accompanies him whenever he visits puts me on edge, filling my restless dreams with shadows, drowning and ghosts of the dead. He never stays long.

The first time I wake properly a familiar woman is washing a cool cloth down my arms. It takes me a while but I eventually remember that I saw her once with Jack and James when I first arrived here. I can't recall her name, but her presence is soothing. She smiles at me when she sees my eyes are open. Doesn't say anything, but she draws the damp cloth over my forehead and I almost die from how good it feels. I drift back into unconsciousness on a peaceful cloud after that.

The second time I wake, things seem more real. The hazy edge that surrounded everything in my tent is gone, replaced with a crisp contrast that makes my eyes hurt. The sounds of Freetown are a soft hum, and somewhere I can hear the slow, rhythmic thwack and splinter of wood being chopped. I lay there in my bed for a good hour before the first strains of a panic attack start to develop inside me. Regardless of my wishes, my brain insists on playing out my fight with Sam, of his head cleaved neatly from his body. Ryka's face, over and over again, as he finished tattooing me and threw down the blade into the dirt, refusing to look at me as he hurdled out of the pit and disappeared into the night.

It feels like Sam's weight is still pressing down on my chest, and there's very little chance it's ever going to let up. A coward to the end, I swing my uncooperative body up in the bed and take my time in reaching underneath, trying to find the answer to this problem. My hand doesn't find anything.

Panic bolts through me as I pat my hand around, trying to locate it. Maybe it got kicked back out of reach. But when I find the strength to lower myself to my knees, swallowing down the dizziness that threatens to help me to the ground more permanently, it isn't there. My halo is gone.

Pacing is out of the question, so instead I drink the full tin mug of water I find by my bed, forcing it to stay down, and think. Where is it? Or, more importantly, who has it? I reach a conclusion pretty quickly—one that makes my hands hurt with how hard I clench them. It takes me a good ten minutes to slowly walk my way over to Jack's tent, and when I get there I don't hesitate. I've had time to get angry, and now I want answers. No one has the right to take my property from me, but it's more than that. He's taking a decision, my free will from me, too. I don't take the time to survey the huge camouflage tent I find myself in. I just move from room to room until I stumble upon Jack, sitting in a high-backed chair, reading.

He opens his mouth to speak but thinks better of it. Completely unsurprised, he points over his shoulder and turns back to his book, sending me in the right direction. Down a partitioned hallway, I find a canvas door tied loosely across an opening. I yank the tie open and stomp into the room. Ryka jumps, dropping the

215

water canister he was trying to stuff into a leather bag onto the bed.

"What?" he snaps, lowering his gaze.

"You know what. What are you doing?" I look at the bag in his hands and the answer seems obvious. "You're going back out into the forest, aren't you?"

He stays silent for a second, but then scowls. "What of it?"

"You're running away."

"I just need some space." He thrusts the water canister inside his bag and a light sweater follows after it.

"Give me back my halo, Ryka."

"I don't have it."

"Don't lie to me!" I stalk across his room, my legs threatening to bail on me with every step, and snatch the bag away from him. "It's not yours to take."

"I told you, I don't have it."

"Ryka!" I'm on the verge of screaming.

He tucks his hair behind his ears and then drags his hand back through it so it needs fixing again. The muscles in his jaw jump as he bites down and releases. "Why do you want it?"

"I don't want it. I *need* it."

"That's utter crap and you know it. You've been doing fine the past few weeks. Things don't change now."

My mouth falls open. "How can you say that? You were there. You saw what happened. I decapitated Sam, for crying out loud!"

"You had to. And besides, that's a good death in the pit."

"You can't possibly be defending what I did." My sheer disbelief doesn't make it into my voice, and I am completely monotone. "You were angry with me, Ryka. You couldn't even look at me!"

"That's because I was petrified! I didn't know how to react. You fell in the damned pit. You fell in the—" He drags his hands through his hair again, and then grips his hands together behind his head, shielding himself with his elbows. "I've never had a reason to be that that scared before, okay? And then you went and killed Sam. You're a Tamji now. You know what that means? Every single match, you can be called to fight, and I'm going to be standing up there on the pit wall feeling exactly how I did the second your back hit sacred ground. So, yeah, I couldn't look at you." He catches me off guard and snatches back the bag. "And now I need some space."

He goes to move around me but I grab hold of his arm. "You don't think I feel the same way when I think about you fighting? Why do you think I was even there in the first place, Ryka? I couldn't bear not knowing what was happening to you." I'm too angry to be surprised that I'm admitting this to him—to myself, to anyone else standing within in a mile wide radius. "Now tell me, if you had a chance to not feel like that, if you could just be numb to all of it, wouldn't you take that chance?"

His eyebrows pinch together, and he looks…hurt. "No, Kit. I wouldn't take it."

"Why not?" I try and see the sense in feeling so much pain and worry.

"Because." He sighs. "Life isn't just fear and horror all the time, y'know? The sweet moments are usually worth the suffering you go through along the way."

I laugh sharply. "I haven't had many sw—"

Ryka's quick when he steps towards me, and I'm surprised when his strong hand cups the back of my neck. He pulls me to him so our chests meet, our hips and our legs. His brown eyes are sad when he leans forward and presses his lips to mine. It's a gentle kiss, lingering and so much sweeter than I ever imagined it would be. My very first kiss. My body seems to know what it's doing, no matter how little experience I have in this area, and before I know what I'm doing I'm kissing him back. He huffs slightly as I lean into him, cautiously reaching up my hand to carry out something I've denied myself for too long. I touch my fingertips lightly over his hair and brush it back out of his face. There's a second when I think he's about to pull away and I can't help but exhale in a sigh.

That seems to light a fire in him. He drops the bag to the floor and buries his hands into my hair, locking hold of my head. The kiss deepens. Breathing suddenly doesn't seem that important when it comes to deciding between a fresh lungful of air and letting Ryka go. I never knew my heart could pump this fast. It goes even faster when he steps me back and I sag onto the bed. He never releases his hold on me. As he positions himself over me, careful to keep his weight off my chest, the pressure from his mouth increases and mine opens in response. His tongue works its way past my lips, and the shock of the sensation, warm and sweet and intense, feels like a jolt of electricity firing through my body. I let out a surprised groan and Ryka responds. I've never experienced anything like this. The sensation is pure and deeply personal, connecting us together in a way I didn't even know could happen. My hands move of their own accord and I find myself clinging onto Ryka. Clinging onto him like I will fall straight through his bed otherwise. His tongue moves in languorous sweeps over mine, and it's natural that I follow his lead. The muscles in his arms flex as he lowers himself just enough that I feel the satisfying weight of him on me, but then he pulls back.

Too breathless to say anything, I just lie there staring up at him with my lips still parted, feeling awestruck. *Damn.* Ryka stares back at me, his brown eyes half concealed by his lowered eyelids. Three seconds pass before he clears his throat. He sits back and perches on the edge of his bed, his back to me. I don't know what I imagined ever happening between the two of us, but it wasn't this. To share something like that and then have him so far away feels wrong. I sit up beside him, our shoulders pressing together, and he sighs. I open my mouth but he shakes his head.

"Don't. You're going to say something snarky or rude, and you shouldn't. I want you to sit here and think about what just happened, Kit. How it felt." His shoulders round in on his body a little, and he seems momentarily self-conscious, which is ridiculous. The great Mashinji Ryka, abashed. The laws of physics will be disintegrating next. He angles his body towards me and leans forward. I'm a statue, too astonished by the last three minutes to do anything other than remain upright as he presses his forehead against mine. Up this close, the smell of him, that wild outdoor scent that is all forest and river and Jada and freedom, rushes my senses and fills me up to bursting.

"You asked me if I would numb out the bad feelings, and I said no. This is why. Because, for me, the possibility that we could be...this," he hesitates before he laces his fingers through mine. "The possibility that there could be something bright, something to look forward to for both of us, after all the suffering and death—it fills me with hope. And it gets better, Kit. It's not just how kissing you feels. It would get so much better than that, I promise you."

He lets go of my hand and moves silently over to the small chest of drawers beside his bed. The top drawer makes a grating sound as he pulls it open and takes out one of his black shirts. He unravels it onto his pillow. The battered silver circle of my halo tumbles out and lies there, glinting in the semi-darkness. He picks it up warily, as though the naked metal is going to burn him. He holds it out, but when I go to take it from him he doesn't let go. We both remain there, him standing, me sitting on his bed, joined together by our fingers looped through the collar.

"It wasn't up to you when they put this on you. You wearing this was something they *did* to you. If you put it back on, they're winning, okay? And you're letting them. You say this is your choice, Kit, and you're right. I'm begging you not to choose this. Choose something else. Choose the possibility that there could be something else worth feeling all the bad stuff for. Choose me."

He uncurls his fingers and lets the halo go. I grip onto it tightly, only because I need something to hold onto, something solid that will keep me grounded. Ryka gives me a small smile, his eyes sadder than ever, and then he picks up his bag and goes.

MEETING

I spend hours sitting in Ryka's room doing exactly what he told me to do. I replay our interaction from the second I stormed in through the door— how angry I was— to the moment he left, trying to work out where I stand now that a whole other bunch of thoughts and screwy feelings have been thrown into the mix. There doesn't seem to be enough nouns for all the emotions I'm experiencing. Sadness, happiness, anger, annoyance, elation: the different strands of sensation are like a rainbow of colours all churning together inside me to create something wholly muddy and unattractive. I'm sure there isn't a name for this. For now, until I learn otherwise, I have officially termed my state of being as 'Ick'.

Jack comes to find me later. Much later, after I've fallen asleep on Ryka's bed. It seemed like an okay thing to do, seeing as he left me sitting here in the first place. The old man smiles briefly when I wake with a start. The smile dims when he sees my halo lying next to me on the bed. "So August figured it out, then? He's skilled, but I didn't think this would be within his capabilities."

"It wasn't," I mumble, trying to shake off my sleep. "He said there were others from the Sanctuary who knew how the halos worked. They helped."

"Oh." The bed creaks, the wood complaining, when Jack sits down heavily next to me. "And what are you planning on doing with it now, Kit?"

He might as well just come straight out with it and ask me if I intend on shackling the thing around my neck again. I glare down at the halo with my hands clasped in my lap, not willing to blink. "I don't know."

"That's okay. Not knowing means you're considering your options, doesn't it? At least you're not blindly rushing to get it back on without even mulling over the alternatives."

I smile, a warped, ugly-feeling thing on my face. He's giving me far too much credit.

"How are you feeling?" he asks.

"I don't know." That's all I'm good for saying right now. Olivia could have probably got a few other syllables out of me, but with her gone I'm feeling pretty flat. "Was the High Priestess annoyed that I didn't fight in the last two days of the matches?"

Jack grunts and looks up at the ceiling of the tent, a burnt orange colour from the lamp he brought in with him. "How could she be? You were delirious. If a fighter can't remain conscious for more than thirty seconds, there's little that even the High Priestess can do about that."

"She's made me Tamji so she can kill me off, hasn't she?" I ask.

Jack scratches at his grizzly white stubble and grunts again. "Likely. We'll work that one out. In the meantime, Ryka won't be back for a couple of days, child. You're more than welcome to stay here if you like."

Surprised by the offer, I'm stuck for what to say. "I don't think so, Jack. But thank you." Sleeping in Ryka's bed would be weird.

Jack laughs. "I meant in Olivia's room. She won't be needing it, after all." There's a hint of bitterness in his voice, although he seems resigned to the fact that his granddaughter is gone. I haven't really processed it. Everyone else has had six days to come to terms with her absence, while I've been spinning around my bed in a catatonic daze. "The choice is yours," Jack says. More choices for me. Great. He rises from the bed and stretches his back. "Shame Ry's not here. We're having a meeting up at the big tent tonight and he's going to be annoyed he missed it. I think you should be there, Kit. Out of everyone, you need to be there."

"What's the meeting for?" I don't like the tone in his voice. Something big has happened, I can tell.

"Just come along, Kit. We're going to be discussing a topic that you're uniquely equipped to provide insight on." He shuffles out the room and leaves me on Ryka's bed, but suddenly it doesn't seem so okay that I'm here.

******

I go to check on Jack later, but he's already made his way up to the meeting. The meeting that he told me nothing about, other than I would want to be there. I really don't want to be there, not one bit. But that doesn't stop me trudging through the mud, skirting around the night fires of some of Freetown's more secluded residents. I'm weak and feel like my bones are made of straw, so my progress is frustratingly slow. It takes a while to reach the massive tent where Jack and the others are waiting, and by the time I get there I'm feeling distinctly unwell. My arm is throbbing like there's too much blood being forced into it. Like it might be on its way to falling off. I haven't even looked under the fresh bandages for fear that gangrene has set in.

Voices ring out into the stillness of the night as I approach the tent, and I think about turning around and going straight back home. That seems pointless now that I've dragged myself here, however. I chew on the inside of my cheek, swallowing down nerves as I push back the tent flap and try to sneak inside without anyone noticing. Unfortunately for me the sound of voices I heard wasn't the hum of a large crowd; it was five people shouting. Their argument stops mid-yell as everyone turns to look at me. Jack and James' faces are sketched in dramatic shadows as they lean into the fire, their elbows resting on their knees, and the woman from before, the one who washed me down, angles her head towards me, softly smiling. The other two men, one portly with ruddy cheeks, the other slim as one of the support posts holding up the tent, scrutinise me with sharp eyes.

"Welcome, Kit," Jack says.

"She's the one you told us about?" Tent Pole asks. His face crinkles as he squints at me. It looks like he's trying to figure out what I am. "*She* killed Sam?"

A hot stripe flares across my cheeks like I've been struck. "Yeah, I did," I say. No point in avoiding what I did to Sam. A whole lot of people saw it happen, anyway.

Jack gets up and collects a chair from the ever-present stack on the left hand side of the room, then sets it down next to him. "Join us, child. We need your expertise."

I frown but do as he suggests, sitting down beside him. This close to a fire indoors, I don't feel warmed. I feel like I'm in hell, unlucky enough to have received an invite to the very front row, right next to the furnaces.

"This is Alistair." Jack points to the chubby man, who inclines his head to me politely. He barely seems to even care that I'm here. "And this is Bartholomew." I feel like sticking to Tent Pole in my head, as Jack introduces the skinny man. He doesn't smile at me. Doesn't offer out his hand. There's something spiteful about the narrow way he picks me over, something calculating. I find myself not liking him very much.

"Now that Kit's here, we can ask her a little more about the Sanctuary. From there we can discuss this matter knowing our chances of success. Ella, you can begin."

Ella, the woman whose name I struggled to remember earlier, shifts in her chair, and the sound of small chiming bells fills the tent. Smiling, she turns to me. "Kit, I'm so pleased you're feeling a little better. How is your arm?"

I shrug. "It throbs."

"That's good. Means it's healing. It'll start to itch soon. That's when you'll know you're well on your way to recovery."

I offer her a weak smile, not so sure I'm as pleased about the prospect of itching as she is. "Thank you for taking caring of me," I tell her.

"Think nothing of it. Anyway, we were wondering if you would be able to tell us of your escape from the Sanctuary, Kit. If you could recount your experience from leaving your home to meeting up with Ryka and finding your way to Freetown, we would be most appreciative."

There doesn't seem to be any harm in telling her the story, so I do, leaving out a few key factors. I don't tell them about how terrified I was when I thought I was going to drown. And I don't tell them about fighting Ryka, either. They listen intently as I recount details about the closed-in fences surrounding the river, and how I was swept away with the floodwater from the rain. Ella frowns with concern when I tell them how I vomited endless on my knees with no one but Jada to keep my company, before I came across Ryka for the second time. Everyone else just sits, taking in the story. No one interrupts. By the time I'm done, I feel sort of stupid. The story doesn't seem very impressive now that I look back on it. Leaving the Sanctuary without a plan, nearly drowning, only to be swiftly followed up by nearly poisoning myself to death with contaminated water. Not the grand tale of escape I would have preferred it to be. Without Ryka's intervention, I probably would still be wandering around the forest, or maybe I would have been snared by one of Jack's traps. I stare at my feet, now beyond caring how dirty my boots are, and listen to the silence that follows. It doesn't last long.

"It sounds like this fence is pretty well maintained," James offers. He's wearing a very full knife belt in comparison to my paltry three blades. They flash as he leans back and crosses his legs at the ankle. "There's a chance we could go down there and cut a way through, but that would negate the 'softly softly' approach."

"Wait, you're going into the Sanctuary?" I gasp.

"We'll explain in a moment," Jack tells me. James ignores my interruption and cracks his neck.

"I still think we're better off sending a two-man team. We could go through the river just as Kit did. That way, the Sanctuary municipality won't be alerted to our presence."

"But getting twenty or thirty people out that way would be impossible," Alastair adds. "A pathway should be cut through the fence where it enters the tree line close to the aqueduct. The breach will be much harder to detect that way."

"I agree," Ella says, straightening out her skirts. "The element of surprise is key here. With such a time sensitive matter on our hands, it would be easy to charge blindly into the city before we're too late. Yet, a subtle entrance is of the utmost importance if we're to accomplish our goal."

I glance around the room, my eyes as wide as they will go. "Which is?"

Jack pats my knee, but everyone else pretends I haven't even opened my mouth.

"I still think this is madness," Bartholomew says. "Who are we to get involved in the Sanctuary's dealings, anyway? They've been aware of Freetown for decades. We receive much-needed trade from them that we'd be hard-pressed to manage without during the wintertime. It's foolishness to bite the hand that feeds us."

Jack stiffens next to me. "The Sanctuary does *not* feed Freetown, brother. I won't have it said that they do. We've been an independent entity for as many years as I care to remember."

"And yet who do we get our wheat from when the ground is frozen solid, Jack? The beets for our livestock? The materials to make our clothes?"

"And where do they get their weaponry for that carnival of a performance they call an amphi-match each month?" James snaps. "This isn't about food for the people of Freetown to you, Bartholomew. It's about the money that lines your pockets. The Sanctuary's money. Tell me, what have you been spending all your currency on within Freetown's limits? The real men living in this town trade in blood and sweat, not gold and silk."

Bartholomew rocks in his chair, hissing under his breath. His fury practically pours off him. From the other side of the fire, I almost admire the way James doesn't even blink at the string of curse words that pour out of the thin man's mouth. "You're a fighter, James. I don't expect you to understand that there are ways to make a living with your mind in place of ending the lives of your fellow town's folk."

James' eyes flash murder, still fixed on the burning fire. "And you are a coward, my friend. I don't expect you to understand that there is honour to be had in making a living with your hands, either in the fields or in the pit, instead of hiding away behind your dusty stacks of papers. But let me tell you this: any time you begin to imagine you can *out-think* me with that big old brain of yours, whatever the venue, please feel free to try and prove it."

"Gentlemen, now is not the time!" Jack runs his hands back through his hair. "Bartholomew, I appreciate that your business will suffer if the Sanctuary discover we have a hand in any part in any of this, but unfortunately that is not what we are here to debate. It's already decided that we will intervene. Right now, we are trying to determine *how*."

Bartholomew's chair creaks as he rises, his stretched out shadow drawing tall and thin on the opposite wall. "I see that the republic is fallen," he mutters. "Good evening, gentlemen."

"The republic is hardly fallen because you can't get your own way, you stupid man," Alastair snaps. He grabs hold of Bartholomew's sleeve and tugs hard so that the frail man falls off balance and lands back in his seat. "Don't cut your nose off to spite your face. There are lives at stake here."

My head starts swimming at this comment. "Whose lives are at stake? Can someone please tell me what all this is about!" My voice rises to a strangled shout, and finally, *finally*, people pay attention.

Ella *tsks* and reaches out to take my hand. The contact is obviously meant to reassure me but just puts me on edge. I tolerate it, though, as she says, "It appears there are some people within the Sanctuary's limits who are in danger of being terminated. The municipality have found out about the cells operating across the city. They know there are somewhere between twenty to thirty individuals whose halos aren't functioning. Right now they have technicians sweeping the city, trying to locate them. It's been decided that we need to step in and help them escape before they are discovered. That's why anything you can give us about the layout of the Sanctuary, as well as access points in and out of the fences, will be a massive help. The information could be vital in saving those people."

I grip hold of my chair until my hands hurt. The burning in my arm gets infinitely worse as my body tenses. "How do you know this?"

"The radio broadcasts," Jacks says. "I told you when you arrived here that we listen to the amphi-match reports. That's not the only thing we pick up. On a daily basis we hear all the radio communication that takes place within the Sanctuary."

My stomach clenches. "So this is real. They're going to kill those people?"

He nods. Cai's face forces its way into my mind. All I can think about is the fact that some of those people were the ones who helped him, protected him, taught him how to camouflage himself in amongst the unfeeling populous. How to survive. "We definitely have to help them," I say. "I have to go with you."

An amused smile tugs at the corner of James' mouth, but no one else finds my statement entertaining.

"That's not happening, child. All we need from you is the information. Like Ella said, anything you can—"

Jack gets cut off when I leap to my feet. "I'm not asking, okay. I have to help. I know the Sanctuary like the back of my hand, every back alley and shortcut through the place. I can't explain that in enough detail, and you aren't going to want to find your way around with a map if the technicians are combing the city, are you?"

Jack huffs out a deep breath and plants his hands on his knees. "You're not going, Kit. Now, you can either help us in this manner, or we can rely on what I remember myself. Which is it going to be?"

"What? You've been inside the Sanctuary?"

Another nod from the old man. "I was like you once. I found a way out and I took it, but that was forty years ago. Things will have changed since then. I don't want to send my people off on an already dangerous mission with old information if we have perfectly good, reliable data to replace it. Will you help us?"

My jaw practically hits the dirt. So that's why Jack has always been sympathetic towards my halo-wearing tendencies. Or at least given me room to consider that I might want to put it back on at some point. He knows how hard it is to deal with the onslaught of fresh emotion because he, himself, has been in my shoes. He used to wear a halo. "Yes," I whisper. "Yes, I'll help you."

"Thank you."

We spend the next hour talking over potential points of entry into the city, and not much is decided. I tell them everything I can but somehow it doesn't seem enough. When we disband for the night, it feels like my legs are rough-hewn rock, heavy to lift and unsteady. Jack lingers behind to talk with Alastair and the rest of us go our separate ways. I'm halfway back to my tent when I realise I'm not as alone as I thought. I freeze beside the copse of silver birch that marks the track leading back to my new home, and listen.

"James," I say out loud.

"You have good ears, Kit. Not much of an advantage in an eight by eight pit, but still, useful." The man himself steps out from the shadows and leans against a tree trunk, absentmindedly chewing on a stalk of grass. He takes it out of his mouth and points it at me. "I thought you and I should have a small discussion."

"About what?" I don't trust him. James has a power-hungry motive for everything, from endlessly working to persuade Jack to let women fight in the pits, to killing off Ryka's father. There has to be some such motive now.

"So distrustful," he smiles.

"You shouldn't have cut off my hair if you wanted me to trust you," I tell him.

"It hasn't occurred to you that I was only trying to help?"

"I doubt that."

The hint of a smile plays across his face. "And I know why. You'd have to be blind to miss what's going on between you and Ryka. From an outsiders' perspective it must be hard to understand how he can have forgiven me for killing his father. But he understands how things are. Freetown's is a harsh reality, but it's ours. People die here. And there's always someone on the other end of the offending blade, right?"

"It's not like that, James, and you know it. It was premeditated. You planned the whole thing with the priestesses!"

He shrugs, but his eyes pierce into me, fierce and challenging. "I never said the priestesses were involved. And are you saying you never strategized in order to win your matches in the Colosseum? Were none of the men and women you killed on the arena floor mothers or fathers?"

Bile leaps up and stings the back of my throat. I fought and killed people of all ages before, when I was under the influence of my halo, and goodness knows the Sanctuary often expected Falin to have children. I look away, mortified that he is probably right. "Just—what are you doing following me, James?"

"You wouldn't believe me if I told you."

"Try me."

"I know Ryka has been watching over you if you're out at night alone. He's not here right now, so I was simply seeing you home safely."

I pull myself up, my hands automatically going to the daggers in my belt. "You don't need to do that."

Focusing on where my hands rest, he steps towards me. "I just wanted to make sure Joshua and his loutish friends didn't chance upon you in a dark corner, girl. My apologies." He goes to turn away, but I call out after him.

"I'm not your responsibility, James."

He smirks over his shoulder. "So the Gods are merciful, after all."

"I'm not Ryka's responsibility either. I can take perfectly good care of myself." I expect James to laugh, but he doesn't.

"I saw you in the pit. I know exactly who you are and what you're capable of." He goes quiet, just staring at me. I shift uneasily and point my thumb over my shoulder.

"I'm going home. You should, too."

He nods, still watching me over his shoulder. "When you locate Ryka, tell him to come and see me. We're going to need to discuss how we're breaking into your old hometown."

"What?" No way is Ryka getting involved in this. It's dangerous, and with that temper of his he wouldn't have a hope of concealing his emotions once he got inside. "That's not a good idea."

"I don't make the rules."

"Well, if he's going, then so am I!"

"You'll have to convince Jack before that happens. I somehow don't think he's going to change his mind any time soon."

I cringe, knowing that what I'm about to say is going to cost me, if not monetarily then definitely in pride. "You could talk to him."

"I can't do that."

"Why not?"

"Because you're not my responsibility." The corner of his mouth twitches like he wants to smile.

I growl, clenching my hands into fists. Gods, this man is difficult. "Please! I—I guess I would owe you."

James' body language changes fractionally, and his smile finally develops. "I see. And you would repay my favour without complaint when I asked it of you?"

"I'm not...I'm not doing anything...*weird* with you, before you even think—"

James barks out a sharp burst of laughter, tipping his head back so that his Adam's apple bobs up and down. "I don't want to have sex with, you strange girl. I've never struggled finding willing participants for that. No, perhaps I'll just ask something of you one day. It will be nothing more than a simple yes."

I scan his facial expression, looking for anything nefarious. It's a pointless task, given that *everything* about James seems potentially nefarious. He's just so confusing. Is being able to go back into the Sanctuary with Ryka, to keep him safe, to repay some of the debt I owe to Cai by helping his friends, worth this deal? Feels like a deal with the devil. I swallow and do my best to shove the niggling *Don't You Do It!* out of my head.

"Fine."

"Wonderful."

"When am I going to have to agree to this 'something'?"

James tosses the grass stem from his mouth and shoves his hands in his pockets, evaporating into the darkness. "Oh, don't worry. It will be very obvious when the time comes."

COMPETITION

Somehow, James makes good on his word, and Jack comes to find me two days later. "You can go, but on one condition," he says, holding up his index finger.

I'm too relieved to object. "Anything."

"You do whatever James and Ryka tell you. And you don't do anything rash that might compromise the plan."

"That's two conditions," I say.

"Two very good, reasonable conditions." Jack frowns at me. "Can you do that? Can you take direction without fighting them every step of the way?"

How Jack knows me this well is a mystery. "Of course I can."

He grumbles but takes me at my word. "I've made contact with one of the cells. The old man in charge, he has a plan to get his people out that might actually work with your help."

"Opa?" I ask. It can only be him.

Jack nods. "You know him?"

"No. But my friend did."

Jack misses my edgy expression. He put his hand on my shoulder. "There's been a lot of movement in the forest today. Ry will be back before lunchtime, mark my words. You should be ready to go. Pack nothing but water and food."

And knives, I think to myself. *Really sharp knives.* With Jack, that probably goes without saying. He hugs me brusquely and leaves, and I go about boiling up enough water to last two days hike through the forest. My bag is packed when Ryka appears around noon, just as Jack said he would.

He stands in the doorway to my tent, awkward and silent, and for a while I pretend I haven't noticed him, even though I have. I just don't know what I'm supposed to say. Our last conversation nearly blew my head off, and I've not come anywhere close to untangling the mess I've made out of everything in his absence. In the end he just comes in and sits down on the edge of my bed as I gather up my stuff. "Did you enjoy your space?" I ask him. It feels kind of petty to be sharp with him but I've felt a little abandoned since he left. After what happened, I don't know, I guess I thought he would want to stick around. He gives me a crooked smile that seems out of place combined with the troubled frown he wears.

"Sometimes, Kit, you can put as much space as you like between yourself and a problem and it won't make a blind bit of difference."

I automatically go to touch my neck but manage to still my hand halfway. I rub the heel of my palm into my solar plexus, wanting the subtle ache there to leave. I have a feeling it's more of an emotional pain than physical ailment, however. "Is that what I am? A problem?"

Ryka closes his eyes and shakes his head slowly. "Not you. Just...everything."

"Oh. Well I could have tried to fix *me* as a problem, but *everything*? That might be a little difficult." I find a small smile for him when he looks up at me. He looks so different without the whole bravado thing keeping his back straight and that cocky grin on his face. Now, he looks a little lost. Confused, just like me. I dump my bag on the floor and note how our roles have reversed since the last time we were together. Him sitting on my bed instead of the other way around, and me getting ready to leave with a bag in my hand. The only difference is that this time, when I go, he's coming with me.

"Are you sure you want to do this?" he asks quietly.

I glance up at him as I pluck Cai's holostick out from underneath my pillow. He flinches and I'm quick enough to catch it. "Yes, I need to. I owe it to those people. Cai wouldn't have made it as far as—" The more I speak, the more Ryka flinches. I straighten, trying to figure out what the hell is wrong with him. "Are you okay?"

He looks away. "Yeah. I just… *Cai…*"

"What about him?"

"It's hard to compete with him, y'know. He has the unfair advantage of being so very *dead*. No one remembers the negatives about people who've kicked it. I'm still very much alive and making mistakes on a daily basis." He stares down at his hands, his hair in his eyes, and I can't help but acknowledge how badly I'm itching to touch him.

"Why do you think you're competing with Cai?" I whisper.

"Because—" He exhales sharply, cracking his knuckles. "You carry that trinket around with you like it's your most prized possession. You fought me to get it back, remember. Every time I see you it's in your hand. Kind of says a lot."

I look down at the holostick, as he said, clenched firmly in my hand. I had no idea he would think of it like that. "I'm sorry," I breathe. "I don't feel that way about Cai. You were right when you said I didn't know him. I just feel so ashamed and guilty all the time. He made a huge sacrifice so I could live, and *I* keep messing everything up, too."

"You haven't messed anything up," he says quietly.

"Really? Cai died so I could feel, so I could escape the Sanctuary and be free of the Colosseum. And where am I now? I've landed myself in the pit, fighting again, except this time I'm awake and I know exactly how horrifying it all is. I'd say that's pretty much the stupidest thing I could have done with the gift he gave me."

Ryka doesn't say anything for a while. He tilts his head as he stares down at his boots and I can't help but focus on the tensed muscles in his shoulders and his neck. The teenager in him seems to be burning off faster and faster every day. He takes a deep breath and finally looks up at me. There's a smile on his face, but his eyes are desperately sad. "So your heart's not broken over a dead guy. That must mean you're head over heels in love with me by now, then, right?"

I laugh, because that's what he needs me to do, although I sense a hint of seriousness in his question. A hint I laugh off nervously. "I'm afraid I probably wouldn't realise it even if I was in love with someone," I tell him quietly. "I have no point of reference to go off."

"Oh, you'll know when the time comes, Kit." Ryka's voice is soft and gentle, so intense. His eyes scour every part of my face and it's the most invasive thing I've ever experienced. I'm addicted to how confronting he can feel. Like he's daring me to look away, but he and I both know that I won't.

"How will I know?" I murmur.

Ryka stops studying the features of my face and locks his gaze with mine. His eyes are piercing when he leans forward and closes the gap between us. "You'll feel breathless," he whispers. Typical that I can't find any oxygen as he says this. He takes my hand and slowly places it on his chest, tracing his fingers carefully over mine. "Your heart will race whenever you're around the other person. It'll burn and feel like it's trying to swell out of your chest. You'll feel like you're brimming over with how much you want to take care of them. Protect them from anyone and anything. Like there's nothing in this world you wouldn't do to keep them safe." Ryka leans closer so that his lips are mere centimetres away from mine. "You'll spend all day every day imagining ways to make them smile. Imagining what their lips feel like on yours. Imagining ways to make them agree to fall as stupidly and painfully in love with you as you have with them."

His voice catches and I can feel his heart thundering underneath my hand. I'm glad he can't feel how mine is matching his beat for beat. I swallow and try to tear my eyes from his but I can't. I feel everything he just described, but I'm too cowardly to ever admit it. I do the next best thing and take the final step, until there's no space left between us. My chest presses against his, my hand trapped in between our bodies, and Ryka seems to hum.

"You'll know, Kit," he breathes, and then he reaches up and cups the back of my neck, pressing his lips to mine. Our second kiss is just as powerful as our first, and I end up curving into him as he holds onto me tight. I'm limp and weak when he finally lets me go.

"It's almost time to leave," he says, clearing his throat. "There's no point in trying to talk you out of this, is there?"

"No."

"Didn't think so." He gazes straight through the tough canvas of my tent wall as though he can see the trees and the river on the other side. "Are you worried?" he asks me. "About the river?" That's what Jack and the others decided—that we should go back the way I came, through the tunnel. I haven't been thinking about it.

"Not really," I lie.

"Will you let me help you this time?" He looks solemn enough that I know he's not trying to be a hero. I let the fixed smile fall from my face and nod slowly.

"That... would be good."

He nods too, apparently satisfied, and collects my hand from his chest, linking his fingers with mine. Even after the last time we held hands when we walked to the Tamji beach, this contains a whole new level of gentleness I wouldn't have thought Ryka capable of. He watches me studying him; I'm intrigued by the way his skin looks so tanned next to my paleness.

"You have a lot of scars," he whispers.

I hadn't even thought about that. I do have a lot of scars. When in the business of knife fighting, you end up with more than you can count. "Yeah, I'm...I'm sorry," I mumble, trying to pull my hand back. I must look like a freak to him.

He lets out a half-hearted laugh. "What are you sorry for?"

"I don't know. Girls here, they're different than me. They wear dresses. They have flowers in their hair, the whole music when they walk bit."

"You don't make any noise when you walk, Kit."

"I know. I'm never going to be like them," I say.

He analyses my face and draws my hand up to his mouth, gingerly pressing his lips against each one of my imperfect knuckles. "I don't want you to be like them. You are who you are. There's no hidden agendas, no games."

I feel my breath catch in my chest as I breathe out. I have no idea how to describe this feeling inside me, but it's a long way from 'Ick'. It's about as far away from 'Ick' as I can get. I swallow as he kisses my hand again.

"*Ryka.*"

"Just tell me if you're going to put it back on, okay? Tell me so I can prepare. I couldn't bear running into you without any warning if you decided to wear it again."

I have no clue what he's talking about for a second. When I realise, my throat closes up at how earnest he sounds. "I'm not going to wear it again," I whisper.

He drops his head and closes his eyes. "Please. Promise me," he says.

My heart pounding again, I do it. "I promise."

"Thank you," he murmurs. "I made you a promise, too. I'm going to keep it."

It's not just how kissing you feels. It would get so much better than that, I promise you.

Suddenly I don't want the halo anywhere near me. I don't want to be able to renege on the vow I just made. I push away from Ryka and rifle through my bag until I find what I'm looking for. Clasping onto the halo, I take hold of Ryka's hand in my free one and pull him out of the tent. "Where are we going?" he says, half laughing. "We have to get moving if we're going to be at the boundary fence by nightfall."

"This won't take a second." I guide him down a path that is much easier to see in daylight, and we end up back at the place where he let me in on his secret. Outside the rear of his tent, I gesture for him to jump down the drop like last time, but this time I don't follow. He smiles up at me, his hair falling loose from his small ponytail.

"I thought you weren't like other girls," he laughs.

"I thought just this once, maybe—" I don't need to say anything else. He takes hold of my waist in firm hands and lifts me carefully down to the pebbly shoreline of the river. This would be the perfect moment to kiss again, but I'm suddenly shy and I duck away from him, biting my lip. "Here," I say, holding out the halo to him. He looks down at it and then shakes his head.

"No. It has to be you."

He's right, of course, but I still shake when I pace up to the fast-running water. Can I do this? Can I cast my security net away and never have it back? It's one thing deciding not to wear it, but it's been under my bed this whole time, a back-up just in case. I run my fingers along the metal, knowing its every dint and scratch. Ryka comes and stands right behind me, so close I can feel his warm breath on the back of my neck. For the first time I'm glad my hair is short. When his hands find my hips and he leans into my neck, I know I am in for some major trouble. Electricity fires through me as his lips whisper against my skin. "You don't have to do this, you know. If you're not ready."

But I am ready. I don't need the halo now. I'm going to try and let Ryka be my safety net, which is as terrifying a thought as it is wonderful. I swing back and fling the collar through the air with as much force as I can muster. The two of us watch from the bank as it loses its fight with gravity and begins to fall, barely splashing at all as it lands in the deepest part of the river.

"You know I'm not diving for that, right?" he says into my ear.

I nod my head, enjoying his proximity. "I don't want you to."

"You two paint a pretty picture," a sharp voice says from behind us. Ryka stiffens, and I place my hands over his, stacked on my stomach. I don't want him to turn around, but in the end we have to.

James' grin looks particularly wide as he leans against a tree trunk, kicking his boots at the earth. "Sorry to ruin the moment, lovers, but we need to leave. There'll be plenty of time for that when we get back." He laughs a little too hard, and I have to fight back the urge to bound up the riverbank and smack him right in his smug face. From the tension in Ryka's shoulders, he feels the same way. We follow James back through the copse of trees to my tent without a word. From there, we meet up with Callum, Max, and another boy I don't know. He is introduced as Raff, and turns out to be the twins' cousin. He does have their dark colouring, but his eyes are a startling green and he's a clear foot taller than either of them. Jack comes out to see us off, and he does his best to hide his smile when he sees my hand interlinked with Ryka's.

"Good luck to you," he says. I get the feeling it's not just our trip to the Sanctuary that he's wishing us well for.

******

The trek back to the aqueduct takes eight hours. Eight hours of running that nearly kills me, with my arm throbbing fiercely and my stomach threatening to purge everything in it. My lack of exercise over the past few weeks apparently hasn't done me any favours. We arrive at the same spot where I crossed through originally, and everything is much the same. Maybe this is its normal state: white water rushing the brickwork in a fierce torrent; foreboding, slick, black water.

"Bad memories," Ryka mutters. "You realise your lips were blue when you climbed out of here last time. Freaked me out."

"You're not helping," I tell him, shooting him a nervous glance. He really isn't. My panic levels are at an all-time high. I inch back from the bank and slump down, not wanting to think about the river or drowning or turning blue. There'll be time for that soon enough. Ryka says something about freshening up and disappears into the forest. James and the other boys pore over the map Ella drew for them based on my detailed descriptions of the Sanctuary. I don't need to look at a map to recall the streets of my childhood; they're all stored in clinical little boxes inside my head, unsullied in comparison to how my Freetown memories have been jammed away. Probably has a lot to do with the emotions tied to each and every moment I've spent there, when I didn't feel a thing in the Sanctuary. Not really.

I flop onto my back and rest my hands on my stomach. There are stars visible through the canopy of the trees, distant pinpricks of light that have never caused me to so much as give them a second glance. Now I find myself wondering what else is up there amongst the deepening bruised blue of the approaching night.

"Mind if I join you?" Max interrupts my thoughts of space and the universe and all the things I don't understand. I'm grateful; my world seems to get bigger and bigger every day and I'm in danger of being overwhelmed. Things were easier when it was just the Colosseum and the Sanctuary's boundary walls. I prop myself up a little as Max joins me, brushing his hair back out of his face. He looks different, although his smile is still mischievous. Maybe it's just the way he tucks his hands into his pockets as he sits down beside me that makes him seem more reserved.

"Do you think we're going to be able to sneak these people out?" he asks.

"I can't say. Maybe. If everything goes according to plan."

Max nods. "Tomorrow night, James says there's a match?"

"Yup. We're meeting the cell leaders there. Jack organised it with Opa apparently. It'll be less conspicuous if we all make a break for it while everyone is walking home. With that many people on the streets, no one will notice such a big group together."

Max nods. "Makes sense. Aren't there going to be technicians everywhere, though?"

"Probably. We just have to do our best to stay out of sight."

"How do we do that?"

I think about this long and hard. "Act indifferent to absolutely everything and everyone."

"So pretend to be dead inside?"

This is a startling statement, but it's true. I don't say anything. Max falls quiet, picking at his bootlaces. "Have you, uh—"

"What?"

He grimaces, but then says, "Have you been up to the Keep at all?"

A hot flush runs through my body. "No, I haven't. I was sick and then—" I trail off, trying to find a way to word why I haven't been up there trying to find Olivia. Max does it for me.

"There didn't seem any point?"

I nod. "She made her choice. She wanted us to respect it. I can't seem to forgive her for leaving, though."

"*You* can't?" he snorts. "I've always known what she intended to do, but it seemed so far away on the horizon. And then all of a sudden she's come of age and they're accepting her. And I'm—"

"Marrying Simone?"

His head tips up and down robotically. I clear my throat and give up on lying down altogether. "Why did you do it, Max? I know you love her. So why did you Claim someone else?"

It takes a long time for Max to respond. He just sits there, very still, staring at my boots like they hold the answers to all his problems. "I guess—" he swallows and blinks for the first time in minutes. "I guess I wanted to make her see what was happening. I thought if it was a reality—that she was going away and I was going to be with someone else—she would realise she was making a mistake. I didn't even think Simone would say yes. I didn't ask her. Didn't even tell her what I was going to do. When she accepted, I panicked. She's a sweet girl, but she's not Livvy. Now I feel like a bastard because she's expecting all this stuff from me and I'm just..."

"Lost." We're getting good at finishing each other's sentences. Max sighs and runs his hands through his hair. "If you go up there, can you, I don't know, can you tell her I'm sorry? I shouldn't have taken it that far. I just thought, even up until the very last second, that she was gonna change her mind. She just stood there and smiled at me. She was crying her eyes out, but she didn't do anything. Just smiled."

I think Max is seconds away from crying himself, and I have absolutely no idea what I'm supposed to do if that happens. I'm praying to all three of Olivia's Gods that it doesn't. "I will if I can figure out which one is her," I tell him. "Olivia did make me promise I would go. Maybe when we get back—"

"You're not going up there, Kit." I nearly jump out of my skin when Ryka emerges out of the shadows behind Max. His hair is wet and pulled back into a fresh ponytail. "I don't want you anywhere near the High Priestess. She's dangerous."

"Dangerous?" I can't help but laugh a little. "She's ancient, Ry. I reckon I could take her."

Max's cheeks go bright red. "You shouldn't speak like that," he says quietly.

"What, you believe in the Gods?"

"Not really, but people have seen things. She's not normal. Best you just don't say anything about the priestesses, even out here."

"I don't get it."

Ryka inhales a deep breath and flares his nostrils. "Just trust me, okay? Max is right. She's not normal, and she's definitely not safe for you to be around."

It's obvious from the looks on their faces that they're not telling me something. "Why, exactly?"

Ryka cracks his knuckles. "Because she's never shown anyone her true face before, Kit. Never, not once in the forty years she's been the High Priestess."

"Is that a big deal?"

Max answers. "They say that if you look upon a priestess' face, even by accident, then you're cursed. And you looked upon the High Priestess' face. That's got to be, like, the mother of all curses."

I flinch, recalling the way everyone at the pit looked away when the High Priestess threw her ceramic mask on the floor. Those women had closed their eyes. Had been crying. I let my head rock back and groan. "Fantastic. I'm cursed now, too."

"Don't believe in that crap. Jeez, what's wrong with you?" Ryka hisses at Max. He sits next to me just as James ambles over.

"It's dark enough," he says. It's true that the day dimmed quickly, and now all I can see of the solid fighter is the outline of his body and the sharp flash of his eyes. "Kit, you first."

"I'll go through with her," Ryka says, getting to his feet. He helps me up, and James doesn't say anything, but I know he's watching us. I don't care about James. The water is all that matters. It looks like thick black tar with the light all gone, and the fact that the surface is flat doesn't do much to cheer me. It makes it seem more sinister, like it's the pure embodiment of evil. Not a good thought when I'm about to submerge my body in it.

"This is going to be cold," Ryka says softly. He drops his bag a second and pulls out his shirt. He slips it on, watching me the whole time. "It's going to be hard to get through the tunnel without using my arms. We're going against the current, okay, so it'll be a fight to make progress. Hold onto the back of my shirt. If you lose grip, don't panic. I'll find you straight away."

I eye him nervously, trying to keep my heart rate from accelerating out of control. "Anything else?"

"Yeah," he grins. "Kick like hell, Kit."

I laugh somehow. Nervous, I'm shaking as we step into the water. He was right; it is damned cold. I suck in a sharp breath as the water swirls over the tops of my boots and floods them, instantly freezing me to my core. My shoulders tense, but Ryka's hand on my arm is warm and reassuring. He gives me a small nod and then we both step forward. The water, deep and terrifying, swallows us whole.

******

Up.

I can't tell which way is up. Water fills my mouth, my nose, my ears. It feels like it's doing it on purpose, trying to fill me up with all its blackness. My lungs start to scream almost instantly, shocked when my chest hits the water. The only thing grounding me, keeping me from losing myself to panic, is the fistful of material I have in my right hand.

I can't see him but I know from the tugging on my arm Ryka's swimming, trying to pull us against the powerful flow of water. It's trying to sweep us all the way back to Freetown and I have no idea whether it's succeeding or not, because I can't see a thing. I have a fearsome urge to scream, and a war rages inside me—my overriding urge to freak out, going head-to-head with my natural instinct to keep my mouth shut tight. It's like the circuitry inside my head has been fried and all I can do is focus on the pressure building behind my lips.

Think, think, think...

...do something... just think...

Ryka told you to...

A smile. Gentle brown eyes.

Kick like hell, Kit.

I kick. Finally, I kick, just like he asked me to. I screw my eyes shut, because that makes it less scary that I can't see anything, and I kick like I'm running from

240

the High Priestess herself. My legs feel like lead weights in the water but I move them anyway, pushing, pushing, pushing. A tumbling motion twists my body over and I feel hands on arms, lifting me upwards.

My face breaks the surface of the water and I drag in a frantic gasp of air that makes both my head and my lungs explode. Fear pulses through me for a second when I open my eyes and it's still dark. I'm neck deep in water. We're in the tunnel?

"It's okay, it's okay," Ryka says. "I'm right here. I've got you." With his arm locked around my ribcage, pressing me to him, he really does have a firm grip on me. "We're halfway, okay? Just take a breath. Get some air into your lungs."

I can't, though. It feels like I'm trapped in a vice and my chest can't expand. "Take...take me back—" I splutter.

"It's okay, just relax. I have you. I'm not letting you go."

"No." I shake my head. "I can't. Just take me back. We'll find another way around."

"We don't have time, Kit. Please, just calm down."

I start struggling against him, gripped by sheer animal instincts, and his hold tightens. "Kit! Don't make me knock you out. Just trust me!"

My arms and legs go still. It takes everything I have but I force my body to relax. "I do trust you. I just—I can't breathe."

I feel his lips against my forehead and even though I can't see him, the contact steels my nerves.

"This will be over in less than a minute," he says quietly. "We've got to go back under so we can get out. Are you ready?"

The current pulling at my legs feels impossibly strong, but I nod. "Okay. Okay, I can do it."

"Good girl." He kisses me once more, his lips pressing against my temple, and then he pulls me down. It feels unnatural to keep a hold of him as he sinks, but I concentrate this time, putting everything I've got into propelling us forward. It doesn't take less than a minute. It feels like it takes ten, although it's probably more like two. My brain feels like a light switch being turned off and on in rapid succession as we rise to the surface on the other side. I'm so disorientated that it takes me a full three seconds to realise it's okay to inhale.

"We're done. We're done. It's okay, it's over," Ryka says as he hauls me up the riverbank. My legs are boneless as my boots scrape against the thick mud, trying to catch a foothold. Ryka does most of the work, pulling me up until I lie flat on my back exactly where I collapsed after the tree pinned me when I first escaped. Once he's got my legs fully up onto the bank, he sinks down next to me. His hand finds mine.

I'm too inundated by relief and adrenaline to figure out why, but suddenly I'm laughing. It's the kind of laughter that shakes your whole body, and I'm so close to hysteria, I can taste it. Ryka puts his hand over my mouth to hide the sound, then his other hand covers his own mouth. He surprises me by joining in, his body shaking with nervous laughter as we both gasp for breath.

"I'm...I'm sorry," I choke out.

His hand tightens around mine, squeezing. "It's really okay."

We've barely stopped when Raff pulls himself up the bank, swearing. "Got mud in my boots! I can feel it squelching between my toes." The disgust in his tone is almost enough to make me laugh again, but the reality of our situation kicks in and I don't. We're back in the Sanctuary.

"Is she okay?" Raff asks.

Ryka pulls me to my feet and sighs. "Yeah. Yeah, she's okay."

******

Soaked to the bone, I'm less entertained two hours later. It seems to take forever to make our way along the path beside the now fenced-in river, and exhaustion begins to set in. By the time the lights that mark the Sanctuary come into view, we're all tired and grumpy, although no one says a word about it. No one says a word, period. My pockets are filled with grit, as are my boots, and I have a feeling it's the reason my eyes hurt so badly, too.

We're all too lost in the rhythmic clomping of our boots to break the otherwise silent journey. Eventually we leave the fenced area close to the processing plant where I saw the Therin eat lunch so long ago.

"We should wait for daybreak here," I say. "There's no cover between here and the city. It'll be suspicious if anyone sees us walking around in the middle of the night."

James grunts. "Fine. But we have to be up and away before dawn. We don't need guards finding us out here taking a nap when we need to be in there." He stabs the hilt of one of his daggers up ahead of us, but none of us need showing.

The Sanctuary is a dusky shadow, barely lit in the distance. My stomach clenches as I realise my mother is in there somewhere. My brother and my father, too. We skirt around the perimeter of the low, single storey building, cautiously checking for guards. We find none, although James won't let us build a fire. Too risky, and we don't want to sleep too comfortably besides. His reasoning makes sense, but I still hate him a whole lot as I curl onto my side on the cold ground, using my bag as a pillow.

"I'm probably more comfortable than that," Ryka says, dropping down beside me. He lies flat on his back, but he turns his head so we're looking at one another. A cautious smile plays across his lips. I don't really know what he means until he lifts his arm up.

"Oh—" My heart does that fluttering thing. I try to make my face do what I want it to but I get the feeling I look like a caged animal.

"It's okay," Ryka laughs. "Just thought I'd offer."

"No, I, uh…that would be good." I don't take my eyes off him as I scoot closer. His eyes seem darker and more intense than usual, and when I rest my head lightly against his chest, he sighs. "You can relax, you know. Your head can't be that heavy."

I breathe out and let the muscles in my neck go, thankful I don't have to keep up the pretence that my head weighs next to nothing. Now the only remaining problem is that I don't know what to do with my hands.

Ryka chuckles and reaches across for my arm; he draws it across him so that my palm rests on top of his ridiculously firm stomach. His arm circles me, his fingers resting lightly on my side, brushing up and down. I shiver at his touch.

"I'm sorry," I say stiffly. "I'm not very good at this."

"Neither am I."

I bite back tired laughter. "You're clearly better than me."

"I'm nervous as hell right now," he says.

I dig my fingers into his belly a little, smiling. "Liar. You've had practice."

Ryka shifts underneath me, making an odd noise at the back of his throat. "What makes you say that?"

My hand goes to his, still stroking up and down my side. "This."

"Just feels right," he murmurs. "Doesn't mean I've ever done it to anyone else."

I prop myself up on my elbow, scrutinizing his face. Big brown eyes look up at me, unblinking. "But you have, haven't you?"

"I've kissed a couple of girls, Kit. I'm not gonna lie about that. But this," he pulls me back down beside him. "I've never done this before."

Even though I've somehow ended up back inside the Sanctuary's boundaries, and I'm exhausted, and I smell bad, and my feet have ridiculously big blisters, I can't help but smile. It's a stupid, goofy smile, and it remains on my face until I pass out.

32

SANCTUARY

"**W**ake up!"

The strained hiss rouses me and I find James bending over us. I'm tangled rather ridiculously with Ryka, our arms and legs wound together. James kicks at Ry's feet with his boot, startling Ryka from sleep.

"We have to go," James clips out. He looks up at the sky, which hasn't started lightening yet. There are still stars out, glimmering faintly, but I know there will be Therin up and preparing for their day, as well as guards who patrol the city. Guards who patrol the compound we are currently sleeping outside.

It takes a moment to free myself from Ryka, embarrassed to have gotten so well and truly tied up in him, and I smile softly when his eyes meet mine. He doesn't say a word. The others are all awake, and it seems strange that we all just get up and start walking. No breakfast, no changing of clothes, no fifteen minutes to get our heads together. Just James pushing us forward.

The sky is gun-metal grey by the time we creep up on the slums skirting the city proper. It's here that we run into our first Falin. I bleach entirely, the blood draining from my face, as the young boy passes us. Ryka stiffens at my side and I hold my breath, waiting, just waiting for him to make eye contact with me. He does, and I notice James' hand move to his knife belt. No question of what he plans to do if this kid recognises me. But he doesn't. He gives our group a bland kind of smile and disappears through the abandoned streets.

"What was he doing out so early? I thought it would just be the servants," James snaps, his eyes narrowing at me.

"I don't know! He was probably meeting his training partner," I hiss, scowling at him. How James expects me to be held accountable for every single person's movements through the city is beyond me. Ryka shakes his head.

"She looks nothing like she did when she left here, James. I'm not surprised he didn't realise who she was."

James scrunches up his nose. "She *is* a lot dirtier."

"I was talking about *her hair*." Ryka's eyes narrow, and my stomach drops. He knows. Somehow, he knows James did it. James doesn't bat an eyelid.

"We're better off getting you off the streets. Which direction should we head in?"

We've already planned this, and a mental map unfolds in my mind as I envisage the best way to reach the old warehouse Cai and I used use for training. Out of the way, close enough to the river to be in a good location but far enough to be sparsely populated, it's the only building Lowrence owns that I know will be empty. Or a least the only person likely to be there is my brother. A sharp pain shoots through my chest when I think about him. What would he do if he saw me? I shiver, remembering the last time we parted ways.

We do our best to be covert as we walk quickly through the streets of the city, and no one seems to notice that we're all wearing shirts or jackets that cover our lack of halos. By the time we arrive at the single storey building, I have given up worrying. There's no point, and the whole repressed curiosity thing seems to be playing out our way. If anyone does think it's odd that the six of us are walking around then they're never going to break habit by even raising an eyebrow. The others don't seem to be able to follow my lead, however.

"They're like zombies," Callum hisses under his breath. Ryka laces his fingers together to create a foot hold for me, so I can stand and take a quick glance in through the windows. Inside the building, all I see are the familiar blue mats and wall of training weapons at the far end of the room.

"Coast's clear," I say, dropping to the ground. Ryka's hand goes automatically to my back and I lean into it a little, if only to let him know I appreciate it. It's strange, but I really do. Over the past week I've grown accustomed to the frequency with which he touches me. I never thought I would enjoy the physical contact, but with him it's different. I like it more than I care to admit.

Max and Raff shift nervously from foot to foot, watching out for people as James chews something over repetitively with his front teeth, taking everything in with sharp eyes. I glare at the muscles working in his jaw, waiting for him to give us the all clear. A stooped old Therin sweeps the street in front of the warehouse, completely oblivious to the fact that we're waiting for him to move along. James exhales dramatically and backs away from the street.

"Are there windows we can break from the back?"

"Yes," I nod. "But there's no need. It won't be locked."

Everyone turns and looks at me. I shrink a little under the weight of all their eyes. "What?"

"Why didn't you just say that?" James snaps.

I shrug. "I thought it was obvious. No one locks anything in the Sanctuary."

"Apart from all the gates and fences," Max mumbles.

"Well, yeah. Apart from those."

The Therin doesn't look up as we let ourselves into my old training room. The dry smell of chalk and cleaning products hits me full-on and it's amazing how quickly I'm transported to a thousand different memories of all the time I have spent here. It's like they're someone else's memories, though. There's nothing to them, no emotion that would tie them to me personally. I re-live all the fights and sparring matches I shared with Cai here and try to find one, just one, where I should have realised his halo wasn't working. There isn't one.

Cai must have worked tirelessly to keep every single feeling in check. I'm angry at him even though I shouldn't be. He had every reason to hide from me. If I had known, I would have reacted in the exact same way my brother did. I would have reported him without a second thought. I stride across the room towards the weapons, feeling stupid for letting myself think about him.

There is one good thing about coming here to the training rooms. I have stacks of knives stored here, none as nice or new or sharp as the ones I lost in the river, but still—I can replenish my knife belt. I pluck the familiar tools down off the wall, running reverent fingers across the wooden and metal hilts as I slip each one into a corresponding sheath around my waist.

"Jeez, girl, you'll hardly be able to walk," James says, stalking purposefully around the perimeter of the large room. There's nothing else in here apart from the mats and us, so I don't know what he's searching for. I just keep on loading up on hardware.

I feel Callum slip up beside me. "It wasn't just talk before, Kit. If we get out of here with our hides, I'm making you the perfect set of knives." He looks on my hurried, mismatched collection with clear distaste. Yeah, they really aren't all that hot, but the points are sharp enough and right now that's all that matters. I nod to him gratefully and catch Ryka frowning.

"We have ten hours before nightfall. We should get some more rest," he says. He rolls his shirtsleeves up so that his tattooed forearms are on show, and I can't help but look down on the two black lines marking my wrists. He put those marks there, but I earned them. I shiver and do the opposite to him, tugging my sleeves down over my hands.

"I'm going to survey the area," James says, dumping his bag. He takes off his weapons and tucks a solitary blade into the back of his waistband. I drop my bag and rub my hands over my face.

"There's something I need to do."

"Does it involve leaving this room?" James asks.

"Yes."

"Then you can forget it."

"But I—"

"What were the conditions of coming with us, Kit?"

I clench my hands into fist, which makes me feel stupid. I glare at him, hating him just that little bit more. He curves a dark eyebrow at me.

"Well?"

"That I have to obey you," I say tersely.

James does his best impression of a pleased smile. "Raff, Max, you come with me. We'll be back in an hour."

The boys follow after James silently, leaving just Ryka, Callum and me behind. I lace my hands behind my head, glaring up at the ceiling, wondering if my teeth might crack because of how tightly I'm clenching my jaw.

Ryka comes and stands close to my back, close enough that I feel his breath on my naked neck again. I sigh and inch closer to him until I can feel his chest is almost touching my back. Almost. "I really don't like that man," I say under my breath.

Callum snorts, but Ryka just *hmmm*s quietly. "You know," he says. "You're forgetting what Jack said."

I turn around and look at him. His hair, as ever, is tumbling into his face. "What do you mean?"

A wicked gleam flashes in his eyes. "He said you had to obey James and *me*."

I open my mouth, grinning a little. He's right, Jack did say that. He reaches up slowly and tucks my hair behind my ear, then softly traces the pad of his thumb under my lower lip. I don't look away from his piercing gaze even though I know it must be making Callum feel awkward. "And if I told you I wanted you to—?" Ryka raises his eyebrows, waiting for me to tell him what it is I want to do.

"Go and find my friend, Penny," I say. I don't mention my brother. I know I'll have trouble getting anyone on board with kidnapping a reluctant Falin, so I figure I'll start with Penny. "She's an Elin, so she's not controlled. Her father beats her. I think she would like to come with us. She's—Cai was her brother."

A wary look travels across Ryka's face, but he doesn't object. "If I order you to come with me to find your friend, Penny, then you have to obey." He is tense now, though, as he always is whenever I mention Cai.

"Is that a smart idea?" Callum asks.

"Probably not. You should wait here in case James comes back. He'll lose his mind if he has no idea where we've gone," Ryka says.

"Forget that!" Callum shifts his body weight, rolling his shoulders back. "It may not be a smart idea, but I never said I wasn't in. My brother seems to think it's okay to participate in hair-brained ideas that ruin his life, and he's supposed to be the smart one. I'm not sticking around for James, no way."

I nod my approval at him and turn back to Ryka. A grim look has set over him. "Aren't you concerned about pissing him off?"

A hint of emotion flickers in Ryka's eyes, disappearing as quickly as it came. But I see it: pure hatred. "No. Now come on." He's so good at hiding that emotion; so good that on a daily basis I have almost thought he looks up to James. Now I know the truth. He hasn't forgiven him for murdering his father. Judging by the intensity of the fleeting expression I just witnessed, Ryka is biding his time. For what, I don't know, but I'm almost glad Ryka's not the pushover James made him out to be.

"Penny lives a couple of houses up from my family," I say. "We'll have to be careful that we're not seen. The casual bystander might not recognise me but my brother or my mother definitely will." My stomach churns when I think about my mother. I haven't missed her in the same way Olivia misses her mother, and that seems like a bit of a tragedy.

We slip out of the training rooms unnoticed, and Ryka surprises me by walking at my side with a completely flat expression on his face. I can't say I feel half as calm as he looks. On the other hand, Callum looks extraordinarily tense. I shoot him a brief smile as we duck our way through the still quiet streets. I also smile politely at the people we pass, because it would be strange if I didn't. Fifteen uneventful minutes later we're standing out the back of Penny's house, and there's a ball of pent-up nerves manifesting itself in my throat. I can't seem to swallow it down. It probably has a lot to do with the fact that I can see the roof of my old house from where I'm standing, and the upstairs windows are overlooking the courtyard we're standing in. I lay my knuckles against the freshly painted white door, the service door this time, hoping to everything holy that a Therin I don't know answers. Slim chance since I've been coming over here to meet Cai nearly every day for the last twelve years, but still.

Ryka's hand goes to the small of my back again as we wait for the door to open. My body hums to life, and I bite my lip. This seems easier with him here. Callum, too. I raise my hand to rap again, but the door swings open and, once more, the same Therin with the cloudy eyes stands before me. This must be her sole responsibility or something. I curse and step forward. Despite her poor vision, my short hair and the layer of filth covering me, she recognises me instantly. Great.

"I just want to speak to Penny," I tell her. She quickly appraises the three of us.

"I'm supposed to tell the Trues immediately if you show up," she states. She cowers into the door like I'm about to attack her. I huff out a sharp breath and take a step forward, which makes her flinch.

"We're not going to hurt you. I just need to talk to her, okay?"

She looks at me and I suddenly realise her eyes are wet. She swallows so that her throat bobs up and down, clutching her shirt collar at the base of her neck. "Is it better? Where you are?" she asks.

Stunned, my eyes flicker to her halo. Looks like Cai might not have been the only one off the Sanctuary's drugs in this household. I consider her question. Is it better where I am now?

Ryka's boots scrape a little as he shifts his body weight. "Yes, it is," he answers for me. I don't miss the hard look he shoots me out of the corner of his eye. I should have answered quicker. I nod sharply, stepping up into the hallway. "Yes."

The Therin shrinks back and lets us slip inside. "Quickly," she whispers. I don't stop to think where I'm going. I move down the hallway, knowing Ryka and Callum are behind. I open the door I'm looking for and all three of us slip inside, the Therin hovering in the doorway behind us. "I'll go and get her," she breathes. "Don't leave this room."

Ryka exhales and sinks down onto the single, narrow bed—the only piece of furniture in the room bar the simple chest of drawers. "Not going anywhere."

The Therin takes one more look at us each in turn, as though she's trying to figure out which one of us is more dangerous, and then pulls the door closed.

"I get the feeling we're all about to die," Callum declares brightly. I laugh a little despite how true that statement might actually be.

"If Penny is who I think she is, she's probably got everyone in this house off their halos. I doubt they'll turn us in," I say. If I knew that with a certainty, maybe my heart wouldn't be hammering so hard in my chest. I chew my lip and sink down on the bed next to Ryka. He runs his hand through his hair, studying me the whole time.

"This is his room, isn't it?

I nod. "Yeah."

Ryka looks away, looks at the plain, pale blue walls with the sun faded patches adjacent to the bed, at the scuffed floorboards and the bookcase that still holds the few books I saw here last time. He looks displeased. "Did you spend much time here?"

"No. I've only been here twice." Two times too many. If Cai were still alive, I would never have had reason to come into his room. He never saw mine, after all. But then, if Cai were still alive I would never have left the Sanctuary. I would never have met Ryka or gone to Freetown, made friends with Olivia or August and Jack. Hell, there's every chance I would be dead by now, killed in the arena. I take

Ryka's hand and we sit in tense silence for a few minutes before the door rushes open and Penny edges in sideways. She's practically on tiptoes, she's so nervous.

"What the hell are you doing here?" she hisses.

I don't answer right away. Her damn father has been at it again; her face is a swollen, purple mess. I clench my fists and stand stiffly from the bed. "You're coming with us." I'd wanted to give her the option, but looking at her now, seeing her like this—I'm not giving her the choice.

"I can't just come with you, Kit! Things have changed around here since you left. My father suspects I helped you leave, he watches me like a hawk!"

Callum pushes off from where he was leaning against the wall. The room seems really small with his tall frame taking up so much space. He flicks a knife over in his hand. "No one will notice if you leave with us tonight. It's a match night. We can sneak you out with everyone else."

"Everyone else?" She looks appalled. "I have people relying on me here. I can't just abandon my responsibilities."

"We'll take them, too," Ryka says. I wasn't expecting that. Opa's group is already big. I strangle out a wheeze when I realise how badly James is going to freak out.

"He's right," I say. "You can bring them with you. How many?"

"Four." She blinks at me. "There are four of us."

"Four won't be too big a problem," Ryka says. "Can you stay home tonight?"

Penny's eyes round out. "Yes. My father hasn't let me go to the matches ever since Cai died. He's embarrassed that I cried over a Falin in front of all of his friends."

Callum knocks his balled up fists on top of one another. A muscle works in his neck. "Wow. Your dad sounds like a complete jerk."

When she laughs, Penny's voice is shaky. She gestures to her face. "You could say that."

I feel like giving her a hug but there's no time, and I still can't help but remember the look on her face as she held Cai's broken body. "We'll be back later for you. Bring only food and water. No clothes, no trinkets, nothing, okay? Wear strong boots and clothes you can move quickly in." I relax a little at the knowledge that we'll be coming by here for her later. That means we can collect my brother. Despite how useful it would have been to study other fighters' techniques, Miranda never wanted us to go to the arena if we weren't called. She always thought it showed weakness to watch the other fighters, and there would be nothing miraculous or mysterious about me if I didn't just show up and beat everybody every single time, without having picked my opponents apart beforehand. At least her ridiculous pride means my brother will be at home tonight. He wasn't on any of the betting screens that we saw. I take a small knife from my belt and hold it out to Penny, but she stops me. She bends to pull out a small, curved fixed-blade dagger from her boot. "Caius gave it to me," she says. "I know how to use it."

There's a bright gleam in her eye when she says this, and I know who she's dreamed about using that knife on. I don't blame her. I want to kill her father myself, if only for his callous reaction to Cai's death. He'd *laughed*, for crying out loud.

"All right. Be ready," I tell her, glancing at Ryka and Callum; both are tensed and ready to move, themselves. "We have to go now."

A desperate look floods Penny's face. "Kit?"

I turn to look at her. "Your father," she says, "he's got people looking for you everywhere. He's so mad."

I draw my lips into a tight line. "He better pray he doesn't find me."

With that we leave Penny chewing on her fingernails and depart the house. The walk back to the training room is silent, and I'm glad. The whole time I think about how close I was to my old home, and whether it was a mistake that I didn't try and grab my brother right then and there.

33

COLOSSEUM

I f James knows we snuck out while he was gone, he does a good job of hiding it. The Sanctuary is teeming, but its energy is flat and missing the charge that snaps through Freetown in the evenings. No laughter, no shouting, no catcalling.

We wear the collars of our jackets up just like Opa told us to. How he is going to find us in this mess of a crowd I have no idea, but Jack seemed sure he would. For the first time ever, I follow the general populace into the Colosseum through the curved sandstone archways, pressed up tight between Ryka and Max. Ryka shoots me the occasional glance but neither of us smile. That would be an immediate giveaway. It also helps that we have absolutely nothing to smile about. Our fingers brush from time to time, though—a small comfort no one notices.

"I didn't think there would be so many people here," Callum mutters behind us. James doesn't turn his head but I know his whole body is on alert, his sharp eyes focused on every single moving object surrounding us. I don't like admitting it, but he's actually really good at this. If there were any other way I would take it, but right now we're counting on James to keep us safe.

"Shut up," he hisses over his shoulder. "You're going to get us caught."

Callum presses closer to his brother's back and does his best to keep his eyes looking straight ahead like James told us to. When the all-too-familiar smell of the Colosseum reaches my nose, my whole body comes alive. It's like ten thousand volts penetrating through my skin, warning me to prepare. Is this what it would have felt like if I'd have fought here without my halo? Probably. My hands itch to go to my knife belt, but it's not there, of course. It's back at the training room along with everyone else's weapons. All I have is the sharp-bladed stiletto that Ryka bought from Callum for me, its heel pressing into the base of my spine like a friendly reminder every time I take a step. At least I have something to defend myself with if we get caught.

It takes us a while to march placidly up the arena steps, trying to find somewhere to sit all together. Technically it shouldn't matter, but we need to keep close enough that we can all run as a group if we have to. The work it takes to keep my face free from emotion is taxing, especially when a Therin stomps on my toes not once but twice. Ryka notices, his deep brown eyes clouding over. Gods, I want to make sure we get out of here alive. It would be a cruel joke if I just figured out how much I care about him only to lose it all in the blink of an eye. Because it would be that quick.

The place is full of guards and technicians with their stupid, ever-present tablets. They're out in full force, and even though I never really paid attention before, I know with a certainty that there are well over twice as many of them as usual. They're out looking for Opa and the others, but that doesn't mean they won't catch us instead.

"Sit there, you two," James whispers. Ryka and I are smooth when we slip onto the end of the stone steps he points to. We sit down, our faces trained to mirror those of the dutiful Therin surrounding us.

Breathe in for three.

Hold for three.

Exhale for three.

Repeat.

It feels like I'm breathing too quickly, even with the pause. No one else picks up on it, though. Miraculously, no one picks up on the fact that there is no silver glinting under my collar either. Ryka's dishevelled hair covers the back of his neck pretty well, so he's safe from prying eyes at least.

"They've sat three rows behind us," he says under his breath.

"Are there guards back there?" I ask.

He nods. "Some. I didn't get an accurate count. They still use guns here?"

"Yes."

"Great."

"It's going to be fine. There isn't going to be a fight," I tell him. Do I believe that? No. Definitely not. But it turns out I'm a grade A liar these days, because he turns and gives me a tight, incredibly polite smile. It makes me feel sick how good he is at this. It would suck for Ryka to be controlled in any way.

"Don't do that," I tell him, raising my eyebrows. My own inane, vacant smile doesn't slip. "It makes me angry."

A flicker of a real smile chases across his lips. "Good."

We wait for a painfully long time while the rest of the Colosseum fills up gradually. I can tell Ryka's desperate to move by the time they start up the fanfare lower down on the arena floor. It's nowhere near as loud up here as I'm used to it. Down there it rattled your bones.

My fingers intertwine with Ryka's, our hands hidden between our bodies. Our shoulders touch and his presence is almost enough to calm the ridiculous surges of panic that come in wave after wave.

"I'd be hopeless down there right now," I murmur.

Ryka shakes his head. "You wouldn't. You'd be better."

"I can barely think straight up here. I'd fall apart in a match."

"You're wrong. You'd react quicker. Your body would take over. A good dose of fear is an excellent motivator when you're fighting, Kit. Trust me."

He's probably right. I wasn't exactly scared when I fought Sam, even though I should have been. I was quick and fluid, and I will be that again if I have to be.

"Citizens of the Sanctuary!" A static crackle tears through the air as the microphone comes to life, startling the both of us. I try to play down how badly shaken I am by fixing my gaze on the loudspeaker situated to our left. Its dirty grey plastic vibrates as the nasal voice speaks again.

"Citizens of the Sanctuary, welcome to the fifth amphi-match of this year.

We thank you for your organized entry into the arena, and for pledging all bets through the appropriate channels. As usual, the matches will commence immediately. We must note there is a revision to the schedules, however. Due to illness, we have reassigned our fight finale this evening. Falin Kitsch of House Kitsch will now be fighting in place of—"

The plastic keeps rattling but I don't hear the words coming out of it. He's fighting. My brother is fighting. How has this happened?

"Falin Kitsch of the Kitsch household?" Ryka whispers.

"Yeah. My brother."

"Damn. What do you want to do?"

I can feel James' hot glare burning into the back of my head. He's expecting me to lose it. I'm not that stupid, though. "Nothing. There's nothing that we can do."

Ryka grunts, and I'm grateful he doesn't say anything else. We sit stiff as statues next to each other as the first fighters come out—a Belcoras daughter, dirty blonde hair and all, pitted against another girl I've never seen before. All I see is her red hair tied back into a neat bun at the back of her neck. She could be a Rosen or maybe a Lightwater. The alarm sounds and they step into the triangle. My knee starts to bounce up and down as I wait for them to get to it. The second alarm sounds and they rush each other, while the Therin make their supportive cooing noises right on cue. I blink fiercely as Ryka stills my knee and removes his hand before anyone can see.

"Are you okay?"

"Yeah. Yeah, I'm okay."

The Belcoras girl and her opponent aren't as quick at picking each other apart as I'd like them to be. There are three other fights between now and my brother's, and if they all take this long then it will be midnight before I get to see him. My memories of him all seem warped now. The halo robbed me of all interest in watching him fight before. I know I always thought I could beat him, but does that mean there are others out there who can, too? Has he just been lucky so far?

"Stop worrying. He's going to win and then we'll get him out of here, too."

I snap my head up at Ryka, narrowing my eyes at him. "We're taking him?"

Tiny lines form in between Ryka's brows. "I know you're planning on it. You may think you're excellent at hiding things from me but I gotta say, your attempts are actually quite pathetic."

I scowl, ignoring his jibe. "James is never going to agree."

"Tough luck for James, then. He's going to have to deal with it."

The crowd below where the Trues sit splinters apart as the red haired girl lunges at the Belcoras girl. The blonde's body goes rigid and she topples sideways, stiff as a board. It would almost be funny if it didn't spell the end of her life. The Therin mark their score sheets even before the alarm sounds, declaring the match over. Finally.

I shudder as some of the pre-mortas kids run onto the arena and lift the limp, bleeding body from the ground. The next fight starts and I don't even pay attention to who is called out of the tunnels. I just sit on my hands and wait. Time stands still as another girl falls into the dirt, her moment in the Colosseum brief albeit more respectable than the first match. I'm blind to anything that's happening below. I'm also blind to the developments around me, and it's only when Ryka pulls me closer to his body that I realize someone is trying to sit beside me. An old man with wispy white hair and deeply worn laughter lines. There is a round, fat stain on his shirt, which pulls tightly across his huge belly. He smiles at me and sits his considerable weight down before I have time to move, and I almost end up in Ryka's lap.

"The prodigal daughter returns," the old man says brightly. I stare at him, leaning away. Not because he's so close, although that is rather annoying; my complete horror is closely tied in with the fact that this man is grinning at me like a simpleton. He's a True. And he's recognized me. My hands clamp around Ryka's leg and I get ready to bolt. That's the only option. That's the only way—

"Calm down, girl," he says, slouching back into the stone cut step we use as a seat. "I sit up here all the time. The guards are used to it."

I open my mouth, but nothing comes out. Ryka thankfully has his faculties about him. "You're Opa?" he asks.

The old man nods. "I am Opa."

Ryka affords himself a little smirk. "So that's why they haven't found you."

Ingenious. The reason they haven't discovered him is because he's not one of the drugged masses. He's part of the system that drugs them in the first place. I'm immediately suspicious.

"Why did you want to meet us?" And why did Cai never mention the fact that Opa was a True in his recordings? It doesn't add up.

"You know full well why I wanted to meet with you. You're the only way out of this gods-forsaken city for my friends." He tosses a handful of red tickertape down onto the crowd below us like most Trues do, laughing in the most obscene way. He waves at one of the guards, who frowns at the old man and realigns his body so there's very little chance he'll make eye contact with Opa again. Clever old bastard.

I shake my head, knowing that James is probably hopping mad right now. Mad he's not the one meeting with Opa. "Why are you supporting the Radicals?" I demand.

"Come, now. That's a horrible name."

"Whatever," I huff. "Get to it. Answer the question."

Opa tilts his head, looking at me. Studying me. He pats his belly and shifts so he's watching the fight. "You're nothing like he thought you would be, you know. He was convinced you'd be this scared little girl who needed protecting. That's clearly not the case. Still all hard edges, aren't you?"

My stomach churns. "We don't have time to talk about Cai. We're kind of in a precarious position if you hadn't noticed."

"Where are the others?" Ryka adds.

"The others are safe. They're prepared to leave with you tonight. As soon as the finale match is called, you all need to go. I'll meet you outside the front of your old house," he tells me.

I frown, shaking my head. "We can't. We can't leave before the end. They'll notice. Plus I have to make sure my brother's okay."

Opa's bushy eyebrows press together to form one scruffy white line. "If we don't move before then, the streets will be teeming with people. I'm an old man, I can't navigate through large crowds quickly. We'll miss our window of oppor-tunity."

"We can come back for him once we've gotten everyone past the refinery," Ryka says, squeezing my hand.

"No!" My ears feel really hot and my eyes are pricking. I bite down the urge to curse. "James will never let us. It has to be now." I shut down and don't look at either of them, mainly because I know they're talking sense and I should just agree to leave, but I can't. He's my brother. Ryka shifts in his seat next to me.

"I swear to you we'll come back for him."

"Would you leave Olivia?" I whisper. That shuts him up. I glare at the back of the Therin's head in front of me, trying to figure out this problem. There has to be a way. The third match is drawing out and Opa is getting twitchy. "Look, I'm about to stage a way out for you. This is kind of a now or never thing."

I refuse to acknowledge that I've heard him, because doing so is like admitting defeat. I'll go along with whatever he does, but I'll be damned if I don't somehow make the situation work to my advantage. Opa takes my silence as a sign and then does something really unexpected. He lists sideways out of his seat and collapses onto the stairs, clutching at his chest. He groans, nice and loud for effect.

"What the hell is he doing?" Ryka squeaks. His voice is so high pitched that I break out into a terrified sweat. The guards that Opa has so conveniently irritated into ignoring us just before are not only paying us attention now, but they're coming straight towards us. And quick.

"Crap!" I grit out.

"My chest!" Opa howls. People on the seats around us are on their feet in seconds, rushing to his side. It's their main purpose in life, after all, to jump whenever a True needs them. Chaos ensues as guards and Therin alike all rush to try and help. Ryka pulls me back through the crowd as an announcement goes up over the loud speakers that the technicians are required in the stands.

"Time to go," he says.

We slip away, fighting a current for the second time in as many days, only this time it's bodies, not water we struggle against. When we reach one of the tiered exits, stairs disappearing into the dark, no one notices us. Ryka grabs onto my wrist and drags me down after him, not looking back once. I do, though. The sound of footsteps hammering after us makes me stumble as I turn to see who is following us. It's James. The tight expression on his face tells me immediately that he's pissed off. Seriously pissed off.

"What the hell happened?" he roars.

"Distraction," I manage, tripping behind Ryka as he hurries on regardless. At the bottom of the stairs I realise we've come out into the tunnels underneath the Colosseum, the ones where I used to warm up before the matches. Ryka falters a second before I point off to the left.

"That way. There's an exit," I say breathlessly. Callum, Max and Raff sweep around James as Ryka tugs me away, but James pauses for a beat, staring at me with a dark look in his eyes, like I somehow engineered all of this madness. My mouth falls open but I don't get a chance to say anything.

"Come on!" Ryka hisses, yanking on my arm. "We've got to get out of here."

We run until it feels like my arm is going to come out of my shoulder socket, and it's only when a Falin steps out into a corridor that Ryka slows his pace. He shoves the Falin out of the way so hard he falls onto his ass as we charge by, but the fighter remains silent. Or close enough. His halo clicks like crazy. Our eyes meet briefly and I recognise him; it's the Belcoras with the mis-matched eyes that I threatened with my knife after Cai died. He looks surprised when he sees me, but he doesn't move an inch. Then we're gone.

"What the hell is that stupid old man thinking?" James snarls once I have directed our group out into the night air. A fanfare kicks up and my whole body locks, knowing what it means. My brother's fight will be next. I dig my heels in so that Ryka has to stop pulling me along. He doesn't even know where he's going anyway.

"Stop!"

The five of them do so, and I wrestle my arm out of Ryka's grip. "I'm not leaving without my brother."

"Kit, I told you, we'll come back once we've got everyone—"

I shake my head at Ryka, ignoring the pleading look in the pooled darkness of his brown eyes. "And I told you, I'm not leaving him."

"Your brother has survived every fight he's been in thus far, Kit. He's going to survive this one. You think he's going to come quietly?" James snaps.

"No." I know he won't. "That doesn't mean we can't *make* him come."

"We barely made it out of there after that incredibly stupid manoeuvre, girl. If we live past tonight then we can talk about sending someone back another time for your family."

I start shaking my head before he's even finished talking. My eyes are unwavering when I lock onto James.

"No."

He rakes his hands back through his hair and scowls at Ryka, dismissing me. "What's the old man's plan?"

"We're meeting him and the others by the river near where Kit used to live. They're going to be waiting for us."

They talk for a moment while I stare back up at the Colosseum. The bright red banners list on the breeze and a jolt of panic rushes through me. Am I being selfish wanting my brother to come with us? Is it just because I feel so alone out there? Undoubtedly. But it's also not fair leaving him here, killing indiscriminately because he's told to. I clench my fist, feeling pain. I look down and see red; there's blood across my knuckles. I must have scraped my hand when I was running. I've already lost so much blood to this Colosseum, too much of it has seeped into the dirt floor and the sandstone walls. I'm furious that it's cost me this ridiculously small amount now. There's no way I want it to claim any more of my brother's.

I'd like to say none of them notice me when I slink quietly away from the huddled group of men, but that would be a lie. Every single one of them does. James pulls himself up straight and comes for me.

"Don't make me carry you kicking and screaming, Kit."

"That's exactly what you're going to have to do," I tell him.

"You're going to get yourself killed. You're going to get all of us killed, too, as well as all the people relying on us to get them out of here tonight. Do you want that?"

His words do make me pause, but not for long. "I know where he will be. I know exactly how to get there. I'm not asking any of you to come with me. I'll go alone. It'll be easier that way. Just go and get the others out. I'll meet you at the refinery."

James glares at me, exasperation clear in his eyes. Max speaks up first. "Just let her go. She's capable enough."

I shoot him a thankful glance. James looks at Max like he's mad, that is until Callum and Raff agree. "She'll be fine," Callum says, nodding at me.

James turns on Ryka. "And I suppose you think this is a great idea, too?"

"No, I think it's a terrible idea," he says. My jaw drops, but Ryka's hand reaches out for mine. "I'm going with her, though. She's right. I would never leave Olivia behind."

Relief. That's what I experience, even though I know he's putting himself in danger for me. I take his hand and press myself against his side.

"Fine. Go, then," James says. "But I'm telling you now, if you get yourselves killed, I won't be held responsible."

"No, not this time," Ryka says quietly. I hear it, though, and James does, too. A sharp, jagged smile spreads across his face.

"We'll see you at the refinery." He turns and melts into the night, swiftly followed by Max and Raff. I catch hold of Callum's hand as he goes to leave.

"Make sure you get Penny and her family, too."

He nods. "Of course."

REUNION

Back in the Colosseum, the thunder of footfall pounds on the arena steps. Everyone is returning to their seats following Opa's production. The fanfare is blaring out loud again, and it can only be ten minutes before my brother is called out onto the match floor. We're almost too late.

"Hurry," I whisper to Ryka, running through the empty passageways. I still can't believe he wanted to stay with me. My heart hurts a little as I consider how much trouble I'm probably getting him into. Actually, it hurts a whole lot. I pause outside the waiting room reserved for the Kitsch family's fighters, panicking.

"My brother's on the other side of this door. He's not going to want to hear what I say. He's going to want to get the guards as soon as I step foot in there. I might have to fight him, so there's a strong chance I'm going to get caught. You should probably go."

Ryka frowns a little and smiles at me. "I'm not going anywhere. It's taking you far too long to realise how I feel about you, Kit. I'm not leaving you. I'm *never* leaving you. If you go, I go."

I shiver at what he says, grateful but at the same time completely blown away. I'm no good with words. I have no idea how to tell him what he means to me, that he's the only reason I'm not a gibbering wreck under the weight of all my guilt. I trace my fingertips lightly across his cheekbone and he dips his head, leaning into my palm. That's enough to make my heart start hammering all over again. He tilts his head and carefully kisses the inside of my wrist. "It's time to do this," he says.

And it really is.

The door handle feels freezing cold in my hand after the searing heat of Ryka's skin. I blow out a shaky breath before turning it and pushing myself forward, not allowing myself time to react. The scene on the other side of the door takes a second to sink in. The sight of my brother, fidgeting with his wrist straps, bouncing on the balls of his feet, isn't what surprises me. That's normal. It isn't even Lowrence, leaning against the wall across the room, or the two guards he has flanking him. It's Miranda. It's the look on her face when she sees me. A horrified, pained expression, like she's being torn apart from the inside out. It's the most emotion I've ever seen her wear, and it's toxic.

"How?" she sighs softly, like all the air is escaping her body. A choked gasp follows. My brother, my father, the guards, everyone turns to look at Ryka and me standing in the doorway, and for a moment no one does anything.

It's then that I hear Ryka exhale. "I don't...I don't understand," he whispers. I catch sight of him and feel the bottom falling out of my world. His facial expression matches that of Miranda's.

"What is it?" I murmur. I don't really need to, though. Dread is cycling through me, gaining momentum, and I can predict the implosion that's about to take place. It's already started.

"You—" Ryka whispers.

Miranda tries to get to her feet, and it's then that I notice Lexa sitting in her lap, her little arms wrapped around the blonde woman's neck. Miranda unravels her daughter and places her absently on the floor beside her. She doesn't move beyond that.

"What are you doing here?" she says.

A confused look passes around the room. Lowrence's eyes land on me and I steel myself, planning how I'm going to take him down if he even so much as *thinks* about stepping towards me. My brother and the guards seem to be waiting for someone to tell them what to do.

"I came for her," he says. Ryka's words ground out a hollow in my stomach. He takes a step but it's not forward, it's sideways, closer to me. His hand snakes around my waist and he grabs hold of my hip protectively. I take my eyes off my wary brother for a moment to look up at Ryka; his eyes are filled with hurt. "Jack said he thought you'd come here. He said you didn't want to feel anymore."

Miranda's head drops and her hair falls into her face. My father finally pushes off the wall and folds his arms across his chest. "Someone had better explain what's going on. You know this boy?" he directs at Miranda. When she raises her head, there are bright tears shining on her eyelashes. She doesn't respond to Lowrence. She takes a step towards Ryka.

"He was right. That's why I wanted to come here. I didn't want to feel anything."

Ryka's body goes stiff. "You're a liar," he snarls. "You're not wearing a halo. You probably never did. You just left us and—"

She shakes her head quickly, holding out her hands. "That's not true. I came here, I…I wanted more than anything to numb all the pain, but when I went to see the technicians I couldn't do it. I knew if they took everything I felt away then I wouldn't remember how much I loved you and your sister. I wouldn't remember how much I missed you."

Ryka's hand tightens on my hip so much so that my skin begins to throb. Not as much as my heart, though. None of this can be true. She can't be….

"You were our mother. You weren't supposed to leave us in the first place. You wouldn't have had to miss us at all if you hadn't left!" Ryka shouts.

So it's true. I feel bile rising at the back of my throat. It all makes total sense. Ryka must have always suspected his mother came here. He'd thought she'd done it to escape her pain. That's why he hates Lockdown, why he hated the thought of me putting my halo back on. It was all because of her. She turned up when I was six years old, for crying out loud. It all fits so neatly that I have to swallow down the urge to scream.

Ryka grabs hold of my hand, shaking like crazy. "Look at you. You didn't waste any time. You've got yourself set up with another little family again. Do you even think about me and Olivia? You know she's gone and interred herself in the Keep because she thinks your martyred yourself to do the Gods' work! She's in there right now, living that life, because you left us to come here and start all over again!"

A strangled sob works free from Miranda. With her hand on her chest, she takes in the two of us standing in front of her. Her eyes fix on me with a look of pure hate. "You brought him here. Why? Do you hate me that much?"

I stare at her blankly. She thinks I knew about this? She's blind if she can't see I'm as stunned as everyone else in the room. And mortified. Lexa starts crying as the second round of fanfare blares drunkenly through the speakers above us. They're calling for my brother.

Lowrence tips his head at the guards and steps forward. "I have no idea what the hell is going on right now, but we need to sort this out later. Son, you have a match to win. And you," he stabs a finger in my direction. "You have a lot to answer for. You're not going anywhere."

Ryka reacts immediately, stepping in front of me. "We're leaving. We came to get him," he says, gesturing to my brother, whose eyebrows inch up his forehead in surprise.

"You're not here to get your halo fixed?" he asks.

The way he asks that, like it would have been the most normal thing to have happened—for me to have come to my senses and returned to be controlled—makes my blood boil. "No! We weren't free, okay? They're using us to kill for sport! We're just money to them. They train us and send us out there to get cut up and die for their entertainment. For their precious social standing! You deserve a name and the chance to make your own decisions!"

My brother just looks at me blankly. "I don't understand."

"Just...can you come with us, please?" I plead.

He looks from me to Lowrence and back again. It's hardly a contest; our father has always been able to threaten us without saying a word. My brother's hand goes to his daggers, the way mine do when I'm unsure.

"Come on, boy. She's not going anywhere. The guards are going to keep these two here until you get back. Then we can iron out this whole mess." He graces me with another hard look. "You have a lot of fights to catch up on before we're square, young lady."

I let out a hard laugh. He actually thinks I'm going crawl back into the arena

266

and fight for him again. I must have really embarrassed him by running away.

"Not. Happening," I spit.

His eyebrow crooks up. "You'll feel differently when you're wearing your halo again." His eyes run up and down Ryka. "And since you're my wife's blood, I will allow you to remain under my roof as well. Who knows, maybe once we have a collar around your neck you'll start behaving, too. Miranda told me about you, you know. Trouble maker from the word go if I recall correctly."

Those words are a really bad move on my father's part. Rage bubbles out of Ryka like it's a tangible thing, infecting me as he springs forward. In two steps he has a knife against Lowrence's windpipe. The two guards spring into action and I have my lone dagger in my hand in an instant. There's no room for error here. It's difficult to fight in such a small space, especially with Lexa present. I may not like her very much, but she's five years old. I share blood with her. Hell, Ryka shares blood with her too.

I feel sick when I slam the butt of my knife straight into the solar plexus of the guard closest to me. I can't think about this whole confused nightmare right now. The only thing that matters is getting out of here. Miranda screams as I take out the winded guard's knees and he sinks to the floor. He pulls out his gun but not quick enough. I lash out with my blade, my movements precision-quick and sharp, cutting at his wrist. His gun clatters to the floor and he has a second to look up at me surprised before I hammer my clenched fist into his face. He goes down without a sound.

"Put the knife down!" the other guard hollers. Unfortunately he's had time to draw his weapon. He's yelling at Ryka, though I doubt he hears him. He's glaring up at Miranda, all the while holding his blade to Lowrence's throat. A thin trail of blood has run down his neck and is dripping onto the floor. My father's eyes meet mine and he holds out his hand, like he thinks I'm going to protect him. I flip my knife over and turn back to my brother, but he's not where he was a moment ago. I panic, just as another burst of fanfare jaunts into life above us. They're going to be coming down here looking for him soon.

"Did you mean it?"

I spin around and my brother is standing in the doorway. His face is blank and I can hear his halo cranking the Sanctuary's drugs into his system. His mouth must be filled with the taste of almonds.

"Mean what?" I say.

A frown flutters across his forehead. "That I can have a name."

I let out my breath and nod. "Yes! You're a person. You shouldn't be referred to like you're someone's property."

"And if I take this off," his hand works its way to the silver halo shining brightly under his collar. "Who will I be then?"

"Whoever you want to be," I say quietly.

His hand falls slack to his side. For a moment I think he's considering it. Really considering it. A shrill shriek snatches my attention away, and that's when things start to unravel. The guard steps forward and presses his gun into the side of Ryka's temple. Ryka reacts by pushing down with the knife so that Lowrence's arms and legs flail wildly, kicking and lashing at the floor.

"Stop!" Miranda wails.

"Who? Who are you telling to stop?" Ryka bites out. "The guard that has a gun to your son's head? Or me, because I have a knife to this piece of crap's throat?"

Her hand flutters to her mouth and tears stream down her face. "Please, Ryka! I love him."

A cold look flashes over Ryka's face. He sinks back a little, easing off Lowrence's throat. "You were supposed to love my father. You were supposed to love *me*."

She buries her face into Lexa's hair, her shoulders shaking. The little girl in her arms is too stunned to cry now. Her crystal clear eyes, just like Miranda's, are round and scared.

"She doesn't love you. She's my mother, not yours."

I mentally reassess whether it would be okay to cold-cock a five year old. If it wasn't for the echoing footsteps fast approaching down the corridor, I might have gone for it.

"I have to go," my brother says.

My heart spasms painfully. "Don't!"

"Your brother knows his duty, girl," my father wheezes. "He knows what his responsibilities are."

"My name is *Kit*," I hiss, "not *girl*."

"Kit?" my brother whispers the word to himself. "Kit, I have to go. If they come in here, they will kill you."

"Just leave with us, okay? It'll be okay. You'll see as soon as we get that thing off your neck."

"Look how irrational she is, son. She's crazed out of her mind. This is why people like you need the halos. It's for your—"

Ryka slams the heel of his palm down into Lowrence's throat. "Don't you dare say it's for his own good," he growls.

Lowrence drags in a gasping breath. "You can't win this, you moron. Haven't you ever heard the phrase, don't bring a knife to a gun fight?"

Ryka shoots upwards in a blindingly quick move; he wraps one of his arms around those of the guard's, and in a second the gun is in his hand and the guard is on his knees, howling with his arm bent behind his back. Ryka shoves him face first onto the ground with his boot, looking positively murderous.

"You were saying?"

Lowrence whimpers. Actually whimpers. Now that the situation is under control, I turn to find my brother. But he's gone.

35

BLOOD

"Are you sure it's locked?" I whisper again. Ryka nods. With my father and Miranda secured in the room behind us, there's no one to warn the technicians at the mouth of the arena floor of our approach. My brother's match is already well under way and the Trues in the stands are making a lot of noise. He must be pitted against another favourite for them to be jeering so loudly. My stomach rolls as we creep up behind the two technicians observing the fight, their faces lit blue from the tablets they use to record every move, every strike my brother and his opponent lands or receives. Ryka nods at me once we have them in grabbing distance; we lunge forward at the same time and drag them back into the darkened corridor so no one can see us as we both utilise the same choke hold. The technicians struggle, clawing at our arms before quickly falling limp. The one Ryka incapacitated turns out to be the woman who conducted my last halo maintenance check. She never let go of her tablet the whole time she was being choked.

We edge forward so we're still cloaked in shadows, but now I can see my brother in the middle of the white triangle painted onto the arena floor. He's in there with that Belcoras boy, the one he must have been training with since I left. My heart kicks into overdrive. Another unfair match. They must know each other's tells by now. I pray to the Gods my brother knows more about misdirection than he used to, because this guy looks like he knows how to fight. I shift anxiously from foot to foot.

"It's going to be okay," Ryka says softly, gripping onto my hand.

I hope he's right. All my brother needs to do is win this match and then we can grab him and run. James and the others will hopefully already have Opa's people on the move by now. It will be a simple case of catching up to them.

My palms sweat as I watch my brother lunge and dart at the Belcoras boy. He's lightning-quick, perhaps quicker than I remember. For nine minutes he looks like he is holding his own, tumbling out of reach whenever the other boy comes at him. And nine minutes is a long time on the arena floor. I can almost feel the lactic burn in my own muscles as he dodges and twists, making sure to put in as many strikes as the other boy gives. The Trues are loving the show, cheering like mad people whenever one of them leaves it until the last second to tuck and roll. My hand fuses with Ryka's, and his gentle mantra, "*he's going to be fine, he's going to be fine*," calms the panic working its way around my body.

I begin to think he really will be fine.

I don't see it coming, and neither does my brother. But Ryka does. His shout echoes out down the tunnel as Belcoras feints to the left, lifting his striking dagger high above his head. My brother blocks up, not registering the dagger in Belcoras' other hand. With both hands above his head, my brother is left wide open for what happens next. The blade slices out across his stomach in a long sweeping motion, renting open his shirt so that a bright red explosion bursts out of him. I can't hold it in; I scream so loud my eardrums feel like they're going to burst. No one hears apart from Ryka, because everyone in the Colosseum, *everyone*, is on their feet, shouting. Looks like a lot of people had money on my brother. He sags to the floor, his hands going to his stomach. When he pulls them away and looks down, they're

HALO

covered in blood. So, so much blood. He topples sideways into the dirt and Belcoras lifts his arms into the air, celebrating his win early.

It's commonplace in cases of stomach wounds. It takes too long for an opponent to die and so the adjudicators allow the win prematurely. I bolt out of the tunnel and race towards my brother's limp body, saying yet another prayer and hoping Belcoras doesn't finish him off before I can reach him. I don't care that everyone can see me. I don't care that hundreds of guards are within shooting distance, perfectly capable of picking me off. All I care about is reaching my brother.

"What the hell are you doing?" Ryka growls beside me. I tear across the dirt floor, pumping my arms so that I can go faster.

"Pretend we're carrying him off," I yell.

"What?"

"Just do it!"

Ryka follows my lead as I drop to my knees besides the crumpled body on the ground. My brother's eyelids are fluttering like crazy. He looks up at me, his lips an unhealthy blue shade. "You shouldn't...you shouldn't..." he gurgles, blood foaming out of his mouth.

"Don't talk, okay. We're getting you out of here. Lay still." I pretend to take his pulse for a second and then I stand. I make a show of turning my body three hundred and sixty degrees around the arena, making sure everyone can see as I hold my thumb up in the air. I don't waste time pausing for dramatic effect before I tip my thumb down, signalling that my brother is dead. The Trues erupt into a furious clamour, screaming and shouting at one another as I take hold of my brother's arms. I glare at Ryka. "Get his legs. We have to get him out of here."

Belcoras is being taken care of by the adjudicator. More fanfare is spilling out of the speakers, so no one notices how openly my brother coughs up blood as we carry him off the floor. Once we're in the tunnel, we stand him up so I can lift his shirt to take a look at his injuries.

I feel a sick twist in my gut when I realise the cut across this stomach is incredibly deep. So deep it makes my chest constrict. "Are you in pain?" I ask him.

He shakes his head. "No pain."

Of course not. The halo takes care of that. My finger nails cut deep into my palms as I thank the stars for that small blessing. With an injury like this, he could

272

easily be dying, but at least he can't feel it. "Let's get you out of here," I breathe.

"You should just go," he rasps.

I ignore him, lifting one of his arms around my neck. "Give him here," Ryka demands. He lifts my brother and carries him in his arms like a child. There's no other way to do it without making his injuries worse. I suddenly feel completely and utterly useless. My hands are covered in blood and my head is pounding.

"Come on, Kit." Ryka leans over to press his lips quickly to my forehead. "It won't be long before they realise your father isn't there." He sets off running with my brother in his arms and all I can do is follow, choking on panic.

36

RUN

The others are gone when we get to the house. The front door is wide open at Penny's place and light spills out over the river. Ryka doesn't stop running, which means I don't either.

"They're ahead of us. You'll have to lead, I don't know the way," he says. I push ahead, not looking at my brother for fear of realising that he's losing his second fight of the evening, or worse still, that he's already lost. We jog all the way through the Sanctuary, not bothering to hide whenever we cross someone's path. By some miracle all the guards are up at the Colosseum. We're at the edge of the Narrows, the ghetto at our back, when we hear the sirens. The wailing sound stretches out into the night, echoing out across the city.

"They know," Ryka pants. He pushes out in the lead now that we're on the path towards the refinery, towards the river. His shirt clings to his back, plastered with sweat, but not once does he slow down. I love him more than life itself for that. He just doesn't give up.

It's a brutal, exhausting run to the refinery, but I'm able to carry on only because I know everything will be okay once we meet with the others. Max or Callum will be able to take my brother for a while and we'll be long gone before they catch us. Or at least that's the plan. Until we arrive and find ourselves alone, that is.

"I thought they would have waited," I moan, pausing to rake in a shallow breath. My arm pulses fire with every determined pump of my heart, but there's nothing I can do beyond trying to focus past the pain. Despite his load, Ryka is faring better than I am.

"You obviously don't know James very well. If I die, he thinks he's got a greater chance of succeeding Jack." He sets of running again, down the fenced-in pathway beside the river.

"What? Freetown is a republic!"

"Doesn't seem to make much difference to James," he says grimly.

None of that makes any sense. "If he wants you dead then why didn't he call you to fight?"

"There's a limited number of times you can pull that trick before people begin to distrust you, Kit," he pants. "If he kills me the same way he killed my father—" he shakes his head. "The people would never back him."

We run forever and I mull over James' betrayal the whole time, imagining what I'm going to say to him if I ever see him again. We're close to the aqueduct when Ryka skitters to a halt. I have to dodge him to avoid slamming into his back.

"What is it?" He puts my brother down gently on the ground and I stifle a sob, not ready to hear him tell me he's dead.

"He's unconscious," Ryka says. "He's still breathing. Pulse is thready but it's still there." He points off into the darkness. "There's a body up ahead. Stay here with your brother." I can't see what he's pointing out but I believe him. My head buzzes as I crouch down to stroke the hair out of my brother's eyes. His skin is clammy with a cold sweat. "Hang in there, little brother," I tell him. I peer up ahead and watch Ryka's dark form shift around. He crouches low for a second and then runs back, shaking his head. There's something in his hand: a gun.

"It's Max," he says, wincing, his hands shaking like crazy. "They've already come down this far after the others. We have to move. Now."

A numb, cold shock thrills through my body, pooling in my stomach. "He's dead? Max is *dead?*" Ryka slings the gun at me and I fumble it. He doesn't answer me, just paces back and forth. The pain on his face is brutal. "I've never held a gun before. I don't know how to use it! Ryka, just stop. Stop! Our friend just died!"

He freezes, staring into the blackness where Max's body lies, a dark inanimate shadow by the waterside. Huffing out a breath, Ryka collects my brother, grunting as he does so, and gives me a tight smile. "We can grieve later, Kit. As for the gun, learn fast. I get the feeling we're going to need it."

I hold the thing like it's liable to go off of its own accord. It's heavy and cumbersome, and I have no idea whether I'll be able to hit anything with it if it comes down to it. Hopefully it won't. I follow after Ryka and he stops in front of Max's body as I pass, blocking the body from view.

"I want to see him," I say, but Ryka gives a small shake of his head.

"Trust me. You don't."

Maybe he's right. Maybe I don't want to see the cloudy expression on my friend's face. I don't argue; I just don't have the heart. The vista changes gradually as we make our halting progress along the riverbank. It's blacker than pitch by the time we reach the aqueduct and Ryka spends ten minutes trying to find the section where the others cut through the fence. He's gone far too long and I begin to get nervous. My brother has turned grey, and his breathing sounds like the wet rasps of a file on metal, like the ones August uses in his forge.

"Don't die. Don't you dare die," I hiss at him. "You haven't even been born properly yet." He lets out a shallow groan and a shiver of adrenalin powers through my torso and my limbs, making me jittery. He's not done fighting. Ryka emerges from the trees after a low whistle to let me know he's coming. The look on his face is grim.

"I found it," he says. "The ground's pretty torn up on this side of the fence. Looks like there was a fight. We're gonna have to be really careful."

Fear floods me on the tail of my adrenalin and I'm reminded of my halo. The synthetic drug used to control our emotions, our hopes and our fears, tasted of sickly sweet almonds when it affected us. In comparison to the metallic blood taste filling my mouth right now, it actually wasn't that bad.

"Okay," I whisper, and we chase through the forest, following the fence line until we come across a five-foot tall gash in the metal links. The ground is torn up like he said, churned, with huge, smeared boot marks. I slip sideways through the narrow rent in the fence, holding back the sharp, snapped metal for Ryka and my brother. We're moving again, letting the dark of the forest envelop us as Ryka sets another torturously fast pace.

It feels like I'm a machine these days, and placing one foot in front of the other and propelling myself forward as fast as I can is pretty much all I'm good for. The night blends to dawn, a cold, bleak kind of morning, and then stirs itself into a grey and dismal day, and we do nothing more than run. Everything becomes a rhythm of fours. The sound of my boots hitting the forest floor, tripping steadily after Ryka, who never complains once about the increasingly heavy burden my brother poses. One, two, three, four. One, two, three, four. One, three, four, two. It's all the same. I'm so lost in the rhythm that I'm almost hypnoti—

The sound of a gunshot startles the birds out of the trees. Ryka drops to the ground quicker than I've seen him move before. "*Kit, get down!*"

I know I have to eat dirt, but I can't seem to get my body to respond fast enough. I'm too busy trying to see where the shot came from. "Kit! Ryka sweeps my legs out from underneath me just as another bullet zips through the air. I feel it buzz my hair and I know without a doubt that if he hadn't sent me to the ground, I would be dead. I gasp and scramble closer to him, dragging the gun out of the waistband of my pants.

"Who's out there?" I pant. "How many?"

"Don't know," he grits out. "Quickly, move!" He rises to a crouch and drags my brother behind a moss-covered boulder. I follow.

"I'm going to scout. Stay here." Ryka disappears into the murky green undergrowth, nothing more than a quick black and gold shadow, and I'm left alone. More bullets rip through the air, but this time they're not aimed at me. They're aimed to the left, where Ryka is. I bite my lip and look over the boulder. I see them: black figures with assault rifles planted against their shoulders, aiming towards the river. Three guards. Their backs are to me, so I move without giving myself time to panic.

I am silent as I sweep behind them. The shortest one doesn't make a sound as I give him the quickest, cleanest death I can; I thrust my dagger swiftly upwards into the base of his neck, and his body spasms and then falls limp. Even though he was good enough to die without gurgling or yelping, the sound of his rifle dropping to the floor tips the others off. They spin and open fire before even seeing me. None of their bullets are even close, although that doesn't stop me from panicking.

I drop and roll, just like in the arena. I scramble to my feet, using the vast trunk of an oak to protect me, and from there quickly assess my surroundings. Nowhere to go to the left. Nowhere to go to the right. My safest option is to head back behind the boulder, but my brother is still there, broken, and I can't lead them straight to him. There's no other option but to wait.

So I wait.

My heartbeat is the sound of thunder in my ears, making it hard to think straight.

"Come out, girl! It'll be better if we can take you back alive!" one of the remaining guards shouts.

I blow out a sharp laugh. Better for whom if I go back alive? Certainly not me. I will die here on the forest floor before that happens. The snap of wood under rubber soles marks their approach, and I continue to wait. The handle of my knife is slick in my hand, ready to strike. The sound of their breath comes out in slow, even draws, and that's enough to tell me these are the medicated, halo wearing kind of troops from the city. No point trying to reason with them. I spin the knife over in my hand once, twice, and then I launch myself from my hiding position.

"*Kit, no!*"

The two men in front of me, faces hidden behind their tinted riot masks, swivel at the waist when Ryka comes burning out of the shadows. They're torn between the two of us for a second, and that's all the time I need. I grapple the muzzle of the gun away from the guard on the left, pointing it to the ground just as his finger squeezes the trigger. The rattle up my arm jars my teeth together as a spray of bullets thud into the ground at our feet.

I yank him closer to prevent him from re-aiming and pull my weak arm back, striking with my elbow. Pain spirals up through my shoulder, and I feel a wet sensation as fresh blood trickles down my arm. My wound is freshly open, and the nausea that washes through me is epic, takes my breath away. Worse, the blow had no effect. The guard wrestles the rifle out of my grip and lifts his booted foot, slamming it into my leg. Too late, I twist and the force of the strike lands on the side of my kneecap, sending me to the floor.

With teeth gritted, I react instinctively. There's no way I can do anything else, with the barrel of the rifle inches away from my face. I draw my dagger upwards and slam it down into the guard's foot. My years of habitually sharpening my knives pays off; the blade sinks straight through his boot like it's butter, not toughened black leather.

The guard gasps in surprise, not pain, and he does the stupidest thing possible. He reaches down and yanks out my knife.

Like I said—stupid.

Blood immediately wells up out of the narrow hole in his boot, a vivid crimson against all the different shades of green. "You'll regret that," I say. He grunts and retaliates with a sharp thrust of his gun. The scuffed metal butt connects with my temple and light explodes inside my head, accompanied with a high-pitched singing that keeps climbing in octaves until I can't hear it anymore. Just feel its presence flowing through me like electricity. My hearing returns when another loud crack fills the air. A gun shot.

"Ryka!" I want to scream. I don't know if he's hurt. That shot could have been the end of him, but it could easily have been the end of the guard he was fighting, too. I scramble up and fly at the man in front of me, drawing the very last of my energy reserves together, and smash into him. We tumble into the dryness and earthy musk of the forest floor, and then we are both fighting for our lives. I finally get it— how being without my halo makes me better. The guard is well-trained and persistent, but I am a hellcat, possessed, and unwilling to fail. His unwieldy body armour makes it difficult for him to move, which is good, but it also makes it hard to hurt him. The Kevlar in his stab vest makes it impossible for my knife to cut through, but I have other options available to me.

Surprised that I still have it, my hand closes around the grip of the gun. I twist myself up and tangle my legs around those of the guard, and then I'm on top of him. I can just make out the wide whites of his eyes beneath his riot mask, a dead giveaway. He knows it's over. He scrambles beneath me, his hands trying to push me off him, but my position is strong. No more time to waste. I wrap both hands around the gun and press the muzzle directly over his heart. The guard goes still.

He stares up at me, panting from exertion now, and I hesitate. The reality of our situation hits me. I can't see it, but underneath the black riot gear, he's wearing a halo. He didn't leave the city walls to hunt me down and exact revenge, or out of a malicious desire to wipe me from the face of the planet. He came because he was told to. And he can do nothing else with those drugs pumping around his body. My hand shakes on the gun handle, rattling it against his chest.

A mistake.

HALO

The guard twists underneath me and lunges, grabbing hold of something. I don't see what, but I find out a second later. My own dagger, the one I stabbed through his boot, is buried hilt deep into my leg. I scream, my cry piercing, not sounding like me at all. With a series of quick, jolting shoves, the guard pushes me from him and crawls to his knees. I tumble onto my back, clutching at my leg like holding it is going to make the pain any more bearable. The guard lifts the visor on his mask and pulls in two laboured breaths before stooping to collect his gun. Where is Ryka? I don't have the stomach to have his lifeless body be the last thing I see before I die. I feel really stupid now. Really, really stupid for never admitting that I love him. Because I do; it's the most powerful thing I've ever felt and I can't deny that this harrowed feeling of regret coursing through me isn't because I'm about to die. It's because I never got to share my life with him.

I squeeze my eyes shut, still holding my leg, and wait for the abrasive sound of his gun signalling my end. It doesn't come, though. When I open my eyes, the guard is still standing, although his body seems to be wavering.

He tumbles to the earth, boneless, showcasing the elegant dagger—Ryka's—buried in the back of his helmet. Ryka staggers forward, his bright blond hair now matted together with blood, and he yanks the blade free.

"Are you ready to go?" he asks me. I just stare at him. Like on the riverbank after we'd made it through the aqueduct, I want to laugh hysterically. But I don't have the energy this time. He heaves me to my feet and I crumple into him, burying my face into his shoulder. I breathe in the smell of him for two seconds, finding enough strength in that to somehow stand on my own.

"Thank you," I say quietly. "Ryka, I'm sorry. I need to tell you—"

"It's okay. I know," he says. I give him a small smile, thanking him silently for not making me say the words. They live there, though, between us. *I love you.*

Ryka binds up my leg and collects my brother, and we leave the bodies of the guards behind us. We head for Freetown. We head for home.

******

We smell something acrid and foul before we see the smoke. It's too dark at first to see much of anything, but as we make our staggering journey towards our destination, the dull orange glow on the horizon spells trouble.

"What's going on?"

Ryka answers my question by quickening his pace. "It's the night fires," he says, but I can tell he doesn't believe that. Another ten minutes later Jada appears from nowhere. She rushes Ryka, slamming into his legs and barks like crazy. Her coat is filthy and she smells like burned hair.

"Where's Jack, girl? Where's Jack?" Jada tips her head to one side and barks again, then disappears into the darkness.

"Gods…" Ryka murmurs under his breath. We find more energy from somewhere and charge the remaining mile through the treacherously black forest. When we break the tree line, complete devastation awaits us. Since arriving here, I had always thought it: an open fire in Freetown was a terrible idea. But after all the death and blood horror of the last twenty-four hours, I doubt this destruction came from a rogue flame. I get the distinct impression this nightmare is an engineered one.

Freetown is burning.

Ryka almost stumbles and drops my brother when he sees it. "You know what this means, don't you?" he exhales.

I take it all in: the screaming and shouting; the still-burning scraps of fabric that float up on the thermals of the fire, savagely beautiful against the night sky. "It means they struck out against us."

"More than that." He shakes his head, a look of cold steel transforming his face. I watch the change come over him, and his determination is frightening. "The Sanctuary have cut us, Kit, and we're bleeding. You know as well as I do what happens next." He turns to face me, and my stomach lurches. There's a promise of pain and blood in his eyes. He takes a step, sucking in a deep breath, and I close my eyes, knowing, just like he said. For the people of Freetown, there is only one answer to this attack, one that will mean death and loss for everyone.

"War," I say softly. "We are going to war."

EPILOGUE

The technician flicks the syringe and a jet of noxious green fluid arcs from the needle. "You're competing again today," she says. Her voice is so familiar. I look up from my position on the surgical steel gurney to find that I recognise her face as well. Above her halo, a thick band of blue and black bruising rings her throat. She gives me a curt smile and takes hold of my arm. The needle tip hovers above my skin while she pauses, studying me with curious eyes.

"I'm going to ask you some questions, Kit. Please answer them as honestly as possible."

I nod stiffly. There's no requirement for me to speak yet, but I want to. I want to find out if her neck hurts, if she's angry at me for knocking her out back in the Colosseum. She pushes the needle into the crook of my arm and presses the plunger down, and fire lights its way up my arm. When it reaches my neck and burns into my mind, my brain starts flickering.

On and off.

On and off.

The Colosseum, the Pit, the Colosseum, the Pit.

"What did you do this morning?" the technician asks. Her fingers wait over the screen of her tablet, ready to mark down my answer. I pull myself out of the Pit and respond, because I'm supposed to. Because I have to.

"I rose with my alarm. I helped...I helped..." I'm struggling to focus. The pulsing in my head is too distracting, my memories too fluid to grasp hold of.

"Who did you help?" the technician presses.

I shake my head and stare down at my hands. There are two neat black lines tattooed into the backs of my wrists.

Sam.

SAM.

Sam.

Sam.

The Pit forces its way back in, and for a moment I am breathless. All I can see, hear, smell is Sam's death, the life that I took from him. It takes a while to regain myself, but when I do everything thankfully seems a little clearer.

"I—I helped my brother. I helped Luca. He's been injured."

The technician nods and taps away on the tablet. A small, bright blue rectangle is reflected in her dark eyes from the screen. "Does that make you sad?" She doesn't look up, just waits for me to answer.

"Yes, I'm worried about him. He might die."

She records this, too, frowning. I shift awkwardly on the gurney and the technician fiddles with the electrodes placed on the insides of my wrists, over my temples, over my heart. She clucks her tongue and reconnects the wires, and suddenly the alarms on the equipment they're connected to start screaming. She snaps her head up and narrows her eyes at me.

"Oh, come on, Kit. It's okay, remember. You have no reason to be afraid."

But I *am* afraid. I'm paralysed by fear as the technician goes and collects a folded black piece of material off an otherwise empty shelf on the opposite side of the room. I know the material immediately; it's one of Ryka's shirts. She begins to unfold it carefully, and I shrink away.

"That's not possible. I threw it in the water! It's gone. He said I'd never have to wear it again!"

The technician carries on slowly laying out the shirt, but she looks up at me and smiles. It's not a friendly smile; it is cold and calculating. "You wanted this," she says. "You wanted it."

She lifts an object out of the shirt, but it's not what I was expecting. In place of my halo is a ceramic mask. It is black as tar and rimmed with a line of white counters, just like the one the priestesses' assassin wore when he tried to kill me.

"That's not mine," I breathe.

The look on the technician's face is almost pitying. "Of course it is, Kit. You fought for this. There's no stopping it now." She stalks forward, holding out the mask, and I go to get up off the gurney but my legs won't work. Nothing works. The pulsing in my head returns, this time slamming so hard I can barely think.

The mask descends, and I can do nothing but lie there as she presses it over my face. My breathing is frantic as it rushes in and out, in and out, the exercise made that much harder by the fact that there is no mouth hole. There *are* eyeholes, however. Through them, the technician smiles, happy with a job well done.

"There. Now you're ready, girl. You're ready to be Claimed."

******

I wake to the sounds of Luca's rattling breathing. Ella still sits on the edge of my bed, watching over him carefully. She's been doing that for days, ever since we returned to find Freetown lit up like a burning torch. The fires have been put out, but half the tent city is now a tattered, burnt-out nightmare. The people have bounced back remarkably, but they are angry. Angry with the devastation the Sanctuary have brought down on their heads, and angry at us for being the cause.

"Bad dreams, child?" Ella whispers, wiping a cloth across Luca's brow. My brother chose that name for himself in one of his rare moments of lucidity.

"Terrifying," I tell her.

She nods her head but says nothing more. My body is stiff when I stand, and I note my arm is still throbbing. I re-opened the wound the High Priestess gave me on the journey back to Freetown, and it doesn't appear to be healing very quickly. The knife wound in my thigh is just as bad, and the pain is something I'm slowly becoming accustomed to. Guess that's part of not wearing the halo anymore. I take just as long to mend as everyone else now.

"He's outside," Ella says softly, tilting her head to wards to the open doorway of my tent. It's both thrilling and worrying that she knows he would be on my mind as soon as I woke. I give her a rueful nod, place my hand briefly on my brother's head to check his temperature—still raging hot—and then go outside to find the *he* that she was referring to.

Ryka's blond hair is the first thing I see, the individual strands that have escaped his messy ponytail floating on the breeze. He looks up at me when I approach, smiling softly.

"Hey, little Kit. Been waiting on you."

I take in the tight pull of his shirt, the soft smile in his deep brown eyes, the way he flicks his throwing dagger over and over in his hand the same way I do when I'm edgy. He seems relaxed but I can read every line of him by now, and I know something's bothering him.

"Are you going to tell me, or are you gonna make me wait?"

He wrinkles his nose and reaches out for my hand, pulling me down into the long grasses beside him. I slump to the ground and wait for him to spit it out. He strokes a finger up and down my arm in a way that makes my skin tingle. I'm only just getting used to people touching me, but this is something different entirely. It's not the brief squeeze of a hug from someone. It's like he's telling me something with the way he traces his finger up and down my skin. I shiver, not because I'm cold or because it's uncomfortable. Because it's the most delicious sensation I've ever experienced. It stops all too soon.

"It's James," Ryka says softly, still staring down at my arm.

When we left the Sanctuary, James and the others were supposed to wait for us. They left before we reached them, fuelling Ryka's suspicions that the highest-ranked fighter in Freetown, the man who killed Ryka's father, was indeed trying to make sure Ryka didn't pose a threat to his chances of becoming the next leader of Freetown. When we returned to find the tent city on fire, Callum, Raff, Penny and fifteen others from inside the Sanctuary's walls had already made it back safe and sound. Callum's twin brother, Max, had been killed, and James was nowhere to be seen.

"He's come back, hasn't he?" I ask.

Ryka nods. "Says he was leading off some of the guards. Wasn't exactly pleased to see me."

I clear my throat, still tickly from all the smoke I breathed in when we helped put the flames out. "Fantastic." There was a moment—a brief, hopeful moment—where the two of us believed he might not come back at all.

"There's something else, I'm afraid."

A sinking feeling takes hold in my gut. "What kind of something else?"

Ryka shakes his head. "I don't wanna tell you. I want to kiss you."

A hot flush prickles at my cheeks and Ryka laughs, skating his fingers across my collarbone where I've turned an unfortunate shade of pink. He seems as fascinated by my reactions to being touched there as I am, myself. My whole life, my halo has taken up residency at the base of my neck, and touching another person in that area was definitely considered taboo. Now, I'm addicted to the way it feels when Ryka's fingers graze my skin there.

It's sensitive. Secret. Intensely personal.

"You can kiss me, but then you have to tell me," I whisper.

A lop-sided grin develops on his face. "Fair," he says, leaning into me. I melt into him, and for a moment I get to forget everything. Forget my dangerously ill brother lying in my bed, the Sanctuary and their attacks on my new home, the fact that the people of Freetown love to hate me, the priestesses want me dead, and that I've landed myself back in the fighting pits. There's nothing but Ryka and the way he tastes like he's been eating oranges. His lips on mine, his breath quickening over my flushed skin, his hands buried deep in my short hair.

"If the world were ending," he says quietly, when he pulls away, "and we were the only people left, I think I'd be the happiest man alive." He cups my face in his hands and kisses me lightly one last time.

"You'd be the *only* man alive," I point out.

"True. Hadn't thought about that." Ryka laughs but the sound of it is melancholy. He finally looks away. "Unfortunately, in the absence of the end of the world, we still have a bunch of people to deal with."

The buzz from his kiss begins to wear off when a frown forms between his eyebrows. "Come on, then. Out with it," I say.

"It's the High Priestess. She wants to see you. I'm supposed to take you up to the Keep."

They say that if you look upon a priestess' face, even by accident, then you're cursed. And you looked upon the High Priestess' face. That's got to be, like, the mother of all curses.

"Why would she want to see me?"

Ryka shrugs and gets to his feet. He offers me his hand, looking down on me with poorly concealed concern. "Apparently she's had a vision. A vision that involves you."

Wonderful. All I can think of, as I take his hand and let him pull me up, is the dream I just had. I don't tell him about it, but the lingering claustrophobia I'd felt wearing that mask is magnified a hundred fold. Once again, it feels like I'm being suffocated. The technician's words ring ominously in my head: *You fought for this, Kit. There's no stopping it now.*

ABOUT THE AUTHOR

Frankie Rose lives in Sydney, Australia, her borrowed homeland. She writes in the paranormal romance, dystopian and contemporary romance genres, and hopes to dip her toes in many more. She is an avid reader, skier and snowboarder, and also loves to climb and hike in the outdoors.

You can reach Frankie at **frankierose101@gmail.com** or visit her website at **www.frankierosewrites.com** for further details of her upcoming projects.

ACKNOWLEDGEMENTS

I have a lot of people to thank this time around. The Halo journey was a bit of a roller coaster, and a whole squadron of people encouraged me and kept hassling me for a finished draft. You guys really got me through!

Let's see, let's see…

My beta readers, you guys were awesome. There were quite a few of you for this project. Carmen, Jessica, Makena, Stacie, Jo-Anne, Jordan, Vicky, and Christina, thank you all so much for taking the time to read through my humble novel in its varying stages. You gals are pretty darned kick-ass! My editor, Julia Park-Tracey, thank you for being super speedy and having such keen eyes! All the Indie-Visible girls, your limitless kindness and steadfast support has been and always will be invaluable.

Chelsea Starling, thank you for being the sweetest, most generous person, with your time, your compliments and with yourself. I love ya girlie, and I can't wait to meet you for real.

Max Henry, formatter extraordinaire, you picked up this task with so little time to complete it and yet still made my books beautiful. I'm so grateful that you were available to work your magic for me! Thank you so much.

Sarah Benelli of Typo Killer, awesome must run in your family. Your hawk eye proofreading caught my typos with unbelievable precision. You are a godsend.

To Nick, without you I wouldn't be able to write. Thank you for supporting me and always, always, always having the faith in me that I usually don't. Having you as my husband, my best friend, is such an overwhelming blessing.

My last thanks goes to you, my readers, who have invested in my work by purchasing this book. I am so very grateful to you all for your continued support. It really does mean the world to me. If you have enjoyed Raksha, I would love for you to leave a review on the site you purchased it from. Reviews really do mean a lot to us authors, and I love reading every single one.

LOVED THE BOOK?

why not leave a review?

Your experiences when reading this book have been uniquely your own. No one else will ever imagine the fighting, the roar of the crowds, the hollow calls of *Raksha! Raksha! Raksha!* quite like you just did. More than anything as a writer, I love when people tell me what they thought of my work and how they experienced the world I dreamed into existence.

The human imagination is an incredible thing.

Share what your mind created from Kit and Ryka's story!

Made in the USA
San Bernardino, CA
25 January 2016